Shiloh san
"Cheney, I love
of my soul. I ha
Will you give m
the greatest honor, and marry me?"

She didn't move, but a single tear escaped out of her eye and slid helplessly down her cheek.

Shiloh, unheeding in the dying light, rose and took her hand. "Here," he said softly. "It's the pearl I gave you, you see. It's the only thing I could think of that would do you justice, Cheney, because it is lovely and it is pure, and it bound us together a long time ago."

He was pressing the ring into the palm of her hand. She looked up at him, stricken. "Sh-Shiloh," she gulped in a raw voice, "I—I am so very honored a-and…and…grateful for your…your…esteem… but I—it's—I…"

She tried, but she could not go on. The realization began to set in, and Shiloh's face twisted with such disbelief and terrible pain that Cheney herself felt it. She swallowed, hard, but the tears began to flow like burning streams down her face.

"You…you're turning me down?" Shiloh stammered. "You…you don't want to marry me? But I thought—no, Cheney! I *know*! I know you love me. Tell me! I thought that I wasn't good enough for you, but now—"

"No, no. It's not that. It was never that and never would be," Cheney cried. "Shiloh, you honestly don't know? You never understood…realized…?"

LYNN MORRIS AND *GILBERT MORRIS*

are a father-daughter writing team who combine Gilbert's strength of great story plots and adventure with Lynn's research skills and character development. Together they form a powerful duo! Lynn and her daughter live near her parents on the Gulf coast in Alabama.

DRIVEN WITH *the* WIND

Lynn Morris
Gilbert Morris

Love Inspired

Recycling programs
for this product may
not exist in your area.

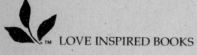 LOVE INSPIRED BOOKS

ISBN-13: 978-0-373-78686-2

DRIVEN WITH THE WIND

Love Inspired Books/June 2011

First published by Bethany House Publishers

This book is dedicated to each of you,
our faithful readers,
with our warmest thanks.

Prologue

Precisely on the first stroke of midnight, the messenger came to the new emergency receiving desk in the west wing of St. Francis de Yerba Buena Hospital. For anyone to come to the emergency wing in the dead of night was not usually something that made the staff particularly happy. But the staff physician on duty, Dr. Cheney Duvall, was glad to see this arrival. As soon as she saw the lovely bouquet of flowers, she knew all about the messenger and his message.

Hi Doc,

I hope to have the honor of escorting you home in the morning. I shall come to the hospital at seven o'clock. Until then,
I remain,

Your faithful servant,
Shiloh Irons-Winslow

P.S. They're called bird-of-paradise, and I think they're my favorite flowers because they remind me of you.

"Mr. Irons-Winslow in town again, I recollect, is he? Sweet sun a-risin', are those flowers? Real flowers?" Nurse Sallie Sisk's eyes widened.

"Yes," Cheney murmured softly, caressing one spiky bract. "They remind me of the sunrise from Mount Haleakala...incandescent orange, so bright you can hardly look at it...sultry purple...deep, mysterious blue..."

Eyeing Cheney shrewdly, Nurse Sisk asked, "You do miss that place, don't you, Dr. Duvall?"

"Hmm? Oh. Yes—well, it makes a definite impression. A memorable impression. Now, Nurse Sisk, would you help me make some small bouquets to put on the wards? There's enough here for four, I should think. So kind of Shiloh to send enough flowers for the entire hospital."

"So kind of you to share 'em, Doctor," Nurse Sisk added.

"Well, this time I want to keep out three of these. They're called bird-of-paradise. And a big bunch of the Hawaiian ginger, please. The scent—"

"Reminds you of Haw-eye," Nurse Sisk finished pertly.

Cheney blushed a little. "Yes. Of Hawaii. Thank you, Nurse Sisk. Now, if you'll attend to the flowers, I'll go make rounds."

He came at seven o'clock precisely, as he had promised. Cheney was watching, though she tried hard not to. He rode out of the raw early-morning mists, and for long moments she could believe that things were as they used to be. He was wearing his faded denims and worn boots and travel- and weather-stained canvas duster. A wide-brimmed gray hat shadowed his eyes.

She decided to go on outside and greet him, for to wait coyly for him, pretending she was not watching for him, was not Cheney Duvall's way. She was glad to see him after three long months, and she couldn't hide it from herself, or him. They knew each other much too well.

"Hi Doc." He slid to the ground and rushed to her. Throwing his arms around her, he lifted her up and spun her around. She didn't protest.

"Hello, Mr. Irons-Winslow." She was a little out of breath.

He was still holding her up close by her waist. She looked down at him, smiling widely. "Are you glad to see me, Doc?" he demanded.

"Yes, I am." Cheney touched his face lightly.

"Good. Then I'll let you down."

"Thank you."

"Oh, and you can call me Shiloh."

"Thank you."

"Welcome."

He took her hand, and she let him. Though his touch gave her the greatest of joy, it also caused her the keenest of pain. In the last six months Cheney had simply let time and circumstances and the certain knowledge of her love for him wash over her and recede deep into her subconscious. The day would come when she would have to face it and deal with it. But that day was not now, not this morning.

"You ready to go, Doc?" he asked as they went inside.

"Would you like to stay and see everyone?" she asked politely. "I know they'd like to see you, and I'm not tired."

"You sure?" He studied her face, the set of her shoulders, her hands. "You're pretty used to nights now, huh."

She nodded. "Yes, and I'm surprised how much I like it. Anyway, Jesty's coming in for the morning shift. I know he'd like to see you. And Dr. Baird, of course, will be very angry with me if I run off with you before he gets here."

One of his perfectly arched brows lifted. "Will you?"

"Hmm? I beg your pardon?"

"Run off with me?"

"Shiloh!"

He shrugged. "Never hurts to ask."

"Oh! You just don't give up, do you?"

"No. And neither do you. But, Doc, that's why I'm here, anyway, you know."

"To...to...ask me to run off with you?" Cheney stammered, her color high.

"Sorta like. You've heard from Mrs. de Lancie, haven't you?"

"Oh. Oh yes, of course. You got her letter, and the formal invitation to the wedding?"

"Yeah, but I wanted to ask if you'd do me the honor of accompanying me on the *Brynn Annalea* to Panama City instead of us going on the Steens' *Maid of Zanzibar*."

"Oh, Shiloh, that would be wonderful! The *Brynn Annalea* will be free next month?"

He grinned. "Not free. But I've got a little sugar run to Panama City set up that'll help cover the trip. If you'll come with me, I'd rather go on the *Brynn Annalea*. Then the *Maid of the Caribbean* can pick us up in Aspinwall."

"Sir, it would give me the greatest pleasure to travel

with you on such a fine ship as the *Brynn Annalea*," Cheney replied.

In the empty foyer he stopped and looked down at her, studying her with peculiar intensity. She met his eyes, then looked away, suddenly shy from the close scrutiny. He started to say something, then changed his mind and gently propelled her to the double doors that opened to the men's ward.

"Dr. Duvall," he finally said with unusual formality, "I don't think you realize what a great pleasure and honor it is for me to hear you say that."

Cheney just smiled, for she could think of nothing at all to say.

Part One

The Foundation of God

*Nevertheless the foundation of God standeth sure,
having this seal, The Lord knoweth them that are his.
And, Let every one that nameth the name of Christ
depart from iniquity.*

—2 Timothy 2:19

Chapter One

The Way of the Sea

Cheney Duvall stared up at the great clouds of soaring sail, though her eyes watered from the sun and salt sting. The *Brynn Annalea* had found a tail of the northeast trade winds, strong and hot, to wend her fast down Baja and push her easily over the Tropic of Cancer. Her sharp prow knifed the water, the jib with the lucky shark's fin mounted on it splashing in the wave crests. She was a beautiful thing, fast, sharp-hulled, streamlined, proud.

And dangerous.

Cheney shouted up at Shiloh, and he was shouting back down at her. Neither of them could possibly hear the other, but both of them kept on.

"You *idiot!* Come down from there *this instant!* You are going to fall and *die!*" Cheney shrieked.

He made an impatient gesture—*Get below, you dumb girl!*—which made Cheney's heart almost stop, for he had let go with one arm to make jabbing "get below" motions to her.

Twelve seamen were perched along the bucking, straining yard, feet kicked back against the footrope, bellies
pressed against the yard, hands gathering up the heavy
canvas. Cheney watched, horrified, as they struggled to
roll the great main royal sail around the yard. Finally it
was wound as neatly as thread on a spool, and the sailors,
with strong and agile movements, passed lengths of rope
around sail and yard and made it fast with hitches. One
by one they started edging back along the yard, making
for the weather shrouds to scamper down.

"Miss Duvall," an authoritative voice spoke behind
her left shoulder. "Until we shorten sail, it's going to be
rough here on the upper deck."

Cheney looked around in surprise at stern, hawk-
like Captain Sloane. She hadn't heard his approach. Now
that she'd taken her eyes off Shiloh, who was flapping
in the twenty-five-knot wind almost two hundred feet up
in the air, she saw that the crew was swarming over the
deck, manning the clew lines and buntlines to haul the
fore and mizzen sails up to the yard. The *Brynn Annalea*
leaped and crashed down, and warm water splashed up
to Cheney's ankles.

"I'm in the way," she said weakly.

Captain Sloane replied evenly, "Yes, ma'am." Captain
Sloane wasn't much for having women on his ship.

Cheney bristled a little. "But…but, Shiloh—I mean,
Mr. Irons-Winslow—he's surely in the way, too! Flapping around up there in this gale!"

Captain Sloane's mouth twitched, though his slitted
eyes didn't reflect amusement. "Miss Duvall, Mr. Irons-
Winslow is the owner of this ship, and if he wants to hang
his laundry from the moonraker, he's got a right to, and

oddly enough, I expect he could do it as well as any sailor on this ship. And, ma'am, this is hardly a gale. It's just a spanking fair wind."

"Oh. Well, I suppose I'll go below."

"Yes, ma'am."

She turned toward the stern ladder, then asked, "Sir, would you please ask Shi—Mr. Irons-Winslow to wait on me at his earliest convenience?"

Captain Sloane glanced back up at the barefoot, shirtless, muscular, and tanned young man as he nimbly monkey-climbed down the netlike shroud. "He'll be a while, ma'am. He wanted to learn how to shorten sail, and he's got four of them to go."

Cheney nodded and went down the ladder, now in a hurry. Her earlier exhilaration was dying as her stomach began to roll along with the motion of the ship. That was the way of the sea, it seemed. Just when you thought you were getting along fine together, she turned on you, laughing, and you ended up seasick.

It must have been hours later when Cheney awoke. All she could see was the golden glow of the lantern above her bunk in Captain Sloane's cabin. It was gimbaled, so it rolled along with the ship. Cheney promptly vomited.

Shiloh was there, smelling clean and outdoorsy, his voice soft, his blond hair glowing from the sun's whitewash. "Easy there, Doc. I've got you. Just lie back now. It's all right—" He cleaned her face with a cool cloth.

Before she passed out again, she reflected how odd it was that she always wanted Shiloh when she was ill, though the memory of him attending her was appalling after she felt well again. He was so soothing, so comforting. He would have made a wonderful doctor, she reflected wearily. But it seemed that instead he was a man of the sea.

The first week out of San Francisco neither Cheney nor Nia had been ill at all as the *Brynn Annalea* glided smoothly south. But the second week, while the ship ran before the stiff twenty-or-so-knot winds, both of them were so seasick that they had to stay in their bunks all the time. Shiloh took care of both of them, much to Cheney's comfort and Nia's horror. Twice Nia tried to get up, but she fell and then tried to crawl, apparently intending to go into the adjoining cabin where Cheney lay like a dead thing. Shiloh threatened to tie Nia to her bunk, so she gave up.

They reached Panama City on a cool April night in 1868, with a hazy full moon that seemed to float just above the horizon. Shiloh regretted that Cheney couldn't enjoy the evening and the memories with him, but she was so weak she only seemed to reach semiconsciousness. He also knew that they couldn't afford to linger long in the lovely old village, for if Cheney and Nia were on land long enough to get their "land legs," they'd get seasick all over again once they were back at sea. This way the seasickness might, as it so often did, run its course and mysteriously disappear.

Shiloh carried Cheney onto the train, and one of his sailors carried Nia. Cheney never even saw the Panamanian jungle where she and Shiloh had had such an amazing adventure three years before.

They crossed the isthmus in record time, and the Steens' clipper *Maid of the Caribbean* lolled along the dock at Aspinwall, faithfully waiting for them. They caught the northeast trades full force, and the clipper sped north.

"That color makes your complexion look a little better," Nia said comfortingly.

"Oh? You mean a gentle moss-green instead of puce?" Cheney asked caustically.

"Mm," Nia replied noncommittally. She frowned as she ran a brush through Cheney's hair, never an easy task. Her thick, waist-length auburn hair had a decided curl to it and normally was shiny and full of body. Now it was matted and dull, and it seemed that a lot of it was breaking off in the brush. "Mr. Irons-Winslow says it's going to rain. I think I'll ask him to catch some clean rainwater to wash—"

"Rain! You mean storm?" Cheney asked fearfully.

"Calm down, Miss Cheney. I don't think so. I think just rain, like a summer shower," Nia said soothingly. "You don't have to be afraid, you know. It seems like Mr. Irons-Winslow knows what he's doing, sailing the ship and finding the way and all."

Cheney managed a weak smile. "Oh, I'm not afraid of the ship going down in a storm, Nia. I'm just afraid that I'll get seasick again—and this time *not* die."

Nia nodded with chagrin. "'Fraid I agree with you there, Miss Cheney. Why can't doctors find a cure for seasickness?"

"If I sail much more in my life," Cheney said forcefully, "I shall dedicate myself to doing just that. Are you finished, Nia? Yes, you're finished. Give it up. This is the best I'm going to look, I'm afraid."

Nia studied her critically. She didn't look as fine as when she was in the full vigor of health, but she still looked lovely. Cheney was tall and slim and lithe, with long white fingers and a graceful neck and carriage. Her eyes, usually a sparkling green, were a little dull, perhaps, and she didn't glow with health and vitality as she normally did. The deep maroon dress brightened her eyes a little, and the fall of ecru lace at the high neckline softened her rather pasty complexion.

"The hat. Yes, the one with the net veil. And here, Miss Cheney, use the rose-colored parasol. The shadow of it will hide some of that paleness…well, maybe a little rouge, too."

"In broad daylight? Shocking, Nia," Cheney teased.

"No, you looking like a haint is shocking," Nia said firmly, brushing an air-thin layer of coral-tinted rouge on Cheney's pronounced cheekbones. "Well, at least you don't look quite so dead."

"Thank you so much," Cheney said tartly. "Why don't you come up with me, Nia? I know you need some fresh air and sunlight, too."

"I'll come. But right now I know Mr. Irons-Winslow wants to talk to you."

Cheney, who was already out the door, turned quickly. "What? What do you mean?"

But Nia merely pressed her lips together and shook her head.

Cheney hurried to the upper deck, squinting in the bright sunshine that she hadn't seen for forever, it seemed. She paused at the top of the ladder, simply breathing in the stringent air. Lifting her face, she closed her eyes and reveled in the clean heat of the sun washing her face.

"Hi, Doc. You look beautiful," Shiloh said, taking her arm.

"You lie, sir, and I'm very grateful for it." She sighed.

"I don't lie," he said mildly. "Ever. Anyway, you feel like a little walk? Or do you need to just sit?"

"Could we sit down? I feel fine, but I'd like to be still and enjoy the sun and the wind for a little." She started toward the stern, but Shiloh stopped her.

"The *Maid of the Caribbean* is more of a businesslike ship than the *Brynn Annalea*," he told her wryly. "The stern has all kinds of serious things like the wheelbox and the counter and stuff. No little castle for passengers and fool owners to sit on. But I've made me a little place to hide so I don't get in anybody's way." It was a sail locker on the port side, close to the bow. Shiloh had piled some blankets up on it and covered it with what looked like an expensive Persian rug. He had to lift Cheney up to sit on it, and she felt absurdly as if she was on some kind of seaborne throne. Easily he jumped to sit beside her and took her hand.

"But, Mr. Scamper-the-Rigging, I thought you were an old sea salt from way back," Cheney said caustically. "My last clear memory was of seeing you up in the sky, hanging on for dear life to some snip of rope."

"Nah. I was shortening the main-t'gallant," he said expansively. "After that, I manfully shortened the mizzen-t'gallant, and then courageously went on to the fore-t'gallant. You wouldn't know what those are, o' course, just bein' a girl and a landlubber and all."

"You're right, and I don't want to know," she grumbled. "Seasickness has a tendency to make you sick, not only of the sea but of anything to do with the sea, such as sails and spars and rigs and clews and bunts and…and… water."

"But not of old sea salts like me, I hope," he said lightly.

"No, not of you," she said, ducking her head. "Where are we?"

"We're almost to the Tropic of Cancer. Over there are the Bahamas. Wish we could see 'em. But we came through the Windward Passage between Cuba and Hispaniola and swung east to catch the trades. Looks like there's some high pressure moving up out of the south, too, that's helping us along. If we can keep it to our backs, we ought to be to New York in four or five days."

Cheney obediently looked in the directions he was enthusiastically pointing, first to the west, where the unseen paradise of the Bahamas lay, and then to the south, where along the bright horizon could be seen a thin, dark purple line. "Thunderstorms?"

"Yeah, but not serious squalls," he assured her. "We'll probably go through some, but I don't think it'll be too tough. You're not scared, are you?"

"Are you?"

"Course not."

"Then neither am I."

He nodded, apparently satisfied. They were silent for a while. Shiloh played with her fingers, taking each one and perusing it, as if to measure its lissome length. Normally Cheney didn't allow Shiloh such intimacies. Their physical relationship consisted mainly of quick fervent hugs and Cheney holding his arm perhaps a little closer than was strictly necessary. She felt so good, however, so at peace and so calm that she allowed this small but personal touch.

"Cheney," he said in a deep voice unlike his own, "do you know what day it is?"

She glanced at him with surprise, but his face was

averted. "Um...Wednesday?" she guessed, a little be-mused.

She saw a wisp of a smile pass over his lips, but he didn't look up. He seemed to be completely absorbed in studying her hands. "Actually, it's Tuesday, but that's not what I meant." Finally he straightened and turned to face her, though he kept a tight hold of her hands with both of his. "It's the twenty-first. It's your birthday."

Her eyes widened. "I can't believe I forgot! But, of course, I've sort of lost the last...the last..."

"Two weeks," Shiloh said gravely. "You've been sick for two weeks."

"And today is my birthday! I feel as if I've just awakened after a long half death, so I suppose it is like a birth day," Cheney observed dryly.

"I got you a present," Shiloh said, childlike, reaching back underneath a fold of the rug. It was wrapped in plain brown paper, but he had tied a seashell on it with some twine. Lovely, tiny, perfect, it was a creamy white scallop with a blush of pink on the wings. "Like the fancy gift wrapping?"

"I love the shell. It's so...pure," Cheney answered softly. "Thank you so much, Shiloh."

"The shell's not the present, Doc," he teased. "I just picked that up somewhere. Been carryin' it around in my pocket."

"It's the best kind of gift. But here—oh, Shiloh! How wonderful! *Bleak House* by Charles Dickens...and it's a first edition? My goodness, it's about—yes, fifteen years old, but it looks brand-new! Wherever did you find it?"

"Just picked it up somewhere. Been carryin' it around in my pocket," he drawled. Actually he had had the Winslow Brothers' shipping agent in London search for months until he had found a first edition, which, though used, was in mint condition. It had cost Shiloh a pretty penny, too.

"I doubt that," Cheney declared. "It weighs five pounds, I think. Anyway, it's my favorite of Dickens's novels." Mischievously she added, "I'm surprised you haven't broken it out before now. I know you must be tired of reading *Hamlet* to me."

"Aw, then it wouldn't have been a birthday surprise. Besides, it was good for me," he asserted. "Never understood a word of Shakespeare till now. And now I dream in Shakespearean English."

Cheney laughed. "Me too. I have been having the oddest Ophelia dreams. Anyway, thank you so much for *Bleak House*, Shiloh. It's a very thoughtful gift."

"Welcome. And maybe you might get the great man to sign it."

"Oh yes! I'd forgotten that Mother and Father are taking the wedding party to his reading at Steinway Hall. Do you really think we might have a chance to meet him?"

"Dunno. Prob'ly Mrs. de Lancie will manage to corner him."

"If anyone can, Victoria can."

Cheney opened the book and, almost without meaning to, as avid readers will, began to read. "Oh no, Dr. Duvall," Shiloh asserted, grabbing the book, closing it, and shoving it back under the rug. "I'm not going to sit here and watch you read. You haven't talked to me for two weeks. I want you to pay some attention to me."

Cheney retorted, "I pay attention to you all the time! I haven't read *Bleak House* in some years, and I—"

"Sorry, Doc," he said, clearly not meaning it. "C'mon,

let's go watch the sunset at the prow." He lifted her down, clasping her waist tightly. His fingers almost met, Cheney was so slim.

They walked to the starboard side of the prow so they could see behind and to the west. The sun had turned into a great orange flame as it seemed helplessly drawn toward the ominous-looking cloud bank that had thickened and widened. They stood in silence for a while, just watching the dying light, which always seemed more lurid, more fiery, just before sunset. To the south, angry whitecaps crested and tumbled on the dirty gray sea.

Staring unblinking into the dazzling sun, Shiloh began to speak. It was an odd speech, for him, spoken in a measured and even tone, without his customary drawl and colloquialism. "My family—it's only just lately that I've been able to say that without stumbling. I've been alone—myself, by myself, for myself—for so long. It's taken a surprising amount of time for my mind to adjust to the fact that I belong to someone, that I have a history and a home."

She stared at him quizzically. "But—this...this is good, isn't it, for you? You sound a little melancholy."

A quick smile touched his firm mouth. "I don't mean to. Certainly it's different for me, the responsibilities and the duties and the care for other people. But yes, of course it's good." He turned to face her, though he still leaned carelessly against the side of the ship. Cheney remained still, watching the sun's first touch of the cloud bank that she knew would swallow it with startling quickness. Sunsets at sea were like that—sudden, without warning.

"Another thing that's good is the...the property," Shiloh went on. "The substance, I guess. It's not only a past for me. It's given me a future. And that, Cheney, is something I never before thought I could offer you."

Cheney froze. She didn't blink. Her thoughts ground to a halt.

They stood silent and still for a long time. Shiloh's look was one of gentleness, of gladness, of unmistakable love. Cheney seemed to be a sculpture, like the figure-head of a ship staring forever into the sea.

Shiloh sank to one knee, took up the hem of her skirt, and lifted it to his lips. Cheney turned to look down at him, her eyes wide and dark. He looked up. "Cheney, I love you to the very core of my soul. I have for a long time. Will you give me the greatest gift, the greatest honor, and marry me?"

She didn't move, but a single tear escaped out of her eye and slid helplessly down her cheek.

Shiloh, unheeding in the dying light, rose and took her hand. "Here," he said softly. "It's the pearl I gave you, you see. I made Nia give it to me so that I could have it set in a ring. It's the only thing I could think of that would do you justice, Cheney, because it is lovely and it is pure, and it bound us together a long time ago."

He was pressing it into the palm of her hand. But, as if it pained her, Cheney jerked back, closed her hand and clasped it against her breast. She looked up at him, stricken. "Sh-Shiloh," she gulped in a raw voice, "I—I am so very honored a-and…and…grateful for your—your… esteem…but I— It's— I…" She tried, but she could not go on. The realization began to set in, and Shiloh's face twisted with such disbelief and terrible pain that Cheney herself felt actual hurting in her breast. She swallowed, hard, but the tears began to flow like burning streams down her face.

"You…you're turning me down?" Shiloh stammered. "You…you don't want to marry me? But I thought—no, Cheney! I *know!* I know you love me!"

He took her by the shoulders and shook her. Then quickly he dropped his hands and clasped her to him gently. "Cheney, Cheney. What's wrong?" he whispered against her hair. "Tell me! I thought that I wasn't good enough for you, but now—"

"No, no. It's not that. It was never that and never would be," Cheney cried. "Shiloh, you honestly don't know? You never understood…realized…?"

He stood back, now watching her with narrowed eyes, warily. "Realized what?"

"Please, wait. Just give me a moment to…collect my thoughts…." She was almost inarticulate from grief and the heavy weight of guilt. It had never occurred to her that Shiloh truly might not realize the constraints placed upon her by her faith.

And all of this time…these last months, when I finally admitted to myself that I was in love with Shiloh, all I could think about was how to safeguard myself, how to protect myself, how to manage my own thoughts and emotions and passions. Not once did it occur to me that Shiloh could be hurt, too, terribly hurt. He looked tight, grim, the skin around his mouth white, his eyes a dark, desolate gray.

"Shiloh—" she began, gulped convulsively, and began again. "Shiloh, dear, I—"

He spoke with a coldness she'd never before heard from him. "Don't condescend to me, Cheney. I've asked you a question. Please answer it."

"A-all right. I'm honored by y-your proposal, Shiloh.

It gives me no p-pleasure, but I'm afraid I must decline. I can't marry you, Shiloh, because you are not a Christian." Tears, hot and accusing, ran down her cheeks and blurred her vision.

"Because—but, Cheney, listen to me!" he said, now pleading. "I'm a good man. You know that! I've always tried to be a good person, to live with honesty and honor. I was brought up by the most honorable and moral ladies I've ever met, except for you and your mother! And I'll—I can go to church with you. That's not a problem!"

Stubbornly she shook her head. "It is a problem, Shiloh. Why can't you—? It's much easier, Shiloh, to be a Christian than it is to—to…try to wear a—a cloak of righteousness. Why can't you see that? Why…why can't you just ask the Lord Jesus into your heart and become a Christian?"

She'd never asked him this question before, not directly. Now she was desolate at his reaction. With a touch of contempt, he retorted, "And if I did such a thing, right now, that would change your answer? You would marry me?"

She dropped her head and whispered hopelessly, "N-no, it—"

"Thought not." Savagely he turned and grasped the rail, his misshapen fighter's hands bloodless. "Please excuse me. I'd like to be alone for a while. Shall I call someone to escort you below?"

"No, that won't be necessary," Cheney said in a voice so arid and choked that she sounded more like an animal than a human. Her fingers were cold, lifeless, as they touched his hand. He started, and like a winter zephyr, they brushed against his palm.

He looked around and down, and she was gone. She'd

given him back his ring—their perfect pearl, their bond, the symbol of their past life together and their future joy.

With a muttered ugly curse, he threw it far behind the skimming ship. It was full dark now. Shiloh never saw it fall into the sea and disappear.

Chapter Two

Family Secrets

Duvall Court, a lone jewel hidden in the wilds of upper Manhattan, was lovely and graceful, as it had always been. Every brick in the circular drive was clean, the seams free from weeds; the pillars in front soared, white and gleaming; the mellow red brick glowed with the patina of comfortable aging. All of the rooms were welcoming. Most of the furnishings and fixtures and accessories were lavish, but never ostentatious. Irene Duvall's talent in decorating reflected exactly the kind of woman she was: warm without being overwhelming, elegant without affectation, tasteful without pretension.

Cheney's bedroom, too, was the same, with the massive sleigh bed, the Honiton lace canopy and coverlet, the bookshelves overflowing with books, the Queen Anne dressing table. As she dressed for dinner she reflected somberly, *How is it now I somehow don't quite feel that this is home? Not that I don't feel "at home"—of course I do—but I'm a grown woman now, and Duvall Court is*

Mother and Father's home. That's the way it should be, I suppose. But where do I feel home is?

With Shiloh, a small, sneaky voice in the back of her mind offered.

"No," she said aloud. *With You, Lord. You are my home.* The mental rebuke carried little conviction, but with a sigh she decided that that must mean it was said in faith. The stab of pain when she thought of Shiloh was very familiar to her now. It was like a deep cut in an awkward place, on the pad of her thumb, perhaps, that she managed to forget at times, but then, too often something rubbed salt in it, and it hurt again.

For this special welcome-home dinner, Cheney had chosen a dress she'd bought in New Orleans the previous year but had never worn. In a shade of sky-blue that particularly complemented her fiery auburn hair and high complexion, the overdress was made of tarlatan, a thin gauzelike muslin, stiffened and gored so as to fit her bodice and waist perfectly. The underskirt, with a medium train, had three rows of crocheted navy-blue Vandyke edging, and Cheney, who had a particular weakness for shoes, had bought a pair of velvet-heeled evening slippers in the same navy-blue shade with pearl buckles. She reflected that the sapphire necklace and earrings Dev had given her—a lifetime ago, it seemed—would look spectacular with the dress. But she didn't want to wear them for a variety of reasons, not the least because it felt, somehow, like another betrayal of Shiloh. She decided instead on an ornate cameo set against a Wedgwood blue, framed in gold and pearls, and pinned it to her corsage, pricking herself as she did.

"Typical," she muttered to herself. She was bemused

at how helpless she was without Nia. However was she to button those thirty-three tiny buttons down her back?

A single quiet knock sounded at her door, and Cheney called out, "Come in, Mother. Please rescue me."

As always, Irene Duvall glided gracefully into the room with only a silken rustle and a faint sweet scent to announce her. "I knew you couldn't dress yourself, darling," she sighed. "I couldn't. Richard had to do my buttons." Irene was wearing a gown of a stunning silvery-gray with white lace and ruffles and white gardenias at her breast and in her hair. She looked like a lovely will-o'-the-wisp.

"Thank you, Mother. I suppose that is one good reason to have a husband around." Cheney shocked herself, hearing the bitterness of her tone.

Irene, who was already buttoning her up, noticed that the back of Cheney's neck turned a dull red. "There, that's done," Irene said with satisfaction. "What else— oh, dear, Nia didn't have time to finish your hair?"

"No, and I know you're just as helpless as I am with that, Mother. Here, just poke some of these in it."

"Cheney, I shall not, as you so vulgarly suggest, *poke* those violets in your hair. I'll send Nia up to you." Irene's tone was severe, but she smiled.

"No, Dally needs her help with dinner. Surely, Mother, we are two intelligent, capable women, and with some forethought and consideration we can ascertain how to put these flowers in my hair."

Irene wasn't too certain of that—she had never, not once in her life, done her own hair—but she could see that Cheney simply wanted her to stay. Irene Duvall was a wise woman, and she knew her daughter. Admittedly, she didn't understand some things about Cheney—they

were two very different women—but she did *know* her.
Cheney rarely confided in Irene. She had always been reserved about her innermost thoughts and feelings, though
she did have a rather flamboyant personality. But Irene
knew how to comfort Cheney, especially since she sensed
exactly what was wrong.

"You're so right, my darling," she said with a show
of determination. "Sit down, and we shall overcome this
adversity of being without maids like two heroines. Here,
I shall put one violet right there. How does it look?"

"Fine, I think. Let us be courageous. Try two right
here, Mother. And what, may I ask, do you plan to
do about the terrible shortage of servants at Duvall
Court?"

The Clarkson family—once slaves of the de Cheyne
plantation in Savannah, Georgia—had been the Duvalls'
servants for years. Now Dally Clarkson was longing to
retire along with her husband, Big Jim, who had put in
twenty-eight years at the Duvall Iron Foundry. Their son,
Demi-Jim, was going to the University of the City of New
York, studying Commerce and Trade, while apprenticing
at a carriage maker's shipping and receiving office. Their
daughters, Tansy and Rissy, were both happily married
and no longer wished to be in service, and besides, Rissy
lived in Charleston. Nia, of course, was still Cheney's
maid, but she was not at Duvall Court unless Cheney
was.

Irene sighed gently as she painstakingly placed two
violets in the curls just behind Cheney's right ear. "I suppose we'll have to hire some more. It's just that I've never
had any servants besides Dally and her family, and Mr.
Jack, of course. It will be so odd."

Cheney eyed her mother with surprise. "Mother, I

can't imagine that a new crop of servants would intimidate you."

Irene smiled. "I'm not certain that 'intimidate' is the word, Cheney. It's just that Dally and Rissy and Tansy and Nia have always been more like family. It's not that way normally. Servants generally present some problems that we have never had to cope with."

"I suppose I must be lucky with Mrs. O'Neil, then, at Steen House," Cheney said airily. "She is not only invisible, but she is mute."

"I beg your pardon?" Irene said blankly.

"The woman's footsteps make no sound. I insist that she must be wearing thick socks. She doesn't go in for these new walking-length dresses, so I have never seen her feet, and I believe it must be true. One rarely catches glimpses of her gliding soundlessly in the darkened halls of Steen House. And she never speaks."

"Of course she speaks, Cheney," Irene scoffed, her eyes alight. "She must."

"I have heard her entire vocabulary. It consists of 'yes, Mum,' and 'no, Mum,' and 'very good, Mum,' and only then if she's directly addressed."

"Many would say that is a particularly virtuous trait in a woman," Irene ventured.

"Many *men* would say so," Cheney retorted. "But I find it a little lonely, so I suppose I do understand what you mean about Dally and Rissy."

"So you are lonely, Cheney?" Irene asked softly.

Cheney started, as though Irene had touched her. To Irene's consternation, she saw her daughter's sea-green eyes, so like her own, grow dark and confused. Cheney dropped her head. "No. No, Mother, I'm not really… lonely. Not…exactly."

Irene waited, but Cheney said no more and did not lift her head. Irene knew this meant that Cheney wasn't going to confide in her, and Irene also knew that she couldn't, and shouldn't, try to force her daughter's confidence. "You only arrived yesterday, Cheney," Irene said gently, "and you appear to be still weary from your long journey and illness. You know that if you don't feel like coming down, everyone will understand."

Duvall Court was entertaining tonight with a formal dinner party to welcome Cheney home. Having received an invitation to the wedding, Irene's two aunts from New Orleans, Tante Marye and Tante Elyse, and Tante Elyse's husband, Gowan Ford, had arrived in New York the week before. Victoria de Lancie, who had spent a month at Les Chattes Bleues and adored the tantes, had urged them to come at least a month early for the festivities. To Tante Elyse's and Gowan's surprise, Tante Marye had been enthusiastic about spending a month or so in New York.

Though they were staying at the Fifth Avenue Hotel, Tante Marye had promptly taken over the running of the Duvall household, much to Dally's consternation. Tante Marye had made all the arrangements for this dinner party herself, enjoining the services of their butler, Monroe, who also served as Gowan Ford's man, and his wife, Molly, housekeeper of Les Chattes Bleues, who had also accompanied the tantes as their maid.

Cheney weighed staying in her room, taking a sleeping draught, and going to bed early. Though she wasn't ill, she was so tired all the time. She almost decided to duck out. Shiloh was to be there, of course, and since the night he'd proposed, their infrequent shipboard meetings had been very constrained. It was so difficult. But then she discarded the idea of not attending because she and

Shiloh were estranged. At any rate, though he was not officially in the wedding party, he had already received and accepted all the invitations from both the Duvalls and the Steens for dinners and social events given for the de Lancie-Buchanan wedding. Cheney would be seeing much of him in the next month, like it or not.

"No," she finally said dully. "I am well, Mother. Of course I'm coming to my own welcome-home dinner. Besides, Tante Marye would never forgive, or let me forget, such a dereliction of social duty."

Irene smiled, but her eyes were a little sad as she put the finishing touches on her daughter's hair. *Blue violets in a wedding are for everlasting love. I suppose Cheney will never marry now.*

Most of Cheney's melancholy disappeared in the merry company. The nine of them had been through such a trying, and even dangerous, time at Les Chattes Bleues in New Orleans that they fast regained much of the intimacy of those eventful days, and soon they were all talking and laughing with the ease of old and close friends. They talked of Les Chattes Bleues, and Cheney and Shiloh particularly asked about Sock and Stocking, their old saddle horses they'd left at the plantation when they'd traveled to San Francisco.

"You mustn't worry about those horses," Gowan Ford grumbled. "Elyse thinks they are twin boys, toddlers, maybe, and she's going to bankrupt the plantation importing white grapes from Italy for them." He was a gargoyle of a man, with a missing arm and eye and ropy scar on his face and coarse silver-and-black hair. His glance, however, at his wife was as affectionate and gentle as a woman's.

Tante Elyse replied, "But, Gowan, you know they don't like those awful watery scuppernongs we grow. They truly pine for good grapes. They get quite thin and pitiful." She was a childlike woman in spite of her age, handsome with clear olive skin and flashing dark eyes and almost black hair without one strand of gray.

Monroe was serving the first course, three raw oysters on the half shell to each diner with Tante Marye's red-and-green pepper sauce. Tante Marye thought a first course of *hors d'oeuvres*—she called it a motley array of vulgar American tidbits, and the use of the French term did not fool *her*—should always be oysters or shrimp.

Cheney knew that this meal would consist of at least ten courses, and her mouth watered, for she did love Tante Marye's formal dinners. The secret to consuming such a vast array of food was that each dish was served in relatively small portions, and then, of course, ladies must never finish all of any dish. Cheney was particularly sorry that she must leave one of the fresh oysters, but she knew that later—along about the seventh or eighth course—she would be glad she did so that she would have room to sample all. Out of the corner of her eye, she noted that Shiloh only ate one oyster—an obvious gesture—and was surprised. He was a big man, and he had a big appetite, and he did love oysters. But Shiloh ate sparingly of the entire meal, merely taking a polite bite or two of each dish. Fleetingly Cheney wondered if his lack of appetite was because he was upset over her refusal of him. But quickly she pushed the sad thoughts away so that she could pretend, at least, that she was having a good time.

The talk turned to Hawaii, and Tante Elyse and Tante Marye demanded endless details from Cheney and Shiloh of the volcanic eruption that had devastated Winslow Villa and the plantation.

"Actually, only about six hundred acres burned, and the lava only covered about ninety acres," Shiloh was saying during the second course, a clear but rich French Soup Maigre. "'Course me and the Doc kinda wished it had been another ninety acres somewheres else." Though he spoke in his normal easy tone, he did not look at Cheney, much less exchange familiar smiles with her.

"It was quite an experience," Cheney added carelessly, for she was determined not to let her mother and father know exactly how dangerous their experience with the volcano had been. It was absurd, of course. Richard and Irene had a fairly clear idea of what Cheney had been through, gleaning some from the extremely offhand reference to it in her letters. The eruption on the island of Maui in the previous October, though not particularly intense, had even been mentioned in the New York papers.

"Oh! I'm sure it was so exciting!" Tante Elyse trilled. "I so long to be in a volcano!"

Her husband growled, "Elyse, you can't be *in* a volcano. It just won't do."

"Why not?"

"Elyse, I really must insist that you do not monopolize the conversation so," stated Tante Marye, a thin, stiff, silver-haired lady.

"But I haven't said much, really. Not nearly as much as I'd like," she added slyly under her breath, taking a ladylike sip of steaming soup.

Tante Marye, as she did so often, either did not hear her or chose not to. "Go on, Shiloh, please tell us all about the volcano."

"We're supposed to call him Mr. Irons-Winslow," Elyse said daringly.

This Tante Marye could not ignore—Elyse giving *her* an etiquette rebuke. "*Shiloh* is what we called him at Les Chattes Bleues, Elyse, and *Shiloh* he shall remain. I have already acquired his permission for using the familiar. If you have not, then you should do so immediately. For shame."

"All this name-callin's kinda embarrassing," Shiloh joked, holding up his hand. "First I didn't have a name, and now I have way too many for one man, not to mention the hyphen. Please, everyone here call me Shiloh. Yesterday, now, and forever."

At this Dev frowned a bit. He was a formal, somber man, and he had never felt comfortable calling other men by their Christian names. Even his adoptive father, Richard Duvall, had had a hard time convincing Dev to call him Richard rather than Mr. Duvall when he reached twenty.

At his side, Victoria, a blond confection in icy mint-green, smiled. "Except for you, Dev. We all know that it is quite beyond your powers to be so informal. I declare, he even calls his housekeeper madam."

"She is a madam," Dev said, unperturbed. "She's married to a perfectly respectable miller named Barentine, who is often afflicted with the catarrh *summat turrible*, has a scar on his head from a fall off a swing when he was a boy that flat knocked his sense outta him, and hopes to own his own flour mill someday, though Mrs. Barentine allows that that's all pie-in-the-sky-on-the-fly." He was watching Victoria as he spoke, and he looked very happy.

"Sounds like Mrs. Barentine allows a lot," Victoria giggled.

"It's shocking," Tante Marye interposed, "how familiar servants have grown these days." Of course, Tante Marye did not cast a foreboding glance at the servants. Tante Marye would never directly look at, or address, the servants during dinner. But Molly and Monroe, standing silently and unmoving by Dally and Nia at the sideboard, exchanged the smallest of long-suffering glances. "Irene, you really must let me help you choose your new staff, and since we are to be here for a month, I will perhaps have a week or two to begin training them."

"That would be such a help to me, dearest Tante Marye," Irene said, most sincerely. For all of her acerbity, Tante Marye managed an extremely complicated household and a large staff of servants, and she did it very well. And, too, the servants did like and respect her, for in spite of her occasional sharp tongue, she was a fair and judicious woman.

"Don't let's talk about servants," Tante Elyse begged. "I want to talk some more about Shiloh." Tante Elyse adored Shiloh, as most women did. "Tell us about your newfound family, Shiloh. The Winslows? I believe their people are British?"

"My...uh...great-great...uh... My ancestor was a man by the name of William Winslow," he said with some discomfort. "Actually, he was born here in America. In 1720. My...uh...people were originally British, but Gilbert Winslow came over on the *Mayflower,* and—"

"My goodness!" Victoria interrupted, her eyes shining. "Shiloh, you mean you are descended from the Founding Fathers? How delicious! American aristocracy, no less!"

"I don't think he was a Founding Father," Shiloh said, his brow wrinkling. "Doesn't that mean, like, those old men who signed the Declaration of Independence and the Constitution and stuff?"

Amused, Richard said, "Yes, I suppose 'Founding Father' does mean that…stuff. But Mrs. de Lancie means that your family was one of the first true American families. The Firstcomers, they're often called."

"Oh. Well, I suppose so. William Winslow returned to England when he was twenty-four years old in 1744. He married a woman named Verity Godwin five years later. Anyway, there are no Winslows left there. I believe there are quite a few Winslows in America that I'm connected with, but I've been having enough trouble with the Hawaiian ones, so I haven't thought much about the American ones."

"What sort of trouble?" Tante Elyse asked innocently.

"All kinds of trouble," Shiloh said with uncharacteristic shortness, casting his first and last glance at Cheney by his side.

After an awkward silence, Gowan said with gruff affection, "Elyse, you're not supposed to ask people about their personal lives or family troubles."

"But whyever not? We're all such good friends here, aren't we? And Shiloh does know such horrible things about us," Elyse said complacently. "Like our *vaudou* infestation. And he did know, dear Gowan, how silly and stubborn you were not to ask me to marry you a long, long time ago. And it was, after all, one of our very own servants who fell madly in love with him and tried to bewitch him and make him fall madly in love with her. And Shiloh also knows—"

"Elyse, stop it this instant. We are certainly not going to air more of our skeletons at this table and in this company." Tante Marye finally caught her breath and bolted upright.

"But that's just my point, Marye. Don't you see that everyone at this table, in this company, already knows—"

"That's enough," Tante Marye said in a dangerously quiet voice.

Tante Elyse fell silent, though she flounced a bit.

Cheney was hurt—Shiloh's coldness to her almost made her feel ill—but still she noted with amusement the little political war going on at the sideboard between the servants. Dally, who normally joined in the Duvalls' dinner conversation with a code of her own—a series of murmurs and grunts of assent or dissent—had been ominously silent throughout the first and second courses. Now the third, swordfish with pepper-and-chive sauce, was her own dish, and she obviously wanted to serve it. But Monroe was blankly stubborn, and it appeared that an actual physical tug-of-war was going on between them with one of the plates. Nia was hiding a smile behind one brown hand.

"Oh, dear Tante Marye," Victoria was saying with ill-concealed amusement, for she did find the tantes delightful, "I must beg to disagree with you. I think we should all tell some terrible story of our relatives or ancestors, for every family has someone who is either a rake or a villain or mad or a card cheat or a horse thief or is just an embarrassment to the family. I, for instance, have a distant elderly cousin who still wears—I swear it!—powdered wigs! He insists on wearing them everywhere, and his coats and cheeks are forever dusted with corn-starch,

for it seems his man is not as skillful as one would wish
with the powder."

Though normally Dev could not take his eyes or his
thoughts from Victoria de Lancie, for some reason his
attention wandered. Perhaps it was the somber, almost
desolate look that briefly marred Shiloh Irons-Winslow's
face when Victoria had said something about rakes and
villains in the family tree. Dev thought darkly that
none of these well-bred people at the table, Shiloh included, knew what it was like to have a true villain in
the family....

*Duane Buchanan had left them, or rather they had
fled, terrified, from him when Dev was only seven years
old. It was odd that Dev recalled so little of his father.
In the infrequent times he thought about him, all Dev
could remember was that he was a big man, thick, with
work-hardened muscles, coarse, tough hands, and a low
roar of a voice. But that was at the end. His mother had
told him that his father hadn't always been like that,
so angry and abusive. Funny, he could remember his
mother before their lives had taken such a tragic turn.
She was not pretty, not exactly, though she was so delicate, with such fine features, that she was like a small
plain bird...a thrush, perhaps, or a swallow.*

*She had spoken often, in those last days before she
died, of her husband and their life before Duane had
started drinking so heavily. There had been good times,
she said. Her life with her husband and son had been full
of laughter and contentment, for she loved Duane Buchanan, and she knew that he had loved her, no matter
what the terrible ravages of alcoholism had done to his
mind and his heart. She was plain and shy, while Duane*

had been a muscular, stormy "Black" Irishman, hand-some and outgoing, and no other men had ever taken much note of her. But when they were both seven years old, Duane Buchanan had announced to Amelia Kay Devlin that he was going to marry her, and he had kept his promise. Ten years later, on a cold day in January, they married. And on October 7, 1835, Devlin Buchanan was born.

They were happy for a while. Duane was a longshore-man at the New York docks and a fire laddie, and though he was still rowdy and ran with his fireman friends some-times, he was never unfaithful to Amelia. Duane seemed very proud of his son, who was like him in all ways, with black, glossy hair and deep dimples and darkly handsome features. Duane had fairly steady work at the docks, in summertime, anyway, and found rowdy fun as a fire laddie.

Amelia had always been an expert seamstress and had gotten a job as a seamstress for a cutter. Cutters—in-house tailors for wholesale firms—were among the city's best-paid workers. The wholesale firms bought cloth straight from the mills to the cutters, who cut it to the desired pattern, then parceled out the sewing to out-workers. Amelia was so good at all aspects of making clothing—including designing and cutting—that her cutter, a timid and nervous man named Ingram Yeager, soon allowed her to do much of the cutting. No one, of course, would ever hire a woman for such a job, or at such a wage, but he did raise her pay, for he began to depend upon her. Amelia made five dollars a week, while the outside seamstresses only made two.

But longshoremen's work was highly erratic, and wild young men who had roamed the Bowery all their lives with their friends were a recipe for a stew of trouble. Duane worked sixteen to seventeen hours a day during the summer, seven days a week, but often he could not find two days' work a month in the long winters. When he had no work, he kept Dev. But it must have been hard, "terrible hard on him," Amelia had told her son sadly. His wife made more money than he did, and he was so young, so full of life and energy and high spirits, and he was saddled with a wife and son and no prospects for bettering himself in the future.

Duane began to spend more and more time with his friends, and they began to call themselves the Bowery Boys. They roamed the streets, a vicious gang of extortionists and vandals and muggers. They stayed out until all hours of the night, carousing and visiting the saloons and oyster houses and brothels. So many of them were in the Bowery volunteer fire regiment that they began to spend more and more of their calls fighting other regiments and sabotaging their attempts at fire fighting than they did actually fighting fires.

Amelia, who understood Duane's feelings perfectly and loved him without measure, rarely reproached him or pleaded with him. Besides, she was too worn-out from working twelve hours a day, then doing housework and tending to Dev, to protest much.

When Duane could get work, he was better. But when he couldn't, he began to sink lower and lower. During the panic of 1837 he didn't work a single day in the last six months of the year. He began to drink, first mainly at night with his friends; then he began to start in the early afternoon after lunch. Finally he started drinking vile-flavored gin for breakfast, graduating to whiskey for dinner and supper.

As his drinking grew worse, so his temperament grew fouler. He began to be abusive, and though he never struck Amelia or Dev, he was belligerent and ill-tempered all the time. He worked sometimes in the spring, but his work habits, as his personal habits, grew slovenly. Amelia took her pay and immediately paid the rent and bought food before going home, for Duane took whatever money she brought to the house and drank it away.

Once, Duane ran out of whiskey money and showed up drunk and belligerent at Jackson & Plant, the wholesaler where Ingram Yeager and Amelia worked. Duane made a terrible scene and kept insisting that Amelia was holding out on him. The tailor, who had no little loyalty toward Amelia, tried his best to intervene, merely a timid plea for Duane to wait until Amelia got home to speak to her. Duane struck him and broke one of his ribs. The general manager of Jackson & Plant, who had never been too enamored with the idea of a woman being an assistant cutter, insisted that Amelia be fired. He refused to give Amelia a reference and threatened poor Mr. Yeager with his own position if he gave Amelia one.

So Amelia finally had to take a job at a boot-blacking production plant. It was filthy, cold, sickening work, for the dust from the blacking was as pervasive as smoke. She only made two dollars a week, for sixteen-hour workdays, seven days a week. She began to buy boxes of the blacking at the discounted price of two cents for the factory workers, and five-year-old Dev became a bootblack boy on the streets.

But it wasn't enough to sustain life. Amelia began coughing constantly, and soon she was coughing up blood at night. They lost their tidy little flat in the Bowery and had to move to a slum tenement. It was a

*filthy, odorous, rat-infested pit. Dev recalled his relief
as he left every day before dawn with his little bootblack
box and bit of rag, for even the cold and hostile streets
of New York were better than the miserable hole he and
his mother slept in. His father they did not see for days
at a time, then weeks, and finally he had been gone for
two months. Though neither of them said it, they hoped
he would stay away for what would surely be a better
Christmas without him.*

Chapter Three

Consultations

Triassic sandstone was pink, but because it contained hematite iron ore, it turned a dignified earthen color as it weathered. In the early part of the century, it had been considered a poor man's substitute for marble, reserved for basements, stoops, and details. Then in the '40s, with that same inexplicable wind that blew change in ladies' fashions, it became stylish and then a luxury item, judged to be more aesthetically pleasing than the artificial whites of Greek Revival.

Two blocks east of Gramercy Park stood a row of modest brownstone two-story town houses, looking much like a row of chocolates, except for the newest, which was completed only three weeks before. It was still pink and might have been likened to the whimsical Turkish delight in a candy box. Dr. Devlin Buchanan lived next to it, and he fervently hoped that the weather would be dour enough in the coming year to color his neighbor's house properly. Dev disliked pink houses, and both his bedroom window and front parlor window overlooked this offense.

Dev was lying in bed, luxuriating in sleeping late and in a leisurely perusal of the *Herald*—though he and Victoria were in the society pages *again*—and in the tray that Mrs. Barentine had just brought him. She had some shortcomings as a housekeeper and cook, but she always produced a wonderful breakfast tray, with toast still steaming in the rack, butter dripping, the coffee thick and almost boiling. She kept a supply of many different kinds of jams and conserves, and though it was expensive, Dev liked the variety. Also, he very rarely ate lunch or dinner at home, so his grocer's bill was negligible. He could afford every kind of jam made in America if he wanted. He was not a wealthy man, but he was comfortable, as his private practice, both here and in London, had been very lucrative. Undoubtedly his skill as a surgeon was mostly the reason he had been so successful, but Dev was also vaguely aware that his grave and professional demeanor attributed much to his success. Women loved having a physician who seemed so far removed from the very personal facets of what was of necessity an intimate physical relationship, and generally, men obediently used the physician that their wives dictated. At the same time, Dev was very handsome. With his dark glossy hair and intelligent dark eyes and flashing dimples, women found him irresistible, especially since he was so unapproachable. He was safe.

He had just unfolded the *Times* and begun to scan the headlines—sighing at the lead-in of the de Lancie-Buchanan wedding party's appearance at Irving Hall the previous evening on page fourteen—when he heard a knock at the front door. He started and almost jumped out of bed, but then he made himself settle back against the pillows and relax. He heard a low murmur of a man's voice and Mrs. Barentine's rather higher and more nasal answer. Her familiar heavy tread came up the stairs. "Dr. Buchanan?" she called uncertainly, knocking on the door.

"Enter," he said resignedly, donning his dressing robe. If Mrs. Barentine had not told the visitor that he was "not in," then it must be a medical emergency or a family member.

The housekeeper came in, a chubby, cheerful woman with round cheeks and a pouty little mouth, carrying the silver salver that held a single white card. Blushing a little, she said in a defensive tone, "He's such a nice young man, and he seemed so disappointed that you were not receiving, sir."

Shiloh Irons-Winslow. The card was plain white with block letters. "Hmm?" Dev muttered to himself. Shiloh had never called on him before. Though they were not enemies, they had never been what one might call friends. When Cheney had first hired Shiloh to be her medical assistant, Dev had positively disliked and distrusted him. He thought that Shiloh was little better than a thug and a bounder, though the fact that Dev was unofficially engaged to Cheney at the time had undoubtedly colored his opinions.

Dev had changed his mind in the last couple of years, however. Shiloh was not the lowlife that Dev had originally thought. Indeed, the man had many qualities that Dev admired, such as loyalty and courage and a sort of inborn integrity that transcended social condition. Shiloh was the same whether he was at a Vanderbilt party or in a tenement slum. Dev's adoptive father, Richard Duvall, had that same innate dignity. Dev had to admit that, like most mortals, he himself changed somewhat with his surroundings, endeavoring to fit in so as not to be out of place, while men like Richard Duvall and Shiloh Irons-Winslow were true to themselves no matter what the circumstances. This quality Dev admired, with no taint of envy but with only a resolution, often renewed, to learn how to be such a man. But still, though Dev thought Shiloh had admirable traits, he had never been able to decide if he *liked* the man or not. Perhaps he hadn't been around Shiloh enough. Well, here was a beginning.

"Mrs. Barentine, show Mr. Irons-Winslow into the parlor and give him some coffee or tea, whichever he prefers," Dev ordered. "I shall be down directly."

He dressed quickly in his habitual three-piece suit and black tie, abhorring that he hadn't shaved yet, and hurried downstairs.

Shiloh rose to greet him, and Dev felt a little better, for Shiloh was dressed in his old Irons clothing—denim breeches, a plain muslin shirt, and worn but spit-polished cavalry boots. He must have ridden over from the hotel. With wry amusement Dev wondered how the high-hat Fifth Avenue Hotel handled a guest clothed in a Western cowhand's costume.

Shiloh glanced at Dev's face—though Dev was unaware of it, his dimples flashed just a bit when he was inwardly amused—and said, "Kind of you to let me in, Dr. Buchanan, since the concierge at the hotel kicked me out."

"Did he?" Dev asked in surprise, waving Shiloh back to his seat in a worn but comfortable armed gentleman's chair. Dev took the sofa across from him. "I'm surprised he didn't have more discretion. They usually know all their paying customers very well, especially the ones who take the fifth-floor suites."

Shiloh shrugged and said dryly, "I hadn't seen this one before, and he seemed to think I was someone's dusty groomsman, or something, and told me to leave by the servants' entrance in the back. Then one of the clerks recognized me, and there was an interesting little scuffle between him and the concierge, but finally I got escorted out the front door by two or three of them, with lots of apologizing and bowing. It was kinda embarrassing. I think from now on I'm just going to head on out the back door unless I'm wearing front-door clothes."

"Front-door clothes," Dev repeated with some amusement. "How do you like them, by the way, Mr. Irons-Winslow?"

"Clothes are the least of it, aren't they? It's all the baggage that goes along with them that's hard to adjust to."

Dev nodded. Shiloh's life had changed drastically since he'd found his family, and it must be difficult to change from a carefree single man, an orphan, to a man with a family and what sounded like complicated properties.

Mrs. Barentine served them coffees, for once in silence, and left the room. Dev waited inquiringly and found that Shiloh wasn't looking at him. He was staring blankly out the window at the pink wall next door. Dev tried to think of something to say. If he asked Shiloh how he was feeling, that would imply he thought Shiloh was here as a patient, which couldn't be true and would be an insult to a social caller. Dev thought about various medical topics, but one could hardly begin a conversation with a caller by saying, "I had an interesting gallstone the other day."

Shiloh stirred, set his cup down with an unnerving crash, and leaned forward, clasping his hands together tightly. "Dr. Buchanan, I'd like to consult with you about a medical problem."

"Oh? Of course I'm at your service, Mr. Irons-Winslow." Now that Dev knew his ground, he immediately reverted from the sociable Dev to the businesslike Dr. Buchanan, "Are you ill?"

Shiloh shook his head. "No, it's my—uh—family." He leaned back restlessly and glanced out the window again, exhibiting uncharacteristic fidgeting for Shiloh. Dev wondered fleetingly why Shiloh was consulting with him instead of with Cheney, but as men are generally not very acute in personal matters, he forgot the half-formed thought as Shiloh began speaking in an impersonal, almost hard voice, much unlike his usual throaty drawl.

"My aunt, Denise Winslow, appears to be losing her mind," Shiloh said bluntly. "During the volcano, she became very agitated and was almost unbalanced. But that's not too unusual, I know. Some people kinda go mad when they're afraid they're going to die." Shiloh had been in the war on the Confederate side, and he'd seen plenty of death—before, during, and after.

Dev responded thoughtfully, "Especially when it comes upon them quickly from an accident or from Acts of God, as Lloyd's of London puts it. Danger with little or no warning can result in panic, a state in which reason does not govern and can be viewed as a sort of temporary madness."

Shiloh nodded with a trace more eagerness when perceiving Dev's understanding and matter-of-fact demeanor. "Sure, that's what I thought it was. Just panic, and then the shock after a disaster. It makes people…strange for a while. But she hasn't come out of it. I mean, she's not running around tearing her hair out and screaming, but my aunt is definitely ill with some sort of mental disorder, I believe."

"I see. Irons—I mean, Mr. Irons-Winslow—you do understand that this is not at all within my area of expertise?"

"I am aware of that, Dr. Buchanan," Shiloh said, matching his formality. "But I hoped that you might be able to advise me about finding a suitable doctor or a private hospital. My uncle and I are fairly certain that if my aunt gets any worse, it will be necessary to…to… make some arrangements for her. And with what little I've been able to read in the medical journals, it seemed to me that London is on the leading edge of research and experimentation with the mentally ill."

Thoughtfully Dev said, "Actually, it's the Germans who have been, for the last decade or so, managing the mentally ill without always having to resort to imprisonment and manacles. As a matter of fact, I know someone right here in New York who is one of the best men in the field. We could go see him now, if you like."

Shiloh was surprised. "We? You mean, you'll go with me?"

"Of course," Dev said, unruffled. "It's my consultation and my responsibility to you."

"Thank you, Dr. Buchanan, I really appreciate it," Shiloh said with evident sincerity.

"Not at all." He rose, looking at Shiloh critically. Once again his guest was staring blankly out the window as a man in prison stares out through the bars. Shiloh had changed, all right. Before, he had been light, careless, easygoing, gliding through life hardly leaving a ripple, always giving the impression that he was just in port for a short time. Now there was a certain heaviness about him, and his face showed care. Dev reflected that families could be a heavy burden, indeed, and it appeared that Shiloh's family did have some terrible problems. It never occurred to him that the Winslows were not the cause of Shiloh's melancholy, and later he would bitterly regret his blindness.

The Bellevue Institution was a walled, twenty-six-acre site overlooking the East River. In its half century of life, Bellevue had included such varied social institutions as a pesthouse, an almshouse, a hospital, a penitentiary, a school, a morgue, a bakehouse, a washhouse, a soap factory, a greenhouse, an icehouse, carpenter shops, a blacksmith shop, and an execution ground. It was still a motley collection of buildings, from the looming three-story blue-stone almshouse to the red-brick hospital to the grim gray three-story penitentiary.

The Insane Pavilion, located on the Twenty-sixth Street side of the grounds, was a nondescript rectangular building with a tiny spare vestibule. It was manned by a burly male attendant with a wooden baton stuck in his belt. When he opened the iron door behind him to fetch Dr. Banckert, an unsettling confusion of catcalls, screams, hoots, whistles, and shouts from the long hallway behind him echoed in the small reception area.

Almost immediately Dr. Banckert returned with the attendant. The doctor was a small man, spare and nimble, with bright eyes, unruly gray hair, and a meticulously groomed mustache. His German accent was thick, which warmed Shiloh toward him instantly because it reminded Shiloh of the Behring sisters.

"Dr. Buchanan, how good to see you. How may I be of service to you today?" Dr. Banckert said warmly, pumping Dev's hand.

"Good morning, Dr. Banckert. I have the honor of introducing to you a colleague of mine, Mr. Shiloh Irons-Winslow," Dev said.

The formal introduction and social niceties proceeded, and Shiloh was flattered by Dev's endorsement of him as a colleague.

When Dr. Banckert understood that Shiloh and Dev had come for a consultation, he hurried them—he was a brisk, quick-speaking and fast-walking kind of man—to his office, a cheerless, windowless cubicle in a squat stone building next to the Pavilion.

As they seated themselves on uncomfortable wooden chairs in front of Dr. Banckert's littered desk, the German physician immediately seemed to shift from a busy little beetle into a still, waiting statue, his hands arranged with odd grace in his lap. Shiloh noticed those kinds of things. Dr. Banckert had what Shiloh had always thought of as healing hands: white and capable-looking with agile fingers and clean cropped nails. Shiloh's own hands were fighter's hands, rough and worn and scarred.

"...Mr. Irons-Winslow and I are curious about the new approaches in treatment of the insane," Dev was explaining. "I'm ashamed to say that I have learned nothing of treatment of the insane other than one or two articles I've read on phrenology."

"Phrenology, pah!" Dr. Banckert burst out with a sudden flurry of energy, waving one hand with derision. "Such drivel! Discernment of bumps on the head—such humbuggery—*Zum Teufel! Nein, nein.* I study Tuke. I follow Pinel."

"And he can dissect a brain faster and neater than anyone I've ever seen," Dev told Shiloh.

Modestly Banckert said, "It's a good skill to have for neurology, *ja?* Not too much good in psychiatry."

"What is psychiatry, anyway?" Shiloh asked curiously.

Leaning forward, his eyes blazing with intensity, Dr. Banckert answered, "We can dissect the brain, break it down into its sundry parts, analyze it, classify it. Now we try to do the same with the mind, Mr. Irons-Winslow, to try to understand it better so that when it grows ill, we can cure it. We are learning how to analyze some problems, as in Pinel's studies. Such understanding has made it possible for us to give mental patients more compassionate care than we used to, though, of course, most asylums are still little better than prisons, restraining all of the patients, regardless of their particular disorder, in the same manner as they restrain the violent lunatics."

"I see," Shiloh said gravely. "And what about the worst cases? The violent ones?"

Dr. Banckert asked, "And do you have a special interest in psychiatric treatment for violent psychotics, Mr. Irons?"

"Yes."

"Professional, or personal?"

Shiloh answered with obvious embarrassment, "Personal. A member of my family."

"Ah. And this family member is your connection by blood?"

Shiloh was nonplussed, then replied, "Oh, I get it. You're thinking sometimes it's inherited?"

"Sometimes."

Shiloh shook his head. "No. An aunt. No blood relation. But I'm— She's my...responsibility."

"I see. And you believe she has some sort of neurosis or psychosis?" Dr. Banckert asked eagerly.

"I don't know what those are," Shiloh answered uncertainly. "All I know is that she's started acting like a homicidal lunatic."

Dr. Banckert leaned back in his chair and steepled his fingers precisely together. "Ah, I see. She has, then, committed murder?"

Confused, Shiloh replied, "Uh—no, sir."

"Then she is not, precisely, homicidal?" Dr. Banckert asked gently.

"Well, no, guess not."

"And she is irretrievably insane during the full moon?" Dr. Banckert went on, his eyes twinkling.

Dryly Shiloh replied, "No, sir."

"And so she is not exactly a lunatic either," Dr. Banckert said in a most kindly manner. "You see, Mr. Irons-Winslow, it is precisely the use of such vague and unscientific terms that have resulted in the cruel methods of treatment that have been used on mental patients. Regardless of the nature of their disorder, they have all been isolated and restrained and ignored as hopelessly deranged. Now we have made a bit of progress in classifying some diseases of the mind as being completely separate from violent lunatics. Mentally diseased persons who are dangerous to themselves or others are generally rare."

"But, sir, she has exhibited some violent behavior," Shiloh said uncertainly.

"And have you ever exhibited violent behavior?" Dr. Banckert asked intently.

"Well...I...yes, sir, I have, but I...I had a good reason for it," Shiloh stammered, feeling a little absurd. Dev was, uncharacteristically, smiling.

"A sane reason for it, you mean?" Dr. Banckert said brightly. "And your aunt's violent act or acts—there was no sane reason for them? With no provocation, no apparent motive, she erupted into violence?"

Shiloh frowned and muttered, "Well, I guess you could say she did have a reason."

"There," the doctor said. "If they have a reason, no matter how repugnant we might find it, it is likely not a psychopathic disease. The true psychopaths, you know, are the ones who have no reason at all. This is a very diluted explanation, Mr. Irons-Winslow, but I must tell you that true homicidal maniacs are very rare, indeed."

"That's some comfort," Shiloh said thoughtfully. "But I still am unclear on what is wrong with my aunt, why she's acting the way she is, and what to do with her."

Dr. Banckert said sympathetically, "I know. I know. These are hard questions, and the answers are complex and intricate. That is why psychiatry is such a difficult field, Mr. Irons-Winslow, and it is also in its infancy. Diagnosis is generally a long-term undertaking, and the cures—when we have them—take even longer. And I cannot possibly do any sort of evaluation of your aunt from talking to you about her condition, no matter how much you tell me about her or the circumstances."

Deflated, Shiloh nodded. "I understand, sir. My aunt is in Hawaii, and there is no doctor of psychiatry available there at all. I just thought it might help if I could talk to someone knowledgeable about the disease."

Dr. Banckert eyed Shiloh shrewdly, then said, "Tell me about your aunt. I might, perhaps, be able to suggest some things to help you and your family to cope, even though I can't help your aunt."

Gratefully Shiloh told him about the volcano, about Denise Winslow's reactions, and her deterioration since that time. He also told Dr. Banckert with stark honesty about his peculiar intrusion into her family and about the behavior and subsequent disappearance of her son, Bain Winslow.

"She has periods of being normal, but even then she seems really depressed," Shiloh said with clear sadness. "Sometimes, she just sits for hours and stares into space, hardly moving. After that, when it seems she'd want to get up, move around, do something, instead she sleeps for long hours. She's begun to drink heavily and to take a lot of laudanum. Recently she actually attacked my cousin Brynn—her own daughter—with a letter opener when Brynn was trying to take away the laudanum. We—that is, my cousin and my uncle and I—had been doing our best to take care of her, and we were doing all right, I guess. She wasn't getting any better, but she didn't seem to be getting any worse—she didn't howl at the moon or froth at the mouth or anything. But when she got violent with my cousin—" Shiloh stopped abruptly, shrugging helplessly.

Dr. Banckert was silent for long moments and drew back into his statue posture, sitting absolutely still and staring into space. Finally he said, "Yes, the violence. That is the hardest question, is it not? For only if we completely understand the causation and can clearly predict it can it be controlled and finally erased." Now focusing on Shiloh with open sympathy, he said, "Sir, I wish I could tell you about your aunt's violent tendencies—why they are manifested, what is the reason, if they will continue, if they will escalate—but I cannot, not without spending a lot of time with her. All I can tell you that may be of some comfort to you is that we are discovering that even the most violent of the insane often respond favorably to gentle care and entreaty, to calm conversation, and most importantly, to a sympathetic listening ear. This does not mean that sometimes they must not be physically restrained, but even in that area we have found more humane methods."

"Oh? And what about that?" Shiloh asked alertly.

"Perhaps it would be best," Dr. Banckert said, rising, "if we would just go to the Pavilion where we house our most violent patients, most of whom will soon either go to prison or to one of the asylums. Here at Bellevue, however, I am allowed to study them for a period before they are shipped out. I have managed to improve their care and the facilities here, though I know that wherever they are sent will not be nearly as pleasant. Still, I find that in these surroundings the patients will talk to me and allow themselves to speak more freely than if they were chained to a wall and wallowing in filth. I will show you that even though we must still be careful for our own and the patients' safety, our methods are much improved over the normal lunatic ward."

They returned to the Pavilion, with Dr. Banckert walking and talking very fast, telling them of the difference between neurosis and psychosis, the characteristics of dementia praecox, of paranoia, of manic-depressive psychosis, using many terms that Shiloh had never heard before and didn't understand.

They passed through the vestibule and the iron door

into a long hallway with more iron doors on each side that led into the separate cells. These doors had barred gratings in them, and through the openings many hands waved and gesticulated. The din was loud at first but seemed to lessen as they passed down the hallway. Evidently once the doctor passed by, the entreaties stopped.

"You see, we must still isolate violent cases," Dr. Banckert explained. "But these cells are as comfortable and comforting as we can make them. We only resort to personal restraints as a very last measure. And we encourage family visits, if at all possible. In some cases we have found that the best surroundings for the disturbed person is an atmosphere as close to homelike as possible. So you see, Mr. Irons-Winslow, perhaps your aunt is in the best situation after all. However, if you will take the time to write a report about your aunt, I will try to make you some concrete suggestions."

"Why, thank you, sir. I'd appreciate that very much."

They heard, among the calls and cries, a strange sound. Somewhere a baby began crying. Dev started, then asked, "You allow infants in here? In the Pavilion?"

Dr. Banckert answered, "Not normally, *nein*. We usually don't allow children to visit. But this is a very interesting case—a man who erupted in sudden, deadly violence without apparent explanation. I truly hoped to be able to classify him, but sadly I don't think he'll live long enough. He's very ill. Let's go in, and you can see one of the cells."

Dr. Banckert motioned to one of the muscular attendants, who then came forward and unlocked one of the doors. They entered a small square room, bare and grim.

Bars covered the single small window. But there were clean sheets on the bed, the chamber pot was empty, the wooden floor clean. A man was half reclining on the bed, staring into space with his eyes half closed. Only after they'd been in the room for a few moments did Shiloh notice that one wrist was manacled, though the chain leading to an iron ring in the wall was light and long enough to allow the man to move about. The man's face was bony, and his complexion was an unhealthy yellow, the cheeks sunken and eyeholes deep. Instantly Shiloh, with his diagnostic instincts, thought, *Liver's shot. This poor mug won't have too long a stay in the asylum or the prison.*

He had a thick shock of salt-and-pepper hair, which, Shiloh noted, was clean and combed, and he saw the washbasin and soap and linen on a small table in the corner. The man's expression was dull, with a hint of what could best be called bewilderment. He didn't speak, but his eyes did track to whoever was speaking at the moment.

By the door in a straight-backed wooden chair a woman sat holding the crying baby. She was probably around twenty-five years old and might once have been pretty in a saucy sort of way. But now her skin was the unhealthy pasty color of a heavy drinker. Her hazel eyes were dull and red rimmed, and she had a slovenly slouch.

Dr. Banckert explained, "As you can see, this man has advanced jaundice and extensive liver damage, presumably from alcoholism. He also periodically exhibits delirium tremens, with the usual symptoms of chills, fever, palsy, and hallucinations. He has a history of explosive outbursts of temper and violent reactions. You see the scar on his neck and his missing right forefinger? Those are from fights, mostly saloon brawls."

"Dart, that's his name," the woman said in a low sing-song voice. "Got it 'cause he put a man's eye out wid a dart."

Dev was staring hard at the man. In a low tone he said, "But it's my understanding that neither delirium tremens nor a history of a high temper and violent behavior is included in Pinel's classifications, and therefore is not currently considered to be true insanity."

"True. This man obviously is violent—but is he a psychopath? No one thinks mean drunks or saloon brawlers are psychopaths. But this man, you see, has had two violent episodes in the last six months that didn't fit into his pattern," Dr. Banckert explained. "Neither incident presented any sort of stimulus to violence—that is, in neither case did Dart have any reason to lose his temper. The first was an interesting incident in which Dart was sound asleep. Evidently he had a nightmare, woke up, and attacked Connie, here. This is Connie Dunleavy, by the way. Dart's friend."

"I'm his wife," she said sullenly. "And you mighta thought it was interesting, mister, but I sure don't. Dart likely woulda strangled me if I hadn't of dashed him upside the head with a flatiron."

"Er…yes, of course," Dr. Banckert said soothingly. "At any rate, when Dart came to, he had no recollection at all of the incident."

"He never done nothin' like that to me before," Connie said in a flat voice that denoted below-average intelligence. "Never did."

"What was the second occurrence?" Shiloh asked.

Dr. Banckert sighed. "The second occurrence is why

he's here. He attacked and almost killed a woman with a child. She was a total stranger to him, passing him on the street in broad daylight, pushing a carriage with her four-year-old son in it. When she passed him by, evidently nothing was exchanged, not even a glance, certainly no words. But Dart suddenly turned and grabbed the woman, threw her to the ground, and beat her face. Then he began kicking her. She sustained serious head injuries, broken ribs, and a broken arm. One of the ribs almost punctured her lungs. Luckily, we were able to get her to emergency surgery quickly. As a matter of fact, this took place not far from here—right down on Madison Square. And Dart did this right in front of a constable. The officer was walking on the street just a bit behind Dart. And Dart knew he was there. He had said something to the constable just a few minutes before."

"He's calm now," Shiloh observed. "Hard to believe he has such a wicked temper."

Dr. Banckert said with obvious frustration, "Yes, he's calm now because I've been obliged to drug him. A new drug—chloral hydrate. Maybe you've heard of it. It has a marvelous calming influence, but it dulls the mind so much that conversation with the patient is worthless as far as being able to evaluate the state of his mind. The patient always drifts into sleep, even with just a slight dosage. Dart's been unreasonable, bordering on hysterical, since he was arrested. He was very agitated this morning, but I knew that Miss Dunleavy was coming with Dart's son, so I was obliged to medicate him."

"Dart don't allus ack so mean," Connie said in a low voice. "Most times he's pretty good to me. He's not happy with the boy, though. Hain't been ever since he was borned."

"The boy is Dart's son, though, isn't he?" Dr. Banckert asked gently.

Connie Dunleavy bristled. "Jist 'cause I don't know him 'cept by Dart, and jist 'cause I'm his common-law wife don't make me no trollop, mister. 'Course he's Dart's son."

Shiloh thought that this must be likely, for the infant—even though most babies tended to look alike—did have a look of Dart about him. For one thing, he had a shock of healthy black hair and dark eyes, which was unusual for babies only three or four months old. Also, he had deep dimples, just as Dart did, dimples that could be seen even when he wasn't smiling.

As Dr. Banckert went on to explain to Shiloh how it was imperative to differentiate between explainable violence and inexplicable violence, Dr. Devlin Buchanan stared at the man lying so still and listless in shackles. As the three men left the cell, Dev stopped, and for a long time he stared down at Connie Dunleavy and Dart's son.

Chapter Four

Kinds and Levels and
Leanings and Sundry Gifts

"I sent Shiloh an invitation to join us," Victoria said with a shrewd glance at Cheney. "But he returned a note with my footman, graciously declining. I must say I'm rather surprised. After all, he's the reason we're connected with Behring Orphanage in the first place."

Cheney said nothing as she stared out the carriage window. They were just about at Seventy-fifth Street West, she judged, though of course there were no street signs here in the wilds of northern Manhattan Island. In fact, there were no streets, only the wide dirt bank of Broadway that rose like a dike above the entrenched squares of land, excavated according to the peculiar philosophy of the Randel Plan. The area north of Sixtieth Street, especially on the west side of Central Park, was still farmland, and the farms generally consisted of shanties with chickens and pigs or perhaps some hardy goats.

Tante Elyse and Gowan Ford were accompanying

Cheney and Victoria to Behring Orphanage at Ninety-third and Broadway, and now, after an awkward silence, Tante Elyse said hurriedly, "I'm sure Shiloh had a good reason for declining your invitation, Mrs. de Lancie. As he is now a man of some means, he must be very…um… preoccupied. With…with his properties and business and family…er—"

"Elyse," Gowan said dryly, "you're blithering again."

"Am I? Oh, dear. I do have such trouble with the art of conversation, particularly when one must smooth over the rough spots," she said naïvely. "And it is awkward, isn't it? Since we all know, Cheney, that you and Shiloh are estranged, and you are so very sad, and Shiloh does seem to be—"

"Elyse," Gowan said severely, "not now."

"Hmm? Oh. Yes, of course. I mean, no, of course," Elyse trilled.

Gowan Ford, as much as he loved his wife and as long as he'd known her, often couldn't tell whether she was feigning such simple-mindedness or not. He had observed that at times her artlessness, instead of repelling people, seemed to make them respond in kind with a startling openness, and he suspected that it was a peculiar kind of gift in Elyse.

But now he wasn't certain whether she truly knew exactly what she was saying, and he didn't want her to blurt out what he'd told her about Shiloh. In the last three nights, since Shiloh and Cheney had arrived in New York, Gowan had seen Shiloh in the Gentlemen's Salon in the Fifth Avenue Hotel. Gowan always stopped in there for a cigar after dinner, for he had some business contacts in New York and often met them there in the evenings. But Shiloh didn't seem to be conducting business. He stayed close to the bar with a group of rowdy young men, drinking and flirting with the barmaids. Last night he'd been in particularly high spirits. Gowan thought that Shiloh was not a messy drunk—he didn't slur his words, or stagger, or anything like that—but his voice got louder, the color in his face was high, and he had a definite reckless, even boisterous, air that was completely unlike him.

Gowan had, of course, told his wife, but he didn't want Elyse to tell Cheney. He tried to puzzle out why—he had little loyalty to Shiloh Irons-Winslow and much loyalty to Cheney Duvall and her family—but some code among men constrained him. He just didn't want to be a tattle, he supposed. Sighing, he thought that the intricacies were too much for him. Probably for any man.

At any rate, Elyse was now talking about Victoria's magnificent gold-and-white carriage, the footmen's livery, the odd desolate scenery after the crowded and lively streets of the city. Cheney had barely responded to Elyse's hints. She sat staring blankly out the window. Victoria was watching Cheney with a hint of regret that she had prodded her friend.

"Yes, Tante Elyse, it's still just like the country right now," Victoria responded, since Cheney was taking no notice of the conversation. "But believe me, the city is creeping northward. I wouldn't be surprised if all of this isn't developed within the next ten years or so. My family has bought several hundred acres surrounding the orphanage, all that we can get our hands on. William Backhouse Astor is snatching up most of it, just as his father did on the Lower East Side years ago. And if that's not an indication of a trend, I don't know my business."

Elyse nodded enthusiastically. For all of her noodling, she was an excellent businesswoman. For most of her life she'd managed Les Chattes Bleues, the de Cheyne indigo plantation outside of New Orleans. "It certainly looks like a shrewd investment to me, Mrs. de Lancie, just from seeing the crowded city to the south. And I was so glad to hear that Richard had purchased several hundred acres surrounding Duvall Court. He said he'd barely managed to grab some of the adjoining plots before Mr. Astor started outbidding him."

Cheney suddenly rejoined the living. "He has? I didn't know that, Tante Elyse. When did Father do this?"

"Last year, while you were in Hawaii, I think," Elyse answered. "Cheney, my darling, you really should start paying more attention to the family businesses and properties. After all, you will inherit everything, along with Dev, of course. In fact, Marye and I have decided to will all of the personal property of Les Chattes Bleues to you and Dev, too, since we have no children."

"Oh—oh, horrors, Tante Elyse, that's in a hundred years," Cheney said with distress. "I'm overjoyed and honored, but I certainly don't want to think about any of that right now."

Very casually Victoria said, "I had wondered, Tante Elyse, if you or Tante Marye had children."

"No, neither of us ever did," Elyse responded wistfully and glanced up at Gowan. "Neither did Gowan, for you know he was so silly he wouldn't marry anyone but me, and now we're so old."

"Elyse, it's not my fault that we got married so late in life," Gowan rasped.

"But of course it is, you ninny," Elyse said affectionately. "If you would have asked me—or even looked my way—when we were young, I never would have married George."

Ford seemed about to retort; then he turned his one good eye—the left—to give her a roguish wink. But Elyse was looking up at him with such shining eyes, such warmth, that Gowan Ford might have been a handsome Prince Charming. "Elyse, I'm not going to have this argument with you for the rest of our natural lives," he grumbled, but with clear affection. "I'm just glad you were fool enough to marry me at all."

"Me, too," Elyse agreed serenely.

Victoria smiled, a little sadly, and prodded, "But do you, Tante Elyse, regret that you didn't have children?"

Elyse was still looking up at her husband's scarred face, her features still youthful, still with a faint trace of Creole sultriness, her always lively expression still and intense for once. "Of course I do, Mrs. de Lancie. Marye has never seemed to mind, but I have my regrets. My life has been so full, however, that these longings have faded much, and I am content."

Gowan Ford had only one hand—his left—and now he reached across with some awkwardness and took his wife's hand and held it, smiling down at her with a tenderness that was intensified by his fierce visage.

And now both Cheney and Victoria, with sad airs, turned to stare out of the glassed windows to the emptiness outside.

Behring Orphanage, the proprietress Jane Anne Blue and her two children, Laura and Jeremy, and Allan Blue, her husband, had a rather entangled history with Victoria and Cheney and Shiloh. Cheney explained the Blues' history to Gowan and Tante Elyse. They had met Allan Blue once, when he brought Sock and Stocking to Les Chattes Bleues for Cheney and Shiloh, but Cheney had never told them the story of his family. Gowan and the tantes did know about Shiloh's history with the Behring sisters, for whom the orphanage was named, though Miss Linde Behring had died in the cholera plague of 1866. Victoria owned the real property and was the patroness of the orphanage.

"And you know, of course—didn't I tell you, Cheney?—that Gowan and I often visit Miss Tanzen Behring at the orphanage in New Orleans," Elyse was saying as the carriage went through the gate. "She's such a lovely woman. I've tried and tried to get her to come out to Les Chattes Bleues for a holiday, but she won't leave the orphanage for even one night."

"She's very dedicated," Gowan agreed, "and it shows. Those are some of the most well behaved, polite, personable children I've ever seen. 'Course we might have known that the Behring sisters would be so gifted after getting to know Shiloh." As soon as he said it, he regretted it, for each time they mentioned Shiloh's name, a shadow seemed to pass over Cheney's face like a small gray wisp of cloud flitting across the sun.

But Cheney had made a determined effort to rouse herself and not to be such poor company, so she replied, "I've always regretted that I didn't meet Miss Etta Behring in Charleston, or Miss Tanzen in New Orleans. I must meet Miss Tanzen the next time we visit. I mean, the next time I visit. Anyway, Tante Elyse, you will love the farm. Victoria has managed to make it into a most wondrous place. It's a working farm, but it's so lovely it looks more like a wealthy estate."

"It is lovely," Elyse said eagerly. "So pastoral…"

After the hollowed-out trenches of northern Manhattan, the farm was like a garden in the wilderness. The rolling acres surrounding the orphanage had been cleared of brambles and thickets, while the hardwoods had been left intact. The apple orchard was lovely now, in early spring, in full bloom. Perky white and yellow jonquils were everywhere in lush clumps, with tiny carpets of white crocuses and purple hyacinth growing wild on the little hills. The road to the farmhouse was earthen and bordered by white fencing all the way up to the house.

The farmhouse—now an orphanage—was a generous two-story clapboard, freshly painted a bright yellow with green shutters framing the windows. Allan Blue was outside wearing a grass-stained apron and holding a shovel. As Victoria's carriage pulled up, he stopped digging in one of the generous flower beds surrounding the house and waved his shovel.

"He looks well," Cheney remarked.

"It's hard to believe that Captain Blue had such an exciting and dangerous time during the war and was such a dashing spy," Elyse declared. "Upon first acquaintance he seems so...clerkish."

"I don't think that's a word, Elyse," Gowan said, his single eye twinkling, "but I do know what you mean."

Allan Blue was indeed a rather nondescript man, slender with mild hazel eyes and a studious manner. Now, however, as he came toward the carriage wiping his grimy hands and grinning, he looked tanned and strong. "I've quite forgiven him for deserting Jane Anne and the children," Victoria said piously.

Amused, Cheney said, "That's very charitable of you, Victoria."

"I must say that Jane Anne made him do everything but dance and sing to get back into the family," Victoria went on, grandly ignoring Cheney. "It was about a year after he returned before Jane Anne would let him move here and join them. I don't believe I've ever seen such an ardent courtship and such conscientious parenting as Mr. Blue carried on during that year."

"How has he been since moving back in with Jane Anne?" Cheney asked.

"Marvelous," Victoria admitted. "A marvelous husband, a wonderful father, and he's been invaluable to the orphans. That's another advantage that Behring Orphanage has over so many other institutions—the children have a father figure. Most all of them have only women."

They alighted from the carriage and sorted themselves out. Allan greeted them all, standing a little back from them. "Please forgive me, ladies, but I am much too grubby to approach you. Today is gardening day, as I suppose you can see."

"You look very well, Captain Blue," Cheney said warmly. He was tanned and fit looking, his unusual honey-gold hair thick and shiny.

"I am better than I have ever been in my life," Allan replied. "Much of it is due to you, Dr. Duvall, and I give thanks every day for you—and Mr. Irons-Winslow. I'm sorry he was unable to come with you, but he sent us a message that he'll be along in a day or two."

He led them to the house and opened the door but refused to go in, as his boots had big clods of dirt stuck to them. A pretty girl with glossy black curls, wearing a black dress and clean white apron, met them.

"Sylvie, announce our visitors to Jane Anne, and mind you do it correctly," Allan said sternly. The girl's full cheeks blushed bright pink as she led them in, and Allan whispered to Cheney, "Practice, you know."

She smiled. "Oh, I know you're a stern taskmaster, Captain Blue." Allan Blue was the gentlest of men.

Sylvie managed to announce them all correctly, though she blushed exceedingly, and her curtsey was more like a bouncy dance step than a discreet bob.

"Thank you, Sylvie, you may go and attend to tea," Jane Anne Blue said and rose to greet her visitors.

Jane Anne Blue was now thirty-five years old, modestly pretty, though she was much too thin. She did look healthy, however, as her brown doe eyes were bright and her complexion was smooth. The worry and stress lines that she had worn when Cheney had first met her were gone. Cheney couldn't help but automatically assess friends in a medical way, especially Jane Anne, for she was fragile.

Victoria performed the formal introductions of Gowan and Elyse, and they all got seated. Eagerly Cheney asked, "But where is Laura? I would very much like to see her. And how is she? Her overall health, I mean. Is she well? Is she getting stronger? What about her rate of growth?"

Jane Anne laughed, a small throaty sound. "Dr. Duvall, it's so kind of you to take such an eager interest, and I would love for you to see Laura later. I don't usually have her with me to receive visitors." Laura was Jane Anne and Allan's youngest child, now eight years old and severely handicapped.

"Dr. Duvall told us about her," Tante Elyse said. "We'd love to meet her."

"Of course. I hope you'll meet all the children," Jane Anne replied. "But right now they are all either in the schoolroom or working. Laura, I'm happy to say, is one of their...um...projects. I had just started letting some of the older girls care for her when Allan came back, but he convinced me to let all of the children, even the boys, learn to help take care of her. He said that it would teach them an invaluable lesson—not only how to care for the disabled but also to have compassion for those less fortunate than themselves. Even the smallest of the children come to see that being an orphan is hard, but that there will always be someone who has worse problems."

"It must be very difficult for you," Tante Elyse said sympathetically.

"It is, in some ways," Jane Anne admitted. "But I must say that Laura herself is not a tragic figure. She is sweet natured and patient, never rebellious, never melancholy, never disobedient. I don't understand the nature of the close relationship that God has with her, but I never doubt that He does. In many ways her life is much easier and more full of simple joys and pleasures than is ours. Indeed, I thank God for her every day. All children are a blessing from God."

Victoria's mouth tightened, though it was likely imperceptible to everyone but Cheney, who happened to be watching her at the time. Victoria said coolly, "I'm glad to hear that Laura is doing so well, Jane Anne. What about Jeremy? Is he working hard on his studies?"

"Oh yes," Jane Anne answered enthusiastically. "It's hard to believe that such a scruffy little rat killer could be so dedicated to his education." Jane Anne explained to Cheney and the Fords, "Allan tutors the boys and I teach the girls. Almost in spite of himself, Jeremy began to get interested in the physical sciences, particularly geology. Mrs. de Lancie has been kind enough to offer him a scholarship to the Columbia School of Mines if he completes his undergraduate studies satisfactorily. We're all thrilled, Mrs. de Lancie, and I must thank you for your extraordinary generosity once again."

"No, don't," Victoria said in a bored tone. "It's not generous at all. I've told you, I just want an indentured servant who is a skilled geologist. When he has completed his degree, Jane Anne, I warn you I'm going to send him to the de Lancie diamond mine in Southern Africa."

"You have a diamond mine, Mrs. de Lancie?" Tante Elyse asked, delighted.

"It's supposed to be," Victoria said dryly. "Though I think I may have more diamonds in my jewelry case than are hidden in this mine."

Cheney smiled. "Oh, you're so blasé about it, Victoria, but that is a magnanimous idea. Sponsoring a college education for the children."

Cautiously Jane Anne said, "It is a wonderful gift, certainly. But it wouldn't be appropriate for all of them, Dr. Duvall. Some of them don't have the initiative, some are more interested in trades, and some, I'm afraid, are just not...not...suited to the more rigorous disciplines."

"They're not smart enough," Tante Elyse told the company cheerfully. "I recognize what you're trying to say so tactfully, Mrs. Blue, for I was never smart enough for pure academics, either."

"Nonsense," Cheney retorted. "You're very intelligent, Tante Elyse. You're an exceptional businesswoman, and that takes a shrewd mind."

"Yes, I know," she said innocently. "But there are many kinds and levels and leanings and sundry gifts of the mind, Cheney dear."

"That is true," Cheney admitted. "Still, I would like to discuss this with you later, Jane Anne. Perhaps I might offer a medical scholarship if any of the children were interested in the field."

"How very generous of you, Dr. Duvall," Jane Anne said warmly. "As a matter of fact, we do have one girl who is only fourteen, but she is a good nurse and has shown some interest in learning more about it. Perhaps you can speak with her."

Victoria said wryly, "Cheney will have her dying to be a doctor if you don't watch her, Jane Anne. Though why any woman would want to subject herself to such abuse, I can't fathom. And once again, Jane Anne, I must insist that you stop announcing my philanthropies, for then I get no points with God, which is the only reason I do them."

Laughing, Jane Anne demurred, "That's not true and also not accurate, Victoria. It's only if *you* do your alms before men that you get no…um…points. You never do that, ma'am, and you have a very charitable heart, which, I am sure, is exactly why the Lord blesses you with such earthly riches."

"Earthly riches, yes," Victoria said with a hint of distant sadness. "And I am quickly learning that there are some things that no amount of riches can ever buy.…" Quickly she focused her cool gaze on Jane Anne again. "At any rate, Jane Anne, there are several matters of business that we need to discuss, and I'm certain that Cheney and Tante Elyse and Mr. Ford would be bored. Perhaps someone may give them a tour before tea?"

Sylvie returned, still blushing and flighty, to take Cheney to the schoolroom, while Elyse and Gowan said they'd like to see the farm. Allan said he'd be pleased to show them around.

When Jane Anne and Victoria were alone, Victoria got right down to business. "How is the baby?"

"She's very well," Jane Anne answered. "She's not colicky; she doesn't seem to be subject to runny nose or cough; her appetite is good. Dr. Buchanan pronounced her healthy and sound. Forgive me, but you didn't speak about Lisa—we've been calling her that—with the doctor after he visited yesterday."

"No," Victoria said shortly. "I—we don't—no. We hadn't spoken of it. At any rate, if we're all agreed that she is healthy, then I shall speak to the Ormonds about her. I'm certain that they'll want to come as soon as I tell them we've got an infant."

Jane Anne nodded, her gentle eyes sad. "Please, Mrs. de Lancie, do ask them to make an appointment ahead of time. The other children mustn't be around, you know. It's so hard for them, especially when they get to the sixes and sevens. The toddlers don't quite comprehend the situation yet, and the older ones have already accepted that they won't be considered for adoption. But the ones who are in between, the six-, seven-, eight-year-olds, they're old enough to understand the adoptive parents' visits, but they're too young to understand that everyone wants to adopt infants."

"I know," Victoria said, sighing deeply. "Last week little Enrico pleaded pitifully with me to adopt him. It was—quite wrenching."

"I'm so sorry," Jane Anne said compassionately. "I try to explain it to them, to teach them not to approach people, but it's very difficult to do so without hurting them terribly."

Victoria nodded; a slight shimmer of tears rose in

her eyes. She swallowed hard, then said in a low, intense voice utterly unlike her fashionably bored crystal tones, "Jane Anne...I feel I must...in good conscience...explain something to you...."

"No, not at all," Jane Anne said with real distress for her friend. "Mrs. de Lancie, I understand all too well your situation. Of course you can't adopt one of the children, for that, indeed, would be a cruel blow to the rest of them. How could you choose one when you are such a...a...guardian angel to all of them? And you are just about to get married, and you'll have children of your own, and..."

At this, Victoria's slender shoulders slumped. She dropped her head and shielded her eyes. "But that's just it, Jane Anne," she said with great difficulty. "I...I...won't have children. I can't. But you're exactly right, I should have known that you knew, that you understood already." With an effort, Victoria regained her formal pose, with her back straight and head high, but her expression was desolate. "I couldn't possibly adopt one of the children, and of course I can't adopt all of them," she said in a barren tone. "And I doubt very seriously if Dev would want adopted children, at any rate."

Jane Anne's eyebrows shot up. "But, Mrs. de Lancie— you mean—" Abruptly she quieted herself, for though she was friends with Victoria, she certainly was not close enough that she could pry into her most intimate affairs. Jane Anne thought it peculiar—even rather ominous— that Victoria and her fiancé had not discussed this, but it certainly wasn't her place to say so. "Yes, I...see," she finished rather lamely. "So, Mrs. de Lancie, would you like to see Lisa and the other children?"

Victoria remained in her tense posture, her face frozen.

"I should like to speak with Mallow and Sylvie and, of course, Jeremy," she answered stiffly. "But no, I don't think I'll want to see the baby again at all."

And Jane Anne Blue understood perfectly.

Part Two

In a Great House

*But in a great house there are not only
vessels of gold and of silver, but also of wood
and of earth; and some to honour,
and some to dishonour.*

—2 Timothy 2:20

Chapter Five

❦

Sweet's House of Exotic Island Princesses

He was called Sweet.

Sweet's real name—though he himself had almost forgotten it—was Johann Zenger. Twelve years ago when he'd deserted his ship to make his way in New York, everyone in Kleindeutschland had thought he was Swedish, probably because of his long, fine yellow hair. He had never bothered to tell anyone he was Bavarian, even when they started calling him the Swede. But then, because of his placid demeanor—in such startling contrast to his ominous bulk—they'd started calling him Sweet. Even that bit of teasing had not ruffled him. After a while he started introducing himself with just the one word: Sweet.

No one who met him could fathom why he should be called that, for no physical evidence presented itself to support the name. He was of average height but of remarkable build, a man with thick strips of glaring muscle in his arms and legs and back. Even his hands were knotted with them. His face was almost a perfect square, and his corded neck was as wide as his head.

Sweet's features were regular, uninteresting, his nose straight and normal, his eyes hooded and of a medium grayish-blue that made them appear to be colorless like thick fog. But it was his lifeless demeanor that made him so noticeable. He rarely spoke, and no hint of expression ever marred his innocuous features. Neither good nor evil seemed to be able to take a firm hold on him. He appeared to be utterly neutral. Now, in his plodding, purposeful way, he was polishing a mirror that was ornate with curlicues and cupids.

Sweet's blandness was particularly startling in this suffocating room. It was a formal parlor, filled with fat sofas and chairs covered in scarlet velveteen, a wool carpet adorned with enormous roses, red rose-patterned wallpaper, and a slightly scarred upright piano. Tasseled pillows littered the sofa, and bright scarves with fringes were draped over the piano, the occasional tables, and all of the lamps. In this overstuffed room, Sweet looked like a great wooden stump.

Reclining on an ornate recamier, a woman watched him with ill-disguised disdain. She had a halo of red hair, a face that could have been pleasing except for the feral cast of her dark eyes, and a viperish manner. "Stop that, Sweet," she snapped. "One of those lazy, stupid girls should have done that."

"But they didn't," he replied in his monotone. "And Mr. Worthington won't like the mirror to be spots." Sweet had learned English from an old Norwegian sailor, whose grasp of the language didn't include all the correct declensions of the verbs. Still, it was miraculous that Sweet had been able to learn the language at all. He couldn't learn to read, though he had tried, and he was aware that he was not at all smart. He'd learned English by rote through sheer determination, repeating for years words, then phrases, and finally sentences.

"Forget Mr. Worthington. You're not his slave," the woman flung at him, then watched him. She loved to bait Sweet and spent many hours trying to calculate how to get a reaction—any reaction at all—from him.

Sweet said nothing. He finished polishing the mirror, then slowly walked around the room straightening this doily, flicking dust from that lamp, plumping another pillow.

With exasperation the woman said, "Sweet, my friend, you need to work on your social graces. Perhaps you should attend my hour of the Art of Polite Conversation with the girls."

Sweet shook his head. "I am no good for that. Mr. Worthington, he knows that I am good for his business and you are good for the nice talk and the grace moves and the pretty fans."

"Grace moves!" she repeated with a gall of bitterness. "Yes, especially my walk!" Her name was Alana Keynes Patterson. She had been born into a respectable middle-class family. But at sixteen, with high spirits and dreams of wealth, she had hit the streets. She'd had a lucrative career for six years, though she had nothing to show for it except a wardrobe of expensive but vulgar dresses, a well-disguised loathing for men, and an even deeper disgust with herself.

Then one day in a drunken stupor almost eight years ago, she'd fallen down the stairs of her "gentleman's" little town house he had rented for her. Her leg had been broken and had then gone septic. Suddenly, with blurring quickness, Alana had only one leg, no career, no money, no town house. The clothes she sold for food had lasted only two months. She had almost starved, until Denys Worthington had rescued her. At least she told herself that, though she knew that Sweet, who had been the steward of the brothel where she worked, had told Mr. Worthington about her and had found her. She had always been rather unkind to Sweet, making him the butt of her acidic jokes, treating him much as a fine lady will treat a tolerated but disgraceful pet dog. Now she was ashamed, and that made her feel guilty, which only increased her bitterness.

Sweet shrugged, a mechanical raising of one thick shoulder. "You are the lady. You teach the girls to be ladies. Good thing for you that Mr. Worthington gives you this job, Alana. You should respect him."

"Pah," she spewed. "He should respect me! He pays me a pittance, and when his girls are trained, he will probably throw me back out on the street!"

"I think not," Sweet answered sturdily. "We go to Bermuda for more girls. They will need learning the fans and the gloves and the eyelashes, too."

In spite of her ire, Alana smiled. Sweet was the most boring man alive, but sometimes his oh-so-solemn pronouncements, in such atrocious English, were amusing.

The heavy brass bell on the front door jangled, and before Sweet could react, Denys Worthington swept into the room, talking already, tossing his hat and gloves and scarf and overcoat onto a chair, then pouring himself a full glass of whiskey from one of the decanters on the sideboard. "I'm late! Hello, Sweet. Hello, Alana. You're looking particularly well."

"Good afternoon, Mr. Worthington," she said warmly,

waving her fan with a grace that was diametrically opposite her sharp attitude with Sweet. "It's such a pleasure to see you."

"Yes, I'm sure," he said laconically, seating himself in a plump armchair close to her. "Everyone's always so pleased to see the boss."

He was surprisingly young for his apparent business success, Alana had always thought, though the first faint lines of dissipation were beginning to mar his full, smooth complexion. Denys Worthington was twenty-seven, about five-ten, elegantly slender. His dark brown hair was always carefully styled, his manicure perfect, his tailoring unexcelled. His cultured British accent gave him an air of masculine sophistication. His careless demeanor didn't fool her, however. Alana knew that she would never trust Denys Worthington, no matter that he employed her, clothed her, and fed her. There was something in him, a carelessness, a well-concealed core of coldness. Alana was an expert in reading men, and she instinctively knew that this man was perhaps one of the most dangerous kind—perfectly self-centered and selfish. Such men would do anything—any betrayal, any cruelty, any harm—to serve themselves.

"Tonight's very important. That's why I insisted on speaking to you two," he said abruptly. "I'm taking a party of three gentlemen to Steinway Hall for the Charles Dickens reading. One is Judge Alston, and the other two are aldermen. I expect all of them will visit tonight, and I have some instructions for you."

Sweet's House of Exotic Island Princesses served only the most reputable gentlemen, but they had not yet entertained any men of stature such as judges or aldermen. Sweet made himself concentrate very hard, so as to imprint Worthington's instructions on his thick mind.

"Sweet, that front stoop is disgraceful. Get a char-woman at once to come clean it, and make arrangements for it to be scrubbed every day. And while you're at it, get her to scrub and polish the bathtubs. I want them to shine like diamonds. That wretched Edna doesn't polish them properly. Speak to her, Alana. With so many women starving on the streets, it does seem we could get a decent maid. Sweet, stock the bar with German beer—Alderman Reese likes it. None of that putrid cheap champagne tonight either. Go buy a case of White Star. Be certain, Alana, that you charge each gentleman by the glass. Don't allow them to buy a bottle."

"Yes, sir," Sweet said laboriously, repeating his instructions under his breath.

Denys looked at him and laughed. "That's about all you can manage at once, isn't it, Sweet? Very well, you may go and get about your business." He took out his gold pocket watch and studied it. "It's getting late, so you'll have to hurry, especially if you can't find an entire case of White Star already chilled. Try Rondel's, but don't put it on my account. Take some cash from the box and get Edna to witness your chit." Sweet plodded out, and Denys turned to Alana.

"Now about the girls," he said darkly. "You've got to instruct them very carefully, Alana. These gentlemen are some of the upperten, and if I can get a stream of them as our patrons, we'll be set for the good life. So these girls must be absolutely perfect tonight. I noticed last week that Oona waves her fan about as if it were a club, Metta simpers instead of flirts, and Lia drinks too much and gets too boisterous."

"I'll speak to them, sir, and tonight I shall watch them closely and correct them discreetly if needed," she said a little stiffly.

He was adamant about such fine details, and though it made her job ten times harder—it was difficult enough to train these ignorant island girls how to walk and wear clothing, much less teach them the more delicate social graces—she did have to admit to herself that the higher the social status of the man, the more polished he wanted his whore. It was just a fact of this life, and it was why Alana had constantly drilled herself in all aspects of Polite Society.

"See that they don't need correction by tonight, Alana," he said harshly. "Though they aren't slovenly, they are lazy, which I won't tolerate. Make them understand that I don't want to be displeased."

"Yes, sir," she said, more submissively this time.

"Good. One last thing, Alana," he said, his dark eyes flashing with some malice. "I saw you flirting with a client last week. Don't ever put yourself forward in that manner again. You are here to guide and supervise the girls. I hardly think it would be good for business if Sweet had to tell some half-drunken besotted client that you aren't actually available because you are an amputee."

Alana's smooth cheeks flushed an angry crimson, and her mouth grew so tight that the skin around her lips turned white. "I understand, sir. What a bad joke that would be."

"Yes, quite," he said in a bored tone, flicking an imaginary speck of dust from his knee. "Now, about the household accounts..."

He droned on endlessly about economizing while

Alana was thinking, *Who is this man? All his airs, all his vile little snubs—he's just a pimp, after all. Even Sweet's a better man than he. Sweet at least knows and accepts what he is. As if I can't tell Denys is probably some kind of con man or lowlife. I saw his other watch, the silver one with the diamond inset that he used to carry, the one with the monogram on it. Either Denys Worthington isn't his real name, or he stole that watch and is just a common thief.*

But Alana was astute enough to know that Denys Worthington was not common, that his well-bred demeanor was genuine, not cultivated, as was her own. There was a difference. There always was some hard-to-define line between true good breeding and self-taught sophistication. Aside from that, Denys Worthington was a man of some means, for he owned a fine ship, had begun a legitimate shipping business, and had leased this house and his own house in Gramercy Park for a full year, paid in advance.

Still, that watch…the initials were not D.W., and he had quit carrying it, though it was a much finer watch than the one he carried now.

So his name must not be Denys Worthington, she reflected spitefully, *and if he must hide his true identity, I hope he's in some misery because of it.*

His name was Bain Winslow.

When he left Hana during the volcanic eruption, Bain was smart enough to know he had to cut his losses and start all over again somewhere else. He went first to Honolulu to take all the money out of the Winslow Brothers' Shipping accounts, and then he'd circled back to Lahaina to clear out the plantation account and both his and his mother's personal bank accounts. Almost as an afterthought he'd emptied the family's secured box, which had quite a sum of Chinese, British, and American currency, some bearer bonds, and his mother's jewelry.

With flush pockets he'd then sailed straight to New York.

The day after he arrived he started visiting the brothels. Three nights passed, and then he found the person—the man—that he wanted.

Sweet was managing a rather shabby brothel in Kleindeutschland. He seemed to care nothing for the women one way or the other. He never sampled the wares, and he never beat them or mistreated them either. He treated them exactly like what he believed they were—valuable property. His relationships with the Johns were all business, too. As long as they paid their dues and minded their own business, they got along with Sweet. If they stepped out of line or caused trouble, he asked them nicely to behave. If they did, he let them go. If they didn't, he told them he would make them behave. If they still didn't, he kept his word, all with the same lack of emotion.

Bain hired him on the spot.

Together they went to the West Indies, picked up six of the most promising girls they could find, and brought them back to New York. Bain leased the three-story brownstone tenement on Mercer Street, cleaned it up, and bought furnishings of fairly good quality, but the decor was garish. After all, one didn't want a brothel to look like one's own home.

Then Sweet told Worthington of Alana Patterson, who was drunk and half dead in the despicable hole of the Old Brewery in Five Points at the time. He brought Alana to the house, cleaned her up and fed her, and Alana started training the girls. Within a month they were presentable. Within two months Sweet's House was very profitable.

Bain was presently scouting around for a new brownstone tenement and was planning a trip to Bermuda to check out the merchandise there. But running a clipper ship took money, lots of money, though only Captain Starnes and the officers were salaried. The sailors he paid by the trip. When a clipper was on regular trade runs, it was no problem to keep the crew with the ship. But Bain hadn't had regular trade runs for the last six months, and he'd lost eighteen sailors already. It was going to take a lot of front money to make a trip to Bermuda. Sweet's was just going to have to get even more profitable in order to help support the *Day Dream*.

On the way to New York, fleeing his home and family and everything he'd ever known and loved, Bain had fought persistently with Captain Starnes to change the name of the ship. Finally Bain had won. He was, of course—as far as Captain Starnes knew—the owner of the ship, and he'd ordered *Locke's* scrubbed off the sides in the equator doldrums. The sailors had scowled and predicted that it would mean bad luck for the ship. Five of them deserted as soon as they docked in New York. But Bain didn't care. He just wanted that accursed name out of his sight and mind.

Bain was also establishing an identity as a legitimate businessman, attempting to set up a run to import hides from Argentina and export finished fabrics from the textile mills upstate. For this reason, he was a silent and unseen partner in Sweet's House of Exotic Island Princesses.

It was because he'd been in Argentina for two weeks

attending to his import-export business that he'd missed the notices in the newspapers' society sections, which generally he read word for word. Unfortunate, that.

Tonight he would find out exactly how bad a turn his luck had taken.

Chapter Six

Portraits

The upper ten thousand were admirably represented at Steinway Hall on this warm April night. New York's elite, more pragmatic than their Old World French Huguenot and Anglo-Dutch ancestors, had learned to accommodate the vulgar *arrivistes,* the "new men" with their merchants' money. In 1852 Charles Astor Bristead, Cambridge-educated grandson of John Jacob Astor, used *The Upper Ten Thousand* as the title for his sketch of elite life in New York City, and the catch-phrase had stuck. Generally it was understood that the uppertens had a net worth of at least ten thousand dollars, kept carriages, went to the opera, had a town house and a country house, and gave balls and parties.

So now in this somewhat republicanized New York, Beekmans, Kents, Van Renssalaers, Stuyvesants, and Lenoxes rubbed shoulders with Vanderbilts, Belmonts, Morgans, Whitneys, and Rockefellers. Some patrician disdain still occurred on the Knickerbocker side, and some bourgeois blustering still occurred on the arrivistes' side, but generally the uppertens were content with their exalted stations.

The de Lancie-Buchanan wedding party did, however, present difficulties to some of the old guard, mostly the elderly matriarchs of the oldest Knickerbocker families. When the splendid wedding party began arriving, filling three boxes in the plush new theater, an elderly LeRoy remarked to her ancient and bejeweled companion, a Goelet, "I see none of the de Lancies are members of the wedding party."

Mrs. Goelet gave the Knickerbocker sniff. "Well, of course not, Mrs. LeRoy. After all, he was her first husband, and you could hardly expect the bereaved family to be a part of this untimely match. After all, Lionel Jann de Lancie died only six years ago. And his wife was in mourning for only a year. Scandalous. But, of course, she is only a Steen."

Mrs. LeRoy's conversation was appropriately meek, for Mrs. Goelet had been a Lispenard, while Mrs. LeRoy had been a Low, and her pedigree was slightly less ancient than that of her companion's. "Her betrothed, Dr. Buchanan, is not of old family—indeed, it seems that nothing is known of his bloodline. He is the ward of the Duvalls and has been, I understand, since he was a child. But I believe that he is quite an esteemed member of the medical profession."

"Yes, although I cannot comprehend this new reverence for surgeons, as he styles himself, though he is a perfectly respected and accredited physician. My mother always had a physician attend us, while the surgeon was called for the servants and the horses."

"I don't quite understand it either, but I do know that Dr. Buchanan has been the de Lancies' and the

Rhinelanders' family physician for several years. I believe he also attends the Livingstons and the de Peysters," Mrs. LeRoy said timidly.

"Does he?" Mrs. Goelet remarked icily, though she made a mental note to make the acquaintance of Dr. Devlin Buchanan. "Still, this wedding party is a motley collection. But what can you expect? Victoria de Lancie is having a maid of honor—in her second wedding! No respectable woman would consider such a vulgar spectacle. And also the maid of honor is that female physician, the Duvalls' blood daughter. I cannot cipher what Victoria's mother is thinking. Even though Josefina married that jeweler, she was a Wilcott."

"She's probably thinking that that Duvall woman is also a de Cheyne," Mrs. LeRoy said with the tiniest hint of triumph. "You do know that Dr. Duvall's mother is Irene de Cheyne, niece of the eighth Vicomte de Cheyne of Varennes?"

"What?" Mrs. Goelet exclaimed, but she did, by decades of long training, recover nicely. "I beg your pardon, but I believe that the present vicomte is the ninth lord."

"Eighth," Mrs. LeRoy repeated with satisfaction. "Do you see the two older ladies in the second and third boxes? That is Marye-Rosarita de Cheyne Edwards, and the other dark-haired lady is Querida Elyse de Cheyne Buckingham Ford. They are the daughters of the seventh vicomte's second marriage to Doña Isabella Maria Rosarita Querida de Galvez, sister to Bernardo de Galvez, who was the governor of Lousiana and viceroy to Mexico in 1785—"

"And they are Irene Duvall's aunts?" Mrs. Goelet interposed, anxious to get the lineage down as pat as her companion.

"Exactly," Mrs. LeRoy replied with only a little huff at being interrupted.

"And so they are the female doctor's great-aunts," Mrs. Goelet murmured, frowning darkly. "Unbelievable. I suppose they are scandalized by their great-niece's choice of a profession, and I'm certain they must be mortified by their family connection to this Steen woman's callithumpian display of a wedding."

"I was introduced to them by Josefina Steen at Taylor's Ice Creamery yesterday," Mrs. LeRoy said smugly. "Neither Mrs. Ford nor Mrs. Edwards seems at all discomfited by their great-niece or her intimate acquaintance with Victoria Steen or, for that matter, with their niece's marriage to Richard Duvall, who is some sort of iron magnate—"

"Very new money, you know," Mrs. Goelet was compelled to remark, for she had not exactly been the topper in this conversation with her longtime friend and was put out by her ignorance of this branch of the House of Bourbon.

"Yes, but he did distinguish himself in the Great War, Mrs. Goelet, and I believe is intimately associated with the secretary of war."

"Ulysses Grant is hardly our kind of people," Mrs. Goelet remarked. "He is, after all, only a common soldier, and I did hear that he drinks heavily and that he actually smoked a cigar in the presence of a lady once. Besides, the Duvalls live all the way up on Park Avenue and East Sixty-fifth! Why, that is positively a wilderness of pigsties and abattoirs!"

"My dear Mrs. Goelet," Mrs. LeRoy said with great superiority, "can it be that you don't promenade in your carriage in Central Park? The land around the park—particularly on the east side—has been developed into some of the loveliest areas on the island. It is my understanding that the Astors are buying up all the lots they can that border the park, and they are considering building up around Fiftieth."

"Astors," Mrs. Goelet repeated with careful enunciation. "They are, after all, only third-generation money." Raising her opera glasses and leaning over perilously far, she scanned the three boxes across the spacious hall. The party was lively, in high spirits, for there were many young people, including in the third box five or six of the city's high-spirited young bloods, sons of the uppertens, rakish young men with loads of new money. "I see Dr. Cleve Batson. He is connected to Dr. Buchanan's practice, is he not? And that is Keenan Bondurant's son, the banker...and Austin Darrow, the attorney. Those other men are the Steen brothers, I see."

"They do make a handsome party, do they not, Mrs. Goelet?" Mrs. LeRoy observed. "The younger Steen men are all personable, and Victoria is, I hear, acclaimed as one of the city's beauties." Victoria had three brothers, none of them striking, but all three were pleasant-looking.

Mrs. Goelet answered stiffly, "To me all of those Steen men look just like Henry, common merchants. Victoria is a beauty, just like her mother, who is, as I said, a Wilcott."

"But that young woman in the second box is Angelique Lyra Steen, Henry's niece by his brother Thomas. Thomas Steen is married to my third cousin, Delia Low," Mrs. LeRoy stated triumphantly, the *coup de grace*. "And Angelique is quite lovely in her own right."

"True, but that would be because of the Low blood,

my dear Mrs. LeRoy, not because of the Steen parentage, as you seem to be attempting to say. Such nonsense. But pray tell me, Mrs. LeRoy, would that very tall, well-favored young blond man in the second box talking to Angelique Steen be Dr. Buchanan? I have never made his acquaintance, but I do understand that he is quite handsome." Mrs. Goelet intended to send a summons to Dr. Buchanan, an imperial order that could not be denied, and arrange for a consultation for a putrid throat. Not that she had a putrid throat just now, but she recalled that she was subject to them in early springtime.

Mrs. LeRoy, with a rare social advantage over her friend, perused the three boxes for a long time. Finally she replied, "No, Mrs. Goelet, that is not Dr. Devlin Buchanan. He is shorter and dark, an elegant man with a dignified comportment. I don't know who that tall young man is...unless..."

"Yes?" Mrs. Goelet demanded sharply.

"Perhaps he may be that man who was, if I understood correctly, some sort of pugilist and was Dr. Duvall's medical assistant. But now he has inherited some properties from a long-lost family connection, and—"

"What family?" Mrs. Goelet asked imperiously.

"I...I cannot recall the family name," Mrs. LeRoy said faintly.

"How very remiss of you, Mrs. LeRoy. How are we to know if he is anyone if we don't know his connections?"

"It's a very confusing story, and I have not been privy to all the particulars from Josefina Steen," Mrs. LeRoy said apologetically. "Indeed, I'm not certain Josefina has complete knowledge."

"I suppose I must call on Josefina myself in order to

find out about these people," Mrs. Goelet said peevishly. She had, of course, been invited to the de Lancie-Buchanan wedding, but she had been planning to travel to her cottage in Sarasota Springs next month so that she would not be obliged to attend. With apprehension she began to realize that she had been unaware of this motley collection's exact standing, and she was particularly piqued that she had not been presented to the two nieces of the de Cheyne vicomte. Desperately she tried to recollect if she had been introduced to the Duvalls. She believed she had met them once, at some ball or cotillion, but she could hardly call on Irene Duvall with such a tenuous connection. And why had the Duvall woman not called on her, which would be the correct social convention—or at least would be if the woman was not a member of the French nobility, for heaven's sake! With dread she hoped that Irene Duvall had not called on her— what if Mrs. Duvall had, and in her abysmal ignorance, Mrs. Goelet had not been "at home"?

Mrs. Goelet's consternation was such that she determined to peruse her calling cards as soon as she got home and to call on Irene Duvall the very next day, though her inability to remedy the shameful situation at present exasperated her. She could hardly summon Josefina and demand introductions, and she would never consider going to the Duvalls' boxes.

She could, at least, summon Dr. Buchanan, obtain a respectable introduction from Mrs. LeRoy, and consult with him on medical matters. With barely disguised irritation she asserted, "Which one is Dr. Buchanan? That is Victoria, is it not, in the first box? Scandalous that he would not be attending her closely. Is he with those young rakes in the third box?"

Mrs. LeRoy's rheumy old eyes sharpened, and she pressed her opera glasses so close that they left little marks on her wrinkled face. "Why…why, I don't see Dr. Buchanan at all. How could the groom possibly arrive so late to one of his own betrothal parties?"

"He is an esteemed physician, much in demand," Mrs. Goelet replied with superiority, forgetting that she had dismissed Dev as a mere surgeon shortly before. "Perhaps he was called away to a medical emergency."

"Perhaps," Mrs. LeRoy murmured speculatively.

But both of them, with the vigilance of seasoned hunters, continued to watch the de Lancie-Buchanan wedding party and clearly perceived that Dr. Devlin Buchanan made no appearance at his fiancée's side that night.

"He is not at all as his portrait would suggest, is he?" Victoria asked Cheney.

Cheney was staring across the partition to the next box where Shiloh was sitting close to Angelique Steen. Shiloh was talking quietly, and Angelique was laughing, a cool wind-chimes sound that carried to the adjoining box. "You don't think so?" Cheney replied dully. "I do. He is a little more polished, perhaps, but still fearless, still defiant—"

One of Victoria's elegantly arched eyebrows raised slightly. "You're thinking of Shiloh's portrait by Homer, aren't you?"

"It wasn't his portrait," Cheney responded faintly. "He just used Shiloh as a model." They had seen the painting *Prisoners from the Front* in a showing of Winslow Homer's work in New Orleans, and though Shiloh said he'd never posed for any painting—and for sure and certain he'd never been taken prisoner—the central figure of the unyielding Confederate soldier had clearly been identifiable as Shiloh Irons.

Victoria said nothing for a few moments as she considered her friend. Victoria had, in fact, bought Homer's painting for Cheney's birthday, but seeing that Cheney and Shiloh were estranged, she had been reluctant to give it to her. Cheney was still watching Shiloh, her shoulders drooped, her usually animated face motionless and melancholy. "Dearest, I was speaking of Mr. Dickens," Victoria finally prodded her. "His portrait in the showroom looks as if he'd be very dignified, very somber. But his readings are quite spirited, are they not?"

"Hmm? Oh yes, his readings." With obvious reluctance Cheney turned to face Victoria. "Yes, he is an accomplished actor, I believe. And yes, his portrait is very sober and venerable, but he does have an energetic presentation. What has been your favorite reading so far, Mrs. Steen?" Cheney asked politely, observing Victoria's mother eavesdropping on their conversation.

"I suppose *Nicholas Nickleby*," Josefina Steen observed. "Such a well-bred young man, with such undeserved hardships. My favorite Dickens is *Our Mutual Friend*. It's really too bad that Mr. Dickens will not be reading from it. The disappearance of John Harmon, you know, quite a mystery." Lovely, haughty, imperious, she gave her daughter, so like her, a hard stare.

"Dr. Buchanan will attend if he can, *Maman*," Victoria said, turning rather quickly to observe the opposite boxes with her diamond-encrusted opera glasses. "He has neither disappeared nor is being mysterious. His note explains his absence."

"Oh yes, the note explains it," Josefina declared, "but it does not excuse it."

Next to Josefina and her husband, the short, rotund, normally jolly-looking Henry Andrew Steen IV, sat Richard and Irene Duvall. Richard looked dismayed, while Irene maintained an elegant composure. "I can see that it would be distressing to you, Mrs. Steen, since none of your family is in the medical profession. My husband and I have grown sadly accustomed to both Dev and Cheney missing part or all of scheduled social events, since they are often summoned to attend medical emergencies."

"Is that right?" Josefina remarked in a bored tone. "I was unaware that Dr. Duvall was in such demand."

"She is," Irene said calmly.

"Of course," Josefina said, idly watching Shiloh, her son Beckett, and his three friends hovering around her niece, Angelique, in the next box. "But then, I still am having trouble understanding. If Dr. Duvall"—here she nodded coolly to Cheney—"Dr. Batson, and Dr. Buchanan are all partners in the same practice, and they are all equally esteemed, I wonder why Dr. Duvall or Dr. Batson might not have attended this emergency for Dr. Buchanan. It is, after all, his own wedding party."

"Mother, that's nonsense. All doctors have their own patients. They don't trade them around like horses, you know. Isn't that right, Cheney?" Victoria said with exasperation.

"Hmm? I mean, I beg your pardon? I'm…I'm afraid I was not attending just now…." Cheney said absently. She had lost the thread of the conversation and had, unconsciously, turned to watch Shiloh again.

"Cheney, dear, are you feeling unwell? Surely that is why you have been paying such scant attention to Victoria and, indeed, to the conversation in general." Irene addressed Cheney, and her soft voice held a stern note that Cheney recalled very vividly from her child-hood when her tomboyish antics had often gotten her into trouble with her mother.

Her cheeks flushing, Cheney turned in her blue velvet seat and addressed everyone. "Please pardon me, I have been unforgivably absent-minded, haven't I? What was the question again?"

"I never know," Richard Duvall sighed under his breath while Irene surreptitiously pinched him.

"Never mind, Cheney, dear," Victoria said quietly, patting Cheney's arm. "Now, since the main objectives of attending the theater are to see and be seen, let us now see who was able to obtain boxes and who was not. Otherwise, we will have nothing at all to talk about during morning calls tomorrow. Look there, I see the Forbeses. Cheney, they have been very loyal patients, haven't they, since that exciting time you saved little Annalea's life? And there, of course, are the Vanderbilts. They still can't buy boxes at the Academy of Music, no matter how much they try to bribe the Board of Patrons. I'm surprised the commodore hasn't tried to hold up the place and rob them of a box at gunpoint. The Astors, the Stewarts, the Grinnells…my, my, the commoners are out in numbers tonight. All right, that about covers the new money. Let's now count the Knickerbockers—you can always tell them by the half mourning, those ancient bloodlines are running thin and weak by now—"

"Victoria, really," Josefina huffed. "You sound like a fishmonger's wife."

Ignoring her, Victoria kept her glasses to her eyes to examine the blood, new and old. "I see Alderman Reese and—oh, that other alderman with the wheezy voice and the dreadful diamond pinky ring. What is his name? I can never recall...something like Blooty? Bloopy?"

"It's Bloomden, as you very well know," Josefina declared. "He did call on you so very often two seasons ago, dearest, that I should think you could recall his name."

"Very forgettable, his name, along with his person, except, of course, for that lamentable ring and his nose whistle," Victoria retorted icily. "But, Mother, who is that with—oh yes, that's Judge Alston, but who is that other gentleman in the party? I can't quite make him out. He's behind Alderman Bloopy...but something...he looks familiar...oh my! In the box next to them—that actress! The one everyone is talking about at Wallack's! And she's alone in that box! How extraordinary! Mother, whose box is that?"

"I'm sure I don't know," Josefina replied stiffly, sipping her fluted crystal glass of champagne. "And neither I nor you need to know who would have the effrontery to make their box available to an actress. Really, it is too insulting. After all, what do those people think the third tier is for?"

Cheney's attention had wandered again in spite of her best intentions and sternest self-admonitions. But she did hear Josefina Steen's dour comment about an actress, and it went straight to her heart.

Actresses are even considered more respectable than women doctors. I know Josefina thinks I should be up in the third tier, too, along with the theater trash and prostitutes and fishmongers' wives. Funny how much more those things have been bothering me lately. I guess since Shiloh's not with me anymore, I just...feel more vulnerable, less self-confident. Oh, bother Shiloh! I simply must find a way to get myself out of this terrible funk.

I'm supposed to be attending to Victoria, anyway. This is her time, and she's been deserted, too. Whatever can Dev be thinking? But Victoria is handling it marvelously. Of course she would never show any personal distress in public, even though we all know perfectly well that all of these people are viciously buzzing about Dev's absence. And meanwhile, here I sit, mooning around like some poor love-mad Ophelia.

From the other side of the partition Cheney suddenly heard Shiloh's voice, low, but close and clear. "She's Ophelia?"

"Yes, of course. Who else in *Hamlet* for such a beauty?" Troy Bondurant replied caustically. "Her name is Minette York. She's a member of the Royal Shakespeare Company, but Wallack contracted her individually for the run, and she's really the star of the play. I could introduce you to her if you'd like."

"Not tonight," Shiloh said firmly. "But I do want to see *Hamlet.*"

As Victoria had said, the main objective in attending the theater was to see and be seen, and certainly everyone in the first-tier boxes—the most important seats—were always examined and studied and dissected down to the smallest detail, particularly during intermission when the lights were up.

One of the august personages in the expensive boxes behaved very oddly during the intermission, but by fate or fortune—neither of which had been particularly kind to him lately—he was not observed.

Denys Worthington, Esquire, was thoroughly enjoying his evening with his friends, soon to be clients, he hoped. In his elegantly British offhand manner he had

reminded them that Mr. Charles Dickens was one of his
countrymen and might have even given them the impression that he was acquainted with Mr. Dickens, which was
as preposterous as if he'd announced that that morning
he'd had breakfast with Queen Victoria. But to Ameri-
cans, England was such a small inbred place, it didn't
seem unlikely at all that one English gentleman would
naturally know every other English gentleman. Mr. Worthington's remarks, made in such a cultured, aristocratic
Queen's English, left the faint scent of continental nobility in their plebian American nostrils, and they were exceedingly impressed, being mere arrivistes.

Alderman Bloomden claimed a distant connection
with the de Lanceys—the disenfranchised British loyal-
ists, not the French Huguenot de Lancies—and this made
him the American *arbiter elegantiarium* of the group. He
knew all about the de Lancie-Buchanan wedding party,
the glittering, lively crowd occupying the three boxes directly across from Mr. Worthington's box.

A dry, thin little man with sparse hair, he affected a
fussy primness that he thought was elegant deportment.
Hungrily eyeing the wedding party, he said in his high
breathy voice, "I don't see Dr. Buchanan at his own betrothal party. I'm not at all surprised, not at all, considering that Mrs. de Lancie, though she is a beauty, is of a
distinctly choleric humor. Perhaps her betrothed is growing weary of her ill temper. Oh, dear, she is looking this
way—" He made a stiff, jerky nod that was a sort of bow,
though he was sitting down. His nose started whistling.

Judge Alston, a plump, expansive man, said caustically, "That de Lancie filly is spirited, all right, but I
don't know as I'd call her choleric. I think your little

whistley nose is out of joint because she wouldn't have you, Bloomden."

"I can't help this affliction," Alderman Bloomden grumbled. "It's a respiratory disorder of the most distressing kind."

"I can certainly sympathize, Mr. Bloomden," Denys Worthington said smoothly, coming to lean negligently against the low balcony railing to face his guests. "Many of our Englishwomen of genteel blood are rather cold and unsympathetic to a man's needs and desires. I'm happy to say that I've found a wonderful haven here in the city with warm and luscious women, most compliant. 'Tis a clean, well-ordered establishment, too, which is important to a man of delicate sensibilities."

"Like me," Alderman Bloomden wheezed sadly.

"Just so. Still, I should like to view this acclaimed beauty and see if she could compete on the Continent. England and particularly France have some of the loveliest beauties in the world. I must pay close attention, for pure comparison, you know," Worthington said airily. The judge guffawed crudely and handed Denys his opera glasses.

Worthington raised them to his eyes and began to check the boxes across the wide expanse of the auditorium, and at that moment Alderman Reese, who had been making odd contortions in order to look at the boxes that were in line with theirs, suddenly burst out, "Look, right next to us, all by herself. It's Minette York, the actress! Hullo, hullo, York! It's me, Alderman—"

His words were cut short because the judge, with rough dispatch, yanked on his coattail hard enough to make Reese stagger. "Sit down, you idiot, you're making fools of us all. I'm sure Mr. Worthington—well, stap me!

Where did he go? Look, you fool, he was probably so embarrassed at your monkeyshines that he headed back over the Atlantic, hotfoot."

But Mr. Denys Worthington had not headed anywhere except to the relative safety of the long curving hallway outside the boxes. As intermission was almost over, it was relatively deserted.

He took deep breaths, his eyes wide and staring, his smooth features tight. *I can't believe it—him! Locke, of all people, in New York, along with that nosy female witch doctor! Steen, that Steen woman introduced me to Locke at Steen House in San Francisco. I knew Henry Steen lived here, but I didn't know Victoria Steen—of course, Mrs. de Lancie! de Lancie!*

But—I thought—why did I think that that woman doctor was from San Francisco? And Locke! Right here, shadowing me like a curse!

Now what do I do?

What can I do?

"Blast them," he growled.

He stood still, now calm but grim, staring down at the plush royal-blue carpet. *First thing I'll have to do is move Locke's—no, now it's just the* Day Dream, *my* Day Dream!—*somewhere. It's practically on display right down on the South Street docks. Maybe to Perth Amboy...*

But what to do about my accursed cousin? Why—how—is he persecuting me like this? He ruined my life in Hawaii and San Francisco, and now that I've got a start on a good thing here, he blunders in along with that terrible woman.

What do I do?

What can I do?

By the time Denys Worthington, Esquire, returned to his guests, Mr. Dickens had almost finished his reading from *Oliver Twist,* the scene where the evil Sikes murders Nancy. The lights were down, and the audience was very attentive to Mr. Dickens. Denys thought—hoped—that neither Locke nor Dr. Duvall would chance to look across at his box. Nevertheless, he drew a chair far back in the shadows of the blue velvet draperies. He thought savagely that Mr. Dickens's reading of the murder scene was chilling, but he could well understand why Sikes, who had been betrayed by the woman, could murder Nancy in cold blood.

Affecting a yawn as Mr. Dickens moved on to Mrs. Gamp of *The Pickwick Papers,* Denys Worthington said, "Gentlemen, I must say I find Mrs. Gamp, like many domineering, interfering women who stick their long noses into men's affairs, to be quite tiresome. Would any of you be interested in seeking more affable female company?"

And so Bain Winslow once again contrived his escape before the final curtain.

Chapter Seven

Dart

Dr. Devlin Buchanan stared at the ruin of a man.

He was still shackled. Vaguely Dev wondered why, for the man had clearly slipped into a coma, that cruel mockery of a peaceful death. With the dispassionate observation that served him so well in his chosen profession, Dev could see that Dart would not linger long in that dark limbo.

Of all of the highest virtues of a man, Dev's most praiseworthy attributes were his senses of duty and honor. Neither tenderness nor vulnerability were part of his makeup. He felt no anger, nor bitterness, nor desire for revenge upon this pathetic half-dead man. He did, in one part of his tidy mind, feel revulsion and even a half-formed sense of dread. Still his sense of duty ran deep, and Dev knew that this man would, perhaps within days, perhaps even within hours, face God. Dev bowed his head to pray for this poor sinner's soul.

The heavy iron door shrieked a lamentation behind him, and the small room, already noxious with the smell of mortal illness, was invaded with the stench of cheap gin and unwashed flesh. Dev, being the kind of man he was, rose and offered the single chair to Connie Dunleavy, who was holding her pale baby.

She sat, her eyes dull, her shoulders bent like an old woman's. "He's dying, ain't he?"

"I hesitate to say, madam. I am not his physician, after all," Dev answered gravely.

She looked up at him standing beside the chair, his handsome face impassive as he watched Dart. He seemed calm, distant, but now up close Connie could see his jaw tensed, the muscles knotted. And on either side of the finely manicured mustache, deep dimples flashed as his jaw tightened. Her bloodshot eyes narrowed. "Then who are you?"

Without looking at her, Dev replied distantly, "My name is Dr. Devlin Buchanan."

A long heavy silence ensued in the bleak room. The only sound was Dart's sickly breathing, small pants drawn as if by animal instinct through his mouth. Dev watched him, forgetting the woman and the too silent child, forgetting the awful surroundings, trying to marshal his whirling thoughts and restive emotions.

Slowly a look of low cunning sharpened Connie's bloated, blurred features. "Buchanan…Buchanan…funny, that. Seems to me like I know that name." Dev gave no sign that he was listening to her, and she sat up a little straighter, tense, and licked her lips. "I'm tryin' to recall, you see, Doctor, as how Dart did once tell me his Christian name, only it were so long ago I been forgetting it, which he riled at me once when I used it."

Slowly the portent of her monotonous whine filtered into Dev's fevered brain. He turned to look at her, and though he was still outwardly collected, his dark eyes burned. He said nothing. Indeed, he didn't think he could speak.

Connie stared up at him, her intense scrutiny wavering beneath his heated gaze, but then ugly defiance made her look like a cornered ferret. "Don't you be gazin' down on me like I'm some low scrub, Mr. High-and-Mighty Dr. *Buchanan*. I bet you got some nob friends, ain't you, and you'd best take care about lordin' it over me and mine. Looks to me like—" she jutted her chin toward Dart "—you might be in for some hard stares and wrinkled fine noses yourself!" Once again the expression, hard and cold, of craftiness came over her. "Don't the Good Book say something like the sins of the *fathers* are took upon the *children?*"

Dev swallowed hard, then dropped his eyes. "Something like that."

"Just so," Connie said with cruel finality.

"What—?" Dev's voice sounded shamefully weak. He cleared his throat, turned again to face her, and began again. "What of it, madam?"

Connie settled back, shifting the baby in her arms with an impatient jerk. "Well, now, I'm considering what of it, Mr. Top-the-Nob Doctor."

In a low troubled tone, Dev said, "I'm not— I don't look down on you, madam, I assure you."

Connie grinned, and Dev could hardly contain his revulsion at her foul breath and broken teeth. "I thought fine upstanding gentlemen didn't tell lies."

Dev's mouth tightened to a straight, painful line. "No. They don't."

She nodded, still grinning hideously. "All right then,

I guess you know what I am, you know what he is, and now I know what you are."

This devastated Dev so deeply that he could hardly breathe. With short, hard steps he went to the single dim window and looked out on the grounds. It was raining. He clasped his hands behind his back so tightly it pained him.

Connie was mercifully quiet for a few moments, then said with studied carelessness, "Dart, he owed me, you know. It's a pure shame he's going to pass without paying me what he owed me. Sold my sewing kit, he did, right afore he went lunatic and knocked that fine lady about so shocking, right out in public."

Dev was in such turmoil that he could hardly understand her words, much less comprehend her implications. "What exactly is your point, madam?" he asked icily without turning.

"Why, my point is, as we have done discussed, that I'm your stepmother, my fine uppity doctor, and—" At these words Dev could no longer contain his disgust. His shoulders jerked ruler straight, and his face blanched. He still had his back to Connie, but she sensed his shame, and like a serpent she was beside him, hissing. "I thought we could conduct some business like quality folk, but then again maybe neither of us is, after all. So I was thinking that you'll be in the way of helping out your poor stepmother, seein' as how your dad left this world with some debts."

"He's not dead yet," Dev muttered with a sudden stab of pain.

"Good as. He owes me. So you owe me—son. That is, 'less you'd be wantin' me to go explain to the good Dr. Banckert just who I am, and who Dart is, and who you are. I'd imagine your friends would be curious about you and your dad, now, wouldn't they? I'll bet that fine cove you was sportin' around with the other day would laugh all night and day at your poor ol' dad, him bein' a drunk and lunatic and a woman beater!"

Dev thought about Shiloh and in a split second knew that he wouldn't care one way or another about Dev's past, but Victoria Elizabeth Steen de Lancie? And her mother and father and brothers? And what about the shame and scandal it would bring on Richard and Irene Duvall, and on poor Cheney, who could hardly afford any more blots on her character?

Dev turned and faced her, and now his clear-cut features were stony. He took out his money clip and savagely thrust the folded bills to Connie. He took care not to let her dirty fingers touch his. "That's all I have. Now begone with you."

Greedily she licked her finger to rifle through the money. "Fifty-eight dollars, that's a might of money to be carrying about in your pockets. It'll do nicely, thank you." Coarsely she thrust it far down into the bodice of her dress. "It'll do—for now, *son.*"

Now in a great hurry, already licking her sodden lips, she went to the door, banged on it, and screeched, "Hey, you great ape! Come let me outta here!"

Dev's mind was numbed, and he watched her mutely. Then, as he heard the turnkey's rasp, he started. "Wait, Mrs.—madam—what about your son? Surely you can't be forgetting him?" The baby was carelessly laid at the foot of Dart's bed.

She turned and sneered, "No, I ain't forgot him, like some people forget their kin." Then, in an abrupt and painful moment of shame, she dropped her eyes and muttered, "I can't take care of him. 'Specially without Dart. 'Tis hard enough for a man to claim his own, much less to take on a woman with another man's child. You— you take him."

Dev thundered, "What? What kind of woman are you to abandon your own child?"

She turned on him viciously. "What kind of man are you—to deny your own brother!"

"Most like it'll take more on an hour to get up to West Ninety-third, sor," the cabbie said apologetically, trying to shield the gentleman with the shabby child from the rain as they struggled to climb into the hansom cab.

"Just get there as quickly as you can," Dev retorted impatiently.

"Yes, sor."

The shutters were closed, and the small cab was stuffy. Dev stared down at the baby and suddenly felt a little dizzy, with some nausea, too. Jerkily he opened the shutters, took long deep breaths, and welcomed the rain on his face, though it was icy cold. He sat there a long time, his eyes closed, trying to compose himself and fight off the sickly sensation in his gut.

He heard, as if from a great distance, a weak cry, almost a sigh. Rousing with some difficulty, he saw that the cold spray was wetting the baby's face, and he was grimacing. He looked like some sort of animal embryo, a newly hatched chicken perhaps. His face was thin and of an unhealthy pallor. For a few moments Dev just stared helplessly down at him. Once again some of the rain blew in, and the baby gasped weakly.

Dev came to his senses, of a sort, and closed the shutters. "Rude of me, isn't it?" he asked the baby, who seemed not to hear him. The child's gaze was unfocused.

"What in heaven and earth am I to do with you?" Dev asked in a desperate whisper.

Dev recalled that he was a physician, and this small being was obviously ill. Feeling on a more sure footing, Dev examined the baby clinically.

He was too small for his age—wasn't he? Dev couldn't recall if Connie had said how old the child was. This started the consternation in his mind again, but impatiently he shoved it aside. "You have jaundice, certainly," Dev said in a dull tone. "And lice. At least you have healthy full hair, though how and why I don't know." Dev had not fully comprehended who this boy was yet, so it didn't occur to him that both he—and his father— had fine thick hair that seemed to thrive no matter their physical state.

Dev, with clumsy fingers—he had never before attended an infant—pried open the boy's mouth and bent to smell of his breath. It was rancid, with the taint of infection, and Dev felt the bile of fury choking him when he realized that the child's breath stank of whiskey. "Putrid infection, probably your throat and tonsils," he made himself say clinically. "And she's been giving you brandy or something, hasn't she? No wonder you never cry." The child blinked stupidly, which seemed to be his sole activity.

Forcing himself to a clinical impartiality, he unwrapped the boy's filthy rag of a blanket and saw that he had no clothing at all, just a thin, sodden, stinking diaper. His entire lower body was broken out in an angry rash, and his legs were so galled that he had three open sores.

Dev stared at those terrible running sores, his throat working, his breath choked. "I'm…I'm…so sorry, little boy. I'm so sorry…."

"I'm…I'm…so sorry, Mama. I'm so sorry…."

Amelia Buchanan had touched her bleeding face with shaking cold fingers and said softly, "It's not your fault, Dev. But, you have to help me now. You have to be strong. Hurry, hurry, while he's out. Get your bootblack kit and your blanket, and put on all of your clothes, my darling. I'll pack up the bread and cheese. Hurry, hurry…."

It was December of 1842, and Dev had turned seven years old that October. Amelia had given her son a shiny silver dollar for his birthday. In spite of their abject poverty, Dev had kept the silver dollar, just to admire, and had thought that he would keep it forever, his present from his ma.

But two weeks previously, Duane had come home and found the silver dollar. Dev hadn't bothered to hide it. Sometimes at night he and his ma played with it, admiring its shine and cleanness. Duane had gone into a towering rage, accusing both Amelia and Dev of holding out on him. Then, thankfully, he'd left.

But just before Christmas Duane showed up again at the Old Brewery where they slept. His hair was wild, he was filthy, and he was so drunk he could hardly see. He could see well enough to grab Dev, however, and demand that Dev give him his pennies he'd earned from bootblacking that day. Dev had tried to tell him that he hadn't made any money—he'd actually taken his five cents and bought some bread and a small lump of cheese. Duane shouted and stamped and shook Dev, and then began slapping him, hard, with his open hand that was like a piece of wood. Amelia tried to stop him, and so, with mad glee, Duane turned on her and beat her, breaking her arm and nose and blacking both eyes.

"I'm leaving, but I'll be back, you two," he said, his words so thick they could hardly understand him. Amelia was barely conscious, anyway. He staggered to the door, wrenched it so hard it threw a hinge, and turned back. "Don't you even think of leavin', Amelia. If you do, I'll find you and bring you back, and you, too, you little scrub."

Now Dev studied his mother anxiously. "Mama, we can't go. His friends would see us and tell him. They know me on the street."

Amelia licked her lips—they were swelling horribly— and said faintly, "We have to try, Dev. He's—the drink's finally driven him mad. We have to get away." Tears slipped down her face.

"But, Mama, you're hurt bad," he said with anguish. "You can't go anywhere. I don't even think you can move."

"Like I said, son, you have to be strong, and you can help me. Now go get me a rag. See if you can find something that's long and skinny to tie up my arm...it's—we'll need to tie it up so it won't move."

They wandered for a day and a night without money, afraid to go to any friends that might alert Duane where they were. They were like two ghosts, haunted and afraid, slipping into the darkness of alleys and doorways so none of the Bowery Boys or Duane's fire laddies would see them.

Finally Amelia said with desperation, "Maybe Mr.

Yeager will help us. He lives on the Upper East Side, somewhere around Fifty-seventh."

The two went north. It was snowing and cold, and Amelia was in frightful shape. They slept in alleys. Dev managed to make two pennies shining shoes, and they bought watery soup. Finally they made it to Fifty-seventh Street, which was not very populated. There were some modest houses, and Dev and Amelia knocked on the doors, but people refused to talk to them, much less help them. Finally they went to a humble white clapboard church with a tiny steeple at Fifty-seventh and Fifth. Exhausted, freezing, with Amelia half dead, they huddled at the doors, waiting for morning. It was four days before Christmas, and it was a Thursday.

The next morning, early, Dev thought his mother had died, she was so cold and still and pale. No one was coming to church on a Friday, but he hoped that the pastor might come. There was no attached rectory, so the church was deserted. But still, someone might come....

"This be it, sor?" the cabbie called down.

Dev jerked, startling the child he held close against his chest. They had arrived at Behring Orphanage, though the evening was so dim and stormy that he could only see the candlelight glowing softly in the windows.

"That'll be two dollars, sor," the cabbie said, smartly lowering the steps.

Dev stared at him, feeling a sudden unpleasant thrill rush through him. He had no money. He had given it all to—his *stepmother.* "W-wait here," he mumbled, barely functioning.

The cabby's round, red face grew suddenly wary, but he saw the man was clearly a gentleman, no matter how

odd his circumstances at the moment. So he didn't protest, but he did follow Dev to the door, just to be sure.

Clutching the child close, Dev stumbled to the door
and knocked loudly. When Allan Blue threw it open, Dev
suddenly was as dumb as if he'd been struck a blow to
the head. His brain was mush, his tongue paralyzed. He
just looked at the younger man vacantly.

Allan Blue had a wisdom beyond his years, and he
did have some finely honed quick survival instincts that
he'd come by, most improbably, in the war. He took a few
moments to recover from his surprise, surveyed the situation, and then took charge. "Dr. Buchanan, how good to
see you. Please, come in. Good evening, sir. Would that
be your cab?"

"'Twould, sor, and I'm not in a great tearin' hurry, you
understand," the honest cabbie said apologetically. "But
there's a matter o' two dollars this kind gent owes me."

Smoothly Allan said, "I understand, and I'll fetch your
fare in a moment. However, I'm sure Dr. Buchanan will
wish to return to town, and we only have an open buggy
here at the orphanage. Would you like to come into the
kitchen, sir, and have some hot coffee and perhaps some
soup?"

The cabbie fiddled with his sodden hat, then said,
"That's mighty kindly of you, sor, but—"

"Of course you will be more than adequately com-
pensated, both for your time and for the cab fare," Allan
said smoothly.

The cabby's face cleared, and somehow Allan managed to usher Dev to the front parlor, get the cabby's
two dollars as surety, direct him to the kitchen, rouse
Jane Anne, who took the baby from Dev without a single

question, and finally repair into the parlor and close the door.

Dev was standing in front of the fireplace, the grate cold and dark, staring blankly.

Allan's mild face drew into small worry lines, but he merely said, "If you would excuse me, Dr. Buchanan, I'll build a fire. Such a cold and damp night."

Dev took a seat on the sofa, moving as if he were an ungainly puppet. The business of fire building, and then the growing warmth and light, served to steady him, however. As the flames grew stronger and the dry tinder began to crackle with a homey sound, Dev finally felt a sort of peace come over him. He was tired, so tired, and he felt the muscles in his neck and shoulders loosening so precipitately that it was almost painful.

Allan studied him with a combination of curiosity and pity, but he judged it best to hold his tongue until Dev spoke.

Finally he did. "That baby—" he swallowed painfully "—is my brother. I mean, he's my half brother. Technically."

"I see," Allan said gravely. "Did you bring him here to leave him?"

"I don't know," Dev said, and he was so openly weary and confused that Allan felt a great rush of compassion for this normally dignified and rather distant man. "I can't think," Dev went on, clearly defeated. "I don't know what to do, and I didn't know where to go."

"You did well," Allan said with reassuring neutrality. "He obviously needs clothing and diapers and food, and since it's so late, you could never find a place to buy them now."

Dev stared at Allan in sudden shock. "Late? What—"

Fumbling, he pulled out a pocket watch and stared down at it with horror, as if it were a snake or noisome insect. "It's…it's…almost half past seven! I've missed the curtain!"

Allan nodded calmly. "I did understand that the Duvalls were taking the wedding party to see Mr. Charles Dickens's reading tonight."

Dev jumped up and looked around the room with desperation, as if he were searching for a way out of a very dangerous place. "I…I…suppose I must—"

Allan came to lay his hand on Dev's shoulder. Dev, who was not at all accustomed to physical expressions, flinched. Allan said gently, "Dr. Buchanan, the hansom cab is still here, you know. We can certainly keep the boy tonight, or perhaps for a few days. Until you can reach some decisions, make some plans."

"Yes…yes…" Dev said with somewhat shamefaced relief. He began smoothing his hair, straightening his waistcoat, in a clear and sad attempt to regain his composure.

A very soft knock sounded at the door, and Jane Anne opened it. "I'm so very sorry to interrupt you gentlemen, but Dr. Buchanan, I felt I must ask your advice about the baby. I tried to give him some milk—anyone can see he's starving—but he cannot tolerate it at all. He vomits it up almost as soon as he's swallowed it. Could you perhaps advise me of something I could do until we can find a wet nurse?"

Dev listened to her, his handsome face growing pale. When she finished, he dropped his head, almost fell back onto the sofa, and buried his head in his hands. Jane Anne, startled and concerned, started to move to him, but Allan signaled her by a stern "no" shake of his head.

"Try goat's milk," Dev said in a muffled voice. "And you will likely need to mix some brandy with it, for the child undoubtedly has an alcohol addiction. The only way to counter that in infants is to wean them very slowly from it."

"I...I see." Hesitantly she went on, "He is very ill, isn't he?"

"Yes," Dev answered. "Yes, he is."

"All right, Dr. Buchanan, I'll try feeding him a little, and then I'll bathe him and dress those sores. That will be all right, won't it?" she asked anxiously.

"Yes, Mrs. Blue. But after you bathe him, call me. I'll make a soothing poultice for the sores."

"Yes, Doctor," Jane Anne said, going to the door. Before leaving she turned and asked hesitantly, "Sir, would you happen to know the child's name? I always feel that they should be spoken to by their given name if possible. It does give them some sense of security, even at so young an age."

Dev looked up, and he was desolate. "I...I...no, no, I'm very sorry to say I never even heard his name. But...I...suppose you should call him Dart. Perhaps he might, in his poor state, have some familiarity with that."

"Dart," she repeated with a small smile. "It's a nice name for a sweet little boy." She slipped out, closing the door softly.

Dev, his gaze searching far out in an unknown distance, said, "Can one of the older boys take a message to Steinway Hall, Mr. Blue? If you would be so kind as to loan me some money, I will send a message to Mrs. de Lancie and the Duvalls, and the boy can come back in the cab. Then I'll take it home...with...Dart."

"Of course," Allan said. "I'll make the arrangements

now. Writing papers are in that small secretary by the window, Dr. Buchanan." He hesitated, then said, "Sir, I don't wish to intrude in your private affairs, and I hope you will not think I am presumptuous, but I believe that I may tell you something I have learned and believe in with my whole heart that may lift your spirits."

Wearily Dev asked, "And that is?"

Forcefully Allan said, "No man can live honorably unless he takes care of his family. And a man's honor is not the image of his family, by what or who his family is. Rather, it is shaped by his actions, by his decisions, and by his doing, always, the right and true thing."

Dev sighed, a deep searching breath from the innermost core. "It's not just—reputation, or status, Mr. Blue." He stood slowly, as if he were elderly. "It's…Mrs. de Lancie, you see. She can't—doesn't—has never wanted children."

Comprehension dawned on Allan's boyish features, and they darkened. "I'm very sorry, sir. That is, indeed, a distressing problem. But, Dr. Buchanan, you are a good Christian man, and Mrs. de Lancie is a fine Christian lady. Surely God will reward you, sir, for your faithfulness and care of your family."

"Perhaps," Dev said bleakly, "but likely Mrs. de Lancie will not now wish to be in my family."

Chapter Eight

"Thus Conscience Does Make Cowards of Us All"

"I'm afraid I'm here under false pretenses," Shiloh Irons-Winslow said.

"Is that right?" Troy Bondurant replied with amusement. "Am I in danger?"

"Just of your time bein' wasted. I'm not violent. Usually."

"I'm relieved for the safety of my person," Troy quipped while studying Shiloh carefully across the businesslike gleam of his banker's desk. "I saw your fights in '66, Iron Man. McCool and Elliott."

"Uh…yeah. But I didn't mean I'm using an assumed name," Shiloh explained. "I really am a Winslow of Winslow Brothers' Shipping. Here, for your own peace of mind." He took three folded papers from his inner coat pocket. "My letters of introduction, sir."

Troy scanned them quickly, only pausing to read one through. He was a fine-looking young blood, a couple of years older than Shiloh, with quick eyes and manner and a certain honed alertness. He was dressed in the single acceptable uniform of men of business: a black suit, a small black necktie, and a discreetly striped waistcoat. The only frivolity about him was his thick, curly dark brown hair and what seemed to be constant amusement lurking in his blue eyes. Laying the papers aside on the gleaming expanse of his desk, he propped his elbows and steepled his fingers. "Your bankers say you're affluent, your shipping agents say you're capable, and your friends say you're hardworking and honorable."

"So they say." Shiloh settled into an easy posture, leaning back in the comfortable armchair. Troy Bondurant reflected that it was always easy to tell the ones who didn't want money or credit—they were relaxed. The other kind always carried some degree of tension about them, no matter how solvent they were.

Shiloh continued, "One reason I came to New York was to explore the possibility of expanding my family's shipping business to the Atlantic. But I've changed my mind." He shrugged carelessly. "Guess I could've let you know and canceled this appointment last night at Steinway. But I guess I didn't really make a final decision until this morning. Rude of me, huh?"

"Not at all," Troy declared. "Let's just make it a social call. I was going to call on you anyway, but I forgot to ask where you're staying." His sharp eyes went to Shiloh's reference letters. Colonel Richard Duvall's, the one Troy had read completely, was on top. "But before pleasure, how about just, as you say, exploring some possibilities? It can't hurt to have some ideas for the future."

"That's all right with me, if you don't mind," Shiloh said easily. "My original scheme was to take one of our clippers and start shipping between the Eastern Seaboard and the West Indies. If that worked out, I had thought I might add another clipper, based in London, for West Indies–European runs."

"Sounds promising," Troy encouraged him. "Two questions—cargo and clippers?"

Shiloh nodded approvingly. He liked a succinct, direct investment banker. "Clipper cargo, as I'm sure you know, has to be lightweight and small bulk, like tea. I was thinking Cuban cigars. Every after-dinner brandy with cigars these days seems to feature Cuban cigars. I'm not much of a con…con… What's that French word?"

"Connoisseur," Troy said, amused at Shiloh's unself-consciousness.

"Connoisseur of cigars," he continued, "but they do seem to suit fine brandy very well."

"Yes, they do, and it's not just an upperten fad," Troy agreed. "All right, that takes care of the Cuba-to-New-York run. How about outgoing?"

Shiloh frowned with concentration a moment. "I didn't really have that worked out yet, but while I was walking here I noticed—"

"You walked from the Fifth Avenue Hotel?" Troy asked, astounded.

"Sure. For a Southern boy, the streets of Lower Manhattan are better than the circus," Shiloh drawled. "Top hats, match girls, shoeblack boys, fine ladies, money changers, bespectacled clerks, monocled gents, bright-eyed maids, horses, hogs, dogs, cheese hawkers, seam-stresses, omnibuses—"

"You're a blooming poet," Troy laughed. "I'll have to take a walk. I don't see it, having lived in it my whole life."

"It takes longer in a cab or even to ride than it does to

walk," Shiloh said. "You must spend half your mornings in a carriage."

Troy nodded. "Reading the papers—all the papers. Anyway, pardon me for interrupting you, Mr. Irons-Winslow. Please continue with your business plan."

"Well, on my way down here I started noticing all the light consumer goods that are so readily available here. Things like pocketbooks, combs, tinware, patent leather, small chests, marble mantels, mustard, writing ink, pencil cases, paint, glass—you know, all the thousands of things that we use every day in our homes and offices and at play," Shiloh explained. "But these simple, everyday items require modern factories and complex machinery to manufacture. Now, I know that the Continent has heavy industry, but I figure most of the West Indies and South and Central America haven't gotten that far yet."

"That's right," Troy said enthusiastically. "But European exports are generally much higher priced than American, for the simple reason that we do have much more competition and therefore lower prices. In addition, those kinds of light consumer goods are usually only sold and shipped in quantity of one or perhaps two related items by jobbers. For example, a jobber might buy six thousand cases of mustard and four thousand cases of vinegar and sell them to Port Lucaya, Grand Bahamas. But that means—"

"That everyone on the smaller Bahama islands must go to Port Lucaya to get a jar of mustard," Shiloh finished. "Right. So I thought, why couldn't I cut out the jobbers and buy the cargo myself, and make it a wide assortment of light consumer goods, sort of a general-store kind of shipment? Then I could sell to one or sixty merchants, and of course, since I'm the shipper, that takes care of my varied distribution."

Shrewdly Troy commented, "I see you've figured out a way to lower your insurance costs, too, as it's a lot cheaper if you own the cargo, and this scheme would allow you to keep using clipper ships. I think you've already answered my second question. With such small-profit dollar shipments, you may not get wealthy, but your clippers would at least pay for themselves."

Shiloh grinned like a small guilty boy. "Yeah. I've found out I'm real partial to those toys. After sailing clippers, barks and brigs are a dead bore, and steamships are a downright sacrilege."

"Clippers definitely are the thoroughbreds of the sea," Troy agreed with understanding. "Anyway, Mr. Irons-Winslow, I must say that you have an astute, fully workable plan here. And I could help you with some related West Indies investment ventures that could mean a higher profit margin for Winslow Brothers'. So why not?"

Shiloh frowned. "Oh, for a number of reasons, some of them personal. One big consideration is that at this time I don't have the extra clipper for an Atlantic run. I had considered moving the one clipper here, but I decided— just this morning, as I confessed—that our Pacific shipping is lucrative enough to keep all three barks and one clipper busy."

Troy frowned, then shuffled Shiloh's papers. "But wait. Your list of business assets includes two clippers— the—let me see—the *Brynn Annalea* and *Locke's Day Dream*. You haven't lost one, have you?"

"Sorta," Shiloh said in his careless drawl.

Troy waited.

Shiloh watched him.

"I see," Troy finally said, though he didn't.

Shiloh continued, "And our family plantation in Hawaii sustained some heavy losses recently."

"Oh? But it is still solvent?"

"Yeah, it's still going strong," Shiloh told him in a less guarded manner. "It was a volcano that destroyed about seven hundred acres. But it wasn't the cash crops that were burned, it was two pineapple fields and lots of jungle, and the lava overran a favorite beach. But it did devastate the plantation house and grounds and out-buildings, so rebuilding is going to take a lot of ready cash." *Which my cousin Bain stole,* Shiloh thought an-grily, though of course he didn't say it.

Troy said, "I understand, then, that just at the moment you're low on investment capital and…er…short one clip-per ship. Just so you may be aware of all your options, Mr. Irons-Winslow, I can tell you that Bondurant Bank-ing and Equities would be happy to assist you in remedy-ing these temporary setbacks and would now or at any time in the future be happy to assist you in this or any other venture."

"Thank you, sir," Shiloh said formally.

"Your servant, sir," Troy said, equally formally. Now he leaned back, his fine leather chair squeaking slightly. "So now that all that dried-up mutton's over, how about some coffee? Tea?"

"You have China?" Shiloh asked.

"Wish I owned it," Troy joked. "My father is trying to buy it, but so far it's a wash. Sorry. Yes, we do have China tea." He rang a tiny silvery bell and ordered refreshments from a clerk who popped his head in, all the while re-flecting that Shiloh Irons-Winslow was quite an enigma. He was the Iron Man, the down-in-the-dirt fighter, he was obviously a Johnny Reb, yet his family was from Hawaii and he was a medical assistant to a female doctor, but he was also an independent businessman. He didn't know French catchwords, but he knew to ask for "China tea," not "Chinese tea." His dress was immaculate, of a fine navy blue close wool, his waistcoat a discreet pinstripe, his watch chain gold, his top hat silk, and yet his hands looked as rough as a plow-hand's.

"I believe we started talking about attending *Hamlet* last night before we were so rudely interrupted by Mr. Dickens," Troy said, smiling. "Are you a Shakespeare fan, Mr. Irons-Winslow?"

"No, I guess you could say I'm a fan of Prince Hamlet of Denmark," he replied lightly. "I gotta be honest, it's the only Shakespeare I've ever read. The Doc—that is, you know my…uh…friend and former employer, Dr. Cheney Duvall? Well, we traveled to New York together from San Francisco. She gets the *Herald Tribune* and the *Sun* out there, and she'd already spotted the announcement of the production at Wallack's. We sorta read it together, like, on the trip. Anyway, it finally started sinking into my thick skull, and now it seems it's like a mirror or model of real life. To me Hamlet seems like the best and the worst of all men. You see what I mean?"

"Don't have a clue," Troy admitted cheerfully. "Never did. Get Shakespeare, I mean, or any poetical kind of stuff. Dickens is much more my speed, and I still have to work pretty hard at that."

Surprised, Shiloh asked, "But didn't you say you'd already been to *Hamlet* three times?"

"Sure. But I guess you might say I'm a fan of Miss Clarissa Howe, who is the loveliest lady-in-waiting you've ever seen," Troy replied mischievously. "And she doesn't have any lines to confuse her or to bore me with, which suits me fine." He eyed Shiloh speculatively for a moment, then went ahead with some hesitation. "I've met Minette York, as I told you. Bluestocking, she is. Like your lady doctor must be."

A shadow passed over Shiloh's clean-cut features, so short-lived Troy Bondurant wondered if he'd imagined it.

"Minette York is an intellectual?" Shiloh prodded him.

"Yes, though she looks like some kind of fluffy small-brained little kitten. Did I tell you that Wallack wanted to put on *Romeo and Juliet* to showcase her, but she particularly asked for *Hamlet?* Said it had such depth, and Ophelia was a part she'd always wanted to play but had never had the opportunity. Seems like *Hamlet*'s not staged much. It's too complex for us...er...Shakespeare illiterates. Anyway, she's one of those most frightening of creatures—an intelligent woman." He gave a theatrical shudder.

Shiloh grinned. "Scary, aren't they?"

"Yes, sir. Anyway, you're here for the de Lancie-Buchanan wedding, right? So you'll be here until then?"

"Yeah, I'm trapped right and proper," Shiloh said lazily, crossing one leg negligently over the other and lacing his fingers over his flat stomach. "I'm not in the wedding party, of course, but I'm sort of obliged to attend all the balls, cotillions—what the devil are those, anyway?—musicales, teas, high teas, and other goings-on for the betrothed couple."

"As Dr. Duvall's escort, I understand," Troy said with elaborate casualness.

"Nah, sorry, but you misunderstand," Shiloh said with the tiniest edge. "What about you? You're at all the de Lancie-Buchanan galas, too, but I know Dr. Buchanan's only groomsman is his best man, Colonel Duvall."

"I've kind of got a double connection, I guess you'd say," Troy answered. "I've been friends with Beckett Steen since childhood, and also I'm good friends with Dr. Cleve Batson. You know, Dr. Buchanan's—and Dr. Duvall's, now I think of it—partner? Sure you know Cleve. He's an usher for Dr. Buchanan, and I'm an usher for Mrs. de Lancie. Anyway, we three and Austin Darrow all kind of make up our own gang."

"Yeah? Like the Upperten Roach Guards?" Shiloh observed dryly. "Or how about the Above Bleecker Dead Rabbits?"

Troy laughed. "Mostly we're just called young jackanapes, or fancy rowdies, things like that. How about joining up?"

"Fine with me," Shiloh answered easily. "If we can do something besides cotillions or musicales. We've got one of those beasts tonight, by the way."

"I know, at the de Peysters'," Troy said, grimacing. "They're awfully stuffy, but they do have almost a million net worth. Anyway, we can get Cleve to make our excuses early—he's oh-so-careful of the elderly ladies that they can't make up enough ailments to get to call him in—and then we'll catch *Hamlet.* At least we can probably make it by the second act."

Shiloh frowned. "I don't want to miss any of it."

"Can't be helped," Troy grumbled. "Social obligations and duties."

"'Thus conscience does make cowards of us all,'" Shiloh sighed.

"Beg pardon?" Troy said blankly.

"Never mind," Shiloh replied, rising. "I'll see you young jackanapes at the musicale tonight."

Not too long ago, Shiloh Irons would have known that he was being watched.

As did many of the hunted in the Great War, he had developed a keen instinct, an almost superhuman awareness of his environment, a sensitivity to the slightest changes in the air or the smell of a place or the thousands of tiny sounds that continually assaulted the human ear, for any of these might herald danger. This visceral alertness was heightened in Shiloh Irons, too, as a fighter. Sometimes he knew what his opponent was going to do even before his opponent did.

But in the richness of the atmosphere of New York City, and perhaps because Shiloh was deliberately numbing himself in many ways, shying away from his pain, he never sensed that danger was near. And Bain Winslow, Shiloh's first cousin, was the worst kind of enemy, one who knew he was weak, despised his own weakness, and therefore would never consider an honest, direct confrontation.

Bain watched Shiloh in the Steens' box at Wallack's Theater, cursing him. Shiloh had come in late with a pack of young bloods—by now Bain knew every one of them, who they were, who their families were—much to the chagrin of the other theatergoers. But then, the Steens were royalty of a sort, and Bain supposed Beckett Steen could hang from the rafters and hoot like an ape if he wanted to.

Bain had six clients with him, possibly very lucrative clients, as they had all been introduced to him by Judge

Alston, who had given Sweet's House of Exotic Island Princesses a glowing recommendation.

Now what shall I do? Slink off? How long am I going to have to run and hide from him anyway! He's like my nemesis or something....

After Bain had seen Shiloh and Cheney at Steinway Hall the previous evening, he had gone to the offices of the *Herald Tribune* and bought back copies of the previous months' editions. Perusing the society pages, he now knew that Cheney Duvall was Victoria de Lancie's best friend and maid of honor; he knew who Dr. Devlin Buchanan was and his connection with the Duvalls; that Shiloh had gained some momentary recognition in New York in 1866 after winning two prize fights, which were sponsored by the Marquess of Queensberry.

Bain had learned that he could find out each evening where his cousin would be, for the *Herald* published both cards of notice of the de Lancie-Buchanan betrothal activities and articles reporting on the events the following day.

They were all supposed to be at that musicale at the de Peysters'! But no, here he is, everywhere I turn! I'm not going to stand for this. I can't be looking over my shoulder for him my whole life, watching for him, wondering if he'll find me. I'll figure out a way to fix him, once and for all!

Bain watched Shiloh obsessively all through Acts II and III of the play. But due to a fortunate circumstance, the box that Bain had rented was at the rear of the theater, while of course the Steen box was second from the stage end. All of the men, Shiloh especially, watched the players instead of perusing the other boxes and the audience. During intermission, all Bain had to do was declare he

was weary of sitting—indeed, *Hamlet* was a long play—
and stand at the back to drink his ices and champagne.

When the play resumed, Bain noted with interest that
Shiloh and Troy Bondurant left the box during Act IV. It
took him a while, but finally he figured it out.

*Of course, they left right after Ophelia's last scene…
so Mr. Irons-Winslow has gone to be introduced to
Minette York… Have to admit that's smart. She's not
in Act V, and after the play she'll be swarmed with suitors…. So Miss Cheney Duvall's escort to all these fine
galas has other interests…. I must find out about this.*

Bain suffered through the rest of the play, for his johns
were too important, and enjoying themselves too much,
to hustle them out early, as he had done at the Dickens
reading. He had visions of walking out of the theater and
coming face-to-face with his nemesis. Licking his lips,
he wondered what Locke—he never thought of him as
Shiloh—would do. Strike him? Have him arrested? His
cousin had powerful friends in New York. Bain would
have to be very careful.

All six of his companions eagerly agreed to visit
Sweet's, and Bain didn't have to hurry them as they left
the theater. He saw no sign of Locke, but only when he
was safely in one of his guest's fine carriages did he
breathe easier.

Soon after they reached Sweet's, when all of the gentlemen had been introduced to the princesses, and the
night was beginning to look kindly upon Bain again—
he'd had three stiff whiskeys, gulping them down one
after another—he took Sweet aside to speak to him privately.

"I have a serious problem, Sweet. There's something
I need you to do," Bain said, taking out his money clip.

"Yes, sir," Sweet said obediently, the permanently vacant look on his face brightening a little. He had a bulldog loyalty to Mr. Worthington, and he was flattered when his mentor asked for his help.

"You know Wallack's Theater? Good. Now there's an actress by the name of Minette York. She's playing Ophelia in the play. She's quite famous, and everyone will know her. Got that?" Bain said very slowly.

"Minette York," Sweet repeated carefully.

"Now I want you to go to the theater and wait at the stage door. There'll probably be lots of people there, and they'll probably ask for her autograph when she comes out, so you'll be able to figure out who she is. Now here's the important part—I want you to watch her, see who she's with. Just watch as she leaves the theater, all right?"

"Do I talk to her?" Sweet asked, his brow wrinkling.

"No, Sweet," Bain said with a trace of impatience. "Just watch her, but the most important thing is to watch the man she's with. I think—I'm fairly sure it'll be a very tall man, strong looking, with broad shoulders and light blond hair."

"Tall, strong, blond," Sweet repeated under his breath.

"That's right," Bain said, sighing. "Now, if she is with such a man, you take a hansom cab and follow them, okay? Miss York, the famous actress, and the tall blond man. You see where they go. Then you come back and tell me. Use the money to take cabs, Sweet. Can you do all that?"

"I can do it, Mr. Worthington," Sweet said. "But what

about the house? High-spirited young gents here tonight, and they bear some watch."

"Alana and I can handle it, Sweet," Bain said, almost kindly. "You just do what I told you."

"I always do that, Mr. Worthington," Sweet said with dignity.

"So you do, Sweet. So you do."

A measure of Shiloh's blindness would have been apparent to one who knew him, for Shiloh saw Sweet outside the stage door but didn't observe him at all. Their eyes even met. In Shiloh's defense, Sweet didn't have the sort of temperament to be sly, so he didn't guiltily look away, which Shiloh might have noted.

Sweet merely perused Shiloh as if he were memorizing him, then gazed at Minette York long and hard. This was certainly not uncommon, so perhaps it could be understood that Shiloh's internal alarms didn't sound.

He took the lovely and talented Miss York to Delmonico's, where she was enthusiastically applauded when they entered. Their supper took three hours, for people kept interrupting them to speak to her or ask her to sign their playbills.

Shiloh didn't even notice the same enormous blank-faced man loitering across the street from the famous restaurant. It was, perhaps, again understandable, since Delmonico's was always very busy after theater hours, and there were many carriages and cabs on the street, not to mention the line of lesser beings waiting to get into the restaurant.

But later, it was not only inexplicable, but it was tragic that Shiloh did not see this man, this noticeable man who couldn't melt into a crowd if his life depended on it. At about three-thirty in the morning Shiloh stood at the window, fighting the beginnings of a hangover with a rancid stomach and aching head and foul taste in his mouth, feeling grimy and smelling sour, and considered the darkest and loneliest hours of night.

He never saw Sweet in the shadowed street below staring up at the windows of Minette York's rooms.

Chapter Nine

With All Their Quantity of Love

In a discreet brownstone at Sixth and West Twenty-fourth resided the offices of Cheney Duvall, M.D., Devlin Buchanan, M.D., R.C.S., and Cleve Batson, M.D. The Duvalls' carriage, that distinctive black brougham with the Duvall Iron Shield on the doors, drew smartly up on the quiet street.

Mr. Jack hurriedly jumped down and tried to open Cheney's door to assist her, but as usual, she had impatiently opened it herself and kicked the steps down. She looked very businesslike this morning in a moss-green skirt and tartan waistcoat with a slender gold chain hanging from the vest pocket. Her mantle was wool, the same shade of gray-green as her skirt, with a bright red, green, and blue tartan lining that matched her tight-fitting vest. "It's all right, Mr. Jack. I'm already out," she said hurriedly.

Mr. Jack frowned darkly. "I'm a-seein' that, Miss Cheney. So you're intendin' to jist go paradin' into a gentleman's abode this early o' the mornin'? Jist goin' right in, are you?"

Cheney stopped on the walk and turned back to him hesitantly. "But—it is my office, Mr. Jack."

"That I know, Miss Cheney," he said with extravagant patience. "But mayhap I'll at least announce you to the gentleman? All's said and done, it is barely six o' the clock."

"Hmm…I see your point. All right, Mr. Jack, I'll wait. Would you be so kind as to ring the bell and tell Dr. Batson that I'm here?"

Mr. Jack looked vastly relieved. As he went up the trim walk, he muttered to himself, just softly enough so that Cheney couldn't hear the words but just loud enough so that she would hear ripples of disapproval. "A body cain't never tell when or about what Miss Cheney Duvall might get her back up, so to speak, and snap her fingers, fie on you. I ast you, why barely six o' the clock? Young ladies what do need their rest ain't got no call to be out stirrin' afore decent folks has had their bit o' toast and coffee. She likely ain't even had that, she's that pale and ghostly." With a decided jerk Mr. Jack rang the bell.

A very sleep-stupored young doctor finally answered, peeping cautiously out the window before cracking the door. "Mr. Jack? Is something wrong?"

"They sure is," he muttered darkly, jerking his thumb over his shoulder. "Miss Doctor Cheney Duvall is a-comin' in."

"Hmm? Oh. Yes, I see. Um…all right," Dr. Batson said with some confusion. "I'll— I shall be dressed promptly—"

"I should hope so," Mr. Jack rasped. "Mayhap I can

keep her occupied for five or so minutes, Dr. Batson, but you'll want to be a-steppin' lively."

Dr. Cleve Batson was not the kind of man to step lively, for he was a very calm, languid young man of twenty-three, thickly built, with reddish-blond hair, freckles, heavy-lidded blue eyes, and a wide, slow smile. Cheney and Dev, after interviewing several candidates for a partnership, had seen that this young man's quiet, relaxed ways were a perfect foil for them, for both Cheney and Dev were rather intense, high-minded doctors. Dr. Batson, on the other hand, seemed to be very reassuring, especially to the elderly and to children. Cheney was competent with all patients—when given the opportunity—but she did, at times, grow bored with the natural and inevitable ailments of the old and the nuisance sicknesses of the young. She was best in trauma situations and with very serious illnesses.

Dev, of course, had worked for years to extricate himself from medical cases so that he might specialize in surgery. The previous year, through Guy's Hospital in London, where Dev had just completed a two-year fellowship, he was—miraculously—invited into the Royal College of Surgeons. Such an august reference had greatly enhanced Dev's reputation and was beginning to change the attitude, expressed so succinctly by Mrs. Goelet, that a surgeon was just a sort of inferior physician.

But Cheney and Dev had managed to establish a modestly successful general practice in 1866, when both of them had been in New York for a period of months during the cholera plague. After the plague, Cheney had wanted to take some time off—she hadn't had a holiday since before she went to medical school—so she had visited Charleston and New Orleans, and then had taken a position at St. Francis de Yerba Buena Hospital in San Francisco. After an extended leave of absence, Dev had returned to London. Unwilling to simply dissolve their partnership and send all their clients elsewhere, they had decided to take in another partner, one who was based in New York and wouldn't be traveling, as Cheney and Dev did. Dr. Batson had managed to walk right in and take over their clients, with the loss of only two families who huffily wanted only Dr. Devlin Buchanan of the Royal College of Surgeons.

Dr. Batson's monthly reports that he faithfully forwarded to Cheney and Dev were splendid. Not only did he maintain their patient base; he had ingeniously almost doubled it. By his humble, compassionate demeanor he had become a favorite of all of the matriarchs of the families, and he had, over a period of months, managed to persuade them to send their servants to him as well. This was relatively unheard of, as it was true that most servants either went to Bellevue for serious illnesses or injuries, or they simply consulted an apothecary for prescriptions. But Dr. Batson managed to convince the ladies that it would be in their best interest in the long run to allow a competent physician to attend the servants, as they would then not be subject to many days off because of sickness. Neither Cheney nor Dev had thought of this excellent way of expanding their practice, and both of them had been very glad they'd chosen Dr. Batson.

But this early gray morning, however leisurely Dr. Batson's comportment might normally be, he was now moving very quickly indeed, running to the window every few moments to see if Dr. Cheney Duvall was sailing up the walk. To his vast relief, she seemed to be enjoying herself, talking and laughing with Mr. Jack and petting the Duvalls' magnificent Arabians, Romulus and Remus. Dr. Batson had time to get dressed, comb his hair, brush his teeth, and run downstairs and put the kettle on before Dr. Duvall came in.

"Good morning, ma'am," he said with composure, moving to meet her in the front reception room while at the same time blessing his housekeeper, Mrs. Slopes, who kept each and every room on both floors as spotless as if they were spit shined.

"Good morning, Dr. Batson," Cheney said, extending her hand for him to shake. She looked weary and drawn, he thought, but then again he supposed everyone in the wedding party was on short rations of rest. Dr. Batson himself was feeling even more lethargic than usual.

In her direct way Cheney went on, "Please accept my apology for intruding on you in this abrupt manner and at such an unheard-of hour."

"Not at all, Doctor, not at all. It is, after all, your own office. Just because you and Dr. Buchanan are kind enough to allow me to board in the apartment upstairs is certainly no reason for you to be inconvenienced," Dr. Batson said sincerely.

Cheney nodded a slight acknowledgment. "Still, it is, I am sure, troubling for you." A shadow of her vivid smile crossed her face, lighting her lovely sea-green eyes a little. "And it is most troubling for Mr. Jack. He convinced me that it would be much better for all concerned—including Mr. Jack—if I brought my maid with me, particularly if I'm to come 'sashayin'' up and bangin' on gentlemen's doors all hours of the night and day.'"

Dr. Batson smiled his wide, delighted grin. It was endearing, to be sure, Cheney thought.

"Mr. Jack is one of my favorite patients," he said.

Cheney's eyes widened. "Mr. Jack is your patient? Why? What's wrong with him?"

"Um…he…he has rheumatism in his left knee, Dr. Duvall," Cleve answered hesitantly. He'd stepped off into a puddle this time, he knew. Mr. Jack was the Duvalls' longtime, most loyal servant, and Cheney wouldn't understand why he preferred Dr. Batson. Like most men, particularly older men, Mr. Jack couldn't imagine letting a lady examine him, not even—or perhaps especially— Dr. Cheney Duvall. Also, Cleve felt the unmistakable pull of conscience. Though he might be a young rake on his own time, he felt very strongly about medical ethics and was particularly sensitive of patient-doctor confidentiality.

Cheney saw his discomfiture, and—uncharacteristically for her—immediately saw the quandary she'd put him in. "I see," she said shortly.

A few moments of awkward silence ensued, but fortunately the teakettle began to screech. "Oh, I almost forgot—will you have coffee or tea, Dr. Duvall?" Cleve asked politely.

"Coffee, if you please," Cheney answered. He went into the kitchen at the back of the house, and much to his chagrin, Cheney followed him. The first floor was all office space. Only the second floor was his private apartment, but Cleve and Cheney didn't know each other well enough yet for him to feel comfortable with her. She was, after all, a lady doctor, and his boss. Vaguely Cleve wondered how Shiloh had managed to live with it for three years.

"…don't want to upset your schedule, but I very much wanted to go over the records to do some catching up this morning," Cheney was saying. "I have engagements all day, and, of course, there's the…um…what are we doing tonight, again?"

"The musicale at the de Peysters'," Cleve said wearily.

With amusement Cheney countered, "Sorry, Doctor. That was last night. Remember? Mozart's Piano Concerto No. 16 in D major? Mrs. Alvin de Peyster, tall lady, large voice, large diamonds, called Wren for some reason I'll never fathom?"

They laughed, and then laughed more, for they discovered that neither of them had an inkling what the wedding party was doing that night. Cleve had just suggested a shooting party, while Cheney thought it must be an egg roll when the dignified and not-easily-amused Dr. Devlin Buchanan appeared in the kitchen.

Cleve was almost speechless, such was his reverence for the internationally renowned Dr. Buchanan. He simply stuttered.

But Cheney wasn't at all impressed with Dev, since he was practically her older brother. "Hello, Dev, you old grumble," Cheney said, taking his arm. "We were just trying to figure out what we're doing tonight to celebrate you and your lovely bride-to-be."

"I don't know," he answered, frowning. "I forget."

Cheney started and studied him carefully. Dev looked—terrible, if the truth be told. His necktie, a thin black silk ribbon, was crooked. He had missed a spot shaving. His eyes were unclear, as if he were in the throes of confusion. And his lack of a courteous greeting— though Dev was sometimes somber, he did have beautiful social graces—told Cheney that something was clearly wrong. "Dr. Batson is making coffee," she said, lightly squeezing his arm. "Let's go sit down and make him wait on us."

"I am, as always, your servant," Cleve said gallantly.

Meekly Dev allowed Cheney to lead him into the reception room. It was a comforting room, designed to reassure the occasional patient who actually visited a doctor's office instead of sending for the physician. It had two facing blue velvet sofas, matching tea tables at either end, with a fine cherry console table by the hall door. No fire was lit yet in the small fireplace, but one was already laid. Dev collapsed onto a sofa while Cheney quickly lit the small bits of tinder and blew until a comforting flame burned.

"I'm tired," Dev said listlessly.

Concerned, Cheney sat close to him. "Dev, what in the name of heaven is wrong? You're not yourself at all! Are you ill?"

"No, no. I'm not ill," he said, rousing himself with an effort. He seemed, for the first time, to focus on her. "I am tired, but I know that everyone must be exhausted with all these wedding festivities. How do women do it, I wonder? Anyway, Cheney, aside from that, I'm—distracted."

"By a patient?" Cheney asked, probing.

"Um...yes. By a patient. I—"

Dr. Batson came in with a tray, the heavy scent of hot coffee steaming up from a silver coffeepot. Cheney and Dev both lifted their faces and sniffed appreciatively in a peculiarly identical way, as if they were twins instead of adopted brother and sister.

"I was just teasing you, Dr. Batson. I'll pour," Cheney said warmly, fixing her coffee with two sugars and heavy cream and Dev's black. "You only brought two cups... won't you join us?"

Fidgeting a little, Dr. Batson cleared his throat and

said awkwardly, "If I might beg your pardon, Dr. Duvall, Dr. Buchanan, I should like to— That is, I haven't— I mean to say, upstairs is—"

"Of course," Cheney said smoothly, knowing that he hadn't had time to shave. "Please take your leave. We can manage."

"Thank you, ma'am," he said and slipped out with vast relief.

"I need to talk to him," Dev said, voicing a vague and tardy objection.

"About your patient?" Cheney asked, signaling him to drink his coffee. He looked as if he were about to drop.

"Yes," he answered dully, staring into the depths of his cup. "My patient."

Cheney's brow wrinkled as she tried to think how best to get Dev to talk to her. It was so difficult to get a man to speak about his problems anyway. Suddenly it occurred to her that Dev never had confided in her. She had talked to him about everything ever since they were small children. But somehow Dev had never seemed to need a confidant. He'd always been so self-sufficient, so capable. With sudden distress Cheney realized that she couldn't recall ever seeing Dev so disturbed. *Could it be the wedding? Could it be that he doesn't want to get married? Or—or horrors, does he, perhaps, not want to marry Victoria? But no, Dev loves her...doesn't he? Then what's wrong, so terribly wrong with him?*

Dev was struggling to focus his thoughts, for he did feel guilty at being such a grumble, as Cheney had so aptly put it. It was rude, after all, not to pay close attention to a lady, especially to his best friend, his sister of the heart if not of the blood...his blood.

My brother. My father. For a fleeting moment Dev

thought that he would blurt it all out, would tell Cheney everything, would ask her to help him think, to make the right decisions, to deal with the inevitable terrible consequences of his shabby story coming out.

But she already looked so upset that Dev rebuked himself for his selfishness. "Cheney, don't think I wouldn't consult with you first," he said quickly, mistaking her distress. "It's just that this patient is an infant, and I know Dr. Batson has had extensive experience with newborns, for he's had six born to our clients in the last year alone. Have you, by any chance, had experience with newborns?"

"Why, no, not much at all," Cheney said, hastily gathering her scattered thoughts. "But, Dev, you have a patient, an infant, that's upsetting you so? It's just that you've been so marvelous to attend all the children at the orphanage, and I know they've had at least two newborns in the last three months."

He dropped his eyes. "This one's different."

"He's—is it a boy?"

"Yes."

"He's gravely ill?"

"Yes."

Cheney desperately wanted to question him further, but obviously Dev didn't want to discuss this patient with her. She wasn't even sure that this patient was the reason for Dev's haunted look. It was uncharacteristic of him; that was certain. Doctors always had to learn to keep a certain emotional distance from their patients. It was their only mechanism of self-preservation. Cheney had had more trouble developing this emotional distance than Dev had ever had.

But he wasn't connecting with her. He was, in a

manner of speaking, pushing her away. He sat close, but he was such a self-contained man, so grave and reserved, that Cheney was at a loss.

Finally, with some awkwardness, she leaned close and, with tiny delicate movements, retied his tie. "It's crooked," she said with weak humor. "I believe this is the first time I've ever seen you awry, sir."

He grunted, a semblance of a laugh. "Oh, I'm awry, all right. I'm certainly awry."

"Oh, Dev," Cheney sighed, then leaned on his shoulder.

Suddenly, with urgency, Dev put his arms around her and pulled her close, hugging her hard. "Cheney—would you—I need to talk to you—"

The raucous doorbell jangled, and a horde of people flooded into the room.

Shiloh Irons stood, one eyebrow raised sardonically, his lips a thin tight line, his arms crossed. Troy Bondurant, somewhat behind him, hurriedly stepped forward, almost tripping in his hurry to see better. Behind him, Austin Darrow, an elegantly thin, snobbish-looking young man, surveyed them coolly, raising a monocle to one sleepy brown eye. Bringing up the rear was the sturdy and shocked Mrs. Slopes, the housekeeper.

"Dr. Duvall. Dr. Buchanan," Shiloh said coolly. "Are we interrupting something—again?"

Cheney and Dev slowly disentangled, neither of them showing any embarrassment at all. They looked at each other. Heavily Dev said, "Now I'm really awry."

"A rye?" Shiloh snapped. "What's that?"

Cheney laughed, and even Dev chuckled as they rose. Complacently Cheney said, "Good morning, gentlemen. Good morning, Mrs. Slopes. Dr. Batson has made coffee, but I think you'll need to make more for our guests. Meanwhile, gentlemen, if you'll excuse me, I do have some work to do." Smiling, she glided out of the room.

She went into her office, pleased to find that Dr. Batson had left it exactly as she'd done it, with the George III barrister's desk, the orderly bookshelves, the neat glass-fronted attorney's bookcase that held medical supplies all in place. The house only had two rooms suitable for offices. Dr. Batson used Dev's normally, but since he'd returned, Cleve had been using Cheney's office. It wasn't of much consequence, since the offices were mainly used for study and for keeping records and medical supplies and for mixing prescriptions.

Cheney sat on one of the red velvet sofas remembering that terrible time she'd contracted cholera, here in this very room. Dev had been magnificent. In fact, Cheney was sure Dev had saved her life. She did love Dev, so deeply.

But thinking of her strong feelings for Dev naturally—and inevitably, these days—made Cheney think of Shiloh. Unbidden and unwanted, hot tears welled up in her eyes.

She rose and with swift, angry steps went to the window, yanking aside the lace curtain to look out, though there was nothing to see. She valiantly fought her tears.

I must...I must stop this grieving! It's unseemly! As if I begrudged You, Lord, for...for not letting me marry Shiloh!

Cheney was generally not the type of person to wallow in self-pity, which she had always told herself was a deceit of the devil's. So she tried to honestly face her feelings and sort them out to understand them, and herself, better.

I love him, there's no getting around that hard fact, but it's— Somehow I have to stop showing my grief. It is sort of a betrayal of You, isn't it, Lord? I mean, You've promised that Your yoke is easy and Your burden is light. For me to mope around, to be so fainthearted, does me no good, and come to think of it, it probably confuses Shiloh. I know he just doesn't understand. But, Lord, it's so hard, so awful. It's the most painful thing I've ever done—to be with him, to see him, to treat him, and be treated like a stranger.... Help me, please....

Then with a plummet of her heart, Cheney's reverie focused on Shiloh. Once again, in her selfishness, she'd forgotten about him and his pain.

What kind of love is this...to pity myself and to forget him? He's hurt, I know he is... He's reckless, running... he looks strained....

And I don't even want to know what he's doing to deaden this hurt. But certainly he's not praying. He doesn't have that solace. Maybe I can— Whenever I think of him, which is constantly, I can make myself turn my pain into prayer. I must. I must pray for him without ceasing....

A quiet knock sounded on her door. Cheney knew it was Shiloh. She took a moment to compose herself, relieved that her tears hadn't spilled. "Come in," she called lightly.

He came in, filling the room as he did, making it look too frilly and crowded. He was so tall, so vital, so masculine, that his presence dominated a room and the people around him. He was splendidly dressed in a three-piece suit with a silk neckcloth and top hat. Still,

Cheney wistfully remembered his faded denim breeches and much-traveled canvas overcoat.

"Hi, Doc," he said, with a touch of wariness. "Can I come in?"

"Of course," she said, turning and smiling brilliantly, if a little falsely.

They sat facing each other on opposite sofas. "I assume this is a social call, not business," she said lightly.

"Huh? Oh yeah. I mean, no. I'm not sick, if that's what you mean." He searched her face uncertainly. "The boys and I are going to a race in the park."

"You are?" Cheney asked. "But—oh, I forgot. It is Saturday, isn't it? No one's working."

"Except you." He shifted restlessly, then with some exasperation, asked, "You haven't read the papers yet, have you?"

"Why, no," she answered. Suddenly wary herself, she asked, "Why? What's in them now? You? Or me?"

"Aw, it's me, like a stupid fool," he said, rising to stride over to her desk and fiddle with a silver letter opener that lay on a stationery chest. He held it up, considering it as if it were some unknown thing and muttered darkly, "'And the spurns / That patient merit of the unworthy takes, / When he himself might his quietus make / With a bare bodkin?'"

"Hamlet," Cheney said quietly, mindful of Shiloh's melancholy. "I...I was so hoping that we might get to go see it, Shiloh. M-might we?"

"No, Doc," he said savagely, turning away. "I saw it last night. You can read all about it in the *Sun*."

"Oh," Cheney said faintly, feeling the suspicious burning behind her eyes again. The *Sun* was a sensational rag, full of ugly unfounded gossip and innuendo. Also, they printed all the news about the theater people and such notorious persons, which more staid papers such as the *Herald* and the *Times* would never include in their society news. "Oh," she said again helplessly, swallowing hard.

They were quiet for a long time, Shiloh with his back to her, Cheney sitting forlornly on the sofa and struggling not to cry. Finally, with determination, Cheney sat up straight, cleared her mind, and ignored her treacherous heart. "You quote *Hamlet* beautifully, Mr. Irons-Winslow. Of course you probably memorized it against your will, I would imagine. How many times did you read it to me when I was seasick? Three?"

"Four," he said, turning, his haggard face brightening a little. "I wouldn't have done it for just anybody, you know. *Hamlet* takes some heavy wading. But now it's kinda like a song or a piece of music. You know how it gets in your head and you can't shut it off? Every time I turn around, I'm spouting some Shakespearean guff."

"I know, but isn't it amazing how so much of it is so well known and often quoted?" Cheney commented. She was actually sick at heart, talking to Shiloh as if he were some stranger she'd just been introduced to. "It...it's so rarely performed, and read even less, but everyone knows 'Neither a borrower nor a lender be.'"

"'To be or not to be, that is the question,'" Shiloh offered.

"'To thine own self be true,'" Cheney quoted.

"'There's something rotten in the state of Denmark,'" Shiloh said, now smiling a little and appearing a little more relaxed. He came and sat back down across from Cheney. "That Shakespeare was a smart fellow, huh?"

"He's generally viewed as such," Cheney agreed heavily.

Mrs. Slopes came in—Shiloh had left the door ajar—carrying a heavy-laden tray of coffee and muffins, fresh and hot, by the fragrance. "Mmm, blueberry. My favorite," Cheney said. "Thank you, Mrs. Slopes."

"Yes, ma'am, Doctor, miss," she said, bobbing. "Shall I serve?"

"No, I will," Cheney said. "I'm sure you have enough on your hands this morning."

"That I do, Doctor, I mean, miss," she said with force in spite of her confusion over Cheney's title. "With them young jackanapes and all—your pardon, Mr. Irons-Winslow." She left in such a huff that Shiloh doubted she meant her apology very sincerely.

Cheney went to the tray, which was so big that Mrs. Slopes had been obliged to put it on the desk instead of the tea table by the sofa. With a sinking heart she saw that three of the morning newspapers were on the tray: the *Sun,* the *Herald,* and the *Times.* Automatically she prepared Shiloh's coffee, studiously ignoring the papers glaring up at her.

But he was right behind her. He had never yet let her serve him.

"I guess I might as well tell you," he said in a curiously dead tone. "Aside from the…uh…article in the *Sun,* Mrs. Steen released the guest list of the Steens' engagement ball."

"Yes?" Cheney said in a voice that scarcely concealed her dread.

"I don't know why she did it—no, that's not true," Shiloh said with disgust. "I do know why she did it. Anyway, Doc, it lists me as Angelique Steen's escort."

Cheney's head was down. With very slow, concentrated movements she dropped one, then another lump of sugar into her coffee. She reached for the creamer and missed the handle. She was appalled to see a tear drop and fall with what sounded like a loud plop in the dreadfully quiet room. "I...I— Would you excuse me for a moment, please? I—" She turned without looking at him and almost ran out of the room.

Shiloh, left desolate behind, watched her helplessly. Then, with longing and a deep sorrow, he whispered, "'I love Ophelia: forty thousand brothers / Could not, with all their quantity of love, / Make up my sum.'"

Part Three

Striving For Masteries

And if a man also strive for masteries, yet is
he not crowned, except he strive lawfully.

—2 Timothy 2:5

Chapter Ten

The Partnership

Miss York,

As a fellow traveler in "the seas and countries different / With variable objects" it would afford me the greatest pleasure to converse with a companion Anglo. I have had the honor of being properly introduced to you by Judge William Alston, but to my sincerest regret, you were much pressed by admirers at the time, and I had no opportunity to speak with you.

Although I am an avid fan, I assure you that I hope to meet and talk with you for reasons purely of an impersonal nature. I do, in fact, have a business proposition that may be of interest to you.

I hope you will receive me at two o'clock this afternoon. Until then,

I remain,
Your humble servant,
Denys Worthington
Gramercy Park

Minette York read the letter again, slowly.

"He does know *Hamlet*," she whispered thoughtfully to herself, "or if not, he has gone to no little trouble to find an applicable quote. And an Englishman introduced by Judge Alston…"

She looked up, her eyes focused far away, remembering. "Oh yes, I recall…not strikingly handsome, but slim and well dressed, elegant. He looked cold and arrogant, as so many of my countrymen do." She smiled, focusing on her reflection in the dressing-table mirror. "Not like American men."

She was twenty years old now, she reminded herself. The reflection in the mirror told her that she looked even younger. She was that type, she knew. She looked wholesome, even innocent, with her big clear blue eyes and pink and white frothy skin and golden-yellow hair that so obligingly curled into any fashionable coiffure, such as ringlets or Grecian curls. Minette never allowed herself to frown and never cried, for that caused wrinkles. She used exotic preparations on her skin—milk, olive oil, essence of myrrh, lily-and-sweet-William water. And on her hair she used almond oil, mint extract, rose-and-rosemary water. She suspected that she would not be in demand, either as an actress or as a gentleman's companion, for many more years. And she knew with certainty that she would not have her youthful beauty for very long. Once the rosebud has opened, it withers quickly.

Her wide blue eyes became unfocused again. "Gramercy Park is a good address, and his note is businesslike in tone, not at all effusive or impudent. Perhaps he truly is a patron of the theater," she murmured, again talking to herself. She had done that since she had lost her only family—her brother, seven years old when he had died of typhus in the poorhouse in London. She had been nine years old, and she'd had no one else to talk to, and no one had talked to her for four years.

"I shall receive him," she decided. "After all, I have nothing to lose. And perhaps, if he truly is a patron and has some work for me—could it be private readings?— I could take better lodgings."

Minette had taken rooms in a house west of Wallack's Theater. It was a little shabby, but it was cheap, within walking distance of the theater, and discreet. Mrs. Cranborne, the widow whose home it was, respected her boarders' privacy and never made any demands except that of the weekly payment.

She went through her rigorous morning toilette with her facials and creams and skin softeners, then brushed her hair until it glowed. Minette couldn't afford a maid, so she did her own hair and cosmetics and dressed herself, vowing that someday she would have a maid, a housekeeper, a house in London, a house in New York, jewels, two carriages, footmen, silk robes, satin slippers....

It won't be from marrying Shiloh Irons-Winslow, she reflected with a distinct pang. *Why am I wasting my time with him? He'd never marry me, and he's not the kind of man to indulge a mistress with houses and silks and satins. I really should find some kind, elderly, lonely millionaire and stop seeing Shiloh.* It occurred to Minette that she never talked to herself aloud about Shiloh Irons-Winslow. The realization made her uncomfortable, and she had to rebuke herself, for she was frowning.

She chose one of her most demure dresses, a morning frock of white muslin trimmed with violet satin ribbons and embroidered muslin flounces. She pulled her hair up and back into thick ringlets with a violet ribbon entwined. The only jewelry she wore was a pair of tiny pearl earrings.

Denys Worthington was meticulously on time, which gratified Minette. She answered the door, and he bowed over her extended hand but did not kiss it. Before he spoke a word, he courteously handed her his card, and Minette studied it: Denys Worthington, Worthington Shipping, Worthington Fine Imports & Exports, New York.

"Please come in, Mr. Worthington," she said.

He was slim and elegantly dressed in a wool suit of a rich chocolate brown and a cream satin waistcoat. "So kind of you to receive me, Miss York. Bit irregular, I know, but you have forgiven me, I hope?"

"Of course, sir. 'Most fair returns of greetings and desires, cousin,'" she said gaily, motioning him to an ancient armchair covered in balding maroon velvet while she seated herself on the sofa.

He smiled, though it was an oddly somber smile for a man so young. "We are speaking Hamletese still, I ken. I'm afraid that I'll suffer for conversation, Miss York. It's a certainty that I don't know the play as well as you do."

But he did recognize the quote. He does know the play. "Forgive me, Mr. Worthington. My old teacher, Mr. Edward Ames, would say that I am showing about," Minette said placidly.

He studied her for a moment, though his perusal was neither rude nor critical. "You have a lovely voice, Miss York, and a perfect Oxford accent. Are you, by chance, from Oxford?"

"No, from London," she replied shortly. "And you, Mr. Worthington?"

"I am a Londoner, too. My family lives in Richmond. Do you know it?" he asked carelessly.

"By reputation only," she answered. "I've never been there, though I do believe the park and the view of the Thames from Richmond Hill are lovely."

"So they are." He watched her again with that assessing look, though it was not at all the type of assessment that Minette was accustomed to.

"I do recall our meeting, Mr. Worthington," she said rather quickly. "I must apologize if it seemed that I cut you off. Sometimes, with so many visitors in such a small dressing room, I quite lose track of where my social obligations lie."

"Not at all," he said automatically. "I appreciate your receiving me, Miss York. As I said, I do have a proposition for you. And it is, I assure you, strictly of a business nature."

"So I understood from your kind note. I must admit, sir, that I am curious. I am not a particularly astute businesswoman, you see."

He looked around at the small, ill-furnished parlor, the cheap chintz curtains, at Minette herself in her nice but inexpensive muslin dress. "So I see, Miss York. I'm aware, as I'm sure you are aware, that you could be much more—affluent."

"Actresses are hardly paid enough for affluence, Mr. Worthington," she said stiffly. "And as for sideline occupations, I never had an interest in any of them."

"I see," he said with a glint of humor in his calculating brown eyes. "Then it seems to me that you might be very interested in my offer, Miss York. I would like to form a kind of partnership—a purely business partnership—with you. In partnerships, you see, both partners are required to invest in the business. Generally it is money or skills or both."

After a moment's silence Minette said quietly, "Pray continue, sir."

"I have the money," he said easily. "And you have the skills."

"Acting, do you mean?" she asked uncertainly.

"Of a sort," he answered. "I believe it is a part you are already playing."

"I don't understand, sir," she said with a hint of impatience. "Please speak plainly."

He shifted, but not with tension. He seemed perfectly at ease, but Minette somehow felt as if she might be the canary in the pretty little cage that the cat's just noticed. Finally he said, "Your pardon, ma'am. If you will indulge me, I must relate some history to you first. I came to New York to begin a trade, an import-export route to the West Indies, New York, and Europe. I own only one clipper, but she is very fine and fast and worthy, and with well-established routes she could make quite profitable runs."

Minette's eyes widened a little, for she had heard something of this business plan before. Bain saw her reaction and immediately pressed on. "But you see, I have a single competitor, a fierce competitor, for the very goods, the same cargoes, even the same routes as I am planning. Naturally, I would like to keep an eye on this competitor." He waited, watching her, but she said nothing. She was, after all, a fine actress, and she kept her face impassive. "His name is Shiloh Irons-Winslow."

"I won't do anything to harm him," she said in a hard

voice. "In the first place, he has been kind to me. And in the second place, he has powerful friends in this city. People like me don't cause problems for people like him and his friends."

"Please, Miss York, I am not some barbarian," Bain sniffed in his most aristocratic tone. "I have no intention of harming the man. I only want to know about his plans, his intentions, his activities. That is all."

She watched him warily, but her anger was dissipating, he could see.

"It would mean—oh, shall we say, twenty dollars per week?" Bain said casually, taking several nice crisp banknotes out of his pocket. Then he sat holding them, watching her.

"That's—that's a very great sum of money," she said in a tight voice, "just to have a good gossip."

He laughed a dry, unpleasant sound. "Yes, that's exactly what it is, Miss York. Just the news about Mr. Irons-Winslow. As a matter of fact, I can read much of it in the *Herald* and the *Sun*. I'd just like, shall we say, a more personal and informed view."

Now, he knew, she was making up her mind.

She looked at the money, and despite the fact that she was an accomplished actress, he could clearly see the longing in her eyes. Twenty dollars a week was likely twice or even three times what she earned from the theater.

"You just want to know…where we go, what he talks about?" she asked, clearing her throat.

"Yes."

A long silence.

"All right," she said, almost a sigh. "I'll do it." She

reached out her hand for the money, but Bain pulled it back slightly.

"Excuse me, Miss York," he said lightly, "but you will be obliged to make your contribution to the partnership before I make mine. I know you've seen him every night since you met a week ago."

She was startled, but then she realized that what he'd said was true. She and Shiloh had been a hot topic in the penny dailies all week, along with the other young men he ran with who were squiring around other actresses. The *Sun* had even dubbed them "The Fine and Dandies," as if they were a social club or some sort of upperten street gang. Minette realized that this must be how Denys Worthington knew so much about her and Shiloh.

"What…what do you want to know?" she asked, licking her lips.

He leaned forward, suddenly intent. "He has spoken to you about his business plans, hasn't he?"

She dropped her eyes. This was harder than she'd thought it was going to be. But, after all, what did she owe Shiloh Irons-Winslow? He'd been nice to her; that was all. He seemed to like her, to enjoy her company. He'd given her some flowers and some candy, but no jewelry, no fine hats or expensive shawls or the like. Once she'd hinted that she would truly enjoy a French tutor, but he hadn't taken the hint, though Minette had been certain that a gift such as that would be more to Shiloh's taste than jewels or furs. Once she'd mentioned that she wished she could afford to stay in a hotel with amenities, such as maid service and a restaurant and bell service. Shiloh had ignored this hint, too. So what did she owe him?

Nothing, perhaps, except respect, which he had given her without fail.

But Minette could not buy a hat or satin slippers or a maid with a man's respect, so she thrust the thought aside. "He didn't speak of it to me, no," she answered in an uninflected voice, as if she were reciting something. "But I heard Troy—Mr. Bondurant—mention something about Cuban cigars and the need for more imports and something about a—oh, I forget what the phrase was. Some American oddity, it was...."

Narrowing his eyes, Bain ordered, "Think of it, Miss York."

She glanced at him briefly and then dropped her eyes again. "It was some kind of store. A...a general store? Does that sound right? Mr. Bondurant said, 'Export the general store and import the cigars, Shiloh. That's your ticket. Take my advice and take my money.' He's an investment banker, you know."

"I'm aware of that," Bain said. He was cold now and short with her. "Listen to me. Have you ever heard what ship Mr. Irons-Winslow talks about using for this import-export venture? Has he ever mentioned any of his ships?"

Minette concentrated, trying desperately to remember. This was, after all, not anything criminal. She certainly couldn't see how this Mr. Worthington's knowing any of this could possibly hurt Shiloh. But it was difficult to recall, for they did drink quite a bit on their late-night excursions, and most of Minette's memories were a little hazy. "I don't recall his ever mentioning the name of a ship," she answered finally. "All I remember is that Troy said, 'One of the barks could do the Caribbean run.'"

Bain sat back, considering. "It sounds as if Mr. Bondurant is talking about it a lot more than Mr. Irons-Winslow is."

Minette looked up in surprise. "Why, yes, he does.

In fact, now that I think of it, Shi—Mr. Irons-Winslow doesn't seem too interested in it at all. Are you certain that he is actually planning to compete directly with you, Mr. Worthington? Because—"

"Don't ever ask me any questions, Miss York. That is not the nature of our partnership," Bain interrupted her sharply. "What about his family? What does he say of his family?"

"His family? Why, he never mentions them to me. He wouldn't, you know. Not to me." She looked back down and picked a little at the embroidered flounce on her skirt. "All I do know is that he…he's in love with someone. Someone else."

"Oh?" Bain asked sardonically. "And you wish it were you?"

The delicate rose-pink of Minette's cheeks flushed a painful scarlet. "I hardly think that is the sort of business information you require, Mr. Worthington," she said as haughtily as she could manage.

"Pardon," Bain said desultorily, "but I am interested in his state of mind, you see. Please tell me more." As if by chance, he shifted his hand a little, and the bills made a nice crisp crackle.

Minette swallowed hard, then went on evenly, "Of course he's never spoken of it—or her, I mean—to me. I just know he is. He's moody, and sometimes when he drinks a little too much, he gets curiously reckless, abandoned, as if he were deliberately surrounding himself, filling himself, with distractions so as to ignore his true feelings."

One of Bain's eyebrows rose with interest. "Really? You have thought much on this, I can see, Miss York, and you show rare insight into a man you've only just met a week ago. By chance, do you have a notion who this treacherous woman is?"

Minette's mouth tightened, and she nodded, a jerky, ungraceful movement. "I'm certain it must be Angelique Steen, that wealthy young debutante he escorts to all of the de Lancie-Buchanan betrothal parties."

"Oh? But he hasn't said anything directly about her or any other woman?" Bain asked carefully.

"No, nothing," Minette said with barely concealed disdain. She was losing her patience, and she felt the beginnings of a headache. "You do see that he would say nothing to me?"

Bain eyed her, then slowly placed the money on the spindly side table by his chair. Rising, he said, "I'll take my leave now, Miss York. But I shall return, probably in a day or two. And then I shall expect a detailed report. Good day, Miss York."

Minette put the money away in an old book of Shakespeare's sonnets that she kept by her bedside. And yes, she did have a full-blown headache by the time she'd gotten the money out of sight.

Chapter Eleven

Night Musing

The following week was unspeakably dreary for Cheney. She was depressed, with all of the accompanying symptoms: loss of appetite, sudden crying spells, lethargy, and sleeplessness. It took all of her energy, it seemed, to just be courteous at the three parties for the wedding she attended during that week. But though she felt listless, she couldn't sleep, and she started staying late at the office, studying, writing, going over patient records and administrative details.

On Friday night she was a little surprised to find that nothing was scheduled for the de Lancie-Buchanan wedding party. They'd had a luncheon at the Union Club—Mr. Henry Steen IV, Victoria's father, was a member and had somehow managed to get the ladies admitted—and Shiloh as usual had been seated next to Angelique Steen. He'd barely spoken to Cheney, and she had avoided him and tried never to watch him and Angelique, or even glance their way. They seemed to be very easy together, laughing often and talking animatedly, and it made Cheney feel as if she were being stabbed in the heart.

With a sigh she tried to focus on the tiny, tidy script in the ledger before her, but the numbers and items all swam together. Rubbing her tired eyes, she reflected that she either needed to refill the oil lamp on her desk—it was flickering weakly—or else just put it out and go home.

Small clicking noises from the front door made Cheney start, but then she realized that it must be Dr. Batson returning home. He peeped discreetly into her office. "Good evening, Dr. Duvall. May I come in?"

"Certainly."

He was wearing full evening dress, with top hat, white tie and waistcoat, full-length satin-lined cape, and gold-topped cane. The Fine and Dandies had been to the Astor Opera House for Verdi's *Il Trovatore*. But as he entered, he stopped short, gazing around, his mild blue eyes widening.

Puzzled, Cheney looked around her office for the source of his alarm, and then almost laughed. The room was dark, for she disliked the glare of gas lamps, and her oil lamp was very low, almost out. On the sofa in front of Cheney's desk, Nia was sound asleep. Laid across her chest was an enormous book, *Gray's Anatomy,* and one of Nia's tiny brown hands was still clutching it, even in her deep sleep. By her side, her left hand still resting lightly on it, was a bleached skull, its white grimace startling in the semidarkness.

Her eyes alight, but with a sonorous voice, Cheney murmured, "'Double, double toil and trouble…'"

Dr. Batson chuckled, leaning over Nia to glance at the book. "'Something's afoot' all right," he whispered, then came to Cheney's desk and asked, "May I—?" He motioned languidly.

"Of course," she answered, obligingly moving some books and papers so he could prop on the corner of her desk. In the previous week she and Dr. Batson had grown much more comfortable with each other. She found him easy to be with and to talk to. He was intelligent, avidly interested in anything to do with the study of medicine, and he was not at all a demanding sort of person.

He glanced back at Nia, then gave Cheney a quizzical glance. "*Gray's Anatomy?* Heavy reading for a maid, isn't it?"

"I've been training Nia for the past—oh, it would be almost a year now," Cheney explained. "She's a marvelous nurse, but I wouldn't agree to apprentice her so that she could theoretically call herself a physician. I disapprove of that convention. But I have, in actual fact, been apprenticing her, as you can see."

"Odds bodkins, my dear doctor of physic," Dr. Batson said, his sleepy eyes twinkling a little, "memorizing the skeletal structure is hardly what I'd call apprenticing. Most physicians never remember it after their examination."

"I do," Cheney said idly. "Don't you?"

"Um—is this a doctor-to-doctor question, or a boss-to-employee question?" Cleve asked warily.

"Neither," she answered kindly. "It's impertinence, I suppose. I happen to have a gift for memorization, but I don't think it's essential for a physician to have *Gray's Anatomy* memorized. But it is important for Nia just now...."

Her eyes rested warmly on the young girl—Nia was actually twenty years old, but she still appeared to be about thirteen. She did look a little absurd, with her prim gray dress and childlike features, holding the enormous book and the whitened skull. Frowning, Cheney continued, "She's been accepted to the New York Medical College and Hospital for Women."

Dr. Batson nodded, for he thought that might be the reason for Nia's strange companions in her repose. Oddly, he had overheard Dr. Duvall and Shiloh arguing about this the previous week. Shiloh had been impatient with Dr. Duvall, and Cheney had been very short with him. It was hardly Cleve's fault that he'd overheard them, for they had argued rather loudly, and this was, after all, a small office. Now, however, Dr. Batson played dumb. "That's quite a step forward, isn't it? After all, there is, I believe, only one other woman of color attending? And Nia must have been accepted upon your recommendation."

"On mine and Dev's," Cheney told him. "More likely just Dev's. Anyway, Nia has convinced me that it really is the only way that she will ever get any accreditation, so I'm supporting it. I just wish that some other institution were open to her, because I despise homeopathy. It's a lot of fatuous nonsense, in my opinion, and she'll get very little training in anything except in their odd philosophy of 'like cures like' and inconsequential prescriptions. So I've made my…um…support conditional. I'm requiring Nia to learn, in addition to her studies at the college, some additional curricula that I think is critical. Anatomy, pathology, animalcula studies, chemistry…"

As she spoke she grew more animated. Cleve studied her, watching her face and expressive hands. He had only met Cheney once in the previous year, when she and Dr. Buchanan had interviewed him. Then she had seemed

to be such a vivid woman, her exotic features flushed
with health, her eyes sparkling, her conversation quick
and incisive and seasoned with a sharp wit. Now, however, Cleve had observed that she was different. Subdued,
almost melancholy. She was thinner than he remembered,
the high cheekbones almost stark, and she had a faint air
of fragility that he never would have associated with her
before. He had spoken to none of their mutual acquain-
tances about it, but Cheney hadn't been in New York very
long before Cleve had come to suspect that Cheney's low
spirits had much to do with Mr. Shiloh Irons-Winslow.
Cleve thought that they must be in love but estranged,
for some reason beyond his understanding. Since Shiloh
had been out on the town with Cleve and his friends for
the last couple of weeks, Cleve had observed that Shiloh
was, without any effort on his part, quite a favorite of the
ladies. Cleve had clearly seen that Shiloh's gadding about
appeared to bother Cheney quite a bit. She was a striking, intriguing woman and certainly would have no difficulty in attracting any number of suitors. But she seemed
isolated these days, as she didn't even spend much time
with her best friend, Victoria de Lancie, Cleve pitied her
a little.

Rousing himself from his reverie, Cleve said, "Well,
I'm certain that Nia will make a fine doctor if you and
Dr. Buchanan believe in her. Mr. Irons-Winslow, too, is
staunchly in her corner, isn't he?"

A shadow passed over Cheney's face, and she dropped
her eyes. "Oh yes, he's always encouraged her, perhaps
more than I have. He says he'll never forget what it's like
to fight against long odds."

An uncomfortable silence fell, and with an effort
Cheney asked politely, "How was *Il Trovatore?* I've heard

that it's a very lavish production, with intricate sets and exquisite costumes."

"That I can attest to," Cleve said in a fashionably bored tone. "As to the music, I'm as ignorant as an alley cat about opera. I can barely tell a tenor from a baritone. I do appreciate the operatic voice, however. It's miraculous, isn't it?"

"Miraculous is the word, Doctor," Cheney agreed, growing more lively again. "The power, in both volume and richness, is so far above normal human ability. I've often speculated about it. Is it atypical muscular development of the larynx, or of the diaphragm? Are the vocal chords different? Is it the lung capacity? I'd love to have an opportunity to dissect a strong tenor."

Dr. Batson was nodding clinically, but they caught each other's eye and then laughed.

"We're a bloody-minded lot, aren't we?" he joked. "Doctors, I mean. Truth to tell, at the opera I'm always studying the singers' sizes, trying to decide if that has something to do with their voices. You know, envisioning their skeleton and muscle mass. Mentally dissecting them. Hope no one knows that instead of being transported to some high artistic plane, I'm having visions of them without their skin on."

"Dev and I do that, too," Cheney admitted, giggling a little. "But we both pretend that we are completely absorbed in the music. At least I do stay awake. Dev always falls asleep."

"Well, you'll have a chance to judge for yourself next week," Cleve said, stifling a yawn with a great effort. "I didn't know until after Troy had already dragged us to Astors' tonight that the wedding party is scheduled to go to *Il Trovatore* next Wednesday. Troy actually likes the opera. The singing, I mean. He won't mind seeing it twice, but I must admit I'm going to find it a little difficult to stay awake the second time myself."

"Oh, I didn't know we were attending *Il Trovatore,*" Cheney said, frowning. "I thought all we had next week, before the Steens' ball, that is, is that…um…what is it? The Ralstons' dinner party?"

Cleve nodded. "Yes, but they're taking us to the opera, you see."

"Oh," Cheney sighed. "Well, the Steens' ball is the last big event before the wedding, isn't it?" Victoria and Dev's wedding was scheduled for May thirtieth, and the Steens' grand ball was two weeks prior, on May sixteenth.

"Yes, some luncheons and dinner parties, but no theater or opera or grand balls after that," Cleve said a little absently. He was studying Cheney, his sleepy eyes narrowed slightly. "Dr. Duvall…Dr. Duvall—" He stopped and cleared his throat uncomfortably.

"Yes, Dr. Batson?" she said with light amusement.

Taking a deep breath as if he were about to plunge into very cold water, he blurted out, "Dr. Duvall, it would give me the greatest of pleasure if you would allow me to escort you to the Steens' ball. Would you consider it, at all?"

Cheney's eyes flew open with surprise. Her first impulse was a polite denial, but then she reflected that it might not be such a bad idea. She and Cleve Batson shared many common interests. He was an agreeable conversational partner, and he treated her with great respect. And there was no danger that Cleve Batson was enamored of her. Cheney may not always be very intuitive about people, but she did at least recognize those symptoms in men, and Cleve Batson evidenced no great passion. In some deep recess of Cheney's mind she also realized that Cleve recognized her hurt over Shiloh and felt sorry for her, but his attitude was neither patronizing nor pandering. He merely liked her, Cheney thought, and found her interesting. It surprised Cheney how much this realization cheered her.

Brightening suddenly, she said, "Why, Dr. Batson, I will gladly accept your escort to the grand ball. Thank you."

Though he seemed surprised, he swiftly recovered, standing to bow gracefully to her. "You honor me, Dr. Duvall. Now, it's very late and I admit I'm tired, but I'd like a cup of tea before I retire. Would you join me? And then, perhaps, you might accept my offer of an escort home."

"I'll take the tea but not the escort home," Cheney said, smiling. "My curricle is at the livery just over on Twenty-fifth Street. I'm quite accustomed to arranging my own transportation. And Nia is with me."

Cleve shook his head. "You mean that in the middle of the night you go over to the livery, by yourself, harness your own curricle, and take yourself home with only Nia as an escort? Your family doesn't worry? Dr. Buchanan doesn't…er…try to dissuade you?"

"Ah, I see," Cheney said with mock gravity. "You're afraid you're going to get in trouble with the stern Dr. Buchanan if you don't baby-sit me. As a matter of fact, Dr. Buchanan is more supportive of my independence than anyone. He knows, you see, that physicians are likely to be called out at all hours, and there isn't always a coachman and footman waiting, or a hansom cab at the curb. Actually, he approves of my learning to handle myself in these kinds of situations."

"All right," Cleve said with open relief. "Then if Dr. Buchanan approves, I won't protest. If you'll pardon me, I'll go put the kettle on."

He left, and Cheney watched him thoughtfully. *So I'll have an escort to the Steens' ball. This is good. Now I won't be mooning around in a corner by myself, worrying about Shiloh and Angelique Steen, or hiding behind Mother and Father. But it's kind of sad. I'll have an escort, and it seems that Victoria won't have much of one. I can't imagine what's wrong with Dev. He's so distracted lately, and he's often late and sometimes leaves early. He says it is a patient with singular difficulties, but I can't find any patient records here that he's documenting. It's just so unlike Dev. He's normally so very conscientious about his duty, especially his familial obligations.*

Dev actually laughed out loud. The sound of it and the realization that he was sitting in a room chortling to himself startled him. But then Dart made the same gremlin face, staring gravely up at Dev as if to see if he would laugh again. And so Dev did.

"You're just a clown, aren't you?" Dev said, poking him gently. His brother's frame seemed delicate, but after a week Dev could already see an improvement in him. Rather clinically Dev noted that the child responded to laughter, and he did seem to pay close attention to the sound of a human voice. These little mental notes may have seemed superfluous to many people, but for Dev, learning to establish a relationship with an infant was a discipline. He had no instinct for it, he knew. After all, children had never played much of a part in his life, and his thoughts about having children in the future had always been vague.

Until I fell in love with Victoria, he brooded. *I had known for years that she didn't want children when she was married to Lionel. She's such a whole person, so complete in herself. She has so many interests, so many things she likes to do. She's active and intelligent. She has her numerous philanthropies and businesses and, of course, her public life, no matter how shallow it may seem. She is an outgoing person, a gracious person, and she is a wonderful hostess and does enjoy a full social calendar—why should she ever want children? Especially...*

But Dev let this observation about his half brother fade away quickly. Dart was sickly, and he was undoubtedly less developed than other children his age—both physically and mentally. That much Dev knew from his medical acumen. The physical symptoms Dev had finally managed to figure out how to treat. Dart had been chronically nauseated, jaundiced, anemic, and suffering from some mild seizures, which Dev quickly recognized as delirium tremens, a result of his addiction to alcohol.

Dev knew that he couldn't medicate Dart for the jaundice and anemia until he found an infant formula that he wouldn't reject. Dev had first tried a wet nurse. His housekeeper's daughter-in-law was nursing her eight-month-old, and she was an excellent sitter. But Dart hadn't been able to keep breast milk down. Dev had then tried Henri Nestlé's new infant formula, but Dart had rejected that, too.

Then, through a trial-and-error process that was almost unbearably tense for Dev, he'd cooked up various potions and experimented on the child. Finally he'd found one that Dart could keep down: a complicated recipe of farinaceous pap, goat's milk, and cow butter that had to be freshly mixed, cooked, and given to Dart when it was warm. Mrs. Barentine's daughter-in-law—also Mrs. Barentine—was a conscientious nurse and would take care of Dart even until late in the night, for she got to keep her little Raymond with her. Dev paid her handsomely, too, for she was discreet and trustworthy, and more importantly, seemed to have a real affection for Dart. But still, Dev could hardly bear to leave Dart with Mrs. Barentine very long at night, for that was when Dart was having his seizures.

Dev still had to mix some brandy in the formula to keep Dart from having a seizure, but Dev had already begun slowly, in the minutest of increments, to decrease the dosage. Dart simply wasn't strong enough to go through an alcohol withdrawal, and it was much more critical that Dev get him strong enough to take cod-liver oil for the jaundice and for the anemia. On this night, the ninth day that Dev had had Dart, the baby had managed to keep down a single drop of cod-liver oil.

"You were a real trooper tonight, Dart," Dev told him, still a little self-conscious at speaking out loud to the infant. Dart gazed up at him with dull dark eyes, but at least he did look in Dev's direction. Dev was holding him in the rocking chair he'd bought the day after he'd brought Dart home, just rocking him slowly and watching him, wondering about him, worrying about him.

He finally allowed the thought to form, the dread that he pushed away so often. *Are you normal? Are you slow or just very calm, or…or are you retarded? Has your brain been damaged by the alcohol? I can only pray that your liver or spleen aren't permanently damaged, but what about your brain—your mind, your emotions, your perceptions, your understanding?*

Suddenly a shock ran through Dev's entire body as if he'd been doused with icy water. He recalled Shiloh's conversation with Dr. Banckert, and the echoes were very loud in his mind.

"And do you have special interest in psychiatric treatment for violent psychotics, Mr. Irons?"

"Yes."

"Professional or personal?"

"Personal. A member of my family."

"Ah. And this family member is your connection by blood?"

It seemed to reverberate in Dev's ears, an ominous bass drum. *Blood, by blood, connection by blood...*

What if my father was actually insane?

What if...it is hereditary?

Dev shut his eyes tight, as if that would erase the thought.

Sensing his sudden tension, perhaps, Dart shifted in Dev's arms, whimpering a little.

Staring back down at the sickly, dull child in his arms, Dev suddenly felt a swell of compassion, of love and tenderness, for his brother.

"Don't worry, little boy," he said hoarsely. "I'll take care of you."

Really? And who's going to take care of me if I start losing my mind and having uncontrollable anger and finally start putting people's eyes out with saloon darts? How would Victoria look with two black eyes and a broken arm?

Desolation, bleak and dark, swept over Dev so swiftly and surely that he gasped. Then, weakly, he dropped his head and pleaded, *God, dearest Father, help me. Just help me...to...be sane...to have peace...and not be afraid....*

A peculiar but blessed silence descended on Dev, and then he heard in his heart: *For God hath not given us the spirit of fear; but of power, and of love, and of a sound mind.*

Dev almost gasped with relief, then repeated the verse out loud in a firm voice. "All right, Dart, you hear that? That's what we're going to believe in. That's what we're going to hold on to. As a matter of fact, I think I'll read Second Timothy to you. Or to me. I probably need it worse than you do."

Later that night after Dart was asleep and Dev lay wakeful in his bed, only one bleak thought intruded on his peace.

Victoria. It's all fine and good for Dart and me to be ready to fight against our father's blood all our lives, but who knows? Christians, good Christians, get sick and die, and sometimes they lose their minds. Should I even contemplate dragging Victoria into such a mortal coil?

"I can't," he whispered, then threw his arm over his eyes wearily. "I won't."

He slept, but he had a nightmare that he and Dart were drowning, and Victoria tried to save them, but she could not.

"Victoria, people are talking," Josefina said stiffly. As if to emphasize the words, she snapped her fan closed with a sharp sound. Josefina had insisted on following Victoria in, even though it was very late and Victoria had immediately started getting ready for bed. They had been to the LeRoys' for dinner, and Dev had excused himself

criminally early. Josefina had not said a word to Victoria
for the rest of the evening, during the ride home, or as
she had followed Victoria up the stairs to her boudoir.

Victoria sighed, rose from her dressing table, and
joined her mother on the satin-and-rosewood love seat
in her bedroom. "I don't care," she finally replied, slowly
and distinctly.

"I do."

"I know."

Impasse.

Josefina gave in first. Though her voice remained
crisp and cool, her dark eyes did soften somewhat. "I
know you won't confide in me, Victoria—you haven't
done that since you were a very small, and if I may say
so, talkative child—but won't you at least tell me if you
and Dev are having any kind of serious difficulties?"

But Victoria didn't even hear the question, for Josefina's words had wrenched Victoria's thoughts around to a
long-ignored sore spot in her mind. *I'd forgotten. Mother
despised for Henry and me to talk much.*

*Funny, I don't recall Beckett or Carsten ever saying
much to Mother, or around Mother, at all. I suppose they
were smart enough to learn from the way she treated
Henry and me for prattling on endlessly, as Mother put
it. Even in the nursery she just wanted to come in, ask a
few questions after our well-being, get straightforward
answers, and then dress us appropriately for dinner. I
wonder, is that how I came to think of children as small
nuisances? Because my mother so obviously did?*

Victoria held no ill will toward her mother for this.
She had never been the type of woman to nurse a grudge
or to dwell on hardship. She and her mother had always
shared a sort of disinterested, dutiful love that might

not be very deep, yet it was real. But since Victoria had
become a Christian, she'd realized that she loved her
mother very deeply and even in a way felt great sorrow
for her. Her mother's life was much like Victoria's had
been—full of wealth and privilege, but shallow, meaningless, and therefore finally hopeless. Now she saw the
faint image of tenderness in her mother's eyes, though
it was heavily veiled, and Victoria—for the thousandth
time, at least—vowed to herself that she would speak to
her mother with love and gentleness instead of the habitual pointed sparring of their lifelong discourse.

"I apologize, Mother," Victoria said rather awkwardly.
"I didn't mean to be so pert. Dev, as you know, has been
extremely busy lately, with some particularly difficult
patients. That's why he seems so inattentive. But no, we
haven't had any arguments, or...or grave misunderstand-
ings."

Josefina's fine porcelain features suddenly became
honed, like a cat who has seen some menace invisible to
humans. "But you are admitting that Dev is neglecting
you."

Fighting her impatience, Victoria answered calmly,
"No, Mother, I'm not saying that, for you—and I'm certain that all of the people who are talking—are imply-
ing that Dev is deliberately drawing away from me in an
open and insulting manner. He is not. He is a busy physician, and I am a grown woman who has long understood
that being a doctor's wife sometimes means sharing his
time and thoughts with his other great responsibilities—
his patients."

"His patients," Josefina repeated carefully. "These patients keep him so busy and distracted that he can't even
meet the social obligations of his betrothal?"

Victoria smiled dryly. "His social obligations are heavy, indeed, Mother. Remember, he is a man who works and can hardly be expected to spend all of his waking hours either preparing for or going to or attending or returning from some social event. He has other duties, and they are more important than a cotillion or a costume ball."

"I see. Then you, Victoria, don't mind being his secondary obligation? You, after all, will only be his wife and, presumably, the mother of his children. It seems to me that you have no clear idea of the harsh reality of—"

But Victoria heard no more of her mother's dire warnings.

I've never told her that I can't have children. How very odd. No, I suppose it's not so odd. Even now I cannot imagine discussing how I went to Cheney for an abortion and ended up having to have a hysterectomy. That fact wouldn't bother her, but discussing it would....

Oh, how I wish I could talk to someone! I feel so confused, so uncertain, and so distant from Dev. It's as if we barely know each other anymore.

She and Dev had come to a decision once their formal engagement was announced that they would forebear being alone together until the wedding. Victoria had been very grateful to Dev for this, as it was one of the ways that he showed his respect for her and his determination not to let her past affect them. Certainly, since their betrothal was so highly publicized, people took great note of these things.

But it did make it very hard on a couple who had become close and loyal friends. Dev and Victoria had confided in each other much since they'd fallen in love. She missed their long private talks together.

And Cheney...she's so melancholy and miserable these days. I can't bear to burden her with my problems.

Victoria had been a Christian for only about a year, and she had, in a way, defined her relationship with the Lord through Cheney. She depended heavily on Cheney's guidance, and though this was not at all a bad thing, perhaps it had resulted in Victoria's feelings of loss and confusion over the ever-widening gulf between her and the man she loved more than anyone else in the world.

Victoria didn't realize that the one Person she needed to pour out her heart to was right there with her, listening to her mind and heart with pity and love, all the time.

John Morrissey's faro parlor and gaming room was elegantly appointed, with plush carpets, sumptuous draperies, rosewood gaming tables, glittering chandeliers, and Baccarat crystal.

The thin champagne flutes broke with a most satisfying musical crash.

Shiloh had hit the loud mustachioed man, who fell backward into a waiter carrying a tray of these fine glasses. Mustache Man, the waiter, another innocent bystander, and the tray of full glasses all fell into a sodden, shard-ridden heap.

Shiloh came to stand over Mustache Man, glaring down at him with fiercely sparking blue eyes. "Stand up, you."

"N-no! You just stand back, sir!" Mustache Man said in his loud bluster, though his voice had risen a full octave. "You're disgracefully drunk. You struck me without the slightest warning."

"Yeah? Well, now I'm warning you. I'm going to strike you again unless you apologize," Shiloh barked, clenching and unclenching his fists.

John Morrissey, the proprietor of this fine establishment, came bustling up to the knot of people. A full foot shorter than Shiloh, John Morrissey looked like a tough pug dog. He reached up and laid a placating hand on Shiloh's shoulder. Shiloh half turned with a jerk, and Morrissey flinched a little but stood his ground. "Mr. Irons-Winslow, back off a minute, here. What's the trouble?" John knew Shiloh from way back. He had been the referee at Shiloh's two fights in 1866.

"The trouble is that this man accused me of cheating at faro," Shiloh growled in a low undertone.

"Mr. Weller, is this true?" John asked, his small eyes narrowing.

His pudgy hand shaking, Weller pointed to Shiloh's bulk looming over him like an enormous bird of prey. "I...I...didn't exactly mean that he was cheating, John, I just meant—I mean—what I said was...something like, 'The odds certainly seem to be in your favor tonight, escorting the lovely Miss York, winning so precipitately. Almost impossibly good luck you're having, young man.' Something like that."

"Yeah, something like that," Shiloh repeated darkly. "Like about forty times." Minette York slipped up behind Shiloh, her eyes wide and innocent, but a tiny greedy and proprietary smile played upon her pouty lips.

"Now, Shiloh, let's just talk to the man. He's a good customer and a reasonable man, aren't you, Mr. Weller?" Morrissey said with bluff good humor. A certain edge crept into his voice as he went on, leaning slightly over the still prone Mr. Weller. "You are a reasonable man, aren't you, Mr. Weller? Surely you can see that such remarks might be misconstrued and that an apology would be the only proper way for a gentleman to make amends."

Pulling a large silk handkerchief out of his pocket and mopping his alarmingly red face, Mr. Weller eyed Shiloh with ill humor. "If I apologize, would you please refrain from striking me again, young man?"

Shiloh shrugged. "Guess so."

"Then I apologize. I did not mean to infer that you were cheating."

Suddenly Shiloh bent to offer the rather plump older man his hand. Mr. Weller flinched. A swift grimace darkened Shiloh's face, and he said with awkward gentleness, "Sorry, Mr. Weller. I…uh…I'm glad I didn't hit you real hard."

"Oh, really," Weller said with injured dignity. "On this end it felt rather like a horse kicked me."

John Morrissey shook his head with relief. "Mr. Weller, you just don't have any idea. I'd say Lady Luck was smiling on you tonight. This is Shiloh Irons, the Iron Man. If he had hit you very hard, you woulda been knocked to Saratoga."

"Oh, dear," Mr. Weller said.

"Sorry," Shiloh mumbled again, helping him struggle to his feet and then bending to dust him off a little. "John, I'll pay for the damages."

John Morrissey smiled. "You sure will, boyo. You sure will."

Chapter Twelve

The Duelists

The Steens' ball for the betrothal of their daughter was glittering, glamorous, and grandiose. At the entrance to the ballroom was a long table covered with a snowy white tablecloth and gentlemen's silk top hats, canes, and gloves arranged in militarily precise rows. The strains of a slow waltz filtered through the twelve-foot-high double doors, which were open but still guarded jealously by two gigantic footmen and a majordomo.

Inside the great ballroom, the scents and sounds and sights were overwhelming. Women glowed in hundreds of butterfly colors, all of the men were striking in full evening dress of white tie and tails, the flowers smelled luscious, the chandeliers glittered like diamonds, the music of the twenty-four-piece orchestra resounded magnificently.

"Tante Marye, it would give me the greatest honor if you would waltz with me," Richard said, his warm gray eyes sparkling. He made an old-fashioned leg, placed one hand over his heart, and bowed.

Tante Marye's face, that most delicate of silken parchment complexions, actually blushed. With great elegance she nodded, then held out her hand. She and Richard danced off, twirling lightly, and Tante Marye smiled brilliantly up at him.

"Did you see that?" Tante Elyse gasped, elbowing Gowan in the ribs. "Gowan, do you see that? If I weren't seeing it, I'd never credit it! After all her mumping about the scandalous waltz—she's still so Regency Era, you know—and Marye never dances! I don't think I've seen her dance for at least fifty years!"

"For such a sweetly rounded woman you sure have sharp elbows," Gowan mumbled.

"Thank you, dear," Elyse said absently. "Irene, Richard is such a divine dancer! Can you believe it? Marye looks thirty years younger. However did Richard get up the courage to ask her to dance?"

"I insisted, I'm afraid," Irene said placidly, waving her fan with exquisite grace. "I saw her watching us during the last waltz, and I was certain she looked wistful for a moment. Perhaps the reason you've never seen her dance is because no one has bothered to ask her to."

"But no one would have the backbone except dear Richard," Elyse said with relish. "Cheney's so like him, isn't she, Irene?"

"Yes, she is," Irene agreed. "She does have his…um… élan."

"Backbone," Elyse repeated, eyeing her husband mischievously. "Grit. Sand."

Gowan sighed. With his black eye patch and thick scars, he looked more than ever like a melancholy dragon. "Where'd you learn those words, Elyse? Marye would slap your wrist if she heard you talking like that."

"I doubt it," Elyse said triumphantly. "Shiloh said it about Cheney. And Marye never criticizes him."

"I've noticed that," Gowan agreed. "He could get away with murder if it was an all-woman jury."

The three turned to watch Mr. Irons-Winslow as he swept gracefully by with Angelique Steen in his arms. It was easy to pick them out of the dozens of couples, of course. Shiloh was always the tallest man in the room. They watched the dancers awhile, swirling in the elegant circles of the waltz. Irene and Elyse talked, as women will, of the other women's clothing while Gowan Ford studied the great ballroom at the Steens' mansion.

It was enormous, easily holding the three hundred people who had been invited to the betrothal ball. Six sets of French doors opened out onto a wide stone balcony that encircled the octagonal room and over-looked the primly geometric French garden. Gowan Ford, who had seen something of pomp and circumstance in the old vi-comte's time, was amazed at the lavishness of this single ball. *Even the aristos of the Second Estate didn't have doings like this,* he reflected. *Maybe the monarchs did, because they had the entire country's fortunes at hand, but a private citizen with this much money? America is truly an amazing place.*

"Gowan, I want you to walk me around the room," Elyse said, her warm dark eyes glowing. "I've never seen such unusual, such luscious, decor. I want to look at everything."

"Victoria designed all of the decorations herself," Irene told them. "She's very creative. May I accompany you? I haven't seen the ice sculptures up close, and Richard says that they are uncanny likenesses."

"The two most beautiful ladies in the room," Gowan

said gallantly. "I'll march the two of you around all night if you want." Even at her age, Elyse glowed. Irene took Gowan's left arm, and Elyse reached up to rest her hand on his right shoulder, as his right sleeve was empty. It was one of the small compromises they'd learned to make, and Elyse carried it off with grace, while Gowan's gruff dignity seemed not at all diminished.

Thousands of flowers lined the walls in great stone urns. Victoria had researched and found a brand-new strain of tulip that was called the Queen of Midnight. It looked black, though it was actually a deep purple. She had imported hundreds of them from the Netherlands, and all of the other flowers—roses, narcissus, crocus, hyacinths—were white. For greenery there were old ivies, deep green, long, trailing, curling, even up the walls, making the ballroom look like a scene from *A Midsummer Night's Dream.*

But the ice sculptures topping the fountains were simply amazing. On one side of the orchestra was a two-tiered fountain, with the black tulips surrounding it and a life-sized ice sculpture of Devlin Buchanan topping it. On the other side was the same double fountain with a sculpture of Victoria, surrounded by orange blossoms. Two servants stood by, constantly renewing the top tier of the fountain with crushed ice, so as to keep the sculptures from melting too quickly in the warm room.

Irene, Gowan, and Elyse stared up at Victoria's likeness. Though Dev's sculpture was very like him, Victoria's was almost uncanny. The artist seemed, in that so-fragile medium, to have perfectly captured her cool elegance, her ethereal beauty.

"It's very like her, isn't it?" Gowan murmured.

"I think," Elyse said softly, "it's more that she is very like that."

As one they turned to watch Dev and Victoria, who were dancing superbly—Dev waltzed with great grace—but who were not looking at each other or smiling at each other or speaking to each other. They danced, every movement, every turn, flawlessly. Victoria did indeed look very like her ice sculpture. She was wearing a satin dress of a very light shade of lavender, trimmed with white Valenciennes lace and pearls, and white narcissus adorned her hair. Dev, with his brooding dark good looks, was a perfect foil for her.

Cheney and Cleve Batson whirled by with perhaps more spirit than grace. Cleve was laughing. Cheney's color was high, and her eyes sparkled. She glowed in an ecru silk glacé gown, wearing her mother's rubies and a diadem of golden roses and baby's breath. They made a startling contrast to the betrothed couple. Cleve and Cheney seemed so alive, so animated, while Victoria and Dev were like two stately Flemish paintings.

The waltz ended, and the couples began to move toward the three long tables that held refreshments. It was getting uncomfortably warm in the room, in spite of the fact that the early spring weather had reverted to a wintry chill outside. Cleve escorted Cheney to the table where Italian sorbets in lovely pastel colors were heaped into crystal glasses. Each serving was topped with a flower of the same hue as the confection.

"Lemon, please," Cheney ordered. A white-gloved waiter handed her an icy glass with purple and yellow pansies. Cheney took a bite with the tiny long-handled silver spoon, and her mouth puckered. Cleve chuckled.

"It is very tart," she admitted. "But it quenches your thirst and cools you off so quickly."

"Then I'll have one, too," Cleve said. "I love drinking the Steens' expensive champagne, but it doesn't quench a true waltzing thirst. Perhaps we could step out onto the balcony and get some air."

"Sir, are you hinting that you are tired of dancing?" Cheney teased, though she took his arm and they headed for the nearest set of French doors. "You've only danced the quadrille, a schottische, and four waltzes, I believe."

"I was injured in the schottische," Cleve said mournfully. "I'm afraid Miss Wyndham trod upon my foot twice."

"Oh, dear," Cheney said, her eyes twinkling. "Is it serious? You're not limping."

"No broken bones, I'm happy to say. I am such a gallant gentleman that I apologized to her both times for clumsily placing my foot under hers," Cleve said airily. "Truth to tell, that's probably what happened anyway. I'm not much of a dancer."

"I enjoy dancing with you, Dr. Batson," Cheney declared. "After all, it's not just the perfection of steps. It's the spirit of the thing that's important. Dev and I had a dancing master who was as somber as a hanging judge, and our lessons were like marching in a funeral procession. He was technically perfect, of course, but it wasn't much fun."

"It's hard to imagine Dr. Buchanan having fun," Cleve mused. Then with a wary look at Cheney he continued hurriedly, "Of course, I mean no criticism of Dr. Buchanan. I admire and respect him very much."

Cheney nodded dismissively. "Of course. As for fun,

however, I must say that I am having a famously good time tonight."

He became very still, and his kind blue eyes searched her face. "Are you, Dr. Duvall?"

She smiled. "Yes, Dr. Batson, I am, and I thank you for your kind solicitations."

"I am, as always, your servant, ma'am." They were leaning against the low balustrade and looking out over the gardens. The night was lovely, though the breeze was cold. A perfect crescent moon shone down on the gardens, and in the sterile light the flower beds looked like etchings in different shades of gray stone.

"What does one do with the flowers?" Cleve grumbled, his spoon clinking loudly as he maneuvered around the blossoms on top of the sorbet. "Eat them?"

Cheney giggled. "I don't think that's the intent. But now that you mention it, my tante Elyse tells me that pansies are edible. Supposedly they have a rather peppery taste."

"Oh?" Cleve gave her a sidelong glance. "I will if you will."

"But—oh, why not? After all, we're doctors. If we poison ourselves, we already know the appropriate dosage of syrup of ipecac."

"A pact," Cleve said solemnly, offering Cheney one of his pansies. "If you get deathly ill, I will remain by your side until the bitter end. If I get it, you must swear never to tell anyone that I died of pansy poisoning."

Laughing, Cheney agreed and scooped up one of her blooms, offering it to Cleve.

"Dr. Duvall," a deep voice interrupted them. Shiloh loomed in the door, dark against the bright lights of the ballroom, his arms crossed. "I believe this is my dance, isn't it? Or are you too much taken up with—by the way, what are you taken up with? Are you two eating flowers?"

"It's—oh, never mind," Cheney said, flushing painfully. "I...yes...it is your dance, I believe, Shiloh." She hurried to take his arm, and with a jerk he turned back to the ballroom. When the light fell on his face, Cheney could clearly see that he was glowering, and his eyes were sparkling in that reckless manner that she recognized all too well. "Dr. Batson and I were just...um...conducting a sort of...um...medical experiment."

"You were feeding each other flowers," Shiloh growled.

Suddenly he came to an abrupt halt. "This is that stupid hopping dance. I don't know how to do this."

"The allemande, Shiloh. It's really very easy," Cheney said in a small voice. "You can see the steps are simple and repetitive."

"I don't know how to do it," he repeated with more force.

Behind them, forgotten, Cleve had trailed them back into the ballroom. Mindful of the rather awkward situation and of his duties as Cheney's escort, he stepped forward and bowed. "Perhaps, Mr. Irons-Winslow, if you'd like to claim another dance, Dr. Duvall will honor me this time."

Shiloh retorted, "And maybe, Dr. Batson, you'd like to go nibble on some more tulips. By yourself this time."

Cheney pressed his arm and said between gritted teeth, "Shiloh! Don't be so rude! Dr. Batson has been the perfect gentleman!"

Cleve looked stunned. He and Shiloh weren't close friends, but they had been together much in the last couple of weeks, along with the rest of the Fine and Dandies. Shiloh had never treated him with such hostility. "Mr. Irons-Winslow, I must protest," Cleve said stiffly, stepping close to them so that he could speak in a low tone. "I don't care about what you said to me—though it was a quite undeserved insult—but you are embarrassing Dr. Duvall."

"I know. I've been embarrassing Dr. Duvall for three years now," Shiloh said, his eyes narrowing. "You've only been embarrassing her for a couple hours. So back up, little man."

"Shiloh! I insist—" Cheney pulled on his arm, trying to get him out in the relative privacy of the balcony. Cleve was standing stubbornly in front of Shiloh, while Shiloh stood immovable, glaring down at Cleve, his eyes narrowed to shards of blue ice.

Dev and Victoria flew by, but as Dev took in the tight, tense tableau, he suddenly stepped out of the widely circling dancers, pulling Victoria along unceremoniously with him.

Coolly Victoria remarked, "I see everyone's having a marvelous time. What is it, Shiloh? Are you and Dr. Batson about to duel over Cheney's honor?"

"Not a bad idea," Shiloh grunted.

"It would give me great pleasure to defend Dr. Duvall's honor," Dr. Batson said sarcastically, much unlike his normal languid tones. "She has been insulted by you, Mr. Irons-Winslow."

"You just stow that stuff, Batson," Shiloh said, bunching his great fighter's fists. "You're the one who took her outside, alone, dillydallied around eating flowers, subjected her to—"

"Eating flowers?" Dev said blankly. "Cheney, whatever has possessed you—"

Victoria laid her hand on his arm lightly, but her whisper was furious. "Dev, leave Cheney alone, for goodness' sake. It would seem that she's having enough trouble controlling these two angry little boys as it is."

"The Doc doesn't control me," Shiloh said, turning on Victoria with barely contained anger. "No one does."

"That's clearly true, Mr. Irons-Winslow," Victoria said, glancing around uncomfortably. The dancers, as they scooted and hopped by, tried to make the steps last as long as they could by the group, eyeing them with voracious curiosity. It was impossible to hear what they were saying over the music and the sounds of the vigorous dance steps on the wooden floor, but a child could see that the three men were angry and the two women were distressed. "Would you at least extend to me the consideration of conducting this ugly little scene outside on the balcony?" Victoria asked tightly. "People are watching, you know."

"Victoria, Shiloh may, in fact, be in the right this time," Dev said, glaring at Dr. Batson.

It gave Cleve a slight feeling of dread, for he loved his position, and Dr. Buchanan was, after all, his employer. But still, Cleve did think that Shiloh was being unfair to Cheney and outright insulting to him. Cleve very rarely lost his temper, but when he did, he simmered on a low boil, and it was hard for him to regain his usual calm. "I beg your pardon, Dr. Buchanan, but you weren't privy to—"

"Dev, I can handle this," Cheney said, yanking hard on Shiloh's arm. It was like pulling on a granite pillar. "Shiloh, listen to me. Victoria's right. We are embarrassing her. If you won't leave it be, at least let's go outside."

Shiloh whirled on his heel, jerking his head in a signal to Cleve, who marched out just behind him. Cheney flitted out after them. After hesitating a moment, Dev followed her. Victoria, her eyes wide with disbelief, turned to the couple dancing ever so slowly by, smiled blankly, then followed Dev out, closing the French doors behind her as quickly and quietly as she could. Immediately she grabbed Dev's arm and yanked hard to separate him from Cheney, Shiloh, and Cleve. "Dev! We can't be out here! This is our betrothal ball—ours, you understand? Mine and yours. It's unforgivable for us to be out here away from our guests and families!"

"Cheney is my family, Victoria," Dev answered sharply. "It's my duty to look out for her."

"Dev, listen to me, please," Victoria pleaded. "Tonight, just now, your duty is to me. I'm not your family yet, but soon I will be. Please come over here with me a moment." He allowed her, with clear reluctance, to lead him a little away from the other three. Now all three of them were arguing. Though Cheney's and Cleve's voices were muted and low, Shiloh's tone was an angry rasp.

"What a distasteful scene," Victoria said in a low voice, ducking her head and smoothing her dress with uncharacteristic nervousness. Two spots of color flared high on her cheeks. "Such disgraceful behavior on Shiloh's part. I'm surprised at him."

Dev eyed her with a cold, calculating look. "Why? I'm not so sure Cleve Batson didn't treat Cheney shabbily by dragging her outside. He knows she's already gossiped about and looked down on by almost everyone here because she's a physician. He shouldn't have put her in a compromising position."

"But Shiloh could have handled it in a more discreet manner," Victoria argued, now with some heat. "He's of good family, and he knows the code of gentlemanly conduct."

Dev's dark eyes narrowed, and he looked formidable, indeed. "Oh, I see. He comes from better breeding stock?"

"That's crude, Dev," Victoria snapped.

"Perhaps. Perhaps I don't know any better, Victoria. My breeding is hardly what you'd call impeccable." He folded his arms, an obstinate expression hardening his fine features.

Victoria was standing as straight and still as her ice sculpture, her eyes flashing dangerously. "You are deliberately twisting my words, Dev. This is ridiculous, and I don't wish to talk about it anymore."

"Excuse me, Victoria, but I don't think it's ridiculous at all. In fact, this topic has become very important to me lately, and I do wish to talk about it." Though he was not conscious of it, Dev sounded very supercilious, even arrogant.

"Here? Now?" Victoria hissed. "Are you insane?"

Suddenly, wrenchingly, Dev's face fell, his shoulders sagged, his hands grew curiously lax, falling to his sides. "No...not yet, anyway," he whispered so quietly that Victoria wasn't sure she'd heard him correctly. Before she could recover, he looked up, and he seemed haggard and much older. "Victoria, maybe you're right. Maybe we shouldn't talk about this, now or at any other time."

"What is the matter with you, Dev? Are you deliberately trying to drive me away?" Victoria demanded.

Then, with a shock she saw the clear intent in his face, in the desolate darkness of his eyes. "You…you are, aren't you?"

Still he didn't answer her. Victoria stared at him, her blue eyes wide with shock and already glittering with tears. He looked back at her, and in him Victoria saw both pitilessness and pity. The thought that Dev, whom she loved and longed for and dreamed of, was looking at her with some kind of sorrow and pity was so appalling to Victoria that she actually felt nauseated.

Swallowing the deathly sickness back down into her roiling stomach, she said in a hoarse voice utterly unlike her own, "You…don't…want to marry me?" Still Dev did not answer. He merely stared at her with that unfathomable, unknown look on his face. Victoria thought that it was like looking at a stranger, a slightly hostile man whom she had never met before in her life.

Her stomach plummeted to the depths. Her breath stopped. Her mind screeched to a pain-filled halt. The two strangers stared at each other for long moments.

Jarringly, with a supreme effort, Victoria recovered her shattered composure, arranged her face into lines of fashionable languor, and nodded shortly to Dev. "I see. Naturally, I need some time to make some arrangements. Or cancel them, rather," she added with a brittle laugh that hurt Dev to the very depths of his heart. "Would you be so kind as to delay announcing that you've thrown me over for a few days? It has upset my equilibrium just a bit. I'm sure you understand."

"Of course you may make any announcement you choose, at any time," Dev said with curious lifelessness. His lips, for some odd reason, felt numb. "I shall, of course, say that you have changed your mind, Victoria, and that you've decided you don't want to marry me."

"I don't need or want your pity," Victoria lashed out.

Dev shook his head sorrowfully. "If you only knew the truth, Victoria, you would never have consented to marry me anyway. Please, let's just leave it at that."

Without another word, Victoria Elizabeth Steen de Lancie, her head held proudly on her long, elegant neck, turned and swept back into the ballroom, smiling with a brittle diamond brilliance.

Dev felt as if he'd been beaten up by a prizefighter, and he sagged against the balustrade, rubbing his gritty eyes. Now Shiloh's and Cheney's voices penetrated to him again. Eyeing them a few feet away, he saw that Shiloh and Cheney were now squared off, as it were, and Cleve Batson was helplessly standing by like an unwanted and unneeded stage prompter.

"Doc, you've gotta stop acting like this," Shiloh was saying, though he sounded calmer.

"Acting like what?" she countered, and now she was furious. "You're the one who's making a spectacle! Not I!"

"I haven't been out moony-gooning around in the shrubbery eating daisies," Shiloh grumbled.

"I keep telling you they were pansies," Cheney flung at him. "And it's hardly any of your business if I want to eat the whole garden!"

"It is my business," Shiloh argued. "You know it is."

"I can hardly see how—" Cleve began.

"I told you, Dr. Batson, I can handle this," Cheney said, turning on him with surprising vengefulness.

"See? You don't even call him by his first name yet,"

Shiloh said loftily. "How do you think it looks, you being out here alone with him?"

"So now I'm out here alone with the two of you, trying to...trying to...oh, what in kingdom come am I trying to do anyway?" Cheney finally finished dramatically. "You two little boys just stay out here and scuffle if you want to. That goes for you too, Dev," she shot over to him, striding majestically through the French doors, banging them backward with a loud crash.

"What'd I do?" Dev said helplessly.

"I dunno, but you're a man, so you're bound to have done something wrong," Shiloh rasped. "I'm gonna go see if they have anything decent to drink in the library. Come on, Batson. Take my word for it, when the Doc's in that high-steppin' state, it's no use tryin' to gentle her down."

"You...you called me 'little man,'" Cleve muttered blackly.

"Huh? Oh. Oh yeah, I did. Sorry. I mean, I apologize, Dr. Batson, for insulting you. Now we don't have to fight a duel, do we?" Shiloh asked, cajoling him. "I mean, since I apologized so pretty and all?"

With gritted teeth Cleve answered, "I'm not suicidal, thank you. And I guess, in a way, you were right, Mr. Irons-Winslow. Not about the little man, but about Dr. Duvall. I should have been more mindful of her vulnerability to malicious gossip."

"Let's forget it," Shiloh said uncomfortably, as men generally are after emotional scenes. "Dr. Buchanan, I see you've been left high and dry, too. Care to join us?"

"Gentlemen," Dev said wearily. "If we could find a

corner with no females lurking there, it would give me great pleasure to join you."

"Women," Shiloh intoned. "Sometimes I think we'd be better off without 'em."

"It seems," Dev said quietly, "that some of them are definitely better off without us."

Shiloh sighed heavily. "You're so right, Dr. Buchanan. You are so right."

Chapter Thirteen

The Players

The Steens' glittering ball lasted until the weary gray hours, so the only guests who stirred the next Sunday morning were the Duvalls, who went to church. Victoria stayed shut up in her room and was not at home to the many callers to the de Lancie mansion that day. Dev, too, stayed at home with Dart, dismissing both Mrs. Barentines, and brooded all day.

Shiloh slept. When he awoke a bleak cold twilight had already fallen, depressing him further. He had a sharp headache right behind his eyes, and his mouth tasted as though he'd been eating dirt. As always, he luxuriated in the *en suite* bathroom with the great claw-footed bathtub and took an almost unbearably hot bath that lasted over an hour, finishing it off with an icy cold rinse. After shaving and using Royal Lyme cologne—an extravagance imported from London that he truly enjoyed—he felt almost human again.

Opening a window, he found that a wintry mist was hanging in the air, a foreboding of a heavy frost. He sniffed, but like his other senses and his keen mind and his uncanny instincts, his sense of smell was dulled. Still, he thought that he could detect a final grasp of winter's cold claw. They were in for a late winter storm, likely with some ice and maybe even snow. Shiloh found himself longing, with a tangible physical pang, for the eternal summer of Hawaii.

When he thought of Hawaii, he thought of Cheney, and frowning darkly he turned and yanked on his old clothes—faded gray Confederate breeches, thin muslin shirt, stained canvas overcoat, and worn cavalry boots. Jamming his old wide-brimmed gray hat on his still wet head, he stamped down to the grand foyer of the hotel and slipped through the steaming, fragrant kitchen and out to the livery stables. It was a long, cold ride to Minette's.

"Shiloh, you must be chilled to the bone," she said, appalled, when he stood in her parlor, his face gray, his eyes dull. "And you're damp, too. Here, give me your coat and hat at once and go sit by the fire."

He gave her an obligatory kiss, then went to collapse into a leather club chair with a matching ottoman and propped up his feet. "Is this new?" he asked, looking around at her as she fussed with his coat. "You've gotten some new furniture, haven't you?"

"Yes," she answered shortly, her back to him.

"I like this chair. It feels good." He rested his head along the back, luxuriating in the warmth of a fine fire and the feel and scent of good leather.

"I'm so glad you do," Minette said, giving him a covert glance. She wanted to add, *I bought it for you,* but of course she could never say such a thing to Shiloh. "Would you like a drink?"

Shiloh hesitated. Minette usually had too sweet wine and cheap gin.

She added in a neutral voice, "I think I'll have a brandy with you. I splurged and bought some Xavier Brothers."

"Sounds fine."

She brought him the drink in a crystal snifter and settled into the chair opposite him, also a new overstuffed chintz armchair. "Are you ill, dearest?" she asked tenderly.

"No," he answered shortly. "I don't get sick. That a new frock? It's pretty. That color of blue suits you. It makes your eyes shine."

She blushed and said, "Thank you, sir, you are kind."

It amazed Shiloh that she could look so innocent, so young, so guileless. He knew she was not innocent and knew that she could be deceptive, yet it intrigued him that she emanated this virginal quality. *No one can fake that, no matter how good an actor. How does she do it? Or why is she like that? Is it just the way she looks, or does she have some internal quality, some soul exercise that absolves her from all guilt? Is that possible? Wish it was—I'd make her tell me how to do it.*

An uncomfortable thought flitted like a small moth through Shiloh's brain. *You know there's only one way to be absolved of guilt, to be forgiven for your sins, and to be clean—the Doc's way, and the Misses Behrings' way, and Richard and Irene's way—God.*

But Shiloh refused to think of God these days. He never had, much. It seemed as if he hadn't had to. He was a moral man, an honest man, in his own eyes. And though his life had been hard, he had always been pretty happy with it. He always thought, vaguely, that being a Christian was the sort of thing that people like the Behrings and the Duvalls did because they had some sort of need that he had never experienced—and never would. Until the Doc had broadsided him.

"Sorry," he said quickly. "What were you saying?"

"Shiloh," Minette pouted, "you really must attend to me. It's hardly fair after I've gone to so much trouble. I've never invited anyone to supper in my room before."

"No? And I guess you cooked all that yourself, slaving away all day?" he teased.

"Well, no, I didn't," she replied good-humoredly. "We should both be grateful for it, too. I'm not much of a cook. Are you hungry?"

"Not very. But it looks appetizing," he added hastily, "and nice." A small table was set close to the fireplace, with a white lace-trimmed tablecloth and several dishes with silver covers. A centerpiece of white lilies and tall slender candles lit the corner romantically. Shiloh noted idly that Minette had the same china as Irene Duvall, that blue Chinese motif—Willow, it was called. But of course thinking about Irene Duvall made him think of Cheney, and he frowned down into his brandy.

Quickly Minette said, "Let's finish our brandy, for it's just a cold supper. Perhaps we'll have another drink. It might give you an appetite. I do like it, and I'm surprised. I'd always understood that brandy was strictly a man's libation. Anyway, Shiloh, please tell me all about the Steens' ball. It must have been the grandest one given this season."

Rousing a little, Shiloh described the decor, the flowers, and the ice sculptures, and told her how nervous he'd been performing the quadrille for the first time. Balls were still, as a rule, opened with that ancient and stately dance, and Minette had taught it to him. "I just knew I'd be walking along on the wrong side of the room or grabbing some poor strange lady to turn her, but I managed to mump my way through it."

With a brittle smile she asked, "Did you open with Angelique Steen?" She regretted it and knew that she shouldn't have done it, but she couldn't stop herself. Minette was falling in love with Shiloh, and she knew beyond all doubt that he would never fall in love with her. He drew away from her, immediately and forcefully, whenever she tried to press for any kind of intimacy. But sometimes she couldn't stop herself, especially from trying to get him to talk about Angelique Steen. He never would, of course. In fact, he always did exactly what he was doing now when Minette mentioned her. He grew distinctly cooler and changed the subject.

"Yeah. Mr. and Mrs. William Henry Vanderbilt were there, and Mr. Vanderbilt, I swear, was a bigger clunk at the quadrille than I was. There was a big stink, I think, because one of the Mrs. Astors didn't come. She was supposedly in Saratoga Springs, but Troy told me that she'll come rushing back to town tomorrow and then leave for the country again before the wedding. Some kinda weird games those people play."

Minette said airily, "But you're one of those people, Shiloh."

"Me?" he said, genuinely taken aback. "Oh yeah. I forget. Guess cause I'm not wearing my front-door clothes. By the way, I hope you're not offended at my dress, that I didn't get all prettied up for you. Sometimes I feel like those neckties are a hangman's noose."

She laughed prettily. "I don't care what you wear,

Shiloh. I never will. In fact, I think you look dangerously handsome and rugged."

"Yeah, that's me, dangerous and rugged," he muttered.
"I feel like an old broken-down nag."

With smooth grace she came to kneel by his chair, caressing his knee. "Finish your drink, and then we'll eat.
Later you'll feel better, I promise," she said brightly.

She's like some woolly little lamb, he mused. *Nothing
like the Doc at all, who's like a cat, one minute purring
and the next spitting and hissing. Never met a woman
like her, never will again, I expect....*

With a jerk he sat stiffly upright. "Minette, I've
changed my mind. Let's go out."

"What? Now?" She almost fell backward.

"Yeah. At least *I'm* going out," he said with rough
carelessness, tossing back the rest of his brandy. "You
can come if you want."

"Well, of course I want," she said, struggling to rise.
Shiloh, ever the gentleman even in ill temper, gently
helped her. She took advantage of it, pressing against
him, raising her heart-shaped face to his and putting her
ever-so-soft hands around his neck. "Are you sure you
wouldn't like to just stay in tonight, darling?" she whispered, going on tiptoe to kiss his lips lightly.

He allowed her to but remained stiff, unresponsive.
"No, I'm really not hungry, and it's a cold supper. It'll
keep, right? I want to go to Morrissey's. Got a mind for
some roulette? I'll stake you."

Her eyes flashed, and she smiled. "Would you, love?
Would you really? All right, just one moment. I must
freshen up." She hurried into her bedroom.

"Hurry up, Minette," he called brusquely. "The 'slings
and arrows of outrageous fortune' await us, you know."

"Yes, yes. Wait for me, Shiloh. I'm coming...."

His chiseled features were, for a moment, tinged with disgust. Minette had no mind for *Hamlet* tonight, and he had no mind for an intimate supper. As usual when he was sober, his mind was consumed, quite against his will, with Dr. Cheney Duvall. Being alone with Minette could not absorb his attention enough to forget Cheney. Perhaps a little roulette and a lot of brandy would.

Cruelly early the next morning Shiloh told the hansom cab driver, "Take me to Harrigan & Hart's first. After that I'm going to Bellevue, and I'll ask you to wait for me while I have a short appointment, and then I'll be going to Duvall Court at Park and East Sixty-fifth."

"Fine wid me, sir," the lean, rawboned driver replied craftily. "If you'd understand, sir, dat I'll be needing to charge you for the waiting-around time." *This flash cove has da grease, that's sure,* the driver thought, smiling as sunnily as he could, considering he was missing most of his bottom teeth.

"Yeah, I do understand that," Shiloh grunted, climbing into the carriage. Immediately he opened the shutter, even though it was a raw, wet day. His senses were not so liquor dulled that he couldn't smell the ingrained dirt in the seats and the odor of other humans who weren't so persnickety about bathing as was Shiloh. He shivered as a gust of icy wind blew into the carriage and stared up at a gunmetal-gray sky. *Looks more like January than May. How I hate this place; how glad I'll be to get away from here...and her.*

But that wasn't strictly true, and Shiloh knew it. His misery was not because he was in New York, and his wretchedness was not Cheney's fault.

She hurt me, yes, he reflected uncomfortably. *But I'm sure making a fine job of hurting myself instead of healing myself. All this stupid racketing around, drinking like some vulgar sot; gambling like the worst fool, knowing all the time that it doesn't really help. It doesn't really do anything but just mask the pain for a little, a very little while...and the price of those few short moments are sure high. I feel—grimy and vulgar, weak and sick. Tough guy, Iron Man, yeah, right. God, I'm so tired, I'm—*

But when Shiloh realized that he might actually be starting to pray, the rebelliousness that was in him, and in men of all the ages, leaped up. He wouldn't go crawling to God like some pitiable, sniveling little boy. He was a man, and soon he would get back his strength and his pride. His eyes suddenly hard, he turned to look out the carriage window and shoved his unwelcome meditation aside.

It was a short way to his tailor's from the Fifth Avenue Hotel—he usually walked—but today he was cold and tired and felt the full dissipation from his late night. He and Minette had stayed at Morrissey's until 3:00 a.m., for she had won splendidly at the roulette wheel. To his surprise, with shy gratitude she'd returned his stake of fifty dollars. The gesture didn't fool him, though. Even in his dullness Shiloh knew that this was just the kind of thing that was calculated to entice him. Minette had been smart enough, early on, to comprehend that Shiloh didn't respond to pretty pleas for gifts or money. He was more generous when it was his own idea.

Wearily he reflected that Minette, at least, was intelligent enough to understand that. Other women never seemed to learn, and he tired of demanding women quickly, no matter how sweetly or seductively they tried to entangle him. Angelique Steen, for instance, had almost driven him mad with her demands for his attention, his admiration, his esteem. It never seemed to occur to her that a man wouldn't be knocked sprawling by her charms. Perhaps most men were. The other Fine and Dandies seemed to be all agog with her beauty, her wit, her grace. But Shiloh found it tiresome to be the sole target of all that intense attention for long.

A small, nasty voice somewhere at the bottom of his mind prodded him that Angelique Steen was already in love with him—or thought she was—and that, in spite of her shallowness, she was going to get hurt. But he couldn't help that. Josefina Steen had thrown them together at every opportunity. He had kept Angelique at arm's length as much as he could, but it was tricky with women. Most of them—particularly the really beautiful ones—did not take kindly to a man being immune to their charms. *Except the Doc. She's beautiful, so striking you can hardly take your eyes off her when she's in the room, and she never preens, never demands adoration—*

"Malediction!" Shiloh growled. "Hey you, driver! Where you goin'? To Brooklyn?"

"Sorry, sir," he called, pulling the horse to a doubtful halt, maneuvering around two other carriages. He had gone two doors past the tailor's. "Having some trouble wid da traffic."

Shiloh jumped out and ordered, "Wait for me."

"Yes, sir, you bet, yer majesty," the driver muttered.

Shiloh came back out, very quickly, wearing a navy-blue caped wool greatcoat. He'd ordered it when he first came to New York, for nights on board ship could be chilly, even in the Tropics. Now, since the weather was turning ugly, he was glad for it. He started back to the cab, then stopped and whirled as if he'd heard an imperative call. Tiffany's Jewelers was right next to Harrigan & Hart's, and in their glass display window something had caught his eye. It was a pearl necklace—rare pink pearls—displayed on black velvet. For a moment he thought how well they suited Minette's pink-roses complexion. Then he remembered his and Cheney's pearl, the perfect pearl, the symbol of their past and their bright future, now at the fathomless bottom of the Pacific Ocean, and he was almost sick. With a muttered curse he pushed into the jeweler's, threw down an immense amount of cash he'd won in a reckless game of poker the night before, and bought a large opal, surrounded by diamonds and hanging on a black velvet cord.

"I'll take it—no, forget it," he muttered to the smiling clerk. "Send it. Give me a card. I'll write down the name and address." With hard strokes he wrote Minette's name and address and signed it, *For my lucky lady...Shiloh.*

Without another word, he stamped out of the elegant store. The clerk avidly read Shiloh's note, then looked after him, wondering how the luscious Miss York—he'd been to see *Hamlet* twice—had managed to make that young gentleman so angry and so generous at the same time.

"Excuse me, sir."

The clerk turned, then bowed obsequiously to the gentleman who had been in the store for some time considering gold cuff links. He was obviously some sort of British aristocrat, and a wealthy one, judging by his clothes. The clerk wondered where he'd disappeared to when the tall angry man had come in and thrown a fortune down on the polished glass counter. Now the British gentleman stood white-faced, his brown eyes sparking with what seemed to be a curious mixture of animosity and wariness. But his voice was languid as he continued, "I was looking at that very necklace, sir, and considering purchasing it for a lady friend of mine."

"Oh, sir, I assure you that we can have another made," the clerk cried. "Quickly, too, I would—"

The slim, elegant gentleman waved his hand with masculine grace. "No, no. Certainly I wouldn't wish to give such a gift to my friend if it so happened that, say, the lady in the next box at the opera had the identical necklace."

"Oh no, of course not, but we could—"

"Perhaps you would, just to satisfy my curiosity, allow me to see who is the fortunate recipient of this magnificent necklace?" A five-dollar bank note appeared between the gentleman's fingers, and in a quick movement he deposited it in the clerk's pocket.

The clerk flushed, but he reasoned that he had lost the commission on the second necklace. "If you would like to look at these necklaces in this case, sir, I am going to go instruct a boy to box this up. If you would excuse me for a moment, sir..." Grasping the necklace, he moved to a curtain behind the display cases, leaving the card Shiloh had written just behind a counter stand displaying marcasite rings.

Bain Winslow read the card, and his smooth, aquiline features darkened. He marched angrily to the doors, but then hesitated, cautiously looking out, up and down the street. Then he left, slamming the heavy glassed door behind him.

Dr. Lyman Banckert's cubbyhole felt overly warm and stuffy to Shiloh, and after the cold, wet air outside it made him feel slightly nauseated. Disgusted with himself, he took deep, even breaths, removed his black kid gloves, and adjusted his tight collar.

"Is it too warm for you, sir?" Dr. Banckert asked, *"Ja,* for me, too, but I don't do this little stove too good—who has winter in New York in May? Anyway, Mr. Irons-Winslow, I must say that this account you wrote of your aunt's situation is very good—succinct, objective, clinical—and you are not even a doctor. You should be, you know. So here is my report," Dr. Banckert said, handing Shiloh a sheaf of papers. "The reason I wanted to talk with you is that I must explain my hesitation in attempting to diagnose and suggest treatment for your aunt in this unconventional manner."

Shiloh nodded. "I understand the limitations of your report, sir, and I'll certainly keep it in mind as I plan my aunt's care. Please don't think that I would, in any way, hold you responsible for my aunt as a patient. I view this as an extraordinary favor, much like a friend discussing family problems with me. Especially since you won't allow me to pay you for what I'm certain was a time-consuming, boring chore."

"Not at all, Mr. Irons-Winslow," Dr. Banckert said smoothly. "As a matter of fact, I found after reading your narrative that it seems your aunt's case is not complicated, not at all. As you will see in my report, I believe that your aunt is neither psychotic nor neurotic, but is simply suffering from a combination of depression and repressed anger. This can be serious, of course, but it gives more hope than if she were exhibiting the symptoms of true mental derangement."

"Depression and repressed anger. Yes…I see," Shiloh murmured thoughtfully, scanning through Dr. Banckert's report. "So you think—and yes, it does make sense—that she simply allowed some of this other anger—at me, at my uncle, at the past—to sort of overflow when Brynn wouldn't let her take more laudanum?"

"I believe so, as it seems that this was an isolated incident," Dr. Banckert said. "I must caution you, however, that there is a possibility that Mrs. Winslow has taken so much laudanum for such a long time that she is addicted to it. Addiction to any opiates can cause the addict to become very violent to obtain the dosage that their bodies and certainly their poor tortured minds need."

Shiloh shook his head. "Brynn swears that she never took laudanum before, not even when she was ill. And it was, as you pointed out, an isolated incident. Brynn and I took the laudanum away from her afterward when she lapsed into the semicatatonic state."

"Yes, after the eruption of anger she became very depressed," Dr. Banckert said eagerly. "But you do see, don't you, that her outburst does have reason, that her behavior is not incomprehensible but it has method? That is one reason I can be fairly certain that she has no real dementia. After all, she only wanted some medicine that would make her serene and forgetful for a while. She didn't attack your cousin because the wolves howling on the moor told her to or because the planet Mercury was aligned with the moons of Jupiter."

Chuckling, Shiloh said, "It makes sense. Of course it does. I can't think why I couldn't see it before."

"Because you haven't been trained, young man," Dr. Banckert said severely. "I don't suppose you'd consider obtaining your medical degree and then looking into psychiatry—no, no, I can see not. No harm in asking, though. I'd dearly love to have an assistant with your insight, but—pah! You young American men, all the fun, all the actresses, all the roulette, all the theater, and the late suppers at Delmonico's… *Ja*, I read the papers, Mr. Irons-Winslow."

Sheepishly Shiloh said, "Well, I do have a job. My family's business, you know."

"I am doing the teasing, you know, Mr. Irons-Winslow. No need to make excuses to me," the older man chuckled. "I just want to let you know that if you ever consider going into medicine, you come see me."

"Thank you kindly, sir. I consider that a great compliment," Shiloh said, rising and pulling on his gloves. "And how can I possibly thank you for performing this valuable service for me? I would ask again that you allow me to pay you something for your time."

"No, no. It is as I said, a consideration from one professional to another. If I have the opportunity to vacation in Hawaii, I shall expect royal treatment," Dr. Banckert said jovially.

"I'll be returning in…in two weeks," Shiloh faltered. It shocked him to realize that in just fourteen days—the day after the wedding—he was going to leave New York and might never see Dr. Cheney Duvall again. Clearing his throat awkwardly he continued, "Why don't you take that vacation, sir? I'll take you to Hawaii, put you up in style in Lahaina for as long as you wish, and then I can make arrangements for your return to New York. It would give me great pleasure."

To Shiloh's surprise, Dr. Lyman Banckert's tired eyes lit up. "Why, that's exceedingly generous of you, Mr. Irons-Winslow. As a matter of fact…as a matter of fact, maybe I will consider it."

"Please do, sir," Shiloh said firmly, offering him his

hand. "Why don't I take you out to supper and try to per-suade you? Shall we say nine o'clock tonight? Meet at Delmonico's?"

"I will be there, Mr. Irons-Winslow. And I warn you, I lost a patient last night, and that always makes me want to take the run away," Dr. Banckert said wearily. "Exotic Pacific islands thousands of miles away sound very good today."

"I hope they sound just as good in a couple of weeks," Shiloh said gallantly. "I mean it, sir, the whole thing. I'll see you tonight, Dr. Banckert. And allow me to thank you again for your kind consideration of me and my family."

Shiloh left, glowering in case the hansom cab hadn't waited for him. But the cab was still there, with the cabbie petting the old horse's nose and picking his own scanty teeth with a shred of wood. Shiloh hurried to get in, for a raw mist hung in the air, dampening his new coat and making it give off that particular smell that wet wool exudes. He clambered into the cab and once again opened both the shutters, for his nose was much more sensitive than most people's.

Across the barren stretch of grounds was the Insane Pavilion, and in the few seconds it took the cab to turn around and leave Bellevue, a scene imprinted itself on Shiloh's mind with that knife-edged attention to detail that was characteristic of Shiloh's keen powers of obser-vation.

A funeral procession was leaving from the Insane Pa-vilion. Six burly attendants were bringing out a casket, cherrywood with brass fittings, which went into a dis-creetly draped hearse. Behind it, in the cold damps, stood Dr. Devlin Buchanan, his aquiline features wiped clean, it seemed, of all emotion. When the coffin was secured, he turned and got into a waiting hansom cab. In the cab sat a young woman with a baby. Shiloh could see the young woman clearly, for she was situated on the side near him as he passed. Their eyes even met. She looked at him with a dull curiosity, and from long habit he nodded and touched the brim of his hat. A faint pleased smile touched her lips—Shiloh had that effect on women—and she modestly looked down, fussing with the baby.

Shiloh's cab left the funeral tableau behind. *Odd. That's an expensive casket, fine hearse, not a rough gig, unusual for the inmates of the Insane Pavilion. And Dr. Buchanan with that pretty young woman...and a baby? No, no. That's not right. She must be the man's widow. Or could the deceased be a woman, the girl's mother or sister, perhaps? Still, she didn't look as if she had the money for that kind of funeral. She looked like a maid, or maybe a respectable shopgirl...that black bonnet, old, not fashionable. Something strange about that scene, can't quite get a good hold on it....*

But Shiloh was, as usual these days, distracted by his own troubles. As the cab made its cautious way through the comparative emptiness of northern Manhattan, he dismissed Devlin Buchanan from his mind in the effort of trying to arm himself against seeing Cheney. Shiloh had not called on the Duvalls once since he'd been in New York, and he hated the thought of imposing himself upon Cheney now. But he must pay his respects to Mr. and Mrs. Duvall.

He stared out the open window at the grizzled gray day, damp, musty smelling, with an invasive chill. "It looks just like I feel," he whispered bleakly.

Since he had realized he'd lost Cheney, Shiloh's world

had been much like the listless scene outside. It seemed to him that there were no bright colors, no perfume in the air, no pleasing sounds, and his tactile senses of taste and touch were dulled to the point of maddening blandness. But then, too, there was the pain. Sometimes he felt a drab ache, as when he and Cheney were in a room full of people, and he struggled mightily not to be aware of her. At other times—and these episodes were happening more and more often—he felt a keen pain, sometimes in his chest, sometimes behind his eyes, when he saw the particular well-known and long-loved tilt of her head, her luscious hair curling along the back of her neck, or her expressive hands making a graceful, definitive gesture even from across the room. It made Shiloh almost ill with longing to watch her walk, her stride confident, her head held proudly, her shoulders straight, and the small breadth of her waist—why, he could span that small waist with his hands—the smell of her hair, always clean, always perfumed with roses and jasmine…her eyes, bright, warm, alive, full of sparks and vibrant colors and promise…

"Gotta stop thinking about her," he growled, gritting his teeth. His head was beginning to ache, and he was cold. Pulling his coat closer around him, he sneezed twice. "Lovely. Bleary eyes, nose runnin', smell like a wet sheep—that'll impress her for sure."

The cab pulled smartly up the brick drive to Duvall Court, its white pillars and mellowed red brick a warm sight. Victoria's carriage was there, and Shiloh had a blessed moment of amusement, for Victoria insisted upon having her driver dressed in the formal costume of the coachman—many-tiered driving cloak, top hat, white gloves. But he was a conservative sight compared to her two ever-present footmen in splendid gold-and-white livery. Her gold-and-white coach looked as if it had ridden straight in on a pink cloud from a fairy tale.

He knocked on the door and was surprised to see a young girl in a black dress and crisp white apron open the door. "Why, Mallow! What are you doing here?" he asked.

Directly inside the door, he saw with a start, stood two large leather trunks with brass fittings and gracefully scripted monograms in what appeared to be solid gold. Shiloh's already nervous stomach plummeted. *Is the Doc leaving? No, not yet—* Then he saw that the elaborate monograms were *B*s—for Buchanan, he guessed, though why Dev's trunks should be in the Duvalls' hallway he couldn't guess. Rousing himself, he smiled at Mallow and began stripping off his gloves, hat, and coat.

She took them, fumbling a little, but smiled up at him saucily. She was a puckish Irish girl, with red hair and freckles and a mischievous sparkle in her green eyes. "Mrs. Duvall hired me, and Sylvie, too, Mr. Irons-Winslow, as the upstairs and downstairs maids. I'm downstairs," she finished proudly.

Dally loomed up behind her, her bulk and the outraged look in her eye quite alarming. "Youse gwine be downstairs in the cellar lookin' for rats if'n you don't quit talkin' the heads off all the callers, Miz Mallow."

"Yes'm," Mallow said humbly, skittering toward the hall closet.

"An' don't be a-hangin' up Mistuh Irons's coat in thet closet. It's wet. I kin see it from here lak you should have, young miss. You go hang it in the kitchen by the stove to dry out summat, and don't be a-fiddlin' and a-faddlin' along, neither," Dally threatened.

"Yes'm…no'm…yes'm," Mallow said faintly and disappeared down the hallway.

Mallow had been with Miss Behring in the old orphanage, and Shiloh had nursed her through a severe case of catarrh. She'd gone on to the new orphanage and still lived there, though she had been working out as a kitchen maid for the last year. She had just turned sixteen, and since the new orphanage was much more roomy than the old, Jane Anne Blue had not had to be as strict about the older children finding lodgings when they went to work.

"I been tellin' that little chile for three days now how to receive gennemen callers, and she been forgettin' it for three days now," Dally grumbled as Shiloh handed her his card and she placed it carefully on a silver platter. "One moment please, Mr. Irons—I mean, Mr. Irons-Winslow, if'n you please."

She disappeared soundlessly through the closed door to the sitting room, and Shiloh was a little surprised. Not at the little formalities of submitting his card for entrance—that was unquestioned courtesy—but that the door to the Duvalls' formal parlor should be closed. Normally when they were receiving callers the door was open, and as often as not, Cheney or Irene or Richard would themselves come into the grand foyer to greet their guests.

In addition, it took long minutes for Dally to return, a closed, stern look resting on her broad face. "They'm be happy to receive you now, Mr. Irons-Winslow," she said, leading him into the room.

An odd scene greeted his mystified gaze. Richard and Irene were seated in two club chairs pulled close to each other. Richard looked somber, and Irene's smooth, elegant features were drawn with unnatural tightness. Tante Marye sat in an old winged armchair, and she looked as severe as if she were about to discipline a particularly naughty child. Next to her on one sofa was Tante Elyse, who appeared about to cry, and Gowan Ford, whose scarred countenance was hard to read, but who seemed, somehow, at a loss. Across from them on a love seat sat Cheney and Victoria. Victoria was pale, but as always she was composed, her back straight, her small, gloved hands gracefully arranged in her lap. But her eyes were a distant icy-blue, and her normally soft, pliable mouth formed a tight, straight line. Cheney was looking at Shiloh imploringly, as if she were pleading with him. But to Shiloh's desperation he had no idea what she wanted, what she needed, what was wrong. He had always known before. Now that was gone, lost, too.

Quickly Shiloh decided just to bluster his way through it. "Hullo, everyone," he said, nodding all around. "Looks like I've landed in the middle of it. By the way, what is it? Anything I've done? Lately?"

"Not this time," Cheney said.

"Please, sit down, Shiloh," Irene said, rousing herself. "How glad we are to see you. Aren't we, Richard?" She turned on him with what was for her a severe glance.

"Hmm? Oh yes, of course, Shiloh. We— What time is it?" Richard said vaguely, fumbling for his pocket watch.

"Richard, you are noodling," Tante Marye said acidly.

Richard looked as guilty as a small boy. "I know, Tante Marye, but—please excuse me, Shiloh, I'm— I was thinking of something else."

"Maybe I'd better come back later, at a more convenient time," Shiloh said smoothly, beginning to rise from the sofa, where he'd gingerly seated himself beside Gowan Ford.

"No!" Cheney said, then flushed painfully. "I...I mean, I'm sure Father was just going to invite you to lunch with us. Weren't you, Father? Isn't that why you wished to know what time it was? To see if it's almost time for lunch?"

"I beg your pardon?" Richard said blankly.

"Of course he was, and I certainly hope you will stay, Shiloh," Irene said, managing a tight little smile. "We've barely seen you these past weeks, in spite of the fact that we're all at the same events for the—" Here Irene's musical voice stopped as completely as if someone had clapped a hand over her mouth, and her glance at Victoria was truly distressed.

"This is absurd," Victoria said brusquely. "Of course I'm going to tell Shiloh. He's almost like family, or would be if he and Cheney weren't having such a terrible falling-out, but that makes no difference to me." This ramble was quite unlike Victoria's usual pointed conversation, and she turned to him, her eyes glittering, her voice hard. "Dev and I have called off the wedding. You needn't know the sordid details, but we did it Saturday night at the ball. I came here thinking that surely Dev had told everyone, but apparently he has not. In fact, no one has seen him since the night of the ball. Anyway, that's why everyone looks so shocked and solicitous."

Shiloh wasn't at all shocked, for the image of Dev Buchanan's drawn face with the despairing look in his eyes at the ball loomed up before him. Somewhere, back in the murk of his mind, Shiloh had known that he and Victoria had had a terrible fight and had flown apart that night. It was his old primitive instinct, his animal precognition, or whatever he had. It was more like a vision than completely understood words or ideas. Shiloh had sensed—or felt or seen—that night that Devlin Buchanan and Victoria de Lancie had been blown away from each other as if by torturous and treacherous winds. But he had managed to dull this knowledge, to ignore it, to drown it in a sea of brandy and loud laughter and Minette York's adoring blue eyes.

Now he couldn't think of a single thing to say. His knowledge of polite society's conduct didn't extend to a situation such as this. He simply looked at Victoria, and his sympathy was so clear and so unforced that she turned away and swallowed hard.

"I just came sweeping in, twittering on about the trunks," she said in a hoarse voice utterly unlike her own gilded tones. "I had no idea that Dev hadn't told you, Mr. and Mrs. Duvall. Please accept my heartfelt regret at having placed you in such an awkward and painful position."

"No, no, Mrs. de Lancie, please don't distress yourself," Irene said in a stricken voice.

Richard was mumbling something nonsensical like "Not at all, not at all."

A horrible silence fell for a few moments, and Victoria looked as if she might shatter into pieces at any time. Everyone else—even Tante Marye—seemed at a total loss. Finally Victoria went on in a dead voice, "I am returning some of the wedding gifts in person, naturally, and taking the opportunity to offer my sincere apologies for any inconvenience the cancellation of the wedding may cause. There will be no announcement in the papers, for my father and I have arranged to have cards of notice printed, and they will be enclosed with the returned wedding gifts. I…I hate to return the lovely trunks, Mr. and Mrs. Duvall, and I…I'm devastated that Dev and I won't be able to take advantage of the trip to France that you so generously provided for us, Tante Marye, Tante Elyse, Mr. Ford. Perhaps you three should go instead and visit the Vicomte de Cheyne? You haven't seen your half brother in many years, I believe." Victoria had regained a weak semblance of her normal polished demeanor.

But the others had not. Tante Marye did manage to mumble, "Why, no, we haven't seen Maxime for many years."

"There, you see. Well, I really must be going," Victoria said with a brightness so false it was painful for everyone. Restlessly she rose, fidgeting with her fan, her reticule. The men jumped to their feet, and the protests began, but with some grace Victoria managed to extricate herself. She hurried out to the foyer, calling Mallow for her cloak in a surprisingly strident voice. With wide, stricken eyes, Cheney finally whirled and followed her, pulling the parlor door closed again with a crash.

The men stood still, as wooden and blank as toy soldiers, while the women stared at one another.

"Well, if that just wasn't the most horrendous thing I've ever sat through," Tante Elyse finally declared. "It was like that awful play, wasn't it, Gowan?"

With an appearance of great weariness Gowan sat down again at his wife's side. "What play, Elyse?"

"Of course you know that awful play, the one where the dead body is right in the middle of the parlor and all of the characters must pretend they can't see it," Elyse explained impatiently. "All of them had to go through the most extravagant steps so as not to tread upon that poor dead woman, and there was her skirt rucked up over her ankles the entire time, and Marye could hardly concentrate on the dialogue because she disapproved so strongly. And then, of course, the conversations were so stilted, so artificial, but funny, you know."

"But I thought you said the play was awful," Richard said, his wide brow wrinkling.

"Oh, it was," Elyse agreed quickly, one of her odd traits that kept everyone off-balance. "Funny and awful. But this, most assuredly, was not funny. It was just awful."

"I want someone to tell me, clearly and without namby-pambying around, exactly what has happened," Tante Marye, who had been in a brown study, suddenly announced.

"I, for one, don't understand at all," Elyse said earnestly.

"What a great surprise," Marye said brusquely. "Please be quiet, Elyse, and let someone with some sense explain this to me. Why have Dev and Mrs. de Lancie broken up? And did she break it off with him, or did he break it off with her?"

Her stern eyes went around the room, but she found no knowledgeable answering gaze. Then with delicate disdain she sniffed. "Well, dear Elyse, it would seem that you are right. There is a dead body in the room, and we can't seem to see it at all."

"Uh—just a minute—my brain's slowly creaking around to working again," Shiloh mumbled. Then he looked up and asked sharply, "Before I came, did Mrs. de Lancie give any reason at all? Did she say anything about *why* they'd broken it off?"

Richard still looked bewildered and worried, and he glanced at Irene. Uncertainly she replied, "Why, no, I don't think so. I think—as she said, she just started talking about returning the trunks, and then when she realized we didn't know about the broken engagement, she just said something like 'Dev and I have decided that we are not suited for marriage.'"

Shiloh frowned darkly.

"You know something about this, Shiloh?" Irene asked alertly.

"Ma'am? Oh—no, no, if you mean do I—I mean, did anyone tell me about it beforehand? Before now, I mean," he stammered. It was extremely difficult—impossible, it seemed—to prevaricate in front of Richard and Irene Duvall. Irene merely looked at him with patience and a sort of pained sympathy, but Richard's mild gray eyes suddenly grew alert. He said nothing, though he regarded Shiloh gravely.

"Aw, *malediction!*" Shiloh muttered under his breath, then plunged in. "It's just that…uh…it was pretty clear, wasn't it, who had thrown who over?"

He waited expectantly, but the only reply was from Tante Marye, who said faintly, "Whom."

"Whom? Oh yeah. Yes, ma'am. Sorry. Whom." Shiloh dropped his eyes for a moment, then lifted his gaze and said to Irene Duvall, "I'm sorry, ma'am. But I'm pretty sure that Dr. Buchanan must have been the one who canceled the engagement. Don't you think so?"

Faintly Irene whispered, "Yes, I'm afraid I do. Do you…do you by any chance, Shiloh, know why?"

"No, ma'am, I sure don't," Shiloh was able to say. He thought that the scene he'd witnessed at Bellevue—the dead person, the young girl, or the baby—might have had something to do with it, but beyond that he really had no idea what was the matter with Dr. Devlin Buchanan.

The door crashed again, open this time, and Cheney came rushing in. Her color was high; her eyes glittered; even her hair seemed to crackle. "Well, this is just horrible! Whatever can Dev be thinking? What's wrong with him? How could he do this to her? She loves him so much, and I know he's madly in love with her!"

"It happens, Doc," Shiloh said dryly.

"Oh—oh—men!" she snapped, stamping her foot. Unfortunately she stamped right on Shiloh's foot, and though he was wearing boots, she was wearing heeled shoes.

"Ow," he mumbled and tried to move his foot, but she was trying to move away, and she stumbled, and the next thing anyone knew, Shiloh was supporting her close in his arms.

She stared up at him, outraged, and he stared back down at her warily. "Well, how...how rude!" Cheney snapped, pushing him. He let her go so suddenly that she almost fell again.

"But you stepped on my foot," Shiloh began, then tried to recover. "Uh...sorry, Doc...Cheney...uh...Miss Irene," Shiloh said, utterly taken aback, his high cheekbones streaked with red, making the V scar underneath his eye etch itself in white.

"Yes," Elyse said with satisfaction, "this is just like that funny play."

Chapter Fourteen

The Wheel Spins

"It's a lovely choker," Mr. Worthington said politely. "But—opals, really. Odd choice, don't you think?"

Self-consciously Minette fingered the cold, smooth stone. "Whatever do you mean?"

"Opals. Surely you know they're considered unlucky," Bain said carelessly. "I'm a little superstitious myself. Wouldn't think of giving a lady opals."

"I'm not superstitious, Mr. Worthington," Minette said coolly.

"No, of course not," he replied vaguely, knowing full well that theater people were notoriously subject to fey beliefs in signs and portents. Settling into the new leather armchair more comfortably, he looked around. "Some nice things I've bought you, Miss York. But this cottage is so shabby. It does look like Mr. Irons-Winslow is in a position to offer to assist you with lodgings more suitable for a woman such as yourself."

It was a mild insult, of course, and before Minette

could catch herself she blurted out, "Mr. Irons-Winslow likes this house. And so do I."

Bain raised a sardonic eyebrow. "Does he, now? Odd, then, that he is staying in the most luxurious suite that the Fifth Avenue Hotel has to offer. How loyal you are, my dear."

Minette shifted restlessly and seemed to be about to make an angry retort, but then she flushed delicately and lowered her eyes.

"Well, then," Bain said briskly, "how is Mr. Irons-Winslow these days? What's on his mind?"

Still looking down, Minette said in a muffled voice, "Nothing much. We've been out so much lately, you see, that we really haven't had many intimate conversations."

"I'm surprised to hear that," Bain said evenly, "since you two have been, from the very first time you met, on such *intimate* terms."

Minette's head snapped up. Bain met her angry gaze with contempt, and again she could offer no self-defense. "I…I was about to have a cup of tea," she said lamely. "Would you care to join me?"

"Certainly, a little touch of home," he said, but his tone was bland, and his eyes suddenly had a faraway look.

Minette rose—almost jumped up—and went into the tiny kitchen. Homey sounds of water running and kettles clanging filtered clearly into the sitting room.

The little fool has fallen in love with him! Bain thought, his tawny brown eyes narrowing. *I knew it. I could see it coming, and now he's given her one stupid little trinket, and she's all gaga!*

Two days ago, when Bain had seen the necklace Shiloh had bought for Minette, he immediately knew he was going to lose his informant. His resentment against his cousin had kindled to an explosive mix of frustration, envy, and finally wrath. It wasn't that Bain was jealous of Minette York. He had never cared for kittenish, pliable young women. He preferred more sophistication, more self-confidence, more maturity. Though no hint of it had ever entered his conscious mind, somewhere in the murky depths Bain felt an attraction for Dr. Cheney Duvall. Even more obscurely, he had felt some stabs of resentment that she had obviously spurned his cousin Locke. Even as he hastily rechanneled his thoughts, a plan, a complex but workable plan loomed in his mind, fully formed and perfect. *Yes…yes! That way, I can fix that snotty female once and forever, and Locke won't be able to do a single thing about it! At least, not if Minette does her part. She's shaky, but surely she'll come around when she sees Locke for what he is. At least, I think she will—no, I'll make sure she will! That tawdry little actress is not going to take a high moral stance with me!* he told himself savagely. *Who does she think Locke is, anyway? Some saint? He's nothing but a scrub like the rest of us! How he can cast such an accursed shadow over me, I'll never know!* he raged silently.

Starting up out of the comfortable depths of the chair, he paced up and down in the small crowded room, his finely modeled features ugly with anger. *He marches into my life, wrecks it, takes over my family, all as if he's lord of the manor—and his women, and his uppity friends—how can life be so smooth for him? Everything comes easy to him, women fall in love with him, and men fawn over him. He's got uncanny luck in business, and I…I should have it all. I'm not the bastard son who's been nothing but a scraggly beggar. I'm the one who should—*

Suddenly a grimace of pain distorted Bain's face, and as if his bones no longer supported his frame, he collapsed into the chair. *I should be like him. That's what I was thinking. But I never will be. I can't be.* Slowly, like an old man, he leaned back and closed his eyes. "Odd," he whispered feebly. *I always thought Father was weak. I always had so much contempt for him, but now I'm beginning to understand. Perhaps he was as overshadowed by Uncle Rory as I am by Locke.*

He wallowed in self-pity for a few moments, then with quick, harsh movements pulled out his cigarette case and lit a cigarette, glowering down at the silver case. It wasn't nearly as fine as his gold monogrammed case, and it was all Locke's fault that he had had to furtively sneak around like some disgraced dog. Well, that was all about to end. He was going to ruin Locke Alan Winslow, and Minette York was going to help him do it.

She finally returned with a silver tea service, the delicious bergamot scent of Earl Grey wafting along with her. "I don't have any crumpets or scones," she said with an attempt at camaraderie. "But I do have this Rum Baba that Shi—I mean, that I have a weakness for. Will you have some?"

"No, and I've changed my mind. I don't care for tea," Bain said rudely. "I'll take some of that excellent brandy you've got over on the sideboard. You can afford it."

Wordlessly Minette rose, poured him a generous snifter of brandy, and returned to her seat. With great composure—yet her childlike face was curiously disturbed, as if the clear lines had been smudged—she poured herself tea and even managed to take a bite of the soggy rich pastry, though it almost choked her.

Taking a deep drink, Bain settled back in the armchair and propped his booted feet up insolently on the hassock. The aftermath of Bain's grim reverie was that he had lost patience with Minette, and he had no intention of coddling her delicate sensibilities. However, he knew she was no fool. She was shrewd and intuitive, and he had already carefully planned his management of her. Minette watched him warily.

"So you have nothing at all to tell me about Mr. Irons-Winslow, hmm?" he asked mildly.

"Well, nothing that would interest you, I'm sure, Mr. Worthington," she replied smoothly. Bain knew that she had taken advantage of tea-making time to prepare herself. "We generally only talk about light topics, fun things, such as the races in Central Park and our favorite games—he prefers poker and faro, while I'm mad for roulette. We talk about Shakespeare. He loves *Hamlet*. But lately we've been talking much about *King Lear*. I've even read some to him."

Bain's gaze grew sharp as he watched her, and incredulously he realized she was telling the truth. His cousin actually did have the most luscious actress in New York in the palm of his hand, and she'd been reading Shakespeare to him! For some reason, this angered Bain even more. His voice laden with malice, he said, "How very cozy! Too bad it's all coming to an end so soon, Miss York."

Her face drained of all color, and her eyes grew as round as silver dollars. "What...what do you mean?"

"I mean," he answered with maddening slowness, "that your little pretend domestic bliss will all be ending very soon. In three days, as a matter of fact, Mr. Irons-Winslow will be returning to his family properties in Hawaii. I have been made aware that he's booked on the SS *Blaze of Glory* to Aspinwall on the twenty-third. That is this coming Saturday, I believe?"

"That…that can't be true," she whispered, licking dry lips. "I don't believe you."

"Ah…he hasn't told you?" Bain asked with feigned distress. "Oh dear. What a gaffe. Still, Miss York, it is the truth. Has he not told you that the de Lancie-Buchanan wedding has been called off? It would seem that the couple has had second thoughts and have broken off their engagement. Evidently Mr. Irons-Winslow feels that he has no reason to stay in New York." He took a sip of the mellow old brandy.

"No reason? But he… I know… I was sure…" she stammered in a desperate half whisper.

Suddenly Bain Winslow knew what she was thinking and was furious with himself for not anticipating this. Still he managed to say carelessly, "Ah yes, the lovely young debutante, Miss Angelique Steen. Who knows? Perhaps they have come to an understanding. Perhaps not. Mr. Irons-Winslow seems to be making a quick get-away from all his entanglements, if you'll pardon the expression."

"I…I don't believe it," she repeated faintly. She looked ill.

"Why should I tell you such a lie?" he asked indolently. "Still, if you require proof—haven't you seen the morning papers?"

"I…I…" She seemed stunned, confused.

Impatiently Bain rose and went to the console table

by the door. "Here, I believe—yes, I did grab up a copy of the *Sun* on my way over here. See that article?"

Her eyes a misty, injured blue, Minette automatically took the paper and read the article in what was called in the impudent *Sun* the "High-Hat Society Section." The article was short and sly. It was about Victoria de Lancie having been seen at Mrs. Randolph Goelet's home for a late supper the previous evening, along with her parents, Mr. Henry Andrew Steen IV and Josefina Wilcott Steen. Conspicuously absent was Mrs. de Lancie's betrothed, the eminent Dr. Devlin Buchanan. The article smirked that it was odd Dr. Buchanan was not attending his betrothed so soon before the scheduled nuptials and particularly odd that he was not present at such an intimate supper at Mrs. Goelet's, considering that he had just been appointed as personal physician to the entire Goelet family. The article went on to cunningly suggest that readers keep an eye on the High-Hats in the de Lancie box at the Academy of Music on Friday night and see who was dancing attendance on Mrs. de Lancie under them. The *Sun* was wagering that Dr. Buchanan's dignified high hat wouldn't be there.

Bain watched as Minette read, digested, considered, fought, and finally surrendered. Her shoulders sagged, and she made a tiny noise, not quite a whimper. Bain took his seat and another sip of brandy, giving her time to wallow in her misery.

She cast the newspaper aside, crumpling it a little because she'd been holding it so tightly. With an awkwardness alien to Minette York she pushed herself out of the pretty chintz chair and went to stare out the window, her face frozen in a white mask.

"As I was saying, Mr. Irons-Winslow has no ties here,

thanks in part to our partnership, Miss York," Bain said with satisfaction, watching her profile. It was immutable, unmarked. She was a consummate actress, after all. "He hasn't managed to encroach upon my business connections—so far. But there is one last thing, and I'm going to need your so valuable assistance."

She swallowed, the only sign of any movement about her. "One last thing," she repeated hollowly. "And what is this one last thing, Mr. Worthington?"

I'm going to utterly ruin him, Miss York. I'm going to make him feel ashamed and guilty and inadequate for a change. I'm going to fix it so that he will never have any standing or credibility or good name—in New York, anyway. And while I'm at it, I'm going to ruin his hopes for any future happiness with that uppity busybody female doctor. I wonder, if I tell you this now, would you suddenly be eager to help me? After all, he has devastated you, too.

But Bain knew that Minette was not at that stage—not yet. Soon he knew that fury would replace the hurt. It was always like that with women like Minette. "Mr. Irons-Winslow has a meeting, a very consequential meeting, with some business contacts early Saturday morning."

She didn't turn around. "And?" she asked coldly.

"And I'll pay you well to make certain that Mr. Irons-Winslow is unable to attend that meeting."

She was silent. Bain waited and watched. The heavy-laden quiet went on and on.

After a very long while she took a deep, ragged breath, and Bain could see the corner of her pouty pink mouth lengthen into a deep slash. Still staring out the window with unseeing eyes, she said, "Very well, Mr. Worthington. But I have two questions."

"I ask the questions, Miss York. Remember?" Bain snapped.

"You will answer these questions," she stated in a faraway voice. "All I want to know is how? And how much?"

Bain smiled, though she never saw it. "Ah yes, of course. Right down to business. That's what I like about you, Miss York. I'll explain to you later how you will do this little favor for me. And since we've done so well together and you've been so helpful to me, I'm prepared to pay you one hundred dollars for this last little task."

"You'll pay me five hundred," she said, still in that careless, weary tone.

He eyed her, weighed her. "Five hundred dollars, Miss York. Half before, half after."

She said not another word. The roulette wheel was spinning.

Part Four
Sound Words

Hold fast the form of sound words....

—2 Timothy 1:13

Chapter Fifteen

Props in the Play

"Farewell and adieu, you fair Spanish ladies. Farewell and adieu, you ladies of Spain…."

What Shiloh lacked in voice he made up for in enthusiasm. Giggling, Minette implored him, "Shiloh, you'll wake up the neighbors, not to mention every dog in the city." Down the deserted street a deep-throated howl had joined Shiloh's serenade.

"You don't like my singing," he said mournfully as he gallantly unlocked the door, then stood aside for her to enter.

"The dog does."

"Yeah, he does. Maybe I should go to his house instead."

"Come in this instant. It's freezing out here, and it's starting to rain."

"It is? It is. Lovely spring we're having in this stinkin' town."

Minette glanced up at his face sharply. It was cold,

distant, though his tone was light. "All cities," she pronounced grandly, "emit a stench."

"'Specially New York," Shiloh grumbled. He began
whistling the song again between clenched teeth as they
went through the complicated process of shedding and
storing cloaks, hats, gloves.

Minette gave him a calculating sidelong look. Shiloh's
eyes glittered, his color was high, and all that night his
conversation had been of no substance but was liberally
spiked with barbed humor about everyone and everything.

*He still hasn't seen fit to tell me he's leaving. Maybe
that stupid old sailor's song is his way of saying good-
bye, the scrub! What's he going to do? Just disappear
without a word?* Every instinct that Minette had about
Shiloh belied this, but she couldn't help but believe Mr.
Worthington. Victoria de Lancie and Devlin Buchanan
had, indeed, called off the wedding. Though it still had
not been publicly announced, Victoria's younger brother,
Beckett Steen, had been talking about it all night as the
Fine and Dandies and their ladies had gone to Niblo's
Garden and then Delmonico's and then Morrissey's.
Shiloh had refused to say a single word about it.

And then there was the fact that the SS *Blaze of Glory*
was indeed sailing tomorrow on the evening tide—Minette had checked the *Herald.* Shiloh had been in rare
form tonight, laughing uproariously at *The Black Crook,*
drinking prodigiously, eating little, gambling outrageously. He had even bought her a bottle of White Star
at Niblo's.

He had also bought her two dozen lilies from a street
vendor with some comment about "pure ladies and pure
lilies," though Minette knew he was not thinking of her.

For some reason he had offered the huge bouquet to Dr. Cleve Batson and had asked him if he'd wanted a bite of two to hold him over before their late supper at Delmonico's, which Dr. Batson stiffly declined. Minette only now recalled that she'd left the flowers at Morrissey's and hoped Shiloh wouldn't realize it. Regardless of his motives, it was a gift, and Minette was the type of woman who thought it very bad form to be ungrateful. But then she reflected that Shiloh had forgotten all about the flowers. She really had no idea where his mind was, but she was certain he was not filled with thoughts about her. She, like the flowers, seemed to be merely a prop in his own private play. With a wrench she reminded herself that probably this was the farewell scene; only he had not seen fit to tell her that.

"Why don't you build up the fire?" she asked, bustling into the sitting room with its dark hearth. "I'm going to have a brandy. I'm positively shivering. Will you join me?"

"Of course, my lady," he said absently, poking at the ashes. He found a secret little cache of live cinders and fed it tiny bits of kindling until it fired. Then he skillfully piled on a pyramid of small logs and placed one big fat one on top.

She glided softly to him, her hair a pale shimmer in the gloom, her eyes huge and dark. She held the brandy snifters close, but didn't hand one to Shiloh as he straightened and reached out for it. He looked at her, his eyebrows raised. "Am I?" she asked softly.

"I beg your pardon?" he said with blank politeness.

"Am I?" she repeated in a whisper so low he could barely hear her. "Am I...your lady?"

He made a mocking half bow, placing his strong,

scarred hand on his chest. "M'lady, I remain, as always, your faithful servant. Now may I have my brandy?"

Her eyes narrowed and her mouth tightened, but since Shiloh was not himself at all, he could neither see nor feel her bitterness. Without a word she held the snifter out to him, and by the time he'd settled down in the chair, her childish features were again soft and pleasing. She stood over him irresolutely for a moment, but then he tossed back fully half the brandy in a gulp, and she settled down in the chair opposite him, sipping slowly, her eyes watchful over the rim of the glass.

"Good brandy," he said with satisfaction, propping his feet up on the hassock. "I'm glad you finally quit buying that putrid raspberry gin, or whatever it was."

"Parsnip wine," she said rather automatically. Abruptly she knelt and started tugging on his right boot. "Here, Shiloh, your boots are muddying up my cushion. Let me take them off."

"Okay," he said lazily, taking another stiff gulp of his brandy. "Wouldn't wanna dirty up your nice cushions."

She struggled to get the tight boots off, looking up at him and smiling brightly. She saw he was studying her owlishly. Then he raised his glass and polished off the last of his brandy. "Such lovely boots, and they are so very wet, my dear," she twittered, wrestling now with the left one. "Mustn't put them too near the fire, though, for it has a tendency to crack fine leather if the heat is—" With a jerk the boot came off, and Minette sat down hard and fast. She looked up at him with the beginnings of a giggle, but it died on her lips.

He was staring down into his glass at the dregs of the brandy. Very slowly he raised his eyes to her. They were heavy lidded and dull, but still they glittered ominously.

"You drugged me," he said in a dangerously low, calm tone. "Why?"

She stared at him and felt the blood rush from her face, leaving her lips cold and dry. He stared back at her with such contempt that she could neither move nor speak. Both of them were motionless, Minette still sprawled awkwardly on the floor grasping Shiloh's boot, while his powerful body seemed to be melted into the soft leather of the chair.

One of the logs shifted, throwing a shower of hot sparks onto the hearth. Shiloh jumped up, his face a mask of rage. He brought one hand up to his forehead, slowly, awkwardly. Then, as if his bones were watery, he folded and collapsed back into the chair. "Drugged me…" he mumbled, as if he were trying to remember.

"N-no…I…no…" she breathed raggedly, making a curiously clumsy wave of negation.

He raised his head and looked as if he could barely see her. Certainly he spoke with great effort, as if something heavy lay on his chest. "Drugged me…for what? Steal my wallet? Never woulda thought you…"

Like a bear who had been stung, he shook his head slowly, then reached over and got his boot, which Minette had propped against the hassock. Minette watched as if she were mesmerized as he pulled it on, then held out his hand for the other. Like a puppet she handed it to him. He drew it on—it took a long time—then, pushing himself against the chair, he stood and began to walk toward the door. He weaved back and forth, and once he stopped midstride, his hand reaching out blindly, obviously trying to keep his balance. She heard a ragged gasp, a long, keen breath drawn in, and he straightened his shoulders and seemed to walk with more confidence.

Only when he'd reached the door and was fumbling to put on his greatcoat was Minette able to move.

"No, Shiloh, please, no. Don't go," she wailed, scrambling up and running to him. She tried to throw herself against him, but in spite of his slow, oddly languorous movements, he managed to push her solidly away.

"Get away from me," he said slowly and distinctly. "For your own good, Minette. Don't touch me."

"No, Shiloh, you can't leave! Please—I can explain, but you…you…no, you can't. You can't go like this—" She was grasping at his coat, pulling at it with all her strength. With a suddenness that threw her back a step, he stopped trying to get into it and shoved it into her hands.

"You want it? You can have it. My hat and gloves and stick, too. Hope y'all live happily ever after." He opened the door, felt his way through it, and slammed it viciously behind him.

She flung it open to run after him, but he had only made one cautious step onto the porch. He looked back at her, and his face was so savage that she flinched as if he'd struck her. Without a word he turned and staggered down the walk, onto the sidewalk, and down the street. Minette stood watching him, her eyes wide with shock. And then the tears started burning, and a great fiery lump rose in her throat. She could feel her heart hammering like a timpani in her chest, hard and doleful. With a great choking sob she turned and fled back into the house. She fell into his armchair, grasping his greatcoat and burying her face in it. It smelled of cigars and Royal Lyme and the scrubbed smell of carbolic soap, and then it began to smell of wet wool, for Minette's tears soaked it through and through.

* * *

"The door is standing wide open, you stupid little fool."

Minette raised her tear-ravaged face. She hadn't heard Denys Worthington come in. She barely heard his cold, crisp voice. She just stared at him dully, then fell back, still holding Shiloh's coat.

Bain Winslow perused her, and the coat, then whirled, cursing, and stamped into her bedroom. He came back out, stopped at the console table that held the brandy, poured himself a drink, and with geometric precision seated himself across from her. "He's not here," he said with a razor's edge to his voice. "Where is he?"

"I don't know," Minette answered, almost choking, and a single diamond teardrop traced her cheek.

Even in his anger, one part of Bain's mind catalogued that Minette was the type of woman who looked lovely and vulnerable when she cried. Her eyes were lustrous, her face pale and soft, her lashes velvety smudges.

"He…he…was here, but…but…" Weeping overcame her again, and she drooped like a wilting flower.

"Get hold of yourself," Bain harshly ordered her. "You're hardly some swooning young maiden. He was here? Did you give him the powder?"

"I…I…" She roused herself and considered him with a dawning suspicion. Nervously she asked, "What are you doing here, Mr. Worthington? I thought the plan was for Shiloh to pass out and stay asleep until the late afternoon. Why should you be here?"

"How dare you question me?" Bain retorted ominously. "Once again—for the last time—did you drug him?"

She swallowed hard. "Yes, I gave him the powder in a snifter of brandy."

"All of it?"

"Yes."

"And?"

"He...he didn't just go to sleep as you said he would," Minette said brokenly. "He knew I'd drugged him. He thought I wanted to steal his money." She sagged hopelessly again, obsessively worrying Shiloh's coat between her fingers.

Bain's sharp eyes narrowed to cold slits. "You said nothing about me, of course."

"No. I was so horrified that he—that I could say nothing. Nothing at all."

She was so openly grieved that Bain believed her. He relaxed just a little. "Then what happened?"

"He left. He just...left."

"He left," Bain repeated sharply. "What do you mean, he left? Did he have a carriage? A horse?"

"He...just walked off."

"Where?"

"He...he was walking so slowly, and it's so cold...and it's still raining, isn't it? He...he wasn't even going toward town...."

"He went that way? Toward the docks?" Bain asked sharply.

"I...I don't know—"

"Answer me," Bain said, leaning forward, his tone ugly. "Did he go in that direction?" He pointed.

"Yes. He was just staggering... I have to..." She stared down at his coat. "He could freeze to death if he passes out, couldn't he? We have to—" She started to rise, but Bain moved so quickly she never even saw him coming. Now he was behind her, pushing her back into the chair with a hand like cold steel on her shoulder.

"Sit down. You'll do no such thing. With his luck, the mayor or the chief of police will probably pick him up," Bain growled. "I can't believe you snarled this up, you little fool." He leaned over her, and she drew away, dropping her head.

"I don't care what you do to me," she whispered. "It doesn't matter anymore."

"Do to you?" he repeated. "Do to you? May I remind you that I have done nothing to you at all except pay you certain sums of money. And that is what your gentlemen callers do, isn't it? You, on the other hand, have committed a criminal act, Miss York. You have drugged a man, robbed him, and possibly intended to harm him."

Her head jerked up. "That's a horrible, beastly lie! All lies!"

"Oh? Clearly all the evidence points to it as the truth," he said icily from behind her, a gritty mutter in her ear. "Mr. Irons-Winslow certainly saw it that way."

The realization of her position—her horrid predicament—came over her slowly, as the shadows grow longer and blacker when the sun sets. Her stomach began to roll with nausea, but it was nothing compared to the acid loathing she felt for herself and for this man who had entangled her in such a malignant maze. She watched him, her head craning back, as he slowly straightened and moved into the shadows behind the chair—Shiloh's chair. Tears began rolling down her face again, but Minette paid no heed. The man behind her paced back and forth like an imprisoned wildcat.

"It's not too late," he said with finality—to the air, it appeared. Now purposefully he went to the sideboard, refilled his snifter with an obscene amount of brandy, and sat down again. "It's not too late, Miss York. Both you and I can have our revenge. I can even make it profitable for you."

"I…I don't understand," Minette sobbed.

"It's very simple," Bain said, leaning back and sipping his brandy as if he were holding forth at a fine gentlemen's club. "Tomorrow you will tell the newspapers that Mr. Irons-Winslow improperly importuned you, and then, when you didn't comply, he beat you. When you do this, I will pay you the other two hundred and fifty dollars. I will even pay your passage back to London."

"Tell them Shiloh beat me?" Minette repeated incredulously. "And leave New York? Are you insane?"

"No, I am not!" Bain roared, his face turning almost purple with rage. "Be careful what you say to me, Miss York. After all, tomorrow you may be lucky to be talking only with journalists. As we have already discussed, you have drugged Mr. Irons-Winslow and robbed him. He could easily have you arrested, and considering the kind of woman you are, you wouldn't have a prayer of getting off without some prison time. Unless…"

Now he leaned forward, his voice as rough as if the words were grit between his teeth. "Unless we ruin him. Unless he is seen by his uppity friends as base and crude and offensive. He's going to utterly ruin you, you know, Miss York. Aside from the fact that he's treated you like a cheap whore, now he'll probably have you imprisoned."

"No, no—it's— It won't work!" Minette was beginning to be afraid. The glitter in Bain's narrowed eyes, the way his words whistled as if with malice between his teeth, his fist clenched so tightly around his cane it looked as if he might splinter it—this man was dangerous. Minette swallowed hard and managed to speak with a semblance of calm. "For one thing, obviously I'm not injured, and—"

Bain whirled his cane in a tight arc. "That could be arranged," he whispered.

She watched him, horrified.

He stared at her with eyes narrowed to tiny slits.

Minette thought she should run. But her legs were treacherously weak, and she couldn't catch her breath.

And after all, there was nowhere to run. She was trapped. She had gambled and lost it all on one spin of the wheel.

Tiredly Minette dropped her head and again brought Shiloh's coat up to her face and breathed deeply. "I won't do it, Mr. Worthington," she said quietly.

The drawn-out moments of silence seemed to last beyond forever to Minette. Then there was an enormous crash, but Minette was so drained she didn't even start. Bain had thrown his cane across the room and broken her hall mirror. She heard him now, his breath fast and savage.

Suddenly he laughed, a coarse coughing sound, and she did look up at him then.

"I should have killed him the first day he showed up," he grated, still with the parody of laughter etched in deep lines on his face. "But I couldn't. Oh no, I couldn't do that, not for all my big talk to my mother and my big thoughts and my big dreams. And now here are my big plans in shabby little rags and tatters again—and it's all Locke's fault!"

"Who *are* you?" Minette asked shakily.

"You have no idea, and you never will, my dear. But it doesn't really matter anyway, because I am nobody, nothing. As are you, Miss York. We're two of a kind. Losers. Both losers."

His normally crisp tones were slightly slurred, and he had lost much of his usual masculine grace, pulling on his gloves with some difficulty. "Yes, we are two people who are just so much flotsam and jetsam tossing around in my brother's wake. Unfortunately—for you, I mean—"

"Brother?" Minette repeated numbly.

But Bain continued with his impetuous, half-drunk monologue, unheeding. "...after all, you have no possible defense for what you've done tonight. And now I know I'm beaten, too, but I can still run, as I've done before. But still, I'll see Locke destroyed, shamed, ridiculed. Then he'll know what he's done to me, how it feels to have everything snatched away from you, a living nightmare. I'll fix that nosy, uppity female, too! She'll be lucky if she's not tarred and feathered. And certainly Locke won't ever be able to look at her again with anything but disgust. Then he can wander the world with everything he ever cared about snatched—"

He seemed to recover himself and stopped talking. He gave Minette a cunning, assessing look. She stared back at him, obviously uncomprehending. With deliberation he put on his fine silk top hat and threw his coat over his shoulders. He seemed to come to a decision. "I must take my leave of you now, Miss York," he said with a mocking bow. "I don't expect we'll meet again."

He left, picking up his stick on the way out and handling it as jauntily as if he were promenading in Central Park.

Minette, staring after him, felt sore, bruised, as if he had really beaten her. She sat motionless, limp, for a long time, her eyes unseeing. Then like a startled cat she jumped out of the chair, dropped Shiloh's cloak, and ran into the kitchen. There, on the tiny wooden table was yesterday's newspaper. Grabbing it, she hurried back into the sitting room, bending over so that she could read by the firelight. Her hands shaking, she ruffled through the pages, stopped, read. Then she grabbed her cloak and reticule and ran out the door.

Chapter Sixteen

Dark and Falling

"How are we going to hide the body?" Nia asked in a conspiratorial whisper.

Over the rim of her teacup, Cheney's eyes narrowed, the low light giving them a villainous glitter. Then she sang a tuneless dirge.

"A pick-axe, and a spade, a spade,
For a shrouding sheet:
O, a pit of clay for to be made
For such a guest is meet."

"That there's some more of that Hamlet's nonsense, isn't it?" Nia scoffed.

Amused, Cheney replied, "Actually it's sung by a character called First Clown, who was a sexton. Speaking of such, the morticians Brown and Carruthers are coming by in the morning to pick up the body."

"You and Mr. Irons-Winslow talking in Shakespeare

all the time—I declare, no one can understand a word you're saying," Nia grumbled. "All the talk I ever hear these days, seems like, is about Hamlet and Ophelia."

Cheney's face fell. For the last several days the penny dailies had been going on and on about the romance between Prince Hamlet of Fine and Dandy and Ophelia. They were talking about Shiloh and Minette York, of course. Evidently Shiloh was spending a lot of time with the actress, for the *Sun* reported on them being seen on the Ladies' Mile, in restaurants, theaters, playhouses. The *Sun* had even intimated in one article that Angelique Lyra Steen was rumored to have said something cutting to Mr. Irons-Winslow—in public—about tawdry actresses, and Mr. Irons-Winslow was reported to have rather quickly taken his leave of Miss Steen. That had amused Cheney in a piercing, painful kind of way. She knew, even if Miss Angelique Steen did not, that Mr. Irons-Winslow would defend even a tawdry actress's honor. Just as he defended vulgar female physicians.

Dr. Batson, when taking his leave of them early that evening, had told them that he and some friends were going out on the town. Cheney knew that was his polite little euphemism for the Fine and Dandies strutting around with their actresses, Shiloh and Minette York included, of course. Cheney sighed, an audible sound of hurt longing.

Cheney was strong though, and slowly she had learned that when she allowed the Lord to bear this burden of grief, she found a measure of peace. As she had determined, the way to do this was to pray for Shiloh when he, and especially his foolish behavior, loomed large in her mind. This discipline had not come easily to Cheney, but as all men and women of God down through the ages had learned, trusting in the Lord implicitly was a process, and usually a slow one.

Now, as visions of Shiloh and Angelique, Shiloh and Minette, Shiloh flushed with whiskey, and Shiloh in drunken brawls at Morrissey's stalked through her mind, Cheney helplessly fought back tears and prayed fervently. *Lord, I know that he's running, that he's searching for something to heal his hurt, for, Lord, I know that he's just as hurt and frightened as I.... But I know, too, Lord, that You are my fortress, You are my strong tower, and Shiloh has nowhere to hide. Speak to him, Lord Jesus, watch over him, show him that with You and You alone will he find peace and a love that passeth all understanding....*

Nia watched Cheney, the distant hurt and worry in her eyes, and knew exactly what she was thinking. She'd known and loved Cheney all her life, but it had always been a distant sort of heroine worship. Nia was younger than Cheney, and Nia's sisters, Tansy and especially Rissy, had always been closest to her. Nia felt helpless, for she didn't know how to talk to Cheney, how to help her. She had never known how, and truth to tell, she would never put herself forward in such a way.

Cheney wandered in her sad thoughts. She missed Rissy, Nia's sister. Cheney might not have confided openly and freely to Rissy about her hurt over Shiloh, but Rissy would have known how to comfort her. Cheney couldn't really confide in anyone, and she sighed, thinking of Victoria. Victoria, too, seemed imprisoned by her grief. She flatly refused to discuss Dev with Cheney, and of course Cheney wouldn't burden Victoria with her troubles with Shiloh. Shiloh and Cheney's break seemed rather inconsequential compared with Victoria and Dev's breakup. Everyone in New York appeared to be gossiping about that.

Finally Nia asked softly, "Miss Cheney, why don't we go on home? It's so late. I'm tired to death, and you must be, too."

With obvious effort Cheney gathered her thoughts. "No, not yet, Nia. I still haven't documented the Forbes file, and I simply must do it tonight while it's still fresh in my mind. But you go ahead and lie down on the couch and nap awhile, Nia. I know you're tired. After all, you did all of the hard work." Cheney and Nia had just dissected a human body. It was Nia's first dissection, and that was always the most difficult.

"It was hard work, that's for sure," Nia said raggedly, passing a tiny hand over her brow.

Cheney studied her. "You know, Nia, you did very well."

"I did?" Nia brightened. "But I—you know I was sick."

"Only at first. At my first dissection, I vomited twice and finally fainted," Cheney declared.

Nia's eyes grew huge and round. "You didn't! But you're so easy, so kiss-my-hand about it now!"

"Now," Cheney repeated ironically. "But I wasn't always that way. You see, Nia, I had to discipline myself not to think about the person, the human being, on the table, because as Christians, you and I know that God's breath of life—the spirit—no longer inhabits that vessel. Now it is, for us, a tool.

"A dissection is one of the most valuable tools you have to learn about the human body, how it works, why it works as it does, and what happens when something goes wrong. Nothing—no book, no teacher, not even years of experience can give you the same insight into the very basis of the science of medicine. Once you have learned this science, you can combine it with compassion to give your patients the most knowledgeable and most sympathetic care possible."

Nia's eyes shone. "When you talk that way, Miss Cheney, I can see the nobility in wanting to be a physician."

"It is a noble profession," Cheney agreed.

Nia responded slyly, "Kinda hard to believe you can feel noble 'bout stealin' dead bodies and cuttin' them up."

Cheney laughed. "You're already learning. Humor helps, too, although not everyone can appreciate our little jokes. And by the way, I didn't steal that body. Dev did."

"He did? But Dr. Buchanan's so…so proper like!"

A shadow crossed Cheney's face, and her weariness returned. "Oh, he didn't actually steal it, Nia. That poor girl died at City Hospital this morning, and Dev has privileges there. You see, Dr. Lyman Banckert, a German neurosurgeon and psychiatrist, was doing a brain dissection along with a lecture on psychiatry today. I wanted us to attend, for Dr. Banckert is one of the foremost experts in both fields. But no women are allowed, not at City Hospital, not even for Dr. Devlin Buchanan, though he did try. So Dev offered to get us a specimen. He knew you'd never done a dissection nor had ever seen one."

Nia said with weary humor, "I'll be sure and thank him for the gift." She yawned, though she tried very hard to stifle it.

"Why don't you go lie down on the couch, Nia, and

nap until I get finished?" Cheney said, rousing herself with an effort. "I'll be about another hour, I expect."

By now Nia could barely keep her eyes open, and her body ached with fatigue and strain. "I don't know how you do it, Miss Cheney. I've just got to rest." She curled up on the couch in Cheney's office.

Cheney watched her affectionately until she fell asleep, which took only a few minutes. Then Cheney covered her with a blanket and got out the file on Mrs. Mason Brackett Forbes. Mrs. Forbes was expecting again, and Cheney wondered how spoiled little Annalea Forbes was going to handle it. Misty-eyed, she thought back to the Vanderbilts' party that wonderful summer when she and Shiloh had saved Annalea Forbes's life....

Cheney thought that there was a fire, because she could hear the shrill, insistent jangling of the fire engine's bells. With vague irritation she wished they would stop ringing the bells; it was waking her up.

Jerking, she sat up, wide-eyed. She had fallen asleep at her desk, and the front doorbell was ringing, shockingly loud in the quiet night. She stumbled to her feet, glancing at Nia, who moved restlessly but did not wake up.

Cheney wasn't a woman who was afraid of calls in the night. She'd answered many of them. But neither was she foolish. Cautiously she looked out the window by the door. A man stood on the porch holding a lantern. He was a big man, thickly built and strong looking, in workman's clothes. There was a woman, too, or perhaps she was a young girl. It was difficult to tell in the dim lantern light. She was dark skinned, but not a Negro, well dressed in a neat and plain dark dress with a clean apron and a thick black shawl. She wore a maid's mobcap. The girl caught sight of Cheney's face at the window and called out, "Dr. Duvall? Please, we need your help."

She had a rich husky voice with a lilting accent that Cheney couldn't place. "Are you…are you ill? Is someone hurt?" Cheney asked, fighting the sleep cobwebs that still entangled her.

The girl came to the window and spoke loudly, looking Cheney directly in the eye. She seemed worried, but she spoke calmly. "I'm the third maid of Mrs. Randolph Goelet. She has fallen ill quite suddenly."

Cheney suddenly felt a little silly shouting at the woman through the window. She felt for the key—the sitting room was completely dark—and opened the door. "My partner, Dr. Buchanan, is Mrs. Goelet's physician, and he is not here," Cheney said. "He's probably at home. Didn't Mrs. Goelet have his home address?"

"Perhaps, but she is too ill to answer questions. Will you come, please, Dr. Duvall?" the girl pleaded. "It is not far. Just up on West Thirty-sixth Street."

Cheney knew the Goelet mansion. It was, as a matter of fact, not far from Victoria's home, which was on Fifth Avenue and West Thirty-fifth. And this girl, though she had an unusual accent and was uncommonly pretty for a third maid, did have the deprecating mien that Cheney was accustomed to in servants.

Still, something about the man bothered Cheney. He didn't frighten her exactly. It was more that he seemed so aloof, so removed. His face was utterly without expression, as if he weren't a part of the scene. He met Cheney's eyes, and there was neither subservience nor disdain nor wariness in his face. It was as if he were looking at a painting of someone he did not know.

Quickly the young girl said, "Dr. Duvall, this is

Rickets, one of the stablemen. He is younger and quicker than the coachman, and we are in such a hurry for my poor lady. She may be dying."

Decisively Cheney said, "All right, of course I'll come. Wait here while I get my bag and cloak." It was freezing cold, and the beginnings of a hard rain had started spattering the steps and walk.

She hurried back into her office and grabbed a heavy wool cloak and her bag, which she always kept well stocked and in order. Hesitating, she considered Nia. *No need to wake her. I'll probably be at Mrs. Goelet's for the rest of the night. I'll just let her sleep.* Nia was tossing restlessly and even mumbling a little, but Cheney was very quiet, tiptoeing out and closing the door soundlessly behind her.

"I'm ready. Go on. Just let me lock up," she told the two. They went on to the carriage while Cheney locked the door and pocketed the key, reflecting that Nia was locked in now, but Cheney's keys were in the house somewhere, in her reticule. Nia would know better than Cheney exactly where her reticule was. In any case, Nia probably wouldn't awaken before morning.

Cheney ran to the carriage, a little surprised that Rickets and the maid were still standing out in the cold rain by the open carriage door. As she reached them she muttered, "Good heavens, what a foul night."

The maid grinned, and it disconcerted Cheney, for it was almost a sneer.

"Now, Sweet," the young girl said in a conversational tone.

Cheney thought in confusion, *Now sweet, now sweet. What does that—*

The man grabbed Cheney's arms, locking them behind

her at the elbows. Cheney dropped her bag, and because she was and had always been quick, she immediately started trying to stamp the man's feet, grunting with exertion.

The maid stepped up, and Cheney started kicking. She connected with something, and the maid cursed, a gutter oath. "You'll pay for that, my fine lady," she snarled. "Hold her, Sweet, can't you?"

"Let me go," Cheney panted, still kicking.

"You wanted to do it by yourself in the carriage, Oona," the man said in a curiously toneless voice. "See, you need my help."

The girl cursed again, then stepped up, dancing between Cheney's kicking heels, and grabbed her by the hair, yanking hard. Then she slammed a cloth against Cheney's mouth and nose.

The reek burned her face, made her cough, made her eyes instantly start squirting painful salty tears.

She only had time for a few little faraway thoughts—small and seemingly disconnected from her, unimportant things—before she passed out.

Cold, so cold, rain...sleet...

Dark and falling...

Shiloh—

Chapter Seventeen

Of Strong Constitution

The steward, splendid in white tie and tails, bent sub-serviently over Victoria de Lancie, murmuring an abject apology for disturbing her. Victoria started, then stared up at the man's worry-lined face. "It's quite all right, Fitchley. What is it?" she whispered as quietly as she could over the music. Her box at the Academy of Music was full, and right beside her the ancient and venerable Mrs. Randolph Goelet was casting dagger glances at Fitchley while trying not to look as if she were eaves-dropping.

He handed Victoria a calling card and mumbled right against her ear, "The lady insists upon seeing you, Mrs. de Lancie. She said to tell you it's an emergency."

Victoria stared down: *Miss Minette York*. It was a silly card with little naked cupids in the corners entwined in red roses. "Very well, Fitchley, tell her to come in."

"She begs most despairingly that you will come down-stairs to meet her, madam," Fitchley said in an agony of embarrassment.

"But—" Mindful of Mrs. Goelet's sharp tongue and equally sharp ears, Victoria rose. "Very well, Fitchley. Let us leave my guests in peace with Corelli."

The meek steward trailed after Victoria as she swept down the grand staircase. Minette York, a slight shadow in a gray mantle with the hood pulled close, fidgeted nervously by the doors. Victoria walked up to her, but before she could say a word the girl burst out, "Mrs. de Lancie, I'm in so much trouble, and so is Mr. Irons-Winslow, and I know he's your friend, and I...I simply couldn't think of anyone else to...to—"

Victoria interrupted her sternly. "One moment. Fitchley? Miss York is very cold and wet. Is there somewhere warm where we can sit down and talk?"

"Yes, Mrs. de Lancie, of course. If you'll just step this way, you are welcome to come into Mr. Kingston's office. He is attending the performance." The steward fussed and fidgeted, but Victoria managed to firmly shoo him out and close the door behind him.

They seated themselves on two uncomfortable chairs—Victoria stiffly, Minette wearily, as if she could hardly hold herself up. "Speak slowly and clearly, please, Miss York. And do begin at the beginning," Victoria said crisply.

"Yes, of course," Minette said with some effort. "I am a friend of Mr. Irons-Winslow, Mrs. de Lancie. He is in some...trouble. And...and I'm afraid that this trouble may also involve your cousin, Miss Angelique Steen." She stopped, obviously at a loss.

Victoria prodded her, "If I am to help you, I must know exactly what this trouble is. That means you must tell me the truth, Miss York. All of it."

Minette passed her hand over her eyes as if she were

trying to wipe something away, then recited in an emotionless tone, "Mr. Irons-Winslow was at my house tonight. I drugged him. My...my accomplice in this plot had assured me that he would simply go to sleep and sleep for many hours. But either the dosage was too small, or Mr. Irons-Winslow is of such a strong constitution that the drug did not act as we expected. It seemed to disorient him, but he certainly was not on the verge of passing out. He...he left my house."

Victoria stared at her, disbelieving. Minette went on weakly, "He didn't take his coat or hat...and I-I'm not certain about the effects of the drug. I'm frightened that he might just pass out. It's so cold tonight...and the rain... the rain is turning to sleet."

"Stop," Victoria snapped. "You're telling me that he left your house drugged, alone, and on foot?"

"Yes, madam, I'm afraid so," Minette said bleakly. "And I don't know where he is."

Victoria sat, her back as straight as a ruler, her head held high, her eyes unseeing as thoughts began to dart back and forth in her head. Minette waited helplessly, watching her. Finally Victoria demanded, "This drug— do you know what it was?"

"No, madam."

"What form was it?"

"Powder. White powder. I dissolved it in brandy."

Now Victoria turned the full force of her crystalline gaze on her, and Minette shrank back. "You say you had an accomplice. Did you two do this to rob Mr. Irons-Winslow?"

"No, madam! I—it's very difficult to explain, but I... never meant—"

"Stop that, Miss York," Victoria admonished her, not

unkindly. "Having hysterics now will do no one any good. Just tell me. Quickly, and in the simplest manner."

Minette nodded and managed, with very little faltering, to tell Victoria about her "partnership" with Denys Worthington, and why he had wanted her to drug Shiloh that night. She even related, in a low, painful whisper, why she was willing to do such a terrible thing to Shiloh.

Her head was bowed, so she couldn't see the clear, strong compassion on Victoria's face. Victoria, too, had once made a fool of herself over a man, and in those dark times of her life she never would have had Minette York's courage to go to a stranger, someone who, most likely, would treat her with utter disdain, if not outright disgust. Theoretically, and quite possibly, for all this poor girl knew, Victoria would have her arrested.

But for all her faults, Victoria had never been a hypocrite, and now she only felt sorry for this heartbroken girl. "It's not true, you know," she said quietly.

"What?" Minette asked, raising her head.

"He's not leaving tomorrow," Victoria said gently. "He wouldn't do that. He would never treat anyone so shabbily. Such cruelty isn't in him."

Minette stared at her, stricken, and Victoria thought she might out into a storm of sobs. But Minette only nodded a little. "I know. I always knew. I just…was afraid."

"Yes, I know," Victoria said. "Now you must tell me all about this Mr. Worthington, and why you think he may do something to harm Angelique."

Minette told her about Mr. Worthington's diatribe. "He was half drunk, I think, and he went on so. It didn't make any sense, really. I…I suddenly found myself concerned for his sanity. I mean, what was he going to do? He wasn't supposed to come to my house tonight, but there he was. Could it be that he was intending to… to harm Shiloh? He was talking about his brother, and I couldn't understand why, but then I realized he was still talking about Shiloh. He couldn't be his brother, could he? Not really, I mean."

"His brother?" Victoria said alertly. "He called Shiloh his brother?"

"Yes, and he kept calling him by some other name, something unusual—what was it?"

"Was it Locke?"

"Why, yes. That was it. He kept on talking about how he would make Locke pay, how he would ruin him, shame him—and about the woman he loved," Minette said sorrowfully.

"He said that?" Victoria said sharply. "He said he would ruin the woman he loved?"

"Yes. He said he'd ruin that…that…uppity female," Minette said, embarrassed. "And I—you see, I know that Mr. Irons-Winslow is in love with your cousin, madam."

"You do? Mr. Irons-Winslow has told you that?"

"No, of course not," Minette said desolately. "He knows I'm in love with him. He wouldn't be so cruel to me. But I just know. I've always known that he's in love with someone else. Of course it's your cousin, isn't it?"

Though Victoria sympathized with Minette York, she had no illusions about her, and in any case she would never discuss Shiloh's personal life with anyone. Sternly she said, "This is very important, Miss York. Did Mr. Worthington ever, at any time, mention my cousin by name? Did he make any direct reference to her at all?"

Minette thought for long moments, chewing on her plump bottom lip. "No…no. Never."

Victoria nodded. "Tell me where you live and where you last saw Mr. Irons-Winslow. Also, if you have Mr. Worthington's address or any information about him, I must know."

Minette gave Victoria her address and the name of the street Shiloh had walked down. "He was going in a southerly direction. And as for Mr. Worthington, I brought his card. He lives in Gramercy Park, you see."

"Does he?" Victoria said coolly, studying the card. Dev lived in Gramercy Park.

Minette was stammering, her pale cheeks coloring a little. "But…but…Mrs. de Lancie—Mr. Worthington— I happen to know that he—"

"Just say it, Miss York."

She took a deep breath and averted her eyes. "He owns a house of…with…that is to say, a house—"

"A brothel," Victoria supplied with some amusement. "I have heard of them, Miss York."

"Yes," Minette said with relief. "It's called Sweet's House of Exotic Island Princesses. I don't know where it is. It's not common knowledge that he's the owner of it, but I hear talk around town."

Denys Worthington was hot backstage gossip because of his connections with many of the higher society men in town, and someone had connected him with the brothel. Minette had, in fact, heard Victoria's own brother Beckett one drunken night trying to talk the other Fine and Dandies into visiting the Princesses, but they had laughed him to scorn. Wealthy, single young men like the Fine and Dandies rarely frequented bawdy houses. They had ready access to scores of more elegant companions, such as dancers and actresses.

Quickly Minette went on, "At any rate, I tell you this because it's very possible that Mr. Worthington would not be at home."

"Very well, Miss York. Now I'm going to get Fitchley to fetch my things, and I'm going to take care of this." She rose, but Minette put out a shaking hand and touched her dress.

"Please...please...you will make sure that Mr. Irons-Winslow is all right? Can you find him?" Minette implored her.

Victoria's face softened, and she clasped Minette's cold hand gently. "I have a friend, a very good friend, who will know exactly what to do. You must go home now. I will call on you tomorrow, if possible, and let you know if all is well."

"You...you would do that? For me?" Minette asked, fresh tears starting again.

Victoria smiled at her, and Minette was amazed at the sweetness of it. "I will do that and better, Miss York. I will pray for you."

Chapter Eighteen

Night Callers

Dev came down the stairs grumbling, fumbling to pull on his dressing gown while holding the lantern he'd just lit. "I'm coming. I'm coming," he said, but quietly, hoping against hope that whatever fool was banging on his door wouldn't awaken Dart.

When he reached the door, he pulled it open to see a man, about six feet tall, with enormous shoulders and legs like tree trunks, all encased in satins and silks. He was wearing a powdered wig. For a moment Dev wondered if he was walking and talking while still sleeping and dreaming. But the icy, wet wind whistling through the open door shattered that illusion.

"Good evening, Dr. Buchanan," the man said politely, as if they were passing on Wall Street.

"Good evening," Dev said warily, trying to peer over the man's gigantic shoulder. He couldn't see anything at the end of the walk but a light blur; still, he knew exactly who this late-night caller was. "Victoria," he breathed, half in distress, half in delight. His heart picked up a slightly faster beat, but no one would have known it from the awful sternness of his face.

Will—for Dev recognized him now as one-half of Victoria's favorite set of footmen—was unperturbed. After all, he had been Victoria's footman-bodyguard for ten years now, and he'd seen many wild escapades in his time. "Mrs. Victoria de Lancie begs that you will accept her apologies for the lateness of the hour and wishes to have an audience—"

"Never mind, Will, I'm here," she announced, sweeping up the steps behind him. "Good evening, Dev."

"Good eve—never mind that! Victoria, what can you be thinking! You can't…you can't be here…now!" Dev stammered. But his eyes widened, devouring her, for she looked as lovely as he had ever seen her. She was wearing an opera cloak of black satin trimmed with ermine, and the fur hood framed her small heart-shaped face as if she were an angel in the best of men's dreams.

"I am here," Victoria announced dryly. "And, Dev, it's beginning to rain. It'll ruin my fur."

"Ruin your—oh, never mind. I give up. Come in. And Will, you and David and Mr. Long come in the kitchen and fix some tea or coffee, if you'd like." The footman wheeled and ran back to Victoria's carriage to tell the other footman and the coachman the good news.

"Thank you," Victoria said, imperially sweeping into Dev's sitting room. "The rain would ruin those satin coats, too."

"Such a tragedy," Dev growled. "Victoria, what are you doing here? How could you be so careless of your reputation?"

Victoria was looking around the room curiously. She had never been in Dev's house, for, of course, unmarried women never called on bachelors in their homes. She picked up a box, a carved sandalwood box that Dev kept on the mantel. She recognized it. It was a gift that the Vanderbilts had given to their male guests at the party on their clipper ship two summers ago. "This is a good room," she said, her eyes soft. "It's like you. Strong and solid and secure."

Taken aback, Dev stared around the room, but then the thunder came back into his face. "Victoria, don't change the subject, please. You shouldn't be here. Whatever possessed you—"

At that moment the front door flew open and crashed mightily against the wall. Will, David, and Mr. Long had tried to come in quietly—the servant's entrance in the back was locked—but the rushing wind had grabbed the door out of Will's strong hands and flung it backward, as if with evil intent.

From upstairs came a baby's cry.

With much muttering, Will and David and Mr. Long shuffled as quietly as they could back to the kitchen.

Dev and Victoria stared at each other. Both of them had eyes widened with surprise. As the baby's cries grew louder Victoria's expression slowly deepened into shock.

"Is that a baby?" she asked, somewhat unnecessarily.

"Yes, it is," Dev gulped.

"Is it your baby?" Vic asked, frowning with fierce concentration.

"Yes—I mean, no! I mean, not precisely—"

Victoria blinked once, twice, then abruptly smiled. It was almost a giggle. "Dev, you look so befuddled. I've never seen you look befuddled before."

"Victoria, I am not befuddled! You are!" he snapped, running his hand through his hair with frustration. One thick lock in front stood straight up, and Victoria almost giggled again.

"Dev, calm down. Now, are you going to go get that child, or shall I?"

Dev took a deep, shaky breath. "I'll go. Of course you can't go. What is she doing here in the middle of the night at my house, anyway? Oh, won't the biddies be clucking about this—" he mumbled as he shuffled out of the parlor.

Victoria heard his step on the stairs, the creak of a door, his voice, quiet and strong; then the baby's crying stopped. In a few moments Dev came back into the room with what looked like a lump of untidily folded blankets. His expression as he came into the room was a strange mixture of shame and defiance.

Calmly Victoria walked to him and pulled back the swaddling so she could see the baby's face. Dart stared back at her blankly, his eyes dark smudges in his thin face. With kittenish suddenness, he yawned. Victoria looked up at Dev. "He looks very much like you," she said in a businesslike tone. "You're certain he's not yours?" Her eyes were twinkling starrily.

Dev blustered, "Am I certain—Victoria! You—you're joking about this!"

"Yes, I am. What is his name?"

"His—? Oh. Dart. Dart is his name."

"Dart Buchanan? What a wonderful name. Here, give him to me, you…you man. You're holding him too tightly, and you've got him trussed up like a roasting fowl."

Bewildered, Dev surrendered the baby to Victoria,

and fussily she adjusted his blanket. He mumbled, "But you're laughing about it. Don't you—? Aren't you—?"

"No," she said decisively. "I was shocked, that's why I asked if he was yours. I know you, Dev. I trust you and believe in you. This child is not yours—at least, he's not your son. Is he your brother?"

Dev gaped at her, then nodded his head. "My...my half brother, actually, but he—I love him."

"Of course you do," Victoria said, seating herself on Dev's sofa as if she were in a royal salon. "Please sit down, Dev, you're making me nervous, twitching around so."

"I'm not twitching," Dev protested weakly, but he did sit down.

"Now then," Victoria said crisply. "I came here because I need your help. So really, Dev, you must pull yourself together."

"I'm trying, but it's not easy," Dev said. "You said you need my help? What's wrong?"

"No, it's not me. Nothing's wrong with me," Victoria said hastily, but she was almost choked with fierce joy when she saw the intense worry in Dev's eyes as he raked her up and down, as if she were going to start hemorrhaging at any moment. "No, it's Shiloh, Dev. He's in trouble. And maybe Cheney, too."

In one instant, Dev's entire demeanor changed. His face was stern, his eyes burned intensely, his words were quick, strong, and sure. "Tell me. Tell me everything."

Victoria proceeded with her story, only stopping once because Dart was beginning to get restless, and Dev fetched his formula. "I'll feed him," he said.

"Nonsense," Victoria retorted, snatching the bottle from him and continuing her narrative.

When she finished, Dev sat very still, frowning and staring into space. Victoria recognized this expression, this stillness—Dev was figuring out what to do, concentrating hard. She had always been glad that Dev was not fidgety, that he didn't pace and fuss and jitter. He was always so steady and sure. She waited, reveling in being able to stare at him without self-consciousness, for she knew he was unaware of her hungry gaze.

"You said Miss York lives on West Tenth? And Shiloh walked south?" Dev asked as if it were a criminal interrogation.

"Yes."

"I think I may know where he's going. Or trying to go, anyway," Dev said thoughtfully. "Victoria, this is very important. Tell me again what Miss York said about the drug."

Victoria shook her head helplessly. "She didn't know anything about it, Dev. It was just a white powder in a packet that she dissolved in his brandy. She didn't know the name of it or how much it was. She said that that Worthington person—who we know is Bain Winslow—joked about giving Shiloh a double dose because he's such a 'great awkward blighter.'" Expressively she rolled her eyes. "The British, they can make 'Good morning' sound like a deadly insult."

"A double dose?" Dev's eyes narrowed. "That's not good, Vic. Not good at all. I hope, I truly hope it was chloral hydrate. You can't overdose on that. At least the quantity required would be so large you couldn't possibly take it in a drink and not notice it. But did she say where they'd been, what they'd been doing tonight?"

"Why no, not really. Why?"

"I just wondered how much Shiloh had had to drink

before he took the drug," Dev muttered, frowning. "The way he's been lately—I'd better take a heroic dose of strychnine to restart his heart and, yes, some digitalis to stabilize—"

Victoria suddenly looked frightened. "But, Dev, you mean…you mean Shiloh could be in danger of—I…I thought he would just be, you know, cold and—"

"I don't know, Vic," he answered shortly but not unkindly. "I won't know until I find him. And I'll find him. But about Cheney…do you think Bain Winslow means to harm her?"

Unconsciously Victoria grasped the baby closer. Dart whimpered a little but didn't awaken. "I honestly don't know, Dev, but I do know that Minette York is afraid of him. To Miss York the most frightening thing was that Bain Winslow showed up at her house while Shiloh was supposed to be unconscious and defenseless. Why? What was he going to do? Certainly not just look at him and snicker. So Miss York definitely feels that Cheney is in some danger; only, of course, she thinks that horrible man was going on about 'fixing' Angelique, as I told you."

Dev said nothing. He merely stared at a distant point beyond Victoria's shoulder, his smooth brow drawn into deep worry lines.

"But, Dev, listen," Victoria went on, "what could that silly little man possibly do? Ride up to Duvall Court and throw rocks through the window? I mean—"

"But that's just the problem, Victoria," Dev said gravely. "Cheney's not at Duvall Court tonight. She's working late at the office. By herself."

"What! Oh, that foolish girl! How many times have I told her to get herself two footmen—oh, never mind all that now," Victoria declared. Busily she began adjusting Dart's blankets, wrapping him more securely, tucking his half-full bottle of formula into her reticule.

Dev flew out of his chair. "What do you think you're doing now?"

Victoria looked up at him, her eyes wide and clear and guileless. "I'm going to your office, of course, to make certain that Cheney's all right. And obviously you can't take Dart with you to look for Shiloh, so I shall take him."

"No! You—this won't work," Dev said, running his hand through his hair again.

"I'm leaving now," Victoria said sweetly, rising and majestically enfolding Dart in the priceless fur of her cloak as she drew it around them both. "You know, of course, that I have Mr. Long and Will and David with me. I declare, I can't fathom why you never get mad at Cheney for dashing all over the world all by herself, but you get angry with me even though I always have at least three attendants at all times."

Suddenly Dev grinned, and Victoria's heart almost stopped as she saw the way his eyes crinkled at the corners and his deep dimples flashed. "It's because I worry about you so much. I'm awfully in love with you, you see, and so I tend to view you as the most precious, most valuable, most wonderful thing I've ever had in my life." His voice dropped as he spoke, and he moved closer to her and finally kissed her lightly, a mere taste of his lips against hers.

She was breathing raggedly, but she managed to say coolly, "I'd love to discuss all this with you later, Dr. Buchanan. After you find Shiloh and I find Cheney. And pray to God that they are both safe and well."

* * *

Nia, a small forlorn figure, was walking alone. Victoria recognized her even in the darkness with a heavy slushy rain falling. Victoria called behind to the footmen, Will shouted, and the lovely gold-and-white coach with the four white horses pulling it came to a careening halt.

"Nia!" Victoria called out imperiously. "Come here this instant, girl!"

She started, and then ran. Will almost threw her into the coach. Her wool cloak was dripping, and Nia was shivering spastically and sobbing. "Oh, thank the Lord, Mrs. de Lancie, thank the Lord! How did you—who's that?"

"It's—his name is Dart. Never mind him now, Nia. What are you doing out walking this late all by yourself? And you're frozen!"

"Oh, Mrs. de Lancie, Mrs. de Lancie, it's awful, just awful! I...I think some bad people took Miss Cheney!" Nia said, gulping her tears.

Victoria sighed. "So it's true." Nia looked astounded, but Victoria demanded, "Tell me everything."

"I...I was asleep on her sofa in the office," Nia said tearfully, but she took a deep breath and went on more calmly. "We had worked so late, and both of us were dead-on tired. I just almost was unconscious, I was sleeping so heavy. Somehow I just knew, sort of somewhere in my head, that the front doorbell was ringing and Miss Cheney answered it. But I was still almost drugged like. I couldn't wake all the way up, and I couldn't stay down in sleep."

"Yes, I know exactly what you mean, Nia," Victoria said, encouraging her.

"You do? Oh, thank heavens, 'cause it sure seems like this is all my fault—"

"Don't start on that, Nia. You didn't kidnap Cheney. You've done nothing but be a loyal friend to her. Now, go on, please."

"All right," Nia said, a little shakily but with determination. "Anyway, I think I heard some talk in the sitting room, and then I kinda knew Miss Cheney was tiptoeing around in the office. It was—nothing sounded—it just sounded normal, you know? So I kind of started slipping back into a deep sleep, but then I heard the front door bang shut. It was like someone shouted in my ear—I knew right then that Miss Cheney was leaving, and she's always supposed to take me with her, isn't she, now? So I jumped up, wide awake, and ran to the door. But… but—" She choked a little, but went on, "Miss Cheney had locked the door and taken the inside key. You understand about the door and key—"

"Oh yes, I understand perfectly." Victoria, in spite of the grave circumstances, sounded faintly amused. "Dr. Buchanan locked me out and himself in just that way one time. Anyway, go on, Nia."

"Well, I ran to the window to look out, and I started banging on it and calling to her. But the man…the man, he was holding Miss Cheney, locking her arms, you see, and that woman, that…that dirty little—"

"I think I know the kind of woman you mean," Victoria said impatiently.

"Yes, that trash clapped something over Miss Cheney's face, and in just a minute she crumpled up like she didn't have a bone in her body. And then that man scooped her up and shoved her in the carriage and…and…" Nia started to cry again.

"Nia, please don't get hysterical," Victoria said evenly. "Listen to me. I'm going to find Cheney and take care of her, you understand? But I need you to help me so I can help Cheney. You must be calm."

"She didn't scream," Nia maundered. "Why didn't she scream?"

"Cheney? You must be joking, Nia," Victoria scoffed. "You should know that Cheney would fight. She always fights, and fights hard."

"Yes, she was fighting them, all right," Nia said with some satisfaction. "Now I'm seeing it in my mind. I saw that tramp hopping around. I hope Miss Cheney kicked her, but good."

"I would guess that she probably gave them some trouble," Victoria asserted, "but nothing like the trouble they're going to be in when I find them."

Nia was still sniffling woefully, but she raised her tearstained face and grimaced. "You'll fix those two, won't you, Mrs. de Lancie? That great hulking pig and that sneaky-pete of a woman?"

In a curiously stifled voice Victoria replied, "Yes, don't you worry, Nia. We'll fix them. First of all, tell me, where were you going? Did you hear them say something about where they were taking Cheney?"

"I couldn't hear a thing, not a single word, Mrs. de Lancie. By the time I got to the sitting room, they were all the way down the walk at the carriage. And it was a plain black carriage, two-horse, no markings at all. But it was a private carriage. Not a hansom cab. All I know is they took off straight south down Sixth."

Victoria asked, "Then where were you going?"

Nia sighed, so deeply it was almost a groan. "Well, I sure enough found Miss Cheney's reticule, thrown down ever-which-way on the sitting room sofa, and it had her keys in it, which is why she took the front-door key, I guess. And it had some money in it. So I was going to walk to Madison Square and see if I could get a hansom cab and go tell Dr. Buchanan."

"You were? Instead of going to Duvall Court?" Victoria asked curiously.

"Why, yes, Mrs. de Lancie. Gramercy Park's a lot closer...and I guess I feel like Dr. Buchanan's the sort of man to take something like this in hand and figure out what to do. I mean, Mr. Duvall could, too, but I could hardly bear to think of scaring Miss Irene to death like this would. Not to mention what my mama's going to do to me when she finds out I let Miss Cheney out alone," Nia worried.

Victoria patted her hand, hiding a smile. Nia's mother Dally was something to be afraid of, indeed, never mind kidnappers in the dead of night. "Nia, you did very well. It was very courageous of you to venture out alone at night, and to Madison Square, yet! That's a dangerous place for a nice, pretty young girl like you, and I'm sure you know that. But you were going anyway. Cheney will be proud of you."

"I...I didn't know what else to do."

"It was the right, the best, thing to do," Victoria said firmly. "Now, you must tell me about these two kidnappers. What did they look like?"

Nia shook her head helplessly. "I couldn't hardly see, Mrs. de Lancie. There was a carriage lantern, but I couldn't see faces very good at all. All I know is that the man had long yellow hair straight down his back, and his big ol' face looked just like a block of bleached wood. That rotten woman was colored. But not a Negro."

"Hmm…you mean, like Spanish, maybe?"

"Darker."

"Like…like…" Victoria sat straight up in her chair. "Like the islands…like Jamaican or from the Bahamas? Like that, Nia?"

"Yes, that's right," Nia said, her eyes lighting up a little. "She was a lot browner than Miss Cheney and the plank-faced big pig, but not as black as me."

"As black as I," Victoria corrected her automatically. She and Cheney both helped Nia with her diction and grammar. "So…I'll just bet she was one of the Exotic Island Princesses. Princesses, my eye—street strumpet is more like it."

Nia made a sharp indrawn breath of shock, but Victoria ignored it. "Here, take Dart, Nia. Have you ever taken care of babies before?"

"Of course. I have nieces and nephews, ma'am," Nia answered smartly, expertly taking Dart from Victoria and holding him just right, with her crooked elbow supporting his head.

Victoria flung open the shutter and called, "David! Come here!"

The young man's head, still with a sodden white wig on it, appeared at the window. He was much younger than Will, only twenty, but he'd been with Victoria for four years. He was so big he had to squat down to look inside. "Yes, ma'am?"

"David, do you know of a place called Sweet's House of Exotic Island Princesses?" Victoria asked innocently.

"Wh-why, ma'am, I—"

"Speak up, David."

"I've...I b'lieve I have heard of such a place, ma'am," he stuttered.

"Have you? Good. Have you, by chance, heard of where this place might be located?"

"Well, it's down on—now you understand, ma'am, that I, that this isn't no personal knowledge of this place— but I have heard somewhere, somehow, that it's down on Mercer Street."

"Thank you," Victoria said smartly. "Tell Mr. Long to take us to Dr. Buchanan's office, and then we're going down on Mercer Street." She slammed the shutter closed, then told Nia, "You're going to stay at the office and keep Dart. I'm going to go get Cheney."

Nia's eyes were huge, her eyebrows straight shocked slash marks high on her forehead. "Mrs. de Lancie, you think that trash took Miss Cheney to a guttersnipe place like that?"

"I'm almost sure of it," Victoria answered angrily. "He said he was going to ruin her...and he still might do that, but not if I get there first."

Chapter Nineteen

The Sad Tale of Her Downfall

Cheney thought she was trying to make her way across a very dark room, inky black, and she was anxious. She was anxious because her hands and legs weren't working right and also because Shiloh had given the patient too much chloroform.

"Too much chloroform, Shiloh," she said, or tried to say. It actually came out in a thick whisper that sounded more like "thoo muth crorfor."

The effort of speaking woke her up, in a sense. At least she opened her eyes and looked around. Yes, she was in a room so dark she couldn't see her fingers in front of her nose.

Were her fingers in front of her nose?

Now something hurt. What hurt?

"Ohh," she moaned softly. She was hurt, she was the patient in the dark room, and she had certainly been given too much chloroform. Cheney knew the too-sweet reek of the anesthetic as well as she knew her own perfume. Her face felt tight and raw, and her mouth and throat were utterly dry and rasping painfully. Groaning, she sat up. Her eyes, too, stung from the drug. For a panicky moment Cheney wondered if she was blind, but with an immense amount of self-control she quieted her thundering heart and tried to take stock of her condition.

I'm not blind...I'm starting to see my hands like white blurs. The skin around my mouth is burned...so is the inside of my nose and mouth and throat—oh, that hurts! They must have used enough chloroform to put down a horse!

"They," she said aloud, startled. It had all come rushing back to her—the pretty island woman, the big man with the face like a blank slab...hurrying out of the office...fighting them...and finally the cloth over her face. "Who were they? And why, why, why?" she whispered.

Now it registered that she was beginning to see details of the room. It was a bedroom, but a bedroom like Cheney had never seen before. It was cheap and garish. The bed was enormous, with faded and moth-eaten velvet hangings—Cheney couldn't tell if they were dark blue or black—and stringy tassels. Dozens of pillows covered in cheap chintz and fringe were littered about the head of the bed and on the floor. An enormous mirrored dressing table with a velvet stool loomed on one wall, but the dressing table was bare except for a fringed shawl. Beside it was a small coal grate, dirty and bare. Behind the bed the entire wall was covered with mirrors, dark wavy mirrors. Cheney couldn't see her reflection—it was too dark—but she could see blurry surreal blobs of dark gray and light gray.

So at least her eyes were still working, though they

felt swollen, her eyelids galled. On the far wall she could see two sets of draperies—windows?

Cheney rose unsteadily and took a deep breath, though it burned as if she were swallowing daggers. She was dizzy from the aftereffects of the chloroform, and her legs tottered like little weak spindles. She swayed in the darkness, noting with dismay that she was so cold she couldn't feel her feet at all, and her breath made little puffs of warm vapor as she panted. Walking as stiffly as if she were crippled, she went to the nearest set of draperies and yanked them aside. She looked down, far down, seeing that she was on the third floor. No escape route here.

The sight of the empty street somehow devastated her. The yellow balls of the streetlamps glowed as warmly and with such welcome as if nothing were wrong, as if nothing had happened, as if she hadn't been drugged and kidnapped and left all alone in this awful place.

Now with sickening chills of fear, she looked down at herself in the weak light. She was barefooted. Her stockings were gone. Her blouse—a plain white one with small tucks—had been unbuttoned and her ribbon tie was gone. Also, her hair was undone and tumbled wildly about her face and shoulders. She felt dirty, horribly vulnerable, and ill.

"What's happening to me?" she asked the darkness fearfully.

No answer came except a nervous voice buzzing in her head. *Well, they didn't kill me when I was passed out. That's a good sign, isn't it? Or is it? Maybe they're going to torture me, do terrible things to me, hurt me, kill me slowly....*

Cheney lurched back to the bed, her legs finally giving

way, and she collapsed. Burying her face in her hands, she felt panic rising, a dark smothering wave that threatened to engulf her, to drive her mad.

"Oh, Lord Jesus," she sobbed painfully. "Help me."

That was all she could manage, over and over again.

As she prayed that desperately simple prayer, she began to feel calm. Not all at once, and not totally. But the roaring, suffocating sea of panic began to recede, to fade very slowly, and Cheney shakily took control of her thoughts, of her mind and emotions and, finally, her spirit. Somehow she realized that the Lord was leading her to that promised place of peace. She clutched at Him. He held her. She began to hear, faintly but surely, that still, small Voice.

Her breathing became less ragged, her heart stopped throbbing wildly, her hands and legs stopped shaking. After a while, she raised her head again and sighed so deeply that it hurt, but it felt as though she was pushing out, with that long breath, all that remained of the fear inside her. "Thank you, Lord," she murmured.

Now she thought of what she should do.

It didn't take her long to decide. Cheney was, and always had been, a fighter.

She staggered to the door—it was locked, of course—and banged on it as hard as she could. "Let me out of here! Right now! Whoever you are, you have made some kind of mistake! Let me out—NOW!"

She listened and thought she could hear the murmur of voices below.

She started beating on the door again, though she knew it was hardly more than weak thumps. "Someone! Anyone! Let me out!"

Abruptly she stopped, for she heard a step, a very heavy, deliberate tread on stairs. Coming toward her.

Even though it was what she thought she had wanted, the sound of that slow, deliberate tread made Cheney wary. She hurried to the far side of the bed and stood stiffly waiting.

She heard a key click in the lock.

The slab-faced man came in holding a lantern. He stopped and closed the door behind him, spreading his legs wide and holding the lantern up high. He stared at her, and once again Cheney thought how blank his face was, how empty his expression.

"I…I…" Cheney tried to speak, but she just couldn't. Her mouth and throat burned horribly, and she hadn't the strength to force out the words.

"You must be quiet," he said.

He studied her, and unbelievably Cheney thought she saw a flicker of concern in his eyes. Not compassion—that was much too strong a word for it—but just a fleeting moment of worry.

Her mind started clicking along fast, and she found her voice. "Sir, I'm very, very cold. Please. Let me out of here."

He looked around the bleak room, then eyed her clinically. He shook his head, but whether in disapproval or in negation Cheney couldn't tell.

"I cannot let you out of here. You must stay here. But just until morning. Then you go."

He turned as if to leave, but Cheney wailed, "Wait!" She was dismayed at the panicky cry, and she made herself continue in an even tone, "Listen to me for a moment, please. I don't know why you've done this. I've never done anything to you or to that woman. I don't even know you. Are you sure you haven't made a terrible mistake?"

In his plodding way he shook his head this way, that way. "No. You are Dr. Cheney Duvall. You are the one."

"The one what?" Cheney demanded.

"You stay here tonight," the man insisted in his leaden manner. "Just tonight. In the morning, you go. Mr. Worthington, he tells me this."

"Mr. Who? Worthington? I don't know anyone by that name. Why would this man want to kidnap me? It doesn't make any sense!" Cheney exclaimed stridently.

The man, unmoved as if she had made no sound, turned again to the door. Cheney pleaded, "At least give me back my cloak, please. I'm very cold."

He turned again, hesitated, and seemed to be considering. Cheney was certain that this process would take a few minutes, so she made herself be quiet and still. But she was starting to shiver, and the man was watching her with calculation, as if he were weighing some unknown cost.

"I don't think—" he began but was interrupted by the sound of someone running up the stairs.

"Sweet! Sweet, are you visiting the doctor? Here, let me in!" a man called through the door.

I know that voice...sounds familiar, Cheney thought in confusion.

Sweet opened the door and, blocking Cheney's view, talked to the man outside in the hallway. "Mr. Worthington, I think you say you can't see her. I think you say she can't see you, too."

"It doesn't matter now, Sweet, doesn't signify at all!" the man said, clapping his hand on her jailer's thick shoulder. His voice sounded almost hysterical, high pitched and giddy, and British.

The man called Sweet stepped outside in the hallway and half closed the door. Cheney could barely hear a low conversation. She heard Sweet's grunts and the other man's cultured lilt.

"Bain Winslow?" Cheney murmured, blinking hard.

"Your servant, Miss Duvall," he said, pushing past Sweet and making a cruel mockery of a bow.

Cheney froze. She watched him, not with fear but with a desperate need to gauge him, to take a measure of him, to know precisely how much danger she was in. Though Cheney wasn't aware of it, her gaze was cool and calculating.

He stared back at her, at first full of drunken amusement, and then he seemed taken aback. He dropped his eyes first, much to Cheney's surprise. Half turning, he said, "Sweet, lock the door and keep the key. Come get me when we're finished."

Swaggering, Bain made his way to the dressing table, set the lantern down, lolled onto the stool, and faced her again. Though he had no hat or coat, he was carrying a stick, a polished ebony cane with a heavy gold vulture-head handle. "Why don't you sit down, Miss Duvall?" he asked sarcastically.

"I...I think I prefer to stand."

He shrugged, took a slim flask from his vest pocket, and drank deeply. "Forgive me. Would you care for a drink?"

"No. No, thank you." Cheney was determined to match his courtesy, however absurd it was. A hundred thoughts and questions buzzed around in her head like a cloud of busy gnats. She was confused and still a little scared. One part of her wanted to cower and scream, one wanted to hide, and one very strong impulse was to pick up something, anything, and bash this smug man's face in.

Though she wasn't aware of it, her eyes scanned the room.

Bain made a wry sound of amusement deep in his chest. "Oh no, Miss Duvall, there's nothing here that you can use to bash my face in. Sweet…"

Cheney was startled, for at that moment Bain Winslow had reminded her very much of Mr. Shiloh Irons. *The way Shiloh knows exactly what I'm thinking sometimes, that same knowing, half-amused expression on his face… so like Shiloh's, even though they look nothing alike.*

"…sure of that, especially after he found the gun in your medical bag. Colt .44 revolver. Deadly thing, that. Where did you get it?"

She weighed him. "Shiloh gave it to me."

A flash flitted through his whiskey-muddied brown eyes, but he said nothing.

Cheney decided she might risk taking the upper hand, at least in this silly, surreal conversation. "Yes, Mr. Irons-*Winslow* gave me the gun. And taught me to use it. If you'll give it back to me, I'll show you."

He stared at her with outrage, and at first Cheney thought he was going to explode. Then his mouth twitched, and he grunted a reluctant laugh. "Miss Duvall, you have got some backbone, 'tis true."

"Mr. Winslow, I'm glad you're amused. But I am not. If you would just give me back my clothes and medical bag and let me leave, it will go much easier on you," Cheney said as firmly and as calmly as she could.

"Go easier on me?" He jumped to his feet, suddenly furious, and cracked his cane on the dressing table. It sounded like a gunshot. "Go easier on me? Nothing has gone easy or right for me since Locke showed up like some…some evil spirit! And now, here I am again, running from the nightmare with nothing in my pocket, and—" He broke off, whipping across the room to stand exactly opposite Cheney across the bed. "Don't dare to tell me you'll make it easy on me, you…you witch!"

Cheney observed him and listened closely, and incredibly, she was somewhat reassured. Normally Cheney was not a very insightful person. She had difficulty understanding people's hidden motives and meanings. But now, as if this sense had suddenly been honed to a fine edge, she thought it very likely that Bain Winslow was not a physical threat to her. His tirade was more like a spoiled child's temper tantrum than a murderous rage.

Quickly she thought, *And what does a spoiled child want when he throws a tantrum? Attention, of course. Talk to him. Get him to talk to you.*

Cheney gave a small sigh, as if marshaling her patience—which, indeed, she was. She made herself relax, her shoulders loosen, her hands fall limply at her sides, her eyes to show nothing but slight interest. "Mr. Winslow, please. This is getting us nowhere. I assume that you have a reason, some plan, something to accomplish in bringing me here this way. Why don't—I mean, won't you please tell me about it? Explain it to me?"

"Why should I?" he blustered, fully as petulant as the naughty child Cheney envisioned in her mind.

"Well, I supposed that is why you are here now. To talk to me."

Bain planted white fists on the bed and leaned across, thrusting his face close to Cheney's. "Talk to you? And how do you know I don't have something more nefarious in mind, my dear doctor?"

Cheney swallowed hard and drew back a little. She dropped her eyes and fidgeted with her skirt. "I suppose...because I know your sister. Brynn loves you." Cheney had not planned on saying this. It seemed nonsensical as it came out of her mouth. But as it turned out, it was exactly the right thing to say.

His cold brown eyes widened, and he drew back with a jolt. Then his lip curled, but with self-disgust, it seemed to Cheney. He took out his flask again, drank, but evidently it was empty, because he threw the flat silver bottle into the dead hearth. Then he paced, his hands clasped so tightly behind his back that his knuckles turned white.

"I don't want to talk about my sister," he muttered.

Cheney sagged with relief. "What do you want to talk about?"

"What do I want to talk about? What haunts me, Dr. Duvall, the dark cloud on every horizon I see, the man lurking in every shadow, the evil nemesis that follows me! My brother Locke!"

Brother? Cheney thought with shock. Bain kept pacing, not looking at her, as if she weren't even in the room.

"Everything that's happened to me is all Locke's fault! I want him to suffer as I've suffered! I want him to feel... helpless, and alone. I want him to feel...shame." He kept his head down as he paced, his voice low and filled with loathing.

"But, Mr. Winslow," Cheney said, bewildered, "I don't understand. What does this have to do with me?"

Now he seemed taken aback. "It has everything to do with you. Locke worships you. I'll ruin you. It'll hurt him."

"Ruin me?" Cheney repeated blankly.

"Yes, of course."

Now Bain seemed to be growing fatalistically calm. He took his seat again on the vanity stool and watched her with what appeared to be genuine surprise at her inability to understand.

"And, though everything hasn't worked out as neatly as I'd planned it, I still believe Locke is going to be ruined, shunned, and despised by all of his pompous little upperten friends." He sniffed disdainfully, took out a fat cigar, struck a match on the dressing table, and lit it, puffing away carelessly. "Pardon me. Do you mind?"

"What? Oh no. I suppose not. After all, it's a small offense in the overall scheme of things," Cheney muttered, her brow creased. Without thinking about it she rounded the bed and sat on it, drawing her bare feet up and to the side to tuck under her skirt. It was totally unconscious, never assumed, the grace and elegance with which Cheney moved and spoke. Finally, in her late twenties, Cheney had come into her mother's inheritance.

She never saw the look of intense admiration that flashed across Bain Winslow's face. Very quick and shadowy thoughts flitted through his mind. He could see how any man could fall in love with this vibrant, courageous woman.

"I'm afraid I still don't understand, Mr. Winslow," she was saying thoughtfully. "You say you're ruining Shi—I mean, Locke? His reputation, is that what you mean?"

Bain frowned and shoved away the perilously admiring thoughts he was having about Cheney Duvall. "That's right. That's exactly, precisely right, my dear doctor."

"How?" Cheney asked plaintively. "What is all this?"

He drew on his cigar, watching her with eyes narrowed

against the blue smoke. She seemed relaxed, merely curious. In a way he was glad, glad that she wasn't afraid, glad that she was talking to him and listening to him in such a reassuring manner. In some deep corner of his mind, Bain realized that Cheney was not looking down on him, was not judging him and finding him wanting.

But oh, Locke did. Locke always did.

His lip curled. "Locke got into a drunken brawl tonight, again. Only unfortunately this time he beat up a woman. A small, frail, defenseless woman. Miss Minette York."

Cheney's eyes grew huge, and her face, especially around her mouth and nose, began to burn painfully. She licked her lips.

"I would imagine that Locke won't be welcome in Mrs. Randolph Goelet's drawing room or Mrs. Josefina Wilcott Steen's box at the Academy of Music after this scandal," he said with malicious amusement. "And then the love of his life, the charming Dr. Cheney Duvall, has a night of rowdy dissipation…and gets caught. It's going to be in the *Sun* and in all the penny dailies tomorrow. With pictures. Photographs, I mean. Real photographs of the fallen woman, half dressed, thoroughly shamed, leaving a—"

"Just a minute," Cheney said slowly. She had barely registered the sad tale of her downfall. "About Shiloh. You…you said he…" She was looking at him beseechingly, and he stared back at her defiantly. Cheney's face changed. She tilted her head, now assessing, now knowing. "Shiloh never did that. He would never do that. I don't care how drunk he was or how angry. He would never, never beat a woman."

She waited, and then was sure, for Bain Winslow's

face now filled with a bitterness so vivid he looked as if his mouth was full of the taste.

Cheney bit her lip and asked tremulously, "Did...did something bad happen to Miss York, though?"

Bain stuck the cigar in his mouth and squinted through the smoke. "You mean, did I do something bad to her?"

Cheney didn't answer.

"What do you think?" Bain asked coolly.

Once again words, strange words, came rolling easily out of Cheney's mouth before they had actually been formed in her mind. "I think you were angry enough to do something to her and make it look as if Shiloh did it, but I don't think you could actually go through with it. I don't think you're truly that kind of man."

"Perhaps you're mistaken," Bain said, but now weakly.

"No, I think you're the one who has made an error in judgment, Mr. Winslow," Cheney said softly, "and so there was always a fatal flaw in your plans. Don't you see? You've misjudged Shiloh, misunderstood him, and you've done no injury to anyone but yourself. Shiloh's friends know him just as I do. They would never believe that he had done such a reprehensible thing. They trust him. They believe in him. That's the nature of friendship. And these other people—the social connections, the balls and parties and cotillions—they mean nothing to Shiloh. He wouldn't care one way or the other what they think or say about him behind his back, and he wouldn't care if he never has to attend another musicale as long as he lives. It's simply not that important to him."

Bain stared at her, clearly in the throes of the bitter-est of defeats. He knew she was right, and of course he knew that such a vicious rumor about Locke wasn't going to materialize anyway. He had just wanted to lash out at her, to belittle her, to make her lose some of her regard for Locke, even if it was just for a little while. Right now Bain had to take even the pettiest of triumphs.

He swallowed hard and ground out his cigar contemptuously on the cheap carpet. "So. Once again I've fought and I've lost, and Locke kicked me while I was down. As for you, Miss Duvall, you are still in a very compromising position. And that will hurt you, and that will still hurt Locke. So I've won at least one round, though Locke, as usual, has the knockout."

Cheney said, almost with pity, "It won't be the first time I've been in a position that's earned me the censure of society. It likely won't be the last. It truly is of little consequence to me."

He stared at her as if she'd suddenly started raving and foaming at the mouth. "But your parents! Your mother!"

Cheney nodded. "Yes, Mother will be distressed. But not ashamed of me. Never ashamed."

He jumped to his feet. "So...so you're a saint, and Locke's an archangel! Yes, yes, I know. Locke's so perfect, so wonderful, he would never, never do anything wrong or even make a mistake! Oh, how I hate him!" Bain snarled.

"I think not," Cheney said simply. "You call him your brother."

With that, his finely modeled features seemed to crumple. He turned on his heel, stumbling, and banged on the door. "Sweet! Come let me out! Now!"

The key-scratch sounded, and then without the slightest backward look, Bain Winslow was gone.

Cheney sat, unmoving, for a little while. Then she thought of how very cold she was and how tired she was. She lay down on the bed, pulled the scratchy but warm velvet coverlet up, and went to sleep.

Chapter Twenty

The Infernal Machine Winds Down

Shiloh's first inkling that he might be in serious trouble came upon him when he didn't fall into the Hudson River.

"Lucky I didn't fall in," he muttered solemnly, looking down into the sleet-spattered black water. "Ophelia drowned. People drown."

After a while, he reflected that it was more than lucky—it was miraculous. He had meant—somewhere back there—to take a left on Washington Street. Instead, he had kept walking, shambling along blindly in the unlit streets and narrow alleys until he had crossed West Street and had almost walked off the end of an empty boat slip.

At this time it also occurred to him that it was a real possibility that he could, and would, drown, should he fall in. His body was betraying him, slowly and treacherously. It didn't belong to him anymore, didn't obey him properly. He knew he couldn't swim. He would be one of those people who drowned if he fell in. He stood at the very edge of the pier, swaying and staring owlishly down. Then, with what might have been comical care under other circumstances, he started slowly sliding backward, one foot toe-heeled behind, then another, and another, until he was away from that edge and that blackness.

His relief was great, and he stood for a long time reveling in it. Finally it occurred to him that now he must put one foot in front of the other and go. But go where? Somewhere—sometime—back there he had had purpose, a plan. But now he'd forgotten both. Still, he did start walking, though it was more like a very old, very drunk man's stumbling shuffle.

"Going to...was going to—where was I going? Somewhere...safe. Somewhere warm." He labored, his face creased in a deep frown. Finally he remembered something.

Duvall Iron Shield.

"Thass not it," he told himself peevishly. "Quit thinkin' 'bout her. Think about the plan."

White pelicans.

What? Something about white pelicans.

"Going to the zoo," he chortled crazily. The sound of his slurred, thick voice and his insane giggle brought Shiloh up short. He stopped, pressed his hands against his head, and with a superhuman effort made himself concentrate.

I'm drugged, and I'm getting worse. I'm lost, and it's cold. Really cold. I can hardly see a thing—at least, I see two or three of things—and I'm moving more slowly all the time. I've got to get a hold on myself. I've got to get moving and stop laughing and get some medical attention. Now, where in blue thunder am I going?

He almost writhed with the effort, but finally he

dredged up his memory of leaving Minette's, concentrating on turning onto Washington...to go...to go to—

White Pelican Tavern! That's it. That's the tavern right by my old shanty! I can go there!

Shiloh wasn't too sure exactly why he felt that his old shack would be safe and warm. It could be occupied. It could be gone. It could be deserted and filthy. Still, he could see it so plainly in his mind, not blurred and confused like everything else was. It seemed like a beacon of light and warmth and security. It was an anchor, like the old anchor with the Duvall Iron Shield forever etched on it that had been left there as if by a gracious Lady Fortune for him to find.

Come too far, all the way to the river, but the cross street to the shanty runs all the way over here, right?

What is the name of that street? Something Catholic... Vespers or Invest or something like that...

He was walking along the docks now, and they were pretty well deserted this time of night. The taverns and brothels and oyster houses and fishermen's shanties were farther south, closer to downtown. There were some boats, most of them small fishing boats, occasionally a larger freighter or barge. Many of the barges had hay piled high, for one of the most lucrative cargoes was feed for the thousands of horses on Manhattan Island.

Warehouses, fisheries, slaughterhouses, and glue factories lined this part of the Hudson River. No comforting streetlamps here. It was a grim, filthy, stinking place. The rain plopped on him, slushy big clumps of part water, part ice. His clothes were sodden, and he was freezing.

Once he heard two or three sets of footsteps, hard, fast steps, and decided that they were the sounds of men running. They passed somewhere close in one of the alleyways, and Shiloh clearly heard a low, hoarse voice cursing someone called Billy. Once, far away, he heard a woman scream, a shrill, frightening wail that was cut off very suddenly. He shivered, telling himself it was from the cold.

He moved more and more slowly. His feet just wouldn't obey his conscious demand that they move faster. He looked down at them, willing them to move, and Shiloh found that he could hardly see his feet. That is, he saw some vague blobs moving in front of him, but his vision was getting very bad, indeed.

Clinically one part of his mind—one of the last parts that evidently hadn't been drug-stupefied yet—told him insistently that he was getting very weak and very cold and very confused, and this meant that he was going to be in real trouble if he didn't get himself out of this fix pretty soon.

This nagging part of his mind kept talking to him, pushing him, prompting him, supplying him with the will to keep walking. But then, in this tiny little tinny babble in the back of his head, a thought formed and grew so large that it shut everything else off.

I'm afraid.

Shiloh stopped walking and stared into the blank night.

Shiloh had never been afraid before. He didn't like it much.

Oh, he'd been in frightening situations before. He had faced death before, many times in the war. But that had been different. Then he'd been actively fighting for his life against an enemy that he could clearly see.

Now he felt helpless, exposed, naked. And scared.

He stood swaying slightly, blinking slowly, unable to shield his eyes from the hard rain that hit his eyeballs from time to time. He reflected that now his thoughts, his line of thinking, once broad and busy, was narrowing and slowing. He could think of only one thing at one time.

He began sinking to his knees.

I don't wanna do this...gotta get up...gotta keep walking.

Why?

I dunno...but I know that's what I gotta do.

He was on his knees, literally. He willed himself to get up but found that he couldn't quite recall exactly how to do that.

He was still working on it when he began to hear noises.

At first he was simply concerned with identifying the noises. It was hard to do. He concentrated hard, listening, screening out the roaring and pummeling in his ears. Finally he thought it was like the murmur of muted voices, for he could hear the giveaway *s* sounds. And rustling. Like clothes. Clothes rustling. If there were clothes rustling, someone must be in them.

He thought something fell on him, for he was falling forward, and he heard a funny whooshing noise. He fell, and fell...and his cheek hit something hard and stinky and gritty. It was very unpleasant.

"Don't, Rock!"

Don't rock. That's right, don't rock. It hurts, Shiloh reflected muddily.

"He's big, if'n he gets up and fights us we'll be in for it."

"He's drunk outer his mind, Rock. And look, he's a

swell, ain't he? We rob him, that's one thing. You kill him, we'll have coppers down here from now till kingdom come."

After a hesitation—it seemed like eons to Shiloh—the Rock answered, "Awright, awright. But you crew clean him out, and I'm standin' here watching. If he so much as blinks, I'll bash him. And I still get my share, too, so don't think about cuttin' and runnin'. I'd find you."

Shiloh felt hard pinches along his waist and thighs and realized that they were turning him over. Desperately he tried to make himself move, to at least try to fight, but he could only wave limply and groan. Once he was on his back, he stared up at the four surrounding him and felt the most sickening shock he'd ever known. "Kids... you're children...little girl..."

"Shaddup," Rock said. He was about fourteen or fifteen, deathly skinny but wiry looking. He was holding a flat wooden club—it was actually an old boat oar— over Shiloh's head. There was another boy, younger than Rock, with a runny nose and enormous dark eyes.

The other two were little girls. One of them must have been about twelve, for she was tall, and now Shiloh realized that she must have been the one who stood up to Rock. The smaller girl couldn't have been more than six years old, filthy, tiny, and with such a look of desolation and hopelessness that Shiloh shut his eyes so he didn't have to see.

"Just...children..." he mumbled.

Rock kicked his side. "Shaddup!"

"Rock," the girl said disapprovingly.

"You shaddup. Just do it, can't you?"

They started stripping him. They pulled at his coat,

and Rock decided that they'd tear it, so he yanked Shiloh
up by the hair, and they peeled it off. They took off his
vest.

Rock, still holding Shiloh in a semblance of an upright
position by his hair, ordered, "Get me that shirt. Allus
wanted a fine shirt like that. What is it, swell? Silk, ain't
it?"

"Dunno, Rock," Shiloh answered.

"Shaddup," Rock said, kicking him in the small of the
back.

The smaller boy, struggling with Shiloh's heavy dead
weight, managed to unbutton the shirt and take it off.
Rock let Shiloh go, and Shiloh heard, rather than felt,
the crack that his head made against the rough street.

Then Shiloh felt tugging on his legs and managed
to look down. The smallest girl was trying to take his
boots.

She'll never get them off, he thought vaguely. Finally
the older girl came to help her, and then they took his
socks, too.

The second boy was going through the coat and vest
pockets eagerly. He looked up. "No wallet or purse. Just
some loose dollars and some coins."

Methodically Rock kicked him again. "Where's yer
wallet, little nimby?"

"Dunno 'zackly," Shiloh answered from far away. "Too
bad, I coulda given you my card...."

"Rock, if he had his wallet, it'd be here," the girl said
reasonably. She had felt along his waist for pockets, but
Shiloh's dress breeches had none. Evidently they didn't
want his pants, and for that Shiloh was very grateful. "I
told you, he's dead drunk."

"Dead," Shiloh echoed.

Rock and the girl laughed, a tragically adult sort of cruel laughter. Shiloh didn't mean to be funny.

And then, without another word, they were gone.

Shiloh lay bare chested and barefooted on the filthy street. He stared upward but could see no sky, no stars, no light or shape or form of any kind.

His whole brain wasn't drug slogged, not yet. Still there was a part of him that understood, that comprehended, that was still a small, very faint voice of reason. But it, too, was fading, narrowing, coming to a point like a light disappearing into the distance. Soon, Shiloh knew, that voice, too, would disappear.

I can't feel my feet...can't feel my legs. Can still sorta feel my arms and hands, though...just can't make 'em work right.

Guess it won't be long before they're gone, too.

Am I dying?

After that thought, there was a terrible time of noise, of clatter, of thumping and buzzing and screeching inside Shiloh's head, and it drowned out his lucid thoughts.

But slowly, as if some infernal machine were winding down, it subsided, and Shiloh began to think again.

Funny...I don't feel the cold now. I don't even feel the wet except on my face....

My life—is this the end of my life? What a waste! What a stupid, foolish, utter, and total waste! Meaningless, empty life...and a shameful death.

No blood...I'm not even bloody.... Thought I'd die... bloody.

"My blood was shed for you instead."

Shiloh was never sure if he heard those words with his ears, his head, his heart, or all of them. But as soon as he'd heard them, he knew—he saw—everything.

He saw that he had not been a good man, that he'd not done one good thing in his whole life. It was all just rags, dirty rags, that he'd thought was fine silk, just as that boy Rock had thought his plain cotton shirt was fine silk. He was ignorant, like a beast, like the boy.

The boy, Rock, was a thief and a robber.

And so was Shiloh. He was a sinner, no better than the worst thief or robber or murderer on earth.

No better than Minette. Just as bad, just as wrong, just as blind as she....

No better man than my cousin Bain. He's a criminal... and so am I. My crimes were different, maybe, but no less evil.

And Cheney—how dumb was I, how stupid, not to see it! Not to know! I thought I was offering her the world, and I wasn't offering her anything but a weak and cowardly life, never seeing what was important, never caring, driven this way and that, whichever way the wind was blowing, that's where my ship went...to nowhere, to nothing....

He was not a nice man. He was not a good, honest man. He was rebellious. He was full of stubborn, blind pride. He had nothing to be proud about. His insides, his guts, his soul, were just as weak and naked and filthy and helpless as his outside.

Yet God had just spoken to him.

To him, personally. To him, privately. To him, on purpose.

It took a great effort, but Shiloh cleared his throat and tried to speak. It came out as a rough whisper, but he did manage to say it all.

"I know what You did for me. I guess I've always known. You, God, came to this earth as a man. You lived and hurt and cried and finally died—for me. I thank You for that, now and forever.

"And I'm sorry, so sorry for my life…for wasting it, for running away from You. I'm sorry for my sins, and they are many, and dark. I ask You now to forgive me. Save me…Lord Jesus, save me…."

He couldn't see anything now. He thought again that he must be dying, but now he wasn't afraid.

He felt warm, and he felt safe.

Chapter Twenty-One

Calling Cards

Cheney dreamed that Victoria was calling her, but for some reason Victoria was angry with her. Victoria was shouting—something angry, something rude.

That made Cheney open one gritty eye, knowing that she was having a nonsensical dream. Victoria was never rude, and she never shouted.

But now, very faint and faraway, she did hear Victoria's voice. And she was shouting.

Wildly Cheney sat up, wincing as she did so. She was sore, as if she'd been tossed around in a barrel. Her mouth and throat felt as if she'd been drinking kerosene. But she ignored all that, for was that—could that be—the voice of Victoria Elizabeth Steen de Lancie out on the street shouting?

Cheney ran to the window, grunting as her muscles protested. The window was locked, and for a moment she thought she would have to break it. But then she found the lock and threw the heavy sash up so fast it made a loud crashing sound. She leaned far out and could see, for it was almost dawn. A large group of people were standing on the walk below, a confused crowd with many people talking at once. Once again she heard, and knew, Victoria's voice. It was raised in anger, but Cheney reflected wryly that it could hardly be called anything so vulgar as a shout. It was more like low harp strings plucked hard.

"Madam! If you don't open this door, I shall have my footmen break it in! Do you understand? Answer me, this instant!"

"Victoria?" Cheney called. But her voice sounded like pebbles in a rusty pipe, so she cleared her throat and tried again. "Victoria!"

Victoria appeared, and Cheney almost smiled. Victoria looked like a vision of paradise in a watered satin ecru formal with a long train—not a speck or smudge on it—and a black satin cloak with luxurious ermine framing her face.

"Cheney! Cheney, are you all right, darling?" she called frantically.

"Yes, yes, I'm not hurt. But I'm locked in!"

"I'm coming. We're coming to get you!" Victoria called, straining to make herself heard over the din. It was hard for her and Cheney to communicate, because Cheney was on the third floor. Thirty-odd feet was a long way to make one's voice understandable.

"Who are all of you people, anyway?" Victoria said, her eyes flashing. It was much too early in the morning—barely dawn—for the colorful women of this district to be out yet. But there were several men. Victoria saw a cunning, ferret-eyed man in a natty but rumpled suit lick the stub of a pencil and scribble on a dirty scrap of paper. "Oh, journalists," she said disdainfully, frowning as if she'd seen a large and loathsome bug. Turning back, she called up to Cheney, "They won't let us in, but Will is going to break in the door. You'll be all right, won't you?"

Cheney waved. "Yes, Vic, I'm fine. No one's here with me."

At that moment a light flashed, a blowsy *poof* sounded, and a ball of smoke appeared. Behind them on the street a photographer stepped out from under his black cloth. Grinning nastily, he quickly started gathering up his equipment. He'd gotten the doctor leaning out the window of a bawdy house, half dressed, her hair awry, her face all red and swollen—and as a bonus, he'd gotten Mrs. Victoria Elizabeth Steen de Lancie, in all her glory, shouting up at Dr. Duvall like a brawling madam.

Victoria turned, and one eyebrow rose with disdain. "Oh no. This won't do at all. Will?"

The giant footman marched to the photographer, who started stammering, "Wait...wait just a minute there, ye thug. That's some—my camera! My camera, all in bits and—no, you can't have the plates—" A tug-of-war ensued, but it was pointless. Soon the glass negatives were thousands of dark bits of glass in the street.

"How much this rig cost you, sor?" Will asked, taking out a wallet.

"Eh? You...you—it cost me twenty-eight—I mean seventy dollars!" the photographer shouted with righteous indignation.

"Here's fifty, sor," Will said woodenly. He returned to the brownstone, and with dispatch he and David had the front door in two pieces, with one sorry piece hanging crazily from the hinges.

They stood patiently waiting while Mrs. de Lancie swept in. A woman, white-faced, with frizzy red hair was reclining on a recamier in the parlor, a lap robe covering her legs. "You must accept my apologies for not getting up to receive you," she said sarcastically. "I'm a cripple."

Victoria said coolly, "How unfortunate for you. I'm so sorry. Would you please direct us to Dr. Duvall's room?"

"I had nothing to do with any of this. I tried to tell Mr. Worthington—"

"Never mind all that now," Victoria said firmly. "Dr. Duvall?"

"She's on the third floor, second room on the left," the woman said. "Mr. Worthington took my keys. I suppose you might as well break that door down, too."

That door was much thinner and lighter than the front door, so Will and David only strong-shouldered it once, and they were in.

Victoria glided into the room, and Cheney rushed to her. "Oh, how glad I am to see you, darling Vic!" She threw her arms around Victoria, hugging her tightly. Victoria was surprised and pleased. Normally Cheney was not at all demonstrative.

"Oh, Cheney, dear, your face—are you hurt?"

"Oh, it's nothing. I'll tell you later all about it," Cheney said, shrugging. Rather blankly she looked around the room, and a yawn overtook her.

Victoria exclaimed, "Cheney Duvall! Is it possible that you've been *asleep?*"

"I was tired," Cheney replied defensively. "Getting kidnapped is very fatiguing, you know."

"Of all the cheek!" Victoria said, staring at her. "I thought I was rescuing you!"

"But you did, you have, Victoria," Cheney said,

placating her. "And I'm so very grateful. Really, it was no joke, not at all. See? I'm very cold, and I wonder where my clothes are. And my shoes. And my medical bag."

Victoria threaded Cheney's arm through hers. "Come along with me, little one. I don't know where your things are, but I'll bet I know someone who does. I don't suppose you were properly introduced to anyone, hmm?" They made their way out into the shabby hallway, Will and David following like immense and stoic guardian angels.

"Hardly," Cheney muttered. "The only new acquaintance I made was that of a man called Sweet. And some maid. She clapped a cloth sopping with chloroform over my face. Really! She used enough to put down a team of oxen!"

"I'm so sorry, Cheney. Your face looks raw and swollen," Victoria said anxiously, squinting to see her in the dark stairwell. "I suppose that must have burned your nose and mouth, too?"

"I'm much better now," Cheney said, smiling at her, "since I've been rescued. But Vic—did you know who really did this to me?"

Victoria nodded thoughtfully. "Yes. Bain Winslow."

"How did you know? And—how did you know I was here? And—" Cheney asked eagerly.

"Not now, dearest. We'll talk about it all later, but right now we need to speak to this lady." They were entering the parlor. The woman was still in the same position on the recamier, ostensibly relaxed. But her face looked ravaged, her eyes had purple pouches underneath them, and her skin was a sickly yellowish color. She was holding a fan, but it was tattered as she had been twisting and torturing it for hours.

Cheney stopped and studied her.

The woman began in a high nervous voice, "Dr. Duvall, I had no knowledge of this, and when I found out, I—"

"First," Victoria said evenly, "Dr. Duvall's clothing and shoes and medical bag. Do you know where they are?"

"In my room. I locked them in there so the girls wouldn't steal anything."

"And your room is—?"

"Second floor, first door," she answered. "And the key—oh, the key."

"I'm sure you'll forgive us," Victoria said sweetly. "Will, David, would you accompany Dr. Duvall upstairs and…er…assist her in recovering her belongings?"

"Yes, ma'am," the guardians replied in unison.

Obediently Cheney went upstairs while Victoria remained in the parlor. Looking around pointedly, then glancing with heavy meaning at the frizzy-haired woman, Victoria waited.

"Oh yes. Where are my manners?" the woman said with the oddest feeling of unreality enveloping her. "Please, Mrs. de Lancie, be seated."

"Thank you." Victoria chose to perch at the very edge of an armchair so overstuffed it looked like a fat animal. Coolly she went on, "I see you know my name. May I have the pleasure?"

"I am Alana Patterson," she replied obediently.

"Well, Miss or Mrs.?"

"Er—Miss."

"Well, Miss Patterson, you have found yourself in quite a painful predicament, haven't you?"

Alana burst out, "Please, madam, just stop playing games with me! What are you going to do to me?"

Victoria repeated calmly, "Do to you? Why, I'm not going to do anything at all to you. Of course Dr. Duvall is the offended party here, so I expect you will be obliged to make explanations as best you can to her."

Alana dropped her head and picked at the tassel to her fan. It was almost bare now, a mere three or four strings. "Is she—will she—is she kind, like you?"

Victoria's eyes reflected her shocked surprise but for only a scant second. "Kind? Yes, she is very kind and very compassionate. Much more so than I. At any rate, I wanted to speak to you privately before Dr. Duvall or my footmen return." Out of her reticule, Victoria took one of her cards. It was a parchment color, and the lettering was dusted with pure gold. With a gold fountain pen she wrote something on the back.

Rising, she glided over to Alana Patterson's chaise and handed the card to her. "That is the address of a house of refuge for unmarried women in distress. It is not advertised, and it is not a workhouse or a sweatshop; neither is it affiliated with any church or denomination. It is simply a place to rest and to make decisions. There are rules that you must abide by, and you will not be able to stay for long. If you should decide to go there, take my card. You will need it to gain entrance."

Stunned, Alana turned the card over and stared down at it in disbelief. "Will they...will they take a woman like me?"

"Yes."

"Can they help me?"

"Yes, if you will let them."

Alana looked back up at her, and tears gathered in

her eyes. "How can I thank you? You are very kind, so kind...."

"Don't tell anyone, please," Victoria said stiffly. "This house is small. They can only take a few women at a time."

"I see," Alana said, her eyes gleaming. "I thought you meant that you didn't want me to tell anyone you were kind."

In a fashionably bored tone, Victoria said, "It would ruin my reputation."

Alana couldn't quite stifle a giggle, a small burst of mirth that sounded much younger than her ravaged face looked.

Cheney came back in then, directing a surprised look at Alana and a suspicious one at Victoria. "Did you find out anything from her?"

"Cheney, dearest, it's so impolitic to speak of people in the third person when they are in the room. Dr. Cheney Duvall, may I present Miss Alana Patterson. Miss Patterson, Dr. Duvall."

Cheney turned to Alana, studying her once again. Cheney was now shod, and by the door David held her cloak. She was still buttoning up her jacket, but she looked rumpled and smudged, and she hadn't been able to do anything to her hair. It was wild and glorious, streaming down her back. Long glossy curls kept falling in front of her face, and impatiently Cheney pushed them back. "Miss Patterson," she finally acknowledged her with a slight nod.

Alana's sallow cheeks flamed. "Ma'am, I can explain—that is, I can assure you, Dr. Duvall, that I had nothing to do with this. I had no knowledge of it beforehand, and when I found out, I tried my best to persuade Sweet and Mr. Worthington to let you go."

Cheney shrugged. "I have no reason to trust you except it is obvious that they left you holding the short end of the stick."

"Don't you mean the cat in the bag?" Victoria corrected her.

"Maybe that's it," Cheney agreed absently. "Anyway, Miss Patterson, I probably know a lot more about Mr. Worthington than do you, so I'm not going to ask you many questions right now. However, I have a friend, a relative of Mr. Worthington's, who I'm certain will wish to question you at length." Cheney looked around at the vulgar parlor. "Do you, by any chance, have any idea where Mr. Worthington is now?"

"No idea at all, Dr. Duvall. Sweet packed everything while Mr. Worthington was talking to you. They left without leaving a forwarding address," she finished ironically. "And the girls, when they saw him and Sweet running like scalded cats, they took off, too."

"I see," Cheney said, glancing again around at the untidy room. "Um...will you be staying here, do you think?"

"I...I—you mean, you aren't going to have me arrested?" Alana asked hopefully.

"I suppose not."

"Then I—no, no. I don't want to stay here, but I—" Alana stuttered.

"I have her address," Victoria said in a bored tone.

Cheney smiled to herself as she sat down on the sofa—dust plumped up from it, a cloud of motes that danced around her—and started rummaging in her medical bag. "Mr. Sweet is a curious kind of man," she muttered. "He left everything in better order than even I had it, even my gun."

"Gun?" Alana exclaimed, alarmed. "Cooee, Mr. High-and-Mighty Worthington didn't half know what he was getting into, did he?" Alana glanced from this fiery woman with a gun to Victoria Elizabeth Steen de Lancie's regal and imperious glamor. Victoria and Cheney ignored her.

Finally Cheney was satisfied that her medical bag was unharmed and in order. "All right, then, I'll be in touch, Miss Patterson, and so will my friend Mr. Irons-Winslow. Shiloh Irons-Winslow." A shadow darkened Victoria's sapphire-blue eyes for a moment, but Cheney was watching Alana Patterson intently.

"Mr. Shiloh Irons-Winslow," Alana repeated meekly. "A nice gentlemanly kind of name, if I may say so."

"Yes, he is a gentleman," Cheney said quietly. "He will be kind to you."

"Will, come here, please," Victoria called, and the footman appeared. He was much older than David, but he was still as strong as a bull. He was a coarse-looking man, with a broken nose and a small scar on his neck, but he was the same height, and his shoulders measured the same as the younger footman's. Victoria liked having matched sets, so to speak. "Would you see if those awful journalist persons are still outside? They are distressing to Dr. Duvall. Please see if you and David can persuade them to leave."

"Yes, ma'am," he said obediently, bowing.

"Cooee, his knickers cost more'n my whole closet," Alana said, forgetting herself completely at the splendor of the footman's white satin knee breeches and coats.

Cheney giggled a little, while Victoria pretended that

she didn't hear, as all very elegant ladies do when they witness a social gaffe. "Miss Patterson," Victoria said in a languid tone, "pardon me, but you did tell me that you were crippled, did you not? May I ask if you need assistance?"

"You're crippled?" Cheney asked alertly. "How?"

Alana asked curiously, "Are you a real doctor?"

"Yes, I'm a real doctor," Cheney said a trifle wearily.

"That explains her rudeness," Victoria put in.

"I'm not rude, I'm just concerned," Cheney argued.

"You're curious, Cheney, and asking such personal questions so bluntly may be considered rude by polite society," Victoria replied placidly.

"Dearie me," Alana said under her breath. She'd never imagined that real ladies, rich ladies, Polite Society Ladies, behaved like this. Of course, none of them did, but Alana had no way of knowing that, having obtained her education in deportment from etiquette books.

"I beg your pardon, Miss Patterson, but I suppose I do have a clinical interest," Cheney said with a weary glance at Victoria.

"It's—of course it's all right," Alana said, embarrassed. "I'm an amputee. My right leg, below the knee. I have a crutch, but it's kept in the kitchen. Mr. Worthington, however, threw it out the back door, I think, when I was arguing with him." Her mouth tightened into a dry scarlet slash. "I suppose he was afraid I'd try to go up to the third floor and let you go, which is absurd. I can barely get up to my own room. Or he might just have done it for meanness. He could be that way."

"Yes, he can," Cheney agreed solemnly. "Do you have a prosthetic leg?"

"No, ma'am," Alana said, ducking her head again.

"Here's my card," Cheney said carelessly. "I can help you get fitted for one and possibly get some financial assistance with paying for it."

Alana looked up at her, utterly bewildered. "I—I can't believe this is happening to me. No one…no one—" She swallowed hard. "No one has ever been this nice to me before. I don't even know you, and you're both so—"

"Really not necessary," Cheney said, clearing her throat and turning away.

"Really not," Victoria said.

Will and David appeared at the doorway and nodded to Victoria.

"We really must be going now," Victoria said, rising like a queen surveying her throne room. "Miss Patterson has a crutch, either in the kitchen or outside in the back, Will. Please fetch it for her. May we, Miss Patterson, call you a hansom cab?"

"No…no, thank you," Alana said in a muffled voice. She had actually started crying, for the first time in years. "I…I want to pack some things, and…and recover a little."

"I will see you soon, Miss Patterson," Cheney said, awkwardly patting her shoulder. "Please, don't be upset. Here is your crutch. And don't lose my card. If you should need anything, you may call at the office or at Duvall Court anytime."

Alana sobbed, her frizzy head bent, and Cheney and Victoria took their rather hasty leave. "Some women get so emotional," Victoria remarked icily. "After all, you were the one who was abducted and frightened half to death and then had to spend the night in a brothel."

Cheney stopped in her tracks, astounded. "Victoria!

Do you mean to tell me that that was a *brothel?* Oh, oh, Dally is going to kill me!"

At that, even Will and David, the two mute statues behind them, laughed long and loud.

Chapter Twenty-Two

Strong Hearts

"It would be difficult," Dev said darkly to himself, "to find a traveling circus in this muck."

The black clouds above were featureless, a solid pall from horizon to horizon. The half-frozen rain almost blinded him, for Dev had brought out his open curricle. He'd considered going for a closed hansom cab, but he knew he was going to need the full range of his keen vision to find a single man walking along the ill-lit streets and Stygian alleys of the Hudson River docks. For a moment he doubted himself. The blankets he'd brought were getting wet, and he could hardly see. And when he did find Shiloh, there was barely room in the stream-lined curricle to fit another person, much less a large, long-legged person who might, perhaps, be unconscious. Shiloh, Dev knew, should really have an ambulance, but one could hardly call out an ambulance to ride up and down the streets looking for a man who was lost.

But quickly Dev dismissed these misgivings. It was done—the course was set. At least the curricle was much faster than a hansom cab or a four-horse carriage. Especially since Dev was driving at a reckless speed, taking corners on one wheel, sliding from side to side on the wet streets. Cheney and her parents would have been startled to see the staid, dignified doctor driving like a drunken rake. But Dev barely thought of it, tooling his well-sprung curricle along in the rain, single-mindedly thinking only of his patient.

Because Dr. Devlin Buchanan was such a methodical and logical man, he had decided to go straight to Shiloh's shanty first. He knew of Shiloh's shanty, had even been there several times. Not on social calls, of course. During the cholera plague of 1866, Dev and Shiloh had not been on what one might call equable terms. But Dev had agreed to be the physician for the fighters in the events sponsored by the Marquess of Queensberry, and as always, he had taken his responsibilities very seriously. After the fights he had called on all of the pugilists—Mike McCool, James Elliott, and Shiloh "The Iron Man" Irons—for several days after the fights to check on their recoveries. Shiloh hadn't seen him and never knew that Dev had called or cared after the McCool fight, for then Jeremy Blue seemed to be taking adequate care of him. But after the Elliott fight, Dev had called on Shiloh three times at his little shack by the docks. By that time Dev had developed a begrudging respect for Shiloh, not for his pugilistic abilities, but because of his work in the quarantine hospital.

Somehow Dev had just known that Shiloh would try to go to the little fisherman's shack. Though Dev had never, and would never, discuss personal things with Shiloh, he understood perfectly how Shiloh felt about the shanty. *It's probably the only place he's ever felt belonged to him,*

Dev reflected. *He kept it clean, bought furniture and curtains. Even though he was only there a few months, it was probably the first time he'd ever had the sense of having a place all his own. Like I felt for so long about the little servant's cottage at Duvall Court. Even after Mother died and I'd moved into the big house, somehow that shabby little cottage felt more like my home.*

It was late on a Friday night, so as Dev expected, the White Pelican Tavern was roaring. He wheeled the curricle up almost on the porch and had a moment's anxiety that one of the rough-looking men staggering around, yelling, shouting, and groping the equally coarse-looking women might just jump in the fine curricle and take off. It would be so easy.

Grimly Dev reflected, *Easy for a block or two, maybe. Then I'd find it, for sure, turned over or in the river. Brutus isn't that easy to drive.* Dev's horse Brutus was of the same bloodline as the Duvalls' Romulus and Remus. They were all high-spirited, fast, and sometimes bad-tempered Arabians. Shrugging, Dev jumped down and, politely declining the proposition of a drunken woman who smelled like old sweat and raw whiskey, went into the tavern.

It was dimly lit and full. The roars of men, the shrieks of women, and the pounding of an untuned piano made Dev's ears hurt. With one quick look around, he could tell that Shiloh Irons-Winslow wasn't in the tavern—not standing up, at least. He was always the tallest man anywhere. Dev tried to see in the dark corners, around the pushing, rowdy crowd. But it was impossible. There were too many people and too little light.

But he did see Hub, the tavern keeper, who had been something of a friend to Shiloh that hot, sickening summer. He shoved his way to the rough wooden bar and managed to plant himself right in front of the tavern keeper's round, sweating face. The man was holding four beer steins by the handles, slopping beer into them from a barrel keg.

"Mr.—" Dev stopped. He realized he didn't know the man's last name, and this bothered him. But gamely he shouted, "Hub! Hub! It's Dr. Devlin Buchanan. Do you remember me?"

The man looked up, his eyes narrowed with suspicion, and shouted back over the infernal din, "Who'm are you?"

"Buchanan!" Dev said helplessly. "Doctor! Oh, forget it." He took out his wallet and laid a crisp five-dollar bank note down, and Hub's suspicious eyes grew as round as his face. "Irons! The Iron Man!" Dev shouted as loudly as he could. "Have you seen him tonight?"

Hub licked his lips, looking longingly at the bill, then slowly recognition made his little pig eyes somewhat less muddy. "The Iron Man, Mr. Irons? Shiloh?"

"Yes, have you seen him tonight?"

Dirty hands reached over the bar. With quick dispatch Hub handed over the beer and deftly caught the coins tossed to him. Now he leaned over to yell in Dev's ear, "Sorry, Dr. Buchanan, now I 'member you. But I ain't seen Shiloh tonight. He visited one morning, doncherno, when I could see straight and think straight widout this rabble. But I ain't seen the Iron Man tonight."

Dev nodded and tucked the bill into Hub's hand. The tavern keeper looked surprised, then yelled, "Thank you. Thank you, sir! Lemme get you something there, Doctor! You look mighty cold and wet."

But Dev merely shook his head and left.

A drunken man and woman were leaning precariously against his curricle, but they were more interested in drinking and clutching each other than they were in stealing the carriage.

The shanty next door was dark, obviously empty. But still, Dev, being the precise man he was, went and checked the front door. It was locked. He tried to look through the cracks in the shuttered windows—not a glimmer of light. Quickly he went around to the kitchen door. It, too, was locked. Shiloh wasn't there.

He hurried back to the curricle, brushing against the man who was leaning against it and sloppily kissing the tawdry girl. Ever the gentleman, Dev muttered without thinking, "Excuse me, please," as he jumped up and flicked the whip over Brutus's back. The couple was so astounded at Dev's appearance, his courtesy, and the sudden disappearance of their prop, that they fell down into the muddy street.

Very slowly, now, Dev drove up Washington Street. Once, by the side of the road, he saw a glimmer of something light colored, so he stopped and leaped out. It was just an ancient lump of wood, aged and sun bleached. Twice he saw unidentifiable lumps on the side of the street, and both times he stopped the curricle, then jumped down to examine them. Both times it was just piles of sodden, stinking garbage—oyster shells, tangled fishnets, soured hay. Finally he just led Brutus and walked, his sharp eyes scanning from side to side.

Several blocks north of the tavern, the district became a slummy industrial area, with great yawning warehouses and stinking factories. Dev was very cold, even with his caped greatcoat on, and the rain pattered off his top-hat brim as if it were a storm gutter. It hindered his vision, so Dev finally snatched it off. Vaguely he was conscious of how much colder he was getting with his head bare and wet, but it didn't really make much of an impression on his conscious mind. He was concentrating too hard on searching for Shiloh.

He walked for what seemed like miles, trying to figure the nameless, unmarked cross streets. He wasn't too sure how far up West Tenth was located, which was the street that Shiloh had been walking along when he left Minette's. He knew that Tenth crossed Washington, and if Shiloh had been heading for the shanty, he would have come straight down this street. But it was going to be difficult to find. Some of the streets had had signs at one time, but they never lasted long. The wood used for the signs was too precious, either as fuel or to shore up an old canvas shanty. Sadly Dev remembered the hay-barge children, the feral little orphans who slept in the hay barges. Many times they stole the precious signs to burn them or to make weapons from the stout wood.

As he went farther north, the condition of the streets and buildings grew a little less bleak, and he began to see some housing. Not fine housing, mostly small dirty shacks, but down these side streets he could see street-lamps. Finally he halted at one of the shacks, not because it was marked, but because it was familiar. He thought very hard and remembered that this was Christopher Street—he'd visited a patient here once, a very elderly woman who had died within hours of his arrival—and the next cross street was Tenth Street. Reluctantly Dev went up to the next street. He turned up Tenth and went all the way up to Bleecker, knowing that one of the anonymous houses he'd passed was surely Minette York's.

No Shiloh.

Thoughtfully he climbed back into the curricle and, struggling a little, for Brutus was impatient with a walking pace, returned to the corner of Washington and Tenth. There he stopped in the middle of the nameless, unremarkable intersection and looked around, feeling the first cold fingers of helplessness—and fear. It surprised him a little that he cared this much for Shiloh Irons-Winslow. He usually was much more pragmatic about his patients. But then, even though he and Shiloh had never had a close friendship, Dev realized that he admired and respected Shiloh. Yes, he finally decided that he did like Shiloh.

I would have liked to have had his friendship, Dev mused glumly.

As soon as he comprehended that he was thinking of Shiloh in the past tense, Dev jerked as though someone had come up behind him and startled him. *Do I really think he's dead?*

Anything could have happened. Someone could have picked him up. He could have gotten a hansom cab and gone, instead, to…to St. Luke's or to someone's house.

But Dev knew that all of those things were highly improbable. No one would pick up a man who was disheveled, apparently drunk, and without any cloak or hat. Shiloh probably didn't have a cent on him. His money was likely in a roomy pocket of his coat. Hansom cab drivers were not noted for their charitable habits. And Dev knew that Shiloh didn't know anyone else who lived close by. The Fine and Dandies all lived across town on the East Side.

Brutus snorted with disgust and stamped impatiently as Dev sat in the curricle for several minutes in the dismal downpour. He was worried, unsure what to do. Dev hated to be unsure of himself. He despised being indecisive. He struggled, trying to discipline his turgid thoughts and uncomfortably strong grief.

Finally his shoulders sagged, and he dropped his head. Ice-cold water poured over him, over his face, down the neck of his coat onto his back. Bleakly he prayed, "Lord, You know that I try very hard to…to do things for myself. I try to be strong, to be courageous, to work to find the right thing, the correct course in my life.

"But now, Lord, I don't know what to do. I'm frightened. I feel weak and helpless. Help me, please. Where should I go? What should I do?"

Much later, Dev was somewhat amused to realize that the Lord God of All spoke to him much in the same way Dev himself thought and communicated. God took it slowly, logically, a step at a time, waiting until Dev comprehended.

All of this self-reliance is admirable, but what is it that God wants of me? My good works? My triumphs, my victories, my strength? No. All of those are as filthy rags to Him.

He just wants me to rely on Him instead of on myself. Let Him bear the burdens. Let Him be the Lord of my life. Ask Him for wisdom to make decisions, to find the right and true course. He wants me to give my life totally to Him.

From now on, Lord, here I am. I don't know what to do. Help me, Lord, please.

No lightning bolt came from heaven, no bush started burning, no thunderous voice shattered the silence. Wearily Dev looked up and around. *I know I've got to keep looking. He's here. He's here somewhere. Should I trace Washington again? No, no. He's not there. He could have staggered miles away by now or into a warehouse or one of those fallen-down shacks. I hope he didn't stumble into the river.*

Dev's head snapped up alertly. What if Shiloh missed Washington and went all the way over to the waterfront? Along West Street? He might not have realized it until he saw the river.

Hope he didn't see it too closely, Lord, Dev prayed grimly, never knowing how close he was to the truth.

"Let's go, Brutus," Dev said, snapping the whip just to make the noise. Brutus had been long ready to go somewhere, anywhere. Dev drove the short block over to the road running along the waterfront. West Street was a curious road—wide in some places, narrow in others, some of it planked just like the docks, some of it two-hundred-year-old cobblestones, some of it neatly bricked, some of it just a muddy cart track.

Dev found Shiloh lying square in the middle of a stretch of brick paving. He was on his back, his head turned slightly to the side, his hands lying peacefully on his naked chest.

Dev grabbed his lantern and his bag and jumped out of the curricle, swallowing hard. He could see Shiloh's face, a stark white wedge in the darkness. Throwing himself to his knees, Dev grabbed Shiloh's wrist. His skin was very cold. His mouth was blue. Even though Dev had been wearing gloves, his fingers were so cold he couldn't feel a pulse.

Muttering to himself, he took out his stethoscope, watching Shiloh's face as he pressed the receiver against his bare chest. Shiloh's eyes didn't flutter. He was completely still. Dev listened for what seemed like a long, long time.

When Shiloh's heart did beat, Dev's dark eyes widened with surprise.

Quickly he pulled out his watch, timing the beats. After one minute he sat back and looked at Shiloh's still form with wonder. "Must have a strong heart," he murmured quietly, though his thoughts were more akin to *Strongest beat I ever heard, not thudding, just like great even strokes on an enormous and sound bell...down to twenty-eight beats a minute. But his heart hasn't weakened at all. Still pulsing that blood all the way down to his feet and up to his brain. That's some heart you've got there, my friend.*

"Still," Dev said to himself, "you can't stay in hibernation much longer. Got to get that heart rate up." He found the kit and the injection of strychnine he'd prepared ahead of time. Tying a tourniquet around Shiloh's arm, Dev noted again, bemused, how strongly and surely the blood in the swollen vein pulsed. Dev gave him the injection, untied the tourniquet, and efficiently stowed everything back in his bag. Without glancing at Shiloh, he jumped up, ran to the curricle, and hopped in to get the blankets. He shuffled through them—he had brought three, but the top one was soaked through—and grabbed the two dry ones.

When he got back, Shiloh's eyes were open.

Dev comically skidded to a halt. He hadn't expected Shiloh to wake up for hours.

"Hello there, Dr. Buchanan," Shiloh mumbled.

"He-hello." Recovering himself, Dev threw the blankets over Shiloh, tucking them around him securely.

"Dr. Buchanan?"

"Yes?"

"Am I alive, or are you dead?"

Dev actually laughed, his deep dimples pronounced. "I'm alive, and you're alive."

Shiloh nodded, contented. "How'd you find me?"

Dev sat back on his heels. "I prayed."

Now Shiloh smiled, and although it was far from his usual complacent grin, it did make his eyes lighten a little. "S'funny, Dr. Buchanan. So did I."

Part Five

A Sound Mind

*For God hath not given us the spirit of fear;
but of power, and of love, and of a sound mind.*

—2 Timothy 1:7

Chapter Twenty-Three

Families Are Worth It

"So...so...that girl Mr. Sweet called Luna or Moonie, something like that—she wasn't a maid?" Cheney asked, her brow wrinkling.

"No, Cheney dearest, she wasn't really a maid," Victoria said, still struggling to hide her amusement. Oh, how she loved Cheney! She'd never thought to meet someone with such an endearing combination of toughness and gentleness, of world-weary understanding and naïveté, of sweet and salt. "But Cheney, dear, whoever or whatever did you think Alana Patterson was?"

"Um...er...I thought she was Mr. Winslow's housekeeper," Cheney said uncertainly. "I did think she wasn't a very good one."

Victoria couldn't contain her laughter, and finally even Cheney giggled a little. "Of course, I should have known, but I had other things on my mind...." She was distracted, looking out the window. "Victoria, where are we going? This isn't the way back to the office." Cheney had asked Victoria to take her back to the office to get cleaned up before she faced her parents', and particularly Dally's, wrath.

Victoria sobered immediately. "We're going to Dev's."

"Dev's!" Cheney exclaimed, then saw Victoria's face. "What...what is it? Did Bain Winslow do something to Shiloh, too? He did, didn't he? Tell me, Victoria!"

Victoria nodded soothingly, then leaned across the carriage to take Cheney's hand. It was icy cold. "I'll tell you, of course. But, Cheney, you're not well, and though we've made a great joke of it, you've been through a terrifying night. Are you sure...?"

Cheney clutched Victoria's hand in both of hers. "I must know. Now."

"All right. Here is all I know."

They had almost reached Gramercy Park before Victoria finished her story. Deliberately she left out any mention of Dart. That was Dev's life, his story to tell, especially to Cheney.

Cheney listened without saying a word, her shadowed eyes enormous, her forehead pale, but the bottom half of her face was an angry crimson from the chloroform burn. Her hair was wild, and her clothes were wrinkled and untidy. Victoria felt pity for her, for she understood very well how self-conscious, and therefore vulnerable and helpless, a woman felt when she was not presentable. But she understood that Cheney wouldn't want to go anywhere to clean up. She would just want to find Shiloh. Victoria thought that in the same circumstances she herself would crawl over broken glass in rags to find Dev.

When Victoria finished, Cheney just said in a choked voice, "Tell Mr. Long to hurry."

They were already hurrying, in fact. Mr. Long and the

two footmen on their sprung chairs behind felt that they'd been hurrying along at a suicidal pace on this carriage for ages and ages. The sleet had stopped, though the streets were still wet and slippery. It was cold. No sun had risen that morning. Only a vague yellow blob hung in the pall of the sky.

"His curricle's here," Victoria breathed.

Cheney said nothing. Before the coach actually came to a complete stop, she had flung open the door, kicked down the steps, and flown out. She was banging on Dev's door and shouting before the surprised footmen had even climbed down.

"Dev! Let me in!" Cheney shouted.

Mrs. Barentine, her eyes popping with shock, opened the door a tiny crack. "Yes? Would you like an audience with the doctor?"

The sight of the prim housekeeper, her gray hair pulled back into a neat bun, her mouth pinched into a very small button of disapproval, did set Cheney back just a bit. "Oh. You must be Mrs. Barentine."

"That I am. And you are—?" The door did not open another inch.

"I'm…I'm—it's rather hard to explain, really," Cheney was saying desperately.

Victoria, as usual, serenely took the situation in hand. "We wish to see Dr. Buchanan, madam. We shall give you our cards, and you will let Dr. Buchanan know that we are here. I'm sure he will receive us."

The door cracked just a bit—Victoria, after all, did look like a relatively sane, respectable woman, though she was outrageously overdressed for morning calls. But Mrs. Barentine still eyed Cheney suspiciously.

"Mrs. Barentine?" came Dev's calm voice from behind

her. "It's quite all right. Well, actually it isn't, but we must go along with the ladies, mustn't we?"

Victoria waited, smiling, but Cheney had just about reached the end of her forbearance. She shoved the door, almost knocking poor Mrs. Barentine down, and threw herself into Dev's arms. He'd been expecting something like this, so he was ready. He hugged her hard and murmured, "He's all right. He's upstairs."

Without another word or a backward glance Cheney flew up the stairs.

"Well!" Mrs. Barentine sniffed. "Well! I never!"

Dev said wryly, "Well, I have. And so will you, I'm afraid. That was my sister, Dr. Cheney Duvall."

"Humph!" Mrs. Barentine grunted disapprovingly. "She don't take after your side of the family, now, does she? Hardly respectable, I'd say."

"Yes. That will be all, Mrs. Barentine."

Dev wasn't paying attention to her. He was staring, bewitched, at Victoria. She still looked lovely, ethereal. She was wearing the same clothing she'd worn last night—it seemed forever ago to Dev—and still she looked as fresh, as untouched, as if she had just now floated down to earth from heaven.

"May I come in, or am I to loiter about here on your doorstep all day?" she asked coolly, but her blue eyes danced as she saw the expression on his face.

Dev sighed. "You might as well come in."

"How can a woman resist such passionate entreaties?" Victoria glanced keenly at him. He was in his shirtsleeves, his vest rumpled, and he was pale. "You look tired," she said quietly as he took her cloak and tossed it onto a chair in the parlor. "Was it difficult?"

Dev's dimples flashed, a sign of his dry amusement.

"I think I'm in worse shape than Mr. Irons-Winslow is."
He was handing Victoria onto the sofa when he stiffened,
his eyes wide. "Good heavens, Vic, I forgot about Dart!
Where's Dart?"

Soothingly Victoria took his arm. "He's fine, Dev.
He's just fine. I left him with Nia at your office. He's just
fine."

"Oh. I should go get him," Dev said, frowning.

"You'll do nothing of the sort," Victoria said, gliding
out of the room.

He heard her go into the kitchen and talk to Mrs. Barentine—whose indignant pipe could be clearly heard.
Dev reflected how nice it was to have someone to help
him. Someone to share with.

Someone to love and to have and to hold forever.

When Victoria came back in the room, Dev burst
out, "Victoria, will you marry me again? I mean, would
you—again—I mean—"

The trill of Victoria's laughter sounded like clear silver
bells. "Dev, please. Your first proposal was so much more
proper. But, yes—I do think I like this one better. Yes, I
will marry you again, so to speak. I would marry you a
hundred times if I could."

He took her in his arms and held her, but gently, for
she seemed impossibly precious to him. She lifted her
head and kissed him. The warmth of her lips, her sweet
spring scent, the spun silver of her hair—

"Well, this just caps the mornin' to be sure," Mrs. Barentine said ominously. Beside her was Mr. Long, Victoria's coachman, who was looking at the ceiling, his
mouth pursed as if he were about to whistle a nonchalant
little tune. He was an older man with fat red cheeks and
just now they were very red indeed.

Dev almost leaped to the ceiling, while Victoria merely sighed as if she were just the tiniest bit annoyed at the interruption. "Mr. Long, please take the footmen and go to Dr. Buchanan's office and pick up Nia and Dart and bring them back here."

"Yes, madam," he managed to say solemnly and hurried out.

Mrs. Barentine was still frowning darkly at Victoria, but she collected herself and disappeared with an indignant whisk of her skirts.

But Dev had already forgotten about his housekeeper and her great offense. His brow was wrinkled. "You know, Vic, there are some things, some terrible things, that I have never told you about my family and Dart, and I don't know if you'll want to marry me—"

"Dev," she said with great patience, "you just asked me to marry you for the second time. Now you're trying to talk me out of it. Really, we must either get married or not, one or the other. I would prefer to get married."

"You would?" he said, trying to comprehend all this joy after weeks of misery. "You truly would? But...but Vic, there is Dart. . . ."

"Yes, Dart," Victoria repeated and smiled as she came into his arms again. "I want to know all about him. What will he call me, I wonder? I know it couldn't be Mother, but do you suppose we could think of some, you know, pet names, such as Mimsy or Popsy? Or—"

Dev stiffened, though he didn't loosen the tight circle of his arms. "No one is ever going to call me Popsy."

"Of course not," Victoria said, gazing up at him wide-eyed.

"Victoria, you seem...almost excited...about Dart," Dev said uncertainly. "You do understand that I'm

going to keep him? Raise him in my household, in my...
life?"

Victoria took his face in her small hands. His beard
was rough, and there were faint blue shadows under his
eyes. She traced one gently. "Of course I understand that,
Dev."

"And you don't mind?"

"Mind?" Victoria was astounded. "Mind? What do
you mean? It's like...it's like a dream that we should have
children of our own. Our own family."

Now Dev was surprised. "You mean, you want children? A family?"

"Of course! I've been agonizing over this for...for-
ever!"

"But I thought we didn't want children, Vic," Dev said,
bewildered. "I thought we said—well, no, we didn't exactly talk about it, but I was sure..."

Suddenly comprehending, Victoria whispered, "You
hoped to please me because I can't have children. And I
was so desperate to please you that I thought I didn't de-
serve to be your wife."

They stared at each other. Finally Dev said, "It seemed
so important at the time. Such immense problems, there
seemed to be. Now I can hardly recall what all the fuss
was about. All I can think is how much I love you, Victoria, and how grateful to the Lord I am that you'll be
with me for the rest of my life."

"Dev, it'll take the rest of your life for me to show you
how much I love you," Victoria murmured.

They were kissing again when Mrs. Barentine entered
with a loudly clanging tray. "Coffee's on," she announced
dryly, "as if anybody cares."

* * *

"Hi, Doc."

Unbelievably he looked much the same. He was very pale, of course, and he was slumped, sitting in an armchair by the window. The sunlight, weak as it was, gilded his hair with a bright aura. Cheney swallowed hard. "Hello, Shiloh."

"Forgive me for not getting up," he said gravely, "but I can't get up."

"You can't? Are you—" She rushed to him, knelt by him.

"Naw, I'm not crippled or hurt or amputated, or anything like that," he drawled, tracing her cheek with his finger and smiling. "I just still get dizzy if I move, too—Cheney, what's happened to your face!" He jerked, started as if he would get up, but, swaying a little, he fell back into the chair.

Cheney jumped up and leaned over him, her hands on his shoulders. "Sit still, Shiloh. It's all right, really. It's nothing, nothing at all. I'll explain later, but first I want you to…"

He was listening, but a heavy length of her loosened hair fell across her shoulders, and he couldn't stop himself from touching it, from tangling his fingers in it. Cheney was only inches away from his face, leaning so close, and he stared at her, directly into her eyes. "You don't know how many, many times I've wanted to touch your hair," he murmured thickly.

Cheney jerked up straight. Shiloh looked confused, but only for a moment. "Sorry, Doc," he said, unrepentant. "You have to make allowances for me. I'm sick."

"You don't seem very sick to me." Looking around Dev's guest bedroom, she saw a plain secretary and a straight wooden chair against one wall. She dragged the chair over, with Shiloh watching her critically.

"It was Bain, wasn't it? He did something to you, didn't he?" Shiloh growled.

"No, actually he didn't do anything to me," Cheney replied calmly. "I mean, he didn't hurt me. Let's just say he...inconvenienced me somewhat. I'm fine, really, Shiloh. I mean it."

"My cousin," Shiloh snorted.

Placing the chair very close to his, Cheney smiled, "You're the one who always wanted a family. With families, you must take what you get and love them anyway."

"Yeah, I know," he said quietly. "Families are worth it."

He took her hand, caressed it for a minute, then pressed it to his lips. Cheney's intake of breath was sharp, but she didn't protest.

After he dropped her hand but still held it tightly, she leaned forward intently and said, "Now I want you to tell me everything."

"Everything? That's a tall order, but lemme see...." He frowned, then recited, "I think you're the most beautiful woman I've ever set eyes on. I'm pretty sure I fell in love with you when we were here, in New York, in the park with Laura Blue. At least, that's when I really realized that I was in love with you and would never in my life love another woman as I do you. You have green eyes that would make a man sell his horse to get to look deeply into them for a while. Your hair is like some kind of precious metal—"

Though Cheney didn't really want him to—she was

blushing prettily—she cried, "Shiloh! Just stop it. You know that's not what I meant."

He nodded. "I know. It's just that those are the things that I've been thinking about mostly last night and this morning. Those are the important things. Some of them anyway."

Cheney was quiet. She couldn't remember ever seeing Shiloh in this quietly introspective mood.

He smiled at her, a gentle smile unlike his own wide crooked grin. "Last night I thought I was dying, Cheney. So I prayed. I prayed and asked the Lord to save me. Not just from death...but to save my soul."

"You...you did?" Cheney breathed. "Was it—was it because you were afraid?"

"Sure," he said, shrugging. "Who isn't, when they finally face God? But I know what you mean. You're asking if I meant it. For life, and not just for death."

He watched her, and she nodded wordlessly, her eyes huge. "I meant it then," he said firmly, looking her straight in the eye. "I mean it now. The Lord showed me the truth about myself, and then He showed me how He could make all those stains on my soul go away, just as though they'd never been. He showed me how life will be different, how I will be different, how I don't have to fight and struggle and lie to myself anymore. He showed me that if He is Lord of my life, He will give me a new life, full of sweetness and joy and peace. And then He promised me eternal life."

Cheney was weeping, tears rolling down her face. He reached out and wiped them away with a touch as gentle as a woman's. "Don't cry, Cheney," he said, pleading.

"Sorry," she said, sniffling dismally. She swiped at her nose but had no handkerchief. Shiloh gave her his. "It's just so…so good I can hardly believe it! Thank the Lord God in heaven above! It's like some wonderful story, some happy, glorious story that I could only make up and think of when I was daydreaming!" Cheney wept a little more while Shiloh watched her, a half smile on his face. She looked up, her eyes red rimmed and swollen. "Oh, I must look a mess, but I have to know, Shiloh, can we get married now?"

For once, Cheney had the satisfaction of seeing Shiloh Irons look absolutely thunderstruck.

"N-now?" he stammered.

"Not right now, you fool," Cheney said, dabbing her eyes. "I mean, would you ask me again? Are you going to?"

"Well…sure, Doc. I mean, I meant to, but gimme a minute," he muttered, frowning severely.

Cheney laughed. "I thought you knew everything I was thinking. You look surprised. Shocked, really."

"I'll get you back," he said slyly. "I'll sneak up behind you when you're not looking and ask you to marry me."

"Sorry, Shiloh," she said, taking his hand and squeezing it. "But from now on I'm going to be looking."

Chapter Twenty-Four

Tender Mercies

They were all together again a few days later at Duvall Court for a somewhat impromptu celebratory dinner. It had been rather odd the way they had fallen in together. Shiloh had insisted on coming to church with the Duvalls. It was the first time Dr. Devlin Buchanan's patient had been up and out, so he decided to accompany him instead of going to church with Victoria's family, as was his custom. Ostensibly Victoria decided that this would be a good week to attend church with her good friend Cheney Duvall.

Tante Marye was a devout Catholic, and Gowan Ford was a devout Methodist. Tante Elyse said she was both, so they had compromised and gone Catholic one week, Protestant the next, and this week they'd woken up and decided to go to the Duvalls' Fifth Avenue Presbyterian Church.

And so Richard Duvall invited them all to dinner while Irene managed to smile and say she'd be delighted, of course they must all come, even though she was secretly horrified. Dinner for nine generally required at least two days of preparation, and Irene was in the process of hiring a new cook. But wisely Tante Marye took her aside and told her not to worry and not to do a thing, that she had a perfectly wonderful idea, and dinner would be served at Duvall Court promptly at eight o'clock. Irene tried to question her, but Tante Marye frigidly told her to go home and rest and be ready to receive her guests at seven-thirty.

And so the nine of them were together again. Mallow, with flaming cheeks and wild-eyed glances at Dally glowering by the sideboard, was serving for the first time. Delicious fragrances of rich food already permeated the air.

"I would like for Shiloh to ask a blessing for this food and for this company," Richard Duvall announced.

Cheney felt a little nervous, but evidently Shiloh was not.

"I'd be honored, sir," he said easily and bowed his head.

"Dear Lord, we ask that You send Your blessings on this food to nourish and sustain us, but also so that we'll always remember that You alone feed us. Thank you, Lord, for each and every person here, for loving friends and lasting friendships. We give You our thanks from our hearts. Amen."

The men echoed the closing amen, and Dev said wryly, "Speaking of hearts, it's difficult for me to believe that yours is made of tissue and muscle and blood corpuscles—"

"Devlin Buchanan!" Tante Marye said, horrified. "Such language at the table!"

His eyes sparkled with merriment. Dev had never

seemed so light-hearted. "It's the truth. His heart sounds like this—" He reached over his elaborate place setting and hit the mahogany dining table hard with his fist. It made a solid loud thump, and the glassware shook and the gold ware tinkled. Before the others could recover, he did it again. Like a delighted small boy he said, "There he was, as pale as death, his heart beating only once about every two seconds. It still was as powerful as a locomotive engine. Mr. Irons-Winslow, you really must donate it for postmortem analysis."

"Sure," Shiloh shrugged, unconcerned. "I won't be needing it then, huh?"

"*O Ciel!*" Tante Marye exclaimed, clutching her napkin to her spare chest.

Tante Elyse said with delight, "How marvelous! Oh, Shiloh, we've heard the story in bits and pieces, but you must tell us everything! Every wretched, frightful moment!"

"Be glad to, Tante Elyse, but I hafta act it out, you see. That requires a lot of fallin' down and groanin' and stuff. Maybe we can do that instead of charades or tableaux later, do you think?" Shiloh was pale, but his eyes were once again a healthy Caribbean blue, and he evidenced no weakness at all.

"Oh yes, let's!" Tante Elyse said, clapping her hands. It was a young girl's gesture, and even though she was fifty-six years old, it became her very well. "I want to play that awful urchin, Rock. Gowan, I shall need a club."

Gowan grinned his gargoyle's grimace. "Of course, Elyse, whatever you want."

"Really?"

"Sure. You know I always give in, in the end. I've decided to just stop fighting it, give up first, conserve my energy."

"Well, that's just no fun at all," Tante Elyse grumbled.

Richard nodded meaningfully at Gowan. "I learned that years ago, Mr. Ford. Makes life so much easier."

"I'm so looking forward to the years I'll take to learn it," Dev said with a sidelong glance at Victoria.

"Oh, I'm so happy you two are back together!" Tante Elyse declared. "But, dear Mrs. de Lancie, will you be able to get everything done—I should say undone, shouldn't I?—to cancel the cancellation? It's only one week until the wedding."

"Six days," Victoria corrected her. "You just wouldn't believe how fast I've been moving. The cards for returning the wedding gifts weren't ready until Thursday. And then on Friday, I just couldn't face it, so I dithered about all day and went to the Academy of Music that night, as you all know. And then Dev and I were reconciled, and since then I've just been floating around. There will be a wedding, whether anyone is there or not."

"We'll all be there," Richard assured her. "As for me, it will be one of the proudest moments of my life."

Victoria said softly, "Thank you, Mr. Duvall. You are so kind."

Mallow was creeping toward the table with two plates, and Richard kindly leaned back so that she might serve him. She was moving so cautiously that Dally whispered *sotto voce,* "You better be a-hurryin' up, girl, or we'll be here all night! They's ten courses, you know!"

Since it was obligatory that the servants were invisible and inaudible at meals with Tante Marye, no one said anything, but Cheney had to hide a smile. Poor Mallow would probably be so glad when Dally retired. Finally she had served all the guests, and her muttered "Whew" was easily heard. Dally rolled her eyes.

"This is marvelous!" Richard said after a bite. "What is it?"

"This is Oysters Marinière," Tante Marye said with satisfaction. "It's a specialty of Madame Gallot's."

"Who is Madame Gallot?" Richard asked, bewildered.

"She is our new cook," Irene said, smiling.

"She is?"

"Yes, dear."

"Have I met her?"

"No, dear. Tante Marye found her only yesterday, and you might say this dinner is her application for employment."

Richard took another bite of the delicious oyster dish. "Hire her, Irene."

"She only speaks French," Irene warned.

"Oh no," Richard groaned. "I'll never be able to ask for anything."

"You could point," Irene teased.

"You could learn French," Tante Marye said severely.

"Maybe Madame Gallot should learn English," Richard said timidly.

"Nonsense," Tante Marye said briskly.

"She's a widow with four children," Irene said conversationally. "And she needs a cottage."

"Four—" Richard blustered, then shrugged. "Why not? It'll be nice to have children around the place again." He smiled at Dev. "Especially since you're taking Dart away. We'll miss him."

"You're taking Dart on your honeymoon?" Cheney asked. "I thought Allan and Jane Anne were going to take care of him while you're abroad."

"I had made those arrangements, but Victoria insists that we take him with us," Dev said proudly. "Isn't she amazing?"

"Yes, she is," Cheney said, winking at Victoria. "Perfectly stupendous."

Dev missed the irony. To him Victoria was all of that.

"Cheney, do not wink. It's not ladylike," Tante Marye said.

"Pardonnez-moi, ma tante," Cheney said, resigned.

Mallow cleared and served the second course, moving a little faster this time. The course was a consommé, a very light onion soup, served in wide bowls on plates. While she was serving Shiloh, Mallow tipped the bowl a little and two drops fell on the cuff of his shirt. She looked at him, horrified, and he winked solemnly at her and shook his head a tiny bit. Cheney glanced at Tante Marye, who certainly saw the incident but said nothing.

"Shiloh winked," Cheney muttered.

"Shiloh is not a lady," Tante Marye said calmly. *"Et toi, mon petit chou, une brebis qui bêle et perd sa bouchée."*

"What's that mean?" Shiloh asked warily.

Cheney translated gloomily, "She said, 'And as for you, my little cabbage, a sheep that bleats loses a mouthful.'"

"She called you a little cabbage?" Shiloh exclaimed. "How do you say it again?"

"That's why I don't want to speak French," Richard said triumphantly. "It doesn't make any sense."

"That's what I say," Shiloh agreed heartily. "Except I do want to learn how to call the Doc a little cabbage. C'mon, Tante Marye, how do you say it again?"

"Mon chou."

"Tante Marye!" Cheney said indignantly. "I don't want to be a little cabbage!"

Shiloh repeated it, but it sounded like "my shoe."

"Mon chou," Tante Marye repeated patiently. "Purse your mouth, Shiloh. *Mon chou.*"

"And it's always like kissy-mouth when you speak French," Richard muttered.

"You told me you thought it was a lovely language," Irene said.

"When you speak it, my dear," Richard said gallantly. "Because you are lovely."

Irene smiled a perfect Madonna's smile.

They valiantly went through the fish course, a steamed turbot with a creamy leek and shallot sauce, and the fourth, saffron and honey leg of lamb. With the fourth course vegetables were served, offered from a large serving dish by Mallow, while the diner indicated if he wished to partake of it.

"I've never understood why the fourth course is often called the remove," Richard commented, his brow wrinkling. "I mean, all of them are removes when you're served like this."

"It is some British oddity," Tante Marye sniffed. "I never call it the remove myself."

Mischievously Cheney said, "Shiloh's British."

"He can hardly help that," Tante Marye said complacently.

"I hardly know it anyway," Shiloh remarked. "I do wish I talked like my cousins and my uncle and aunt, though. They sound so veddy veddy high-hat." He shook his head regretfully. "Even my cousin Bain, although he's such a scrub."

"Oh, I am *so* happy someone else besides me brought this up," Tante Elyse said, beaming. "Where is your cousin now, Shiloh?"

Shiloh shook his head. "No tellin', Tante Elyse. Dr. Buchanan and Mr. Duvall have been kind enough to make inquiries for me while I was lazin' around pretending to be sick, but they couldn't find a trace of him."

"Not at the docks," Richard added. "At least, no passenger by the name of Bain Winslow or Denys Worthington or even Mr. Sweet was booked on any ship that left Manhattan on Saturday."

Shiloh shrugged. "He probably paid cash and used another name would be my guess."

"Perhaps he jumped a tramp steamer or pirate ship, and—" Tante Elyse began excitedly.

"Elyse, I don't think there are pirate ships docked in Manhattan," Gowan grumbled.

"There may be," Elyse said slyly. "If Mr. Winslow brought Shiloh's clipper ship that he stole and has been conducting illegal trade on the high seas, which it would be, of course, since the ship does not belong to him, even if he were hauling Bibles, then it would be a pirate ship, wouldn't it?"

"Well…" Gowan Ford hesitated, confused partly because of his wife's odd syntax and partly because he thought she may be right.

"But *Locke's Day Dream* isn't here," Shiloh said wistfully. "I wish she were. I'd love to see her again."

"We checked on that, too," Richard explained. "No ship by that name or registered in the name of Winslow Brothers' Shipping or Worthington Shipping has been here in the last year. Of course, he could have forged the ship's registry. As long as he paid the harbor fees, they probably wouldn't have cared enough to check closely."

"Then where is your ship, Shiloh?" Tante Marye asked. "Don't you think that Mr. Winslow brought her here?"

"Yes, ma'am, I do," Shiloh said slowly. "But I think he's sailing in her right now to someplace far away from me."

Shiloh sounded bewildered and a little hurt, so quickly Tante Elyse trilled, "Your cousin sounds like such a debonair, tragic villain. Cheney, I simply must know all about Mr. Winslow. What does he look like? Does he look like Shiloh? Is he as handsome as Shiloh?"

Cheney shook her head. "No, he doesn't look like Shiloh at all, and no, he isn't nearly as handsome. He is fine looking, in a snooty blue-blooded kind of way, as British men seem to be sometimes. You know, all thin-nosed and pale and Byronic."

"You think he looks like that?" Shiloh exclaimed. "I thought he looked like...like a scrub."

"He's a male version of Brynn," Cheney explained, "and so of course he is fine looking. You just think he looks like a scrub because you think he is one."

"Don't you?" Shiloh shot back.

Cheney's brow furrowed, and she stared down at her half-finished turbot. "I think...I think he does bad things, yes. But when I was talking to him, I came to understand him a little. I feel rather sorry for him."

"Cheney, how could you possibly pity him when he

had abducted you and frightened you half to death?" Victoria cried.

"Because I came to see that he was constantly comparing himself to Shiloh," Cheney answered slowly. "And he was constantly coming up short. It's not so much envy, you see. It's more that he tortures himself with his own weaknesses and inadequacies as compared to Shiloh."

"How do you know all that?" Shiloh asked intently. He and Cheney hadn't had much time to talk in the last few days, and she hadn't told him this.

Thoughtfully Cheney answered, "He calls you his brother."

A silence descended. Mallow began quietly retrieving the fourth course.

Finally Richard said, "I'm very proud of you, Cheney. To have compassion on a man who has done you so much wrong, that is rare indeed. 'Forgive those who trespass against us' is one of the most difficult commandments."

"Boy, that's the truth," Shiloh said fervently. "It's gonna take me a while to get that one under my belt."

Cheney said quietly, "I think you've already forgiven Bain. I think you would like to find him and tell him that you've forgiven him and try to help him."

He stared at her, bemused. After a few moments he asked, "How come you know all this stuff? I'm the one who's supposed to know all the stuff."

"I know stuff," Cheney said complacently. "Lots of stuff."

Slyly Tante Elyse said, "Oh, Cheney, we know you do. For instance, now that you've spent a whole night in one, I simply must know—what does the inside of—"

"Elyse! Assez! Tais-toi!" Tante Marye managed to

say in spite of the fact that she had just taken a bite of the fifth course.

"Qu'est-ce qu'il y a?" Elyse asked innocently.

"Alors!" Tante Marye threw her hands up in the air, a very Gallic gesture. *"Tu ne parles pas des demi-mondaines!"*

"C'est ça," Tante Elyse said sulkily. Then slyly she whispered to Cheney, *"Il faut que tu dises à la première occasion."* Of course Cheney was across the table, so everyone heard.

"Amazin' how much French you can pick up just listening," Shiloh commented with a grin. "I think I understood 'bout all of that."

"Really, I don't know why I try," Marye breathed wearily.

"I don't either," Tante Elyse said complacently.

Ignoring her, Tante Marye asked, "Cheney, dear, are you quite well now? After that dismal experience?"

"Oh, Tante Marye, I'm wonderful!" Cheney exclaimed. "I feel better than I've felt in…in forever!"

She and Shiloh exchanged sidelong looks, and then Cheney happily started cutting her roasted quail into small triangles.

"Cheney, don't tell me that you're full already," Irene said sternly. "We have five courses to go."

"Hmm? Oh no, I didn't realize…." Hastily she took a triangle bite.

"I don't think that Cheney has lost her appetite because she is unwell," Tante Elyse said knowingly. "I think it's because she has a secret. Does she, Shiloh?"

"Aw, c'mon, Tante Elyse, I did want to at least talk to Mr. and Mrs. Duvall first," Shiloh pleaded.

Tante Elyse nodded. "Then I shan't tell."

"Zut alors!" Marye exploded. "Elyse, you have already told!"

"Yes, I know," she replied serenely. "But what does it matter? We all know. We're just pretending that we don't."

And there seemed to be no answer to that.

By the time they finished all ten courses, everyone was almost comatose, but Madame Gallot had been unanimously approved. They all retired to the drawing room, and there, to Tante Elyse's everlasting delight, they play-acted Shiloh's dramatic night, and she got to play Rock. Gowan even got her a club, one of Richard's umbrellas. Cheney was the older girl, Victoria the younger girl, and Richard played the younger boy. They struck ridiculous poses and thought of outrageously complex and villainous lines and had great fun. Even Tante Marye laughed and applauded. Dev consented to play himself, and he made a most daring and swaggering rescue of Shiloh.

When Mallow brought in tea and coffee and bonbons, they settled down, and Shiloh told them all about how he had felt, how afraid he was, and how God had spoken to him and comforted him, and how he had prayed and given his heart to the Lord. He ended by saying, "It was the worst and best night of my life."

They visited until very late. This group always had so much to talk about, and they enjoyed one another's company as if they were a very close-knit family. Finally, however, only the Duvalls and Shiloh remained.

"Come into my study, Shiloh," Richard said cordially. "Tante Elyse reminded me—twice—that I must make an opportunity to speak with you very soon. How about now?"

"Yes, sir, I'd appreciate it if you aren't too tired," Shiloh agreed readily.

Cheney rose, but Irene stood up and slipped her arm about Cheney's waist. "Where are you going, dearest?"

"I want to go, too," Cheney insisted. "Shiloh said he wants to talk to you, too, Mother, and I'm not going to sit out here like some little schoolgirl in the headmistress's office."

"No, dear," Irene said sweetly, tightening her hold on Cheney's waist. "Richard, you and Shiloh please go on. Shiloh, I do appreciate your sensibilities, but I believe that you and Richard should speak privately."

"Thank you, ma'am," Shiloh said with ill-disguised relief. The two men took their leave rather quickly.

"But I want to hear!" Cheney argued. "It's about me, after all!"

"No, dear, I think this is about Shiloh," Irene said gently. "Now, suppose you tell me all about it? I'd like that so very much."

"You would? Oh, Mother, it's so wonderful, I just can hardly think of how to begin…perhaps with a day in the park, with Laura Blue…."

Shiloh settled down in one of the leather club chairs in Richard's study. He liked this chair, for it faced the painting of Cheney on the wall. She was about sixteen, he thought, dressed in a riding habit, holding the reins of an Arabian horse. It was a very good likeness of Cheney. It captured her spirit and the fire in her eyes.

Richard settled down into the chair opposite Shiloh's and followed his gaze. "Excellent, isn't it?"

"Yes. Because she is," Shiloh said.

Richard nodded.

"Sir, I love her," Shiloh said simply. "I've loved her for a long time. I want to marry her, I want us to have a family, and I want to be with her as long as I live."

"I'm glad, Shiloh," Richard said. "I know that Cheney loves you just as much. Maybe more. Sometimes I think women feel things more keenly than we do."

"Our ease, but our loss," Shiloh said, staring into the fire.

"Too true, and wise of you to see it," Richard remarked.

"Wisdom…yes, that's a pearl beyond price," Shiloh mused. "I don't have much of it yet." He shifted in his seat and looked intently at Richard. "Did you know that I asked Cheney to marry me when we were traveling here to New York?"

Quietly Richard replied, "I didn't know. That is, Cheney didn't tell us. But we thought that must have been what happened. And Cheney refused you, didn't she?"

"Sure. She had to. I see that now," Shiloh said with a sad smile. "But look what it took for me to see it. The good Lord almost had to kill me. Anyway, Colonel Duvall, what I want to explain to you is that I just can't marry Cheney right now. Don't get me wrong—I really want to, very badly—but somehow I don't feel it's the right thing to do."

Richard's eyes lit up. "Shiloh, that's the best thing I could ever hear you say. You see, the only reservation I would ever have about you and Cheney getting married right away is that you're such a brand-new Christian. You haven't gotten truly grounded in the Lord yet. Of course, I know you're saved. I know you'll follow the Lord all your life, and I already respect you as a man. But always, with everyone, there is a sort of—settling in, of finding your day-to-day path with Him."

Shiloh listened closely, and slowly the light of revelation made his eyes gleam brightly. "Yes, that's exactly it. I didn't know how to put it into words. I do need to understand exactly how to have a daily life with Him. It's all very dramatic, you know, to be snatched from the jaws of death and all, but it's not really a guide to everyday living. I need to figure out the...the footsteps. One, then another, and another..."

"Exactly," Richard said with satisfaction. "You do know a lot of stuff."

A grin flashed, but then Shiloh sobered again. "The thing is, Colonel Duvall, I can't figure out how long this is going to take. I mean, it's not like when you get through X days of school, then hey!—you're a graduate!"

Richard laughed. "No, you don't ever graduate, Shiloh. It's a lifelong learning process."

Shiloh frowned. "Colonel Duvall, beggin' your pardon, but I don't want to wait till I'm dead before I marry Cheney. Couldn't you give me some kinda estimate?"

"Oh yes, I see what you're getting at," Richard said. "Sorry, Shiloh, but I can't do that. You see, one of the things you'll learn is to hear the Lord's voice and know His will. When you're ready, He'll tell you, and you'll know in your heart that it's His truth."

Shiloh nodded slowly, thoughtfully. "It is hard, though, not to be able to set a date. That would kinda set it in stone for me, you know?"

"Shiloh," Richard said dryly, "I don't think you'll have to worry that Cheney will marry someone else while she's waiting for you. I think—I do know my daughter pretty well—that she'll have more joy in waiting for you than most women would have in a lifetime."

His new slow, gentle grin creased Shiloh's face. "Yes, sir, I think you're right. After all, she waited for me for three years, didn't she?"

"I think she's waited for you all her life," Richard said quietly. "And then, even when it seemed that it wasn't possible for you to love each other, she still believed in you. She believed in your love for each other, but most of all she believed in Christ's love, which is full of tender mercies. I think, deep down, she knew that Christ's love would conquer even your strong and proud heart."

Chapter Twenty-Five

Love, Which Conquers All

Seven-year-old Dev waited, watched, hoping against hope, fighting without weapons, believing without knowing....

And at dawn someone did come. It was two men in a work cart. One was a small man, wiry and sinewy, and Dev was astonished to see that as he drove he was weeping. The other was a giant black man.

They went past the church to the cemetery behind. Dev watched. The two men dug a grave, and the black man drew out an ornate white cross. Soon a fine carriage drove up. An attractive couple dressed in fine clothing got out of the brougham. The big black man single-handedly pulled a small casket out of the carriage, too. The four of them went to the grave and had a prayer. Then the small white man sang "Jesus, Lover of My Soul" in a fine tenor voice that never wavered, though the tears rolled steadily down his face.

The couple seemed devastated. The tall, fine-looking husband didn't weep, but his face was a study in grief.

The woman, who was wearing a heavy veil and leaned heavily on her husband, wept silently, her slim shoulders bowed and shaking.

After the short memorial, the couple returned to the carriage while the black man stayed behind to cover the grave. Dev watched, stricken, as the small man hurried to open the carriage door and pull down the step. The woman, with her husband almost lifting her, had her foot on the first step....

"Wait," Dev tried to cry, but it only came out as a small boy's whimper. So he ran, his heart pounding with fear, but his feet skimming over the snow.

"Sir—ma'am—sir—" he said, skidding to a stop by the three.

The small, wiry man frowned and took a step toward him, as if he were trying to shield the sorry sight from the couple's eyes. "Here, you, boy, get along now," he said, though not unkindly. "Mr. Richard and Miss Irene don't need to be attending to any beggars today"

The woman laid her gloved hand on his arm. "It's all right, Mr. Jack," she said in a weary but musical voice.

The well-dressed gentleman stepped up. "What's the matter, son? Are you lost?"

Dev dropped his head, then remembering himself and his station, he snatched the ratty stocking cap off his head. "No, sir," he breathed without looking up. "My m-mother and I...are waiting for the reverend, sir. But I...I just wanted to tell you how sorry I am that you lost your baby, sir...ma'am. I...I want to be a doctor when I grow up...so I can take care of people that get sick... and get...hurt."

The four stood in a wintry, bleak tableau.

The woman, in a heaven-light cloud of scent, suddenly stepped in front of Dev, threw back her heavy gray veil, and put one hand under his chin, raising his face.

Dev thought that if there were any such things as angels, this lady must look just like they do. Not only was she beautiful to look upon, but her green eyes were deep wells of great sadness and great gentleness bruised, yet still there was a calmness and serenity that Devlin Buchanan had never seen in his seven years and thought he would never see in all of his wretched life.

"What is your name?" she asked softly.

He swallowed hard. "Devlin Buchanan, ma'am."

"My name is Irene Duvall, and this is my husband, Richard Duvall," she said. "It is very kind of you to be sorry for our loss. We've just lost a son, you see. That's why we are here in the churchyard on this cold and snowy Thursday morning. And why are you here?"

"My...mother and I...are waiting."

Miraculously she smiled a little. "You're waiting for what?"

Tears suddenly filled the boy's eyes. "For help."

Richard and Irene Duvall exchanged glances. Now Richard didn't smile, but some of the heavy care seemed to have been lifted from his noble features, and he nodded slightly to her. "We need help, too, Devlin," he said in a deep leonine voice. "It may be that the Lord has put us together in this place, at this time, so that we may help each other."

Dev was so startled that his tears stopped. "Me? Help you? I could never do that!"

Richard Duvall's slow gray eyes took in the boy's thin, careworn face. "But I think you will, Devlin. I believe you will."

* * *

Dev studied Irene Duvall, who smiled back at him. She glowed today with happiness for him. He thought that she looked even younger and more lovely than that first time he'd seen her, the angel in the frozen churchyard. She'd been an angel to his mother, too, those five years that Amelia had managed to hang on to life after Richard and Irene had taken them in and built them a small cottage out back, much like Dally and Big Jim's cottage. Dev's mother had sewn for Irene, and Irene had been a friend to her. After she died, Irene had become a mother to Dev, and Richard had been his father.

I knew Irene couldn't have any more children. I remember well the monthly doctor's visits for so long, and Richard's sadness and Irene's pale, tear-washed face afterward. It must have been terrible when she lost the little boy at seven months. They even named him, just to bury him. They named him Alan. Funny, I don't think to this day that Cheney knows about Alan—she was only one and a half years old—but I know Irene felt that I was sent to her from God that cold, sad day. And I have thanked God every day of my life for her and Richard and Cheney. And now I have…

He lost his train of thought then, because Victoria had finally come into the church and was slowly making her way up the aisle on her father's arm. She was smiling at Dev serenely.

Dev took a last glance at Irene, at Richard by his side, at Cheney on the other side of the pastor, and at Nia holding Dart up in the gallery.

Then he smiled back at his bride.

Thank You from my heart, Lord, for all of these loves, but especially for Your love, which conquers all.

Amen.

Chapter Twenty-Six

There Go the Ships

After the wedding, Shiloh Irons-Winslow returned to Hawaii, accompanied by his good friend Dr. Lyman Banckert. Dr. Banckert had a sort of working holiday in Lahaina, fishing and swimming and lazing on the beach, and attending Mrs. Denise Winslow three times a week. After a month he told Shiloh, *"Ja,* I have the answer to her. Let us walk on this so lovely beach, and I will tell it to you."

It was late evening, and they strolled along the beach, staring out hungrily over golden Auau Channel, the sun setting behind them. Shiloh looked back for a moment, thinking that Cheney had the colors of Hawaiian sunsets in her hair, but then he made himself pay attention to Dr. Banckert.

"Your aunt is a selfish and bitter woman," he said firmly. "She has evidenced no symptoms at all of true dementia. *Nein, nein,* let me say it. She has evidenced symptoms of several of them, at different times, and rather badly."

"You're saying she's just faking it?" Shiloh asked, astounded.

"*Ja, ja.* She is faking it," Dr. Banckert said, rolling the idiom around with satisfaction. "Oh, she is very unhappy, my friend, and prone to depression, but ha! Who is not, at times? She has lost a great deal recently, it is true. Her home, many irreplaceable possessions, which are the fabric of her past, and of course there is the unhappiness of her marriage. Where is your uncle, at the way?"

"By the way," Shiloh corrected him absently. "He's in Shanghai on business. He won't return for a couple of months."

"Ah yes, and stay for two days, *ja?*" The doctor shrugged fatalistically. "It is sad. I loved my wife for thirty years, and we fought most of that time. But it was good fights, you see? We show our love this way, sometimes."

Shiloh grinned widely. "Dr. Banckert, I know exactly what you mean, believe me."

"So, there is this woman, she is unhappy, she is bitter, she marries the wrong man and thinks she loves his brother all her life, and—"

"She told you that?" Shiloh exclaimed.

"Of course she didn't. I know this, though, because I get her to talk to me, and I listen." He glanced up at Shiloh. "You must always listen, listen, listen to people. They will tell you everything if you just listen. You have the gift, you see. They will talk to you, and you will listen."

Shiloh nodded thoughtfully. "But what am I to do with her? As you know, my cousin Brynn has an understanding with Dr. Baird. But she refuses to leave her mother because she seems so ill. It's very hard on Brynn and Walker."

"You listen to me," Dr. Banckert said solemnly. "I think much of this playacting is exactly for the reason you are saying. Mrs. Winslow does not want her daughter to get married and leave her alone. It is an understandable fear for a woman whose husband has, for all intents and purposes, deserted her. She may never see her son again. You, she cannot tolerate. Bad reasons—bad for her, bad for her husband, and bad for you—but she can hardly bear to set the eyes on you. You look much like your father, Mrs. Winslow says."

"But then, what the blue thunder am I supposed to do?" Shiloh blustered. "Please tell me, Dr. Banckert."

The old man said with pity, "I am so sorry, Mr. Irons-Winslow, but I cannot. You understand, *ja?*"

Shiloh sighed. "Sure, I understand. It's my decision to make, and mine alone." The sun was going down over the peak of Puu Kukui looming behind them. Shiloh looked back once again to see the last moments of brightness. He saw his and Dr. Banckert's footsteps thrown into clear relief in the flat, hard light, a path stretching back farther than he could see.

Then, as clearly as if he were repeating the words aloud, he heard his own voice. *"It's all very dramatic, you know, to be snatched from the jaws of death and all, but it's not really a guide to daily living. I need to figure out the footsteps. One, then another, and another...."*

Shiloh laughed a little at himself. Dr. Banckert heard nothing, absorbed in the beauty of this dying day and the siren's song of surf. Shiloh began to pray.

* * *

He was still praying, though a little less eagerly and a little less patiently, two weeks later.

Shiloh and Dr. Banckert had returned to Hana, where Shiloh put the doctor on the Winslows' bark *White Crow* for the first leg of his return to San Francisco. Tang Lu's boardinghouse was doing a bustling business now, but of course Shiloh always had a room there, even if Tang Lu had to toss out one of the captains. After the volcanic eruption, Shiloh and his uncle had lifted the restriction that the crews couldn't come into Hana, so both the Winslow Guest House and the Zeisses' upstairs rooms were full most of the time. And Alena Zeiss's General Store was doing a booming business. Konrad Zeiss was still keeping the plantation going, and it was still more than a full-time job.

Shiloh decided to stay for a few days, for he liked the quiet village of Hana much better than he liked the busy but shabby town of Lahaina on the other side of the island. He walked the beach, remembering the dark days of the volcano, how terrible, yet wonderful, it had been for him and for Cheney. He looked down where the lagoon had been, and where Bain's and Brynn's streams had run freely. The lagoon was poisoned now, and the streams and the beach were nothing but black, cold, crumbly lava.

Dead, all dead, he thought sadly. *Lost to me forever... like the pearl, Cheney's pearl, that I so foolishly threw away.*

He stopped, for a thought, unbidden, had come to his mind. It was a glimmer of light, of hope, in all the sadness that he felt. Then he thought with wonder, *This is*

*God's voice. He's trying to tell me something, to teach me
something.... What is it, Lord? Where are You?*

He struggled, standing on the rise over Brynn's stream,
frowning. Like the last sight of a train going far away at
night, the light glimmered faintly, but Shiloh couldn't
grasp it, couldn't keep a hold on it. Frustrated, he stared
down at his dusty boots.

Beside his right boot he saw a tiny spot of green.
Shiloh fell to his knees, then got down on his hands to
be able to see it closely. It was so small. He discovered
a plant, just a whisper of a seedling in a sea of choking
blackness, a little three-lobed leaf on a stalk as small as
a pin.

Straightening, Shiloh sat back on his heels and smiled
a little. Then he said quietly, "'Therefore if any man be in
Christ, he is a new creature: old things are passed away;
behold, all things are become new.' This whole place
died, but it lives again. Just like me."

It was the first of many lessons he learned in those
weeks of solitude. He began to scramble the heights of
Mount Haleakala, sometimes walking all the way around
to the Winslows' fields, often seeing Konrad Zeiss and
talking with him. But when the press of business wasn't
urgent, he walked alone, praying and reading the Bible
that he always carried now in his knapsack. Tang Lu
packed food for him, and he carried a canteen, but mostly
he drank from the thousand springs on the mountain.
Except for the thin line where the lava had choked some
of the springs, the rest of the vast mountain had plenti-
ful sweet water.

Early one morning he decided to go all the way up to
the high sandalwood grove that he and Keloki had tended
so gently. Shiloh had not been there since the volcano

erupted. He thought that the two trees were just above the fissure where the lava had come streaming out, but he wasn't sure. It was close, anyway, and he thought that the trees either might have caught fire, or if not, they were so delicate they had probably withered from the extreme heat.

He set out, going straight up the mountain behind the guesthouse. The sandalwood grove was, he knew, over to his left, because it had been almost directly in a line behind Winslow Villa. Shiloh had never come this way before, had never explored this part of the mountain. But he didn't want to go over to where the villa had been and go up from there. He hated crossing the blackened lava fields.

It'll be hard to find, he reflected. *I only ever went to it from Keloki's house at the village and once around the bridle path with Mr. Zeiss. It's only about twenty square feet in these miles and miles of wilderness.*

Then he realized that the bridle path traced a wide circle around from the north pineapple fields, and he should eventually hit that. If he followed it on around, it should take him within feet of the sandalwood grove.

He walked—or climbed—steadily, without even breathing heavily, for it was as Devlin Buchanan had said—he had a heart like a locomotive engine. He drank from a small stream that he knew trickled lightly all the way down to drain into the ocean at a point just south of Hana. He decided to follow it up awhile, for it ran a fairly straight course. The sound of the icy-cold water bubbling merrily was soothing to Shiloh.

At about five thousand feet he was surprised to see that the stream abruptly ended. It was flowing from underneath a large rock overhang into a small stone-

encircled pool about thirty feet wide. At the south end
of the pool two jagged rocks stood tall and pointed, like
spires. Evidently it had been a weak spot in the field of
stones, for the water had worked an opening between
them to allow the little stream to escape all the way to
the Pacific Ocean. Idly Shiloh noted how beautiful the
place was. The pool was at the end of what looked like
a sizable level shelf. Haleakala had many great craggy
plateaus along its massive sides, but most of them weren't
visible because of the thick forest and undergrowth.

Shiloh walked on and soon hit the bridle path. He followed it slowly, carefully watching the forest on his right
for familiar landmarks.

He found the sandalwood grove about noon. His heart
beat a little faster—he did love those trees—as he followed the faint footpath up a little higher. First he saw
the hut, and then he saw the trees.

They looked much the same as they had that last fate-
ful day he had seen them, the day that Konrad Zeiss had
ridden up to tell him that he was fired and no longer
wanted on Winslow Plantation. That day Shiloh and
Keloki had watched frightened bats, thousands of them,
starting and flying away in broad daylight. Shiloh hadn't
known then that he was standing over a running lake of
fire.

Quickly he walked a little farther south, past the
hut. He'd gone, perhaps, only a hundred feet when he
saw below him the first dark scarring of the lava fields.
Straining, he scanned it closely and realized that he was
looking at the very end of the fissure. He could barely
pick out the beginnings of a jagged crater, not very wide,
it seemed, for all the terror it had spewed forth.

Returning to the small clearing with its two stunted

trees, Shiloh felt comforted. He sat down between them and simply enjoyed the silence, the warmth, the ever-bright colors of Hawaii. Closing his eyes, he sniffed, and his nose, sensitive again, picked out the different scents: hot, metallic-smelling rocks; the tang of the sea; the deep rich smell of good dirt; the crushed perfume of the Hawaiian ginger he sat upon, for it was so prolific it was considered a weed in the islands. He even thought he smelled the heady, mysterious fragrance of sandalwood, though he knew in his mind that that was impossible. It was only the precious heart of the tree, after it had died, that gave the priceless perfume.

"Thank You, Lord, for all this goodness," he said quietly.

He sat awhile, not moving, his mind idle and content, just soaking in all the sensations of this place he loved.

But then, with the sigh of a man of the world with many cares, he picked up his burdens and began sorting through them again.

What am I going to do? I've just got to stop mooning around here like the Monk of the Mountains.

Aunt Denise. What can I do with her? Where could she go? Could I hire a nurse—no, it'd take two or three nurses to give round-the-clock care, seven days a week. She'd hate it. And she'd hate me.

And then there's my cousin Bain. Wasn't it something, the way the Doc nailed that down? A small unconscious smiled played on Shiloh's firm mouth, a sure sign these days that he was thinking of Cheney. *Bain Winslow, my—he called me his brother. How I wish I could find him, talk to him. I could help him. I know I could…maybe someday.*

What about Brynn? Aunt Denise keeps her in turmoil

all the time, and Brynn worries about her, tries to please her, tries to help her. She can't continue to live like that. She shouldn't *live like that. She and Walker should be able to get married and build a good life for themselves.*

But where? Where would they live? Brynn's life is here, and Walker's is in San Francisco. What would they do? How can I—

Shiloh sat upright, his blue eyes wide. "What?" he exclaimed to the empty air. "Here I am stewing away about Brynn and Walker and Bain—what about me and Cheney? We've never even talked about…about actually living together! How dumb is that?"

Pretty dumb, he sourly answered himself. *All I think about is getting married. I wanna get married. Never once did I think that there'd be a day after we got married, and another day after that, and so on…for 'bout a hundred years, I hope. We can settle that easy, I think. Me and the Doc been wandering a long time…funny, but I don't really care where we live as long as I'm living with her. But she's got her family there in New York, and I've got mine here all the way across the world. Maybe we could live in the middle, like Dodge City. It'd sure be easier if I had one of the ships in the Atlantic, though. That way we could travel back and forth so easy….*

"Lord, this is hard," he grumbled. "I mean, I've got all these family problems—"

As soon as the words were out of his mouth, it hit him like a speeding train. *Family—family! I've got a family!*

He ruminated on that for a while.

"Okay, Lord, I see. You're right," he said humbly. "I'm

very, very thankful that I finally have a family, even Aunt Denise. Thank You."

But I do have problems, a part of him nagged. *What's the secret here? Is there some code or something that I've missed? I know You're here, Lord, I just know that....*

In his mind echoed Richard Duvall's voice in the quiet of his library six thousand miles away. *"You see, one of the things you'll learn is to hear the Lord's voice and know His will."*

"I don't hear a bloomin' thing," he muttered, "except a fool out here in the woods talkin' to trees. All right, Lord, I'm listening." He shut his eyes tight.

He waited expectantly, then impatiently, then angrily.

Still he heard precisely nothing.

But Shiloh, for all his faults, was generally a good-natured man and his petulance only lasted for a short time. Realizing he was hungry, he searched his pack for whatever goodies Tang Lu had put in for him. Today she'd fixed him up with a fresh pineapple—already peeled and diced, of course—wrapped in a ti leaf, two mangoes, some of Alena's delicious Hawaiian sweet white bread, and some pork chunks that Tang Lu had baked on sticks for easy eating. He said a short and to-the-point blessing, as Richard Duvall had taught him. For his first course he chose the pineapple, and his fingers got sticky as he picked up the juicy chunks.

He considered his Bible and wondered what to read while he ate. Shiloh had started to read through the Bible on his way back to Hawaii from New York. It had been a fast read-through, really just a sort of absorption of words rather than concepts, but Shiloh had been surprised and pleased at how much of it had actually stuck

382 Driven With the Wind

in his mind. When he finished he decided to read it thoroughly and so started in the logical place—at the beginning. He'd found, however, that it was very hard work, and he started including a daily reading of a psalm and five proverbs, just, as he lyrically thought, as a sort of dessert and savory after the meat.

"I want to read that verse about the sea again," he said dreamily, sniffing, picking out the sea salt on the light breeze. The Psalms were marked by a lock of Cheney's hair bound with a white ribbon, and he caressed it with pineapple-sugared fingers for a moment when he opened the book. Then he began to read Psalm 104.

After a while, he raised his head, his eyes unseeing, his bread and meat forgotten. "'He appointed the moon for seasons: the sun knoweth his going down,'" he repeated softly. Then he read and ate more.

A smile touched his lips briefly. "'There go the ships: there is that leviathan, whom thou hast made to play therein.' You even know when the whales play."

He read the psalm, then read it again. Then he raised his eyes to the blue sky so near and prayed. "It's all planned, isn't it? It's all in perfect order. Perfect order. Lord, I want my life to be like that. I want it to go the way You plan it. I want all of my decisions, all of my thoughts and ways and footsteps, to be in Your perfect order."

When Shiloh returned to the guesthouse sometime later, he had found no answer to any of his questions. But he wasn't worried anymore. He wasn't desperate to know all of the answers immediately. He still thought, still considered different things, possible solutions to his family problems. And he still longed for Cheney with a yearning that was almost a physical hurt. But he didn't plead piteously with the Lord to let him marry Cheney soon. He had realized that he'd almost been accusing the Lord of keeping her away from him—when Shiloh had meant, all the time, to be learning how to cling to Him first.

I'm going to do that now, he thought firmly. *I'm going to learn how to give You my burdens and let You carry them, Lord. I'm going to learn that where I'm weak, You are strong. I'm going to remember that I'll never be lonely again, because I have You for my friend, You who are even closer than a brother.*

To Shiloh's surprise—and joy—trusting God brought an immense relief to him. He even shrugged, as men do when a very heavy burden has been removed from their backs.

Two days later he rose before dawn, as he'd been accustomed to do while in Hana. Tang Lu was always already up, and she served him a private breakfast in his room. The boarders were served breakfast at seven o'clock in the dining room.

On this day, however, he was surprised to hear Tang Lu's soft knock at his door only a few minutes after he'd gotten up. She must have heard him moving about. "Come in," he called softly, as he was dressed and was just splashing his face.

She came in, shut the door quietly, and made a pretty bow. "May I speak with you, Mr. Irons-Winslow?" she asked, her eyes modestly downcast. She was dressed in her everyday work clothes: a black tunic, black pants, white stockings, flat soft shoes. Shiloh had brought her a satin *cheong-sam* from Lahaina, a blue one with yellow flowers and dragons on it. It was the only time he'd ever

seen Tang Lu blush. She'd worn it while serving him and
Dr. Banckert their dinner that night. Shiloh had made
her blush again when he told her how pretty she looked.
But of course she wouldn't wear it for everyday. Shiloh
thought that, as thrifty as the woman was, she would
probably never wear it again but would save it for one of
her daughters.

"Sure, Tang Lu," he said a little sleepily. "But are you
sure you don't want to wait till after breakfast? I know
you've got a lot of work to do in the mornings."

"No, please," she said.

"Okay." He sat down on the bed and motioned her to
the single chair in the room, a dreary brown horsehair
armchair. She perched on the very edge of it, her ankles
primly together, her hands twisted in her lap.

"I have been praying," she said quietly. "I have been
very bad."

"I'll never believe that," Shiloh said, teasing her. But
she remained somber, so Shiloh asked, "What is it, Tang
Lu? I'll help you. You know that."

She nodded. "I know that, yes. You are good friend,
Mr. Irons-Winslow. The Winslows have always been good
friends to me. And that is one way I have been so bad. I
have not been such good friend to the Winslows."

"But, Tang Lu——" he stopped, for she opened her
mouth but then clapped it shut again. Shiloh realized
that she would never, never interrupt a man, much less a
Winslow. "Sorry," he said uncomfortably. "Please, you
just go ahead and say your piece, and then we'll argue."

Her eyes flickered with a mere second of amusement.
Tang Lu was not a fool, and she did have a sense of
humor. Still, she grew grave again as she continued, "I
am obligated to my parents. I only just now realized that,

Mr. Irons-Winslow. In the Chinese way, I think only of my husband's parents, of him, of his children, and of his first wife, and I think it is sad that my parents don't have a son to care for them. But I think it's not my place. Do you see?"

Tang Lu's parent's, Tang Sun and Chen Guifei, had been the Winslows' personal servants for many years. Now they were the only two servants Brynn and Denise had at the house in Lahaina. Tang Lu's father, called "Sunny" by the child Brynn, was over sixty years old. Her mother, Chen Guifei, or just "Fay" as Brynn had dubbed her, was fifty-five. They worked hard, and the work was difficult. Keeping a household and especially being a servant to Denise Winslow these days would tire a herd of young servants.

"I do," Shiloh reassured her. "I have learned since coming to Hawaii that this is how the Chinese people think, how they are taught. It's perfectly understandable that you've been that way."

"But no more," she shook her head vigorously. "I am praying for my parents, and then I see—pffft! Like Chinese fireworks! Take care of them, Tang Lu, you wicked, ignorant woman!"

Shiloh grinned. "Tang Lu, there's not a wicked inch of you."

"Thank you," she said with dignity. "So this wickedness now I want to be gone, and I see what I must do."

"What's that?" Shiloh asked with interest.

"I want Mrs. Winslow to come live here at the guesthouse. I want my parents to come with her. They can all live here with me. I can take care of my parents, and we can all take care of Mrs. Winslow," Tang Lu said firmly.

"What? But...but, Tang Lu, my aunt—" Shiloh blustered, astounded.

He was wrong, though, about one thing. Tang Lu did interrupt him. "Mr. Irons-Winslow," she said softly, "this is what the Lord has told me to do. It is not your burden to bear anymore."

"But I can't make it your burden, Tang Lu," Shiloh argued.

"It does not make my burden," Tang Lu said, smiling one of her rare dreamy smiles. "It takes the burden away."

He stared at her. "You know, now because I'm a Christian, that actually makes sense to me. You're sure?"

"Very sure."

"She'll make you miserable."

"Yes, she will try," Tang Lu agreed with another, very slight twitch at the corner of her mouth. "But she will not succeed."

"All right, Tang Lu," Shiloh relented. "Of course we'll pay you, and pay you well. That'll take up two of the rooms, of course, so you'll only have the two left. It'll halve your income."

"I have an idea, too, about that," she said modestly. "Perhaps we will talk about this second idea later."

"No, go ahead and give it all to me at once," Shiloh said lightheartedly. He was suddenly feeling almost giddy.

She searched his face for a long time. "The second idea I have is with Alena Zeiss. We would like to build a hotel here in Hana."

He thought about it awhile. "You know, that's not a bad idea, not a bad idea at all. We don't have many rooms here, do we? And we do have passengers sometimes from the barks. If we had a hotel, the barks could stay here overnight, and you'd get some of that money instead of it going to Lahaina, hmm?"

"There are people wanting to move here, Mr. Winslow," she said, now excited. "Sailors, some of them with families, love Hana. They would need a place to stay while they are finding their houses. And who can know *gaijin?* They visit here, they like it here, and they stay here with all their dollars, maybe."

He grinned. "Tang Lu, I think that's a great idea. I've been beatin' my head in trying to figure out a way to help Alena. But she won't let me." Alena was Shiloh's illegitimate first cousin, Logan Winslow's daughter by a Hawaiian woman.

"She would never ask you. She is too proud," Tang Lu scoffed. "But I am not."

"So who's better off?" Shiloh declared. "Okay, Tang Lu, let's do it. I'll have to talk to my uncle, of course, but I'm sure that he'll go along. We'll figure out how to finance you later."

She clasped her hands together, her slanted brown eyes shining. She looked very young. "Oh, thank you. Thank you a thousand times, Mr. Irons-Winslow."

"No, Tang Lu, it's I who must thank you, for today you have done me a—no, two—very great services," Shiloh murmured. "It's a debt that cannot be repaid with money."

She bowed a little, then sat expressionlessly watching him.

Finally he asked, "Is there something else? C'mon, Tang Lu, you might as well go on."

She blinked but said with reluctance, "Yes, there is a third idea."

"Let's hear it," Shiloh exclaimed heartily. "I'm ready for anything now."

"All right. I had not planned to say this third idea to you. I think, though, that the Lord has shown it to me now while we are talking."

"Go on, then. It must be a good third idea."

"I hope so. It is this. Will there ever be another Winslow Villa? I know it is not my place to ask, but I must, for the third idea."

"Well, I had always planned to rebuild," Shiloh said slowly, "and just the other day I saw a good spot for it right up above Hana by a little pool."

"Good," Tang Lu said with encouragement. "Because the third idea, you see, is not really my idea. It's your cousin Brynn's. We write letters to each other. In Brynn's last letter she said to me, 'If only Winslow Villa were still there! It's a dream of ours, of mine and Walker's, to live in Hana. I would have the plantation to run, and Walker would be the doctor in Hana. But maybe it will be years before this happiness comes, if it ever does. Winslow Villa is gone, and if my cousin Locke did rebuild it, of course it would be his, and he might not like us to live with him. And then, of course, my mother is so ill.' That," Tang Lu finished, "is Miss Brynn's third idea."

Shiloh stared at her, his eyes wide and blank. "You mean—Walker wants to live here? In Hana?"

"Oh yes, sir."

"And my cousin still wants to work the plantation?"

"Yes, sir."

Shiloh was quiet for a long time, and Tang Lu, because she was a patient and quiet woman, sat still and waited.

At last he spoke, his eyes crinkling at the corners as he grinned his old Shiloh Irons wide, crooked grin. "Tang

Lu, you're the most wonderful woman in the universe, and I think I love you. Will you marry me?"

She rose, her face still and composed. "Pffft," she said dryly. "Like Chinese fireworks, you are, Mr. Irons-Winslow. Big flash, then gone. You'll leave me for Doctah Duvall tomorrow, no?"

"Maybe not tomorrow," Shiloh replied impudently. To Tang Lu's shock and secret delight, he jumped up and enveloped her in a hug that almost squeezed the breath out of her.

"Thank you, Tang Lu," he whispered. "Thank you from my heart, now and always."

The next few days were very busy for Shiloh. He talked to Brynn, wrote to his uncle, wrote to Walker Baird, met the ships, met with Konrad Zeiss and Alena, tended the plantation, met with Tang Lu, met with his bankers in Lahaina, and still found time to take long walks in the paradise twilight.

Late one night he was back again at Hana, for the Winslow bark *Petrel* was due in, and he wanted to meet her. The ships returning from San Francisco always carried letters from Cheney to him. Sometimes she wrote to him twice a day. He stared into the sitting-room fire, sniffing the fragrant incense of the sandalwood chips he'd thrown in. He was reading *Macbeth,* but Shiloh wasn't really concentrating very well. "I miss you, my heart," he murmured, seeing Cheney's face in the bright flickering flames.

Lord, I know that it's not time yet. I do miss her, but I trust You. I know that somehow, something is undone. No, that's not it. I know that there is still something that You have for me, something to tell me. And when You do,

I'll hear You, and I'll know Your voice, and I'll know the truth.

He watched the flames for a time but grew restless. He thought he might join Keloki and Ulu Nui up on the bluff, for they were throwing papala spears to greet the bark. Shiloh loved this dramatic tradition, and Keloki and Ulu Nui always volunteered for it.

An urgent knock came on the door, and before Shiloh could jump up, Tang Lu had answered it. He went out into the tiny foyer, but Tang Lu was already closing the door. She turned to him and handed him a creased, slightly grimy letter. "For you from the *Petrel*. They sent a messenger before they even got docked."

It was addressed to Winslow Brothers' Shipping, and it was marked, "Extremely Urgent." With a shock Shiloh saw that it was from Captain Geoffrey Starnes in New York.

Captain Geoffrey Starnes was the captain of *Locke's Day Dream*.

Shiloh ran back into the sitting room, and Tang Lu discreetly closed the door. Tearing the letter open with shaking fingers, he read hungrily.

Dear Mr. Winslow:

It is with some apprehension that I write to you, for I find myself in a rather odd position, and the thought has occurred to me that perhaps I have been in grave error and have possibly even committed a crime. If this is the case, I am at your service, now and in the future, to answer for my actions. I await your pleasure at the above address in New York.

I do not wish to attempt to defend myself in this

communication. That is not why I am writing to you. Therefore, I will not go into how Locke's Day Dream *came to be in Perth Amboy, New Jersey. At this time I think it only necessary that you know how and why she is in peril of being confiscated by the New Jersey Port Authority.*

Mr. Bain Winslow had docked her in New York on the South Street Harbor. Then, in April, he came to me and told me that she must be berthed in Perth Amboy, New Jersey, immediately. It was a costly move—you are aware, Mr. Irons-Winslow, that with a clipper it takes just as full a crew to move her five miles as it does to move her five thousand—and Mr. Winslow at that time used all of the ship's treasury to make the move.

I did not see him again until early in the morning of Saturday, May twenty-third. He came to my rooms in an excited state and demanded that we take the Day Dream, *as he insisted upon changing the name of the ship, to the West Indies immediately. Immediately! Of course I was obliged to tell him that not only was it impossible for the ship—she was not outfitted nor supplied for any journey—but it was impossible for the crew. I, myself, had not been paid for the month of May. Many of the crew had deserted, and many had simply taken other ships because I could give them no assurance of when* Locke's Day Dream *would sail again.*

Mr. Winslow was very angry and kept insisting that we leave right then, that morning. But of course it could not be done, and I was finally obliged to tell him, rather strongly, that it was hopeless.

And so he finally left my rooms. I have not seen him nor heard from him since.

I have been paying the harbor dues, Mr. Winslow, but I must tell you that I have no more money except for rent and food. If the dues are not paid by next month, the Perth Amboy authorities are going to begin confiscation proceedings on Locke's Day Dream.

It finally occurred to me—I am not a very insightful man—that perhaps Mr. Winslow did not, in fact, have the authority to be in possession of the ship, and from these musings came my apprehension that perhaps I have acted wrongly. I wrote to you immediately for instructions. I do wish to assure you that the ship is fine. I check on her almost every day.

Please accept my sincerest apologies if I have committed any errors, or if I have, unknowingly, been an accomplice in the mismanagement of Locke's Day Dream. *I assure you that that, more than anything, causes me the greatest of distress.*

I will await your instructions, sir. Until then,

I remain,
Your faithful servant,
Capt. Geoffrey Starnes

Shiloh's eyes were so bright they looked like Arctic ice in the eternal sun. He threw back his head and laughed for sheer joy. "Oh, good man, good show, Starnes! Bless you a thousand times. I'm going to double your salary! Triple it! And…and…I think—yes, I'm sure! I'm going to give *Locke's Day Dream* to Cheney—for a wedding present!"

* * *

It was the middle of August, and San Francisco was hot and close. Even the nights were stuffy. The temperature fell, but the air still felt heavy. It was Saturday night, and Cheney's new emergency wing had taken in three gunshot wounds, one stabbing injury, one strangling victim, a woman in labor, a child bitten by a dog, and an elderly man who'd had a heart attack. Cheney had lost him, but he was the only one, and for that she was grateful. She was deathly tired.

Wearily she dragged herself to the office that once was Shiloh's, and as always, it made her miss him terribly. Now it belonged to a new head of nursing, an older man named Jones. Cheney had only seen him once or twice and had been unimpressed. Of course it would have been hard for her to be impressed with anyone trying to take Shiloh's place. The man had, courteously enough, offered the use of his office to the doctors on the night shift, as Shiloh had always done. It was a nice place for them to gather with some of the nurses for coffee breaks and discuss the patients when they had time. They hadn't had time on this night, but Cheney had left her cloak and reticule and bag in there, and she dragged herself there now to fetch them.

The room was dark, and since no one had used it tonight, they'd brought no lantern in. She took a tentative step inside, waiting for her eyes to adjust. As they did, the first thing she saw was that Shiloh was sitting in the chair behind the desk and staring out the window, just as he always used to do.

She blinked hard, then blinked again.

"Hi, Doc," he said softly. "Did I scare you?"

"Hi," she said, as if in a dream. "No, you didn't scare me."

"Good." He rose, his shadow broad-shouldered, his hair a faint silver glimmer thrown into relief by the moonlit window behind him. He moved to her and took her in his arms. It wasn't until then, really, that Cheney was sure he was indeed there.

They held each other tightly for long moments, and then Shiloh pulled away, tilting her face up to his. He watched her, savoring the outlines of her face, the wide, clear forehead, the exotic tilt of her eyes, the thick swath of lashes, the mysterious mark of beauty high on her cheekbone, the determined jaw. "Will you marry me, Cheney?" he asked quietly.

"Y-yes, Shiloh. I will marry you."

"I love you, Cheney. I love you so much," he said hoarsely.

"I love you, too, Shiloh. Yesterday…now…and forever."

Epilogue

It was a year to the day that Shiloh had first proposed to Cheney. On her twenty-eighth birthday, April twenty-first, 1869, Shiloh Irons-Winslow and Cheney Duvall exhanged their vows.

Though the wedding took place in Cheney's humble home church, the Fifth Avenue Presbyterian Church, it was a very grand wedding.

For one thing, Cheney had, for once in her life, indulged her richest dreams in deciding upon a wedding dress. She and Victoria had designed it, and Angelique of New Orleans had made it. Cheney chose a rather simple basic design—a high neckline, a tight-fitting waist, a very slight bustle, and a long train. The icy white satin seemed to radiate its own light. Luxuriously thick and heavy, it was so rich that the finished dress, by itself, weighed eleven pounds. But it looked as though Cheney were wearing a living, sparkling river. The only trim was frothy white Brussels lace at the neck and the hem.

Cheney's veil was billowy and long, of an Alençon lace net so light it moved with her breath. Her hairpiece—a tiara—and the entire twelve-foot length of the veil were studded with thousands and thousands of pearls.

Instead of an elaborate bouquet or brand-new ivory-bound prayer book, Cheney carried her old Bible that her father had given her when she was sixteen. A simple arrangement lay on top of it—a single white rose with ivy and orange blossoms cascading down from it.

She kissed her father, then lowered her veil. They began their stately walk, the last one she would take as his daughter. Cheney felt like laughing and crying at the same time, but deep within her flowed a wellspring of joy, quiet and sure. She was, at last, going home.

When she stepped into the church, she caught her breath. Once again, Shiloh had surprised her with a birthday gift. She had ordered very modest flower arrangements of white roses and ivy, but now this plain little church that seated only one hundred people on hard wooden pews was riotous with dazzling flowers.

The church, from the pew ends to the altar to the rafters, was filled with thousands of bird-of-paradise flowers that Shiloh had imported especially for this day. He had also brought in yards and yards of white Hawaiian ginger. Their spicy-sweet scent, even more than the sight of the flame flowers, brought the heavenly sunsets from Mount Haleakala to Cheney's mind, and she thought it was so fitting, so perfect, for Shiloh to do this. He had found so much that was precious in Hawaii, and now he was giving it to her. He gravely watched her coming to him, his eyes wide, as if he were seeing visions. Beside him stood his uncle Logan Winslow.

Cheney and her father started walking, and Cheney thought that she would only see Shiloh, but she was wrong. She saw everyone. On the back rows—the last two—sat Dally and Big Jim Clarkson with all their family. Rissy and Luke had traveled from Charleston with their eight-month-old son, Vess. Mr. Jack sat beside them, nodding at Cheney and furtively wiping a tear from his eye.

There was her friend Sharon Batemen Carter with her husband, Josh, all the way from Arkansas with Sharon Rose and their new baby, Elijah, named after Josh's father. From even farther—Washington Territory—Lydia Thornton, the pretty and plainly dressed missionary, had traveled with her unlikely friend Georgia Jakes, now Mrs. Dean Wharton. Georgia still looked much like a saloon girl who was playing it straight for one afternoon. Her husband was an old grizzled man, and he looked very happy. Powell and Martha Jane Drake were present, with Kelvey and Stony. Cheney had been writing to them all for four years.

She looked over to her beloved tantes. Tante Marye was crying, but Tante Elyse beamed radiantly. Gowan Ford was smiling at his wife, though he did look up dutifully at Cheney as she slowly walked by.

Allan and Jane Anne Blue, with Laura lying beside them dressed in pink lace, had come, too. Gangly, half-grown Jeremy grinned mischievously at Cheney as she passed by.

On the groom's side Mr. and Mrs. Walker Baird sat close together. Brynn was glowing as much as she had at her own wedding, two months previously. All of the Fine and Dandies, scrubbed and on their best behavior, sat together. Cleve Batson impudently winked at her. Miss Etta Behring from Charleston and Miss Tanzen Behring from New Orleans had both come. Incredibly, sitting next to them, was General Nathan Bedford Forrest. His sharp fox eyes were filled with appreciation as Cheney glided by. But seated next to him was his half brother, Shadrach Forrest Luxton, and Cheney saw that he had grown into a fine man. His eyes were shadowed a little with sadness, but he smiled at her, a genuine smile of gladness for her happiness.

Standing at the altar, waiting for her father to join them, were her mother and Dev, whom Cheney had asked to stand with her parents as her brother. Cheney reached Shiloh, and her father, with a small sigh, stepped behind her.

Shiloh smiled at her, and she could smile back, though her eyes were dewy with unshed tears. She handed her Bible to Victoria, and then she and Shiloh knelt. Shiloh took her hand and held it all through their promises to each other. He wasn't supposed to do that, but Cheney was glad that he did.

Though she had known it would happen, and she had even said the words secretly to herself many times in the long months past, she was still spellbound when Shiloh turned to her and vowed in a strong, sure voice, "With my body, I thee worship. With all my worldly goods, I thee endow. With this ring, I thee wed, in the name of the Father, and of the Son, and of the Holy Ghost."

In all her life, Cheney could never recall one word of her marriage ceremony except those promises of Shiloh's and one more sentence that rang out like the bells of heaven:

"And now, in the sight of God, I pronounce you husband and wife."

* * * * *